KNIGHTS TEMPLAR

DAUGHTER OF WAR

by S.J.A. Turney

1st Edition

For Sarah

Who aspires to great things through history

Published in this format 2018 by Victrix Books

Copyright - S.J.A.Turney

First Edition

The author asserts the moral right under the Copyright, Designs and Patents Act 1988 to be identified as the author of this work.

All Rights reserved. No part of this publication may be reproduced, stored in a retrieval system or transmitted, in any form or by any means without the prior consent of the author, nor be otherwise circulated in any form of binding or cover other than that which it is published and without a similar condition being imposed on the subsequent purchaser.

Also by S. J. A. Turney:

The Damned Emperors

Caligula (2018)

Tales of the Empire

Interregnum (2009)
Ironroot (2010)
Dark Empress (2011)
Insurgency (2016)
Emperor's Bane (2016)
Invasion (2017)
Jade Empire (2017)

The Marius' Mules Series

Marius' Mules I: The Invasion of Gaul (2009)
Marius' Mules II: The Belgae (2010)
Marius' Mules III: Gallia Invicta (2011)
Marius' Mules IV: Conspiracy of Eagles (2012)
Marius' Mules V: Hades Gate (2013)
Marius' Mules VI: Caesar's Vow (2014)
Marius' Mules VII: The Great Revolt (2014)
Marius' Mules VIII: Sons of Taranis (2015)
Marius' Mules IX: Pax Gallica (2016)
Marius' Mules X: Fields of Mars (2017)

The Ottoman Cycle

The Thief's Tale (2013)
The Priest's Tale (2013)
The Assassin's Tale (2014)
The Pasha's Tale (2015)

The Praetorian Series

Praetorian – The Great Game (2015)
Praetorian – The Price of Treason (2015)
Praetorian – Eagles of Dacia (2017)

The Legion Series (Childrens' books)

Crocodile Legion (2016)
Pirate Legion (2017)

Short story compilations & contributions:

Tales of Ancient Rome vol. 1 - S.J.A. Turney (2011)
Tortured Hearts Vol 2 - Various (2012)
Tortured Hearts Vol 3 - Various (2012)
Temporal Tales - Various (2013)
Historical Tales - Various (2013)
A Year of Ravens (2015)
A Song of War (2016)

For more information visit http://www.sjaturney.co.uk/
or http://www.facebook.com/SJATurney
or follow Simon on Twitter @SJATurney

LLEIDA
FRAGA
BARBERA
SANTA COLOMA
VALLBONA
VALLS
CADENETA
BARCELONA
ROURELL
TARRAGONA
EBRO BATTLE
CATALUNYA 1198

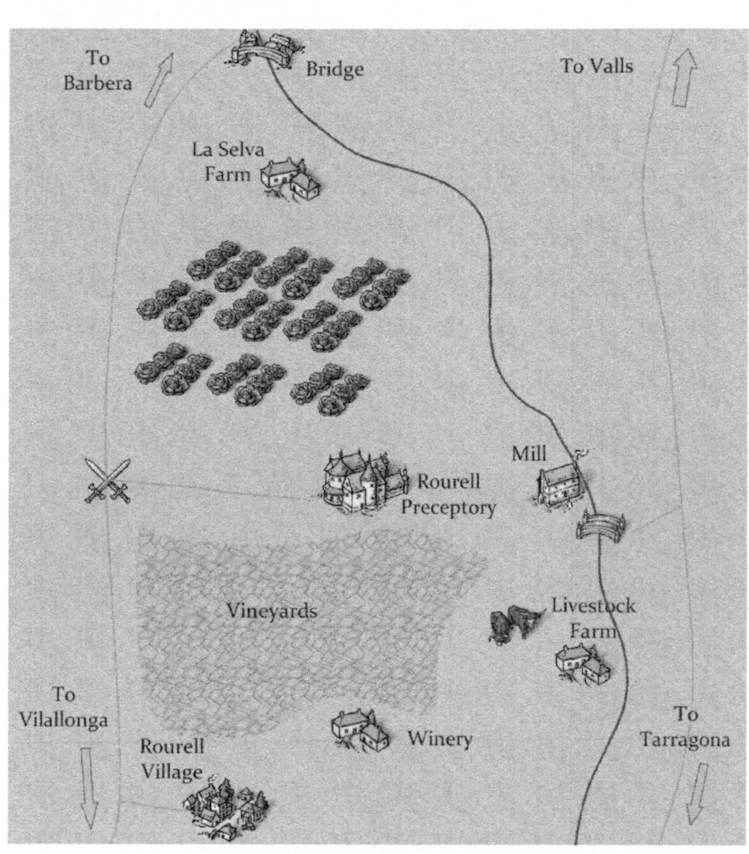

To Barbera
Bridge
To Valls
La Selva Farm
Mill
Rourell Preceptory
Vineyards
Livestock Farm
To Vilallonga
Rourell Village
Winery
To Tarragona

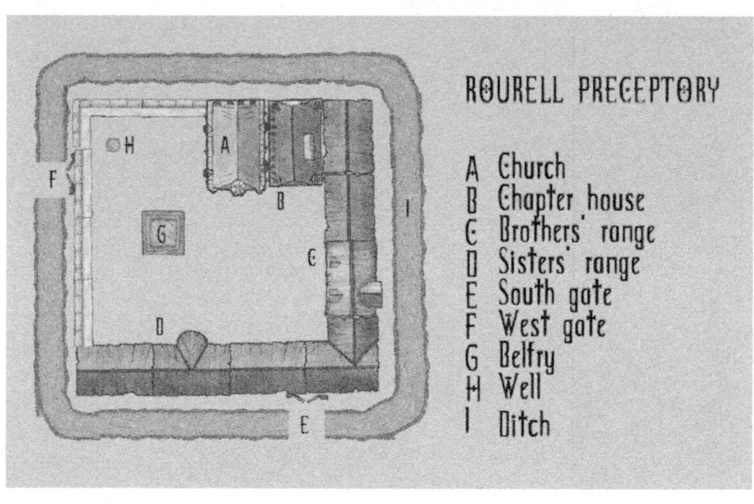

ROURELL PRECEPTORY
A Church
B Chapter house
C Brothers' range
D Sisters' range
E South gate
F West gate
G Belfry
H Well
I Ditch

PREFACE

The Templars have gone far beyond a historical group of Catholic warriors founded to protect pilgrims in the Holy Land. They have become part of legend and, like all legends, the truth is often nebulous or distorted. Despite their importance, they were only around for two hundred years. To put that in perspective, the Plantagenet family provided monarchs for a century longer. In the sweep of history, it is little more than the blink of an eye, yet they have made their mark on the human consciousness.

Over the years, this strange and impressive organisation has been the subject of endless treatises, novels, films and more. They appear, sometimes as heroes, occasionally as villains. Sometimes they are shown as rigid soldiers of God – monks with swords protecting the pious from the heretic. Sometimes their trials and the many accusations made against them by wealth- and power-hungry crowns are brought to the fore and they themselves are depicted as heretics, occultists and more.

I have attempted in this book to avoid such temptations. To make the Templars neither exemplars of rigid piety nor secretive heresy. I have attempted to produce a tale based on a realistic appraisal of the order. True medieval characters rather than heroes or villains.

With this in mind, I will state from the outset that the very existence of female Templars, though not well documented and perhaps not officially sanctioned, is very real. The two female characters I have used are historically attested people, for all the seeming flight of fancy that such women might have existed.

Cartularies have survived that document admissions and transactions within the Templar order, and it is from these documents that the characters have come.

The Templars were much more varied and complex than simply knights with white cloaks and red crosses.

Welcome to the Order of the Poor Knights of Christ and the Temple of Solomon.

Welcome to Spain.

PART ONE: LOSS

CHAPTER ONE

EBRO BASIN, KINGDOM OF ARAGON

YEAR OF OUR LORD 1198
SUMMER

Arnau de Vallbona spied the enemy at the same time as the rest of the company of Santa Coloma, a roar of righteous ferocity rising from every throat, audible even above the deafening thunder of hooves. The mail coats of the waiting Moors gleamed in the searing Iberian sun with a brilliance that Christian chain shirts never seemed to achieve – a shimmering piscine argent that rippled beautifully. Their lines were an explosion of colour, their banners fascinating – an illegible scrawl of Arabic script beneath images of swords and crowns and crescents and stars. Their helms, combined with chain coifs, revealed so little of their swarthy faces they might easily have been Christians, but for their banners and the quality of their mail. White, hungry eyes shone out from the darkness flanking their helmets' nose guards as they levelled their maces, hammers, swords, lances – a challenge, a threat.

The arid umber-coloured ground rumbled away beneath Arnau and his companions as the small mounted force of knights and men at arms bore down on the Moorish raiders who had plagued the region this past year and more. The border with the Almohads who controlled Valencia had created a fluid and dangerous region, ever mobile and changing, and raiders were far from uncommon, but this particular force had drawn Aragon's ire upon the brutal burning of a church in the spring. Pedro II, King of Aragon and Count of Barcelona by the grace of God, had commanded three of his more belligerent nobles to gather a force with which to bring the raiders to justice.

Three companies had rolled south to seek the enemy – that of Pero Ferrández d'Azagra, Lord of Albarracin; of Don Atorella; and of Arnau's own lord, the aged warrior beloved of Christ, Berenguer Cervelló de Santa Coloma. The ego of the Lord of Albarracin had led him to assume he would achieve overall command of the force, and his pride had been somewhat dented when the king brushed the arrogant noble aside and sent someone entirely different to lead the campaign – a glorious figure who now rode at the head of the cavalry and had drawn Arnau's eye throughout the ride, inspiring him and quelling his doubts and fears.

The army had chased around the dry, brown borderlands for two weeks, often catching wind that the raiders had been seen in the area recently or were tantalisingly near. Twice, they had even caught up with the enemy, only to lose them again as they deployed the mass ranks of foot soldiers. The raiders were an entirely mounted force, far too quick and manoeuvrable to trap into a full fight with infantry, and on each occasion they melted away into the hills and valleys, whooping, before the Christian force could be brought fully to bear against them. Consequently this time, when the enemy had been spotted, the bulk of the infantry had been left with the wagons and the horses issued forth to join battle or chase the raiders into the swift waters of the Ebro to drown. Albarracin had been scathing, displeased with the peril of matching only cavalry against cavalry, which would cancel out all the advantage in numbers the Christians could claim, though the army's leader had simply straightened and proclaimed his faith in God and their sureness of victory.

The enemy was not a force of organised, devout Almohad warriors. The Almohads, who had crossed the straits from Africa and imposed a powerful caliphate upon the previously fragmented Moorish *taifa* states of Iberia, were truly a force to be reckoned with. Zealous and clever, they had all but halted the Christian reconquest for half a century now. Yet it was not they who awaited the cavalry, but a rabble of vicious Moorish raiders who had taken advantage of the rough borderlands.

Arnau had tried throughout the ride to hate the men they would face, and had found that he could only do so if he focused on that aspect. Not that they worshipped a heresy, but that they were raiders who killed and thieved as a matter of course. That they had burned a church with the priest still inside. *That* made them bad men.

Arnau was as God-fearing a young man as could be found in the county of Barcelona, and he kissed the feet of the Virgin's statue in the village chapel every day. He had sat vigil in that same sanctuary. He took the Eucharist, and believed with an undying passion in the divinity of the trinity. But he had been born in the days when the Moor's dominance of the region was still fresh in the minds of all. When the after-effects of four centuries of Moorish control were still being unpicked from society, largely unsuccessfully.

The streets still often carried their Moorish names. The land was irrigated with their ingenious systems. The arches to be seen in grand buildings were still distinctly theirs. Even their delicate bath houses still functioned, though few God-fearing Christians would trust their flesh to such a place, with their cloying steam and rough masseurs. But that great fall of a culture in the region as the Moor had been driven back south had created a strange rift between Christians young and old. Those who had spent their lives under the dominion of the Moor, which had been lifted less than half a century ago, were often still fervent and spiteful in their denunciations. To them the Moors were the soldiers of the Antichrist walking the Earth, who had imposed their twisted beliefs upon the true people of Iberia. Men like Arnau's father, in fact, seeking a final end to the *musulmán* and his ways. Men like the French and English lords who sought repeatedly to take sharpened steel to the Holy Land and wrest Jerusalem from the clutches of the Saracen.

Those younger men like Arnau, though, who had been raised among the ashes of that world, lived a more complicated life. They watched the Moors who had remained living as little more than slaves in the new regime, being beaten for failing to adequately farm land that their families had cultivated as free people for

hundreds of years. It was hard to hate them. So much easier to pity them. After all, as the fifth Book of Matthew preached:
You have heard it said 'an eye for eye, and a tooth for a tooth'. But I tell you not to resist an evil person. If anyone slaps you on the right cheek, turn to them the other cheek also.
Arnau hardened his heart. Blessed Matthew could afford clemency. He had not been burned in a church by such men. Forget the Moorish boys begging for a crust on street corners, a cross carved in their forehead with their own thumbnail to deny their origin and encourage passing Christians to help them. Forget the grave of the gentle imam in Vallbona that was still spat upon daily, despite his having been a kindly old man who had helped Arnau's own grandfather to ease his pain in his last years. Forget that Aragon and Catalunya had been their homes for more generations than any man could remember. *These* men were raiders and priest-burners, beyond pity.

'Who is your master?' cried the man leading the charge.

'*God* is our master,' roared every voice in the company of Santa Coloma on the left flank, as well as those beyond in the other two units that formed the army. And well they might. A man might turn from God's grace on a drunken night when he thinks he might get away with it, and he may think he serves no master but himself in the half-light of dawn. But riding into battle, truths were hammered home into the heart and mind, and never more so than when a man like *this* one led the fight. For, even beleaguered as they were, and with diminished numbers after the disastrous defeat at Alarcos, the Templars were ever the heart and soul of the fight against the infidel.

And more so than the fact the men they faced were murderous raiders, *he* was what cast aside all uncertainty in Arnau… the Templar. All thoughts of charity for the Moor turned to dust as the man leading the charge in the white tunic with the eye-catching red cross couched his lance and roared a passage from the Psalms.

'A sinner beholdeth a just man and seeketh to slay him. But the Lord shall *not* forsake him in His hands!'

When such a man bellows such a glorious thing it flows through the veins, setting light to every nerve. The blood is up, riding into battle, whether a man be sword-virgin or blood-soaked veteran, and it takes little to turn a pious and thoughtful man into a berserk butcher. Thus was it for Arnau. The mass of Moors charging them could have been Christians. They could have been Jews. They could have been women and children, and he would have gleefully released his sword on the word of that glorious man with the red cross who led them.

Battle was joined a moment later. The unnamed Templar disappeared into the colourful melee of Moors ahead of any Christian companion, heedless of peril, his soul entrusted to the Lord. Arnau felt the righteousness of their cause at the sight. All the more so because the man was an impregnable, impervious, soldier of God. Even ahead of the army and surrounded by the enemy, he was alive and delivering divine justice with the edge of a blade. Arnau could hear the Templar singing his devotion to God as he cleaved limbs and hacked flesh and broke bones.

Arnau was consumed. Gone was the young man who had felt sorry for the Moor of the street corner begging for scraps. Here was Arnau de Vallbona, warrior of Christ and son of the righteous reconquest. He noted only at the last moment that he had, in his glorious pursuit of the Templar, strayed from his own company and towards the army's centre. Still, there was no chance of altering direction at this point, and an enemy was an enemy, after all.

Horse hit horse and man hit man. A spear clacked off his shield and took several links of mail from his arm in passing. Arnau raised the mace that was his weapon of choice. His arm came up and then down sharply, the heavy points of the iron head carrying brutal death. The weapon struck, smashing and bending the corner of the Moor's hastily raised circular shield. He saw that shield fall away, accompanied by a scream that was muffled by layers of leather and chain. The shield arm had shattered under the blow. The Moor lifted his sword in desperation, still wailing at his broken arm, but he could not deflect Arnau's second blow. The mace came down again and this time crunched into the meeting of shoulder and neck. He felt bones break again under the weight of the dreadful weapon, and the enemy's chain veil was ripped aside in the process, revealing bared white teeth, caging in the ongoing scream.

The Moor could do nothing. His shield arm dangled, the weight of the iron disc dragging it down, and his curved blade toppled from the fingers of an arm broken at the shoulder. The man was almost past Arnau already, his horse driving on despite the impending demise of its rider, and the young soldier had to turn and reach hard to swing the mace once more. It struck the man in the face, and while Arnau was spared the view of the damage he inflicted as the man was carried away by his desperate horse, as the mace came round seeking a new target, the horrific mess on the iron points told its own tale.

A lance with a perfect point came from nowhere and passed by Arnau so close that he felt the breeze of its movement. A sword came down. His shield went up, the black lion of Vallbona catching that curved blade. The Moorish sword skittered across the face of the shield, defacing that proud animal, and Arnau roared some unintelligible imprecation as he smashed the blade away and brought round his mace in a wide arc, slamming it into the man's unprotected chest, the points digging deep into the mail shirt, snapping ribs, crushing lungs.

The rider lolled to one side in his saddle and Arnau moved on. He cast his gaze about, trying to take stock of the situation in a split second. The forces were more or less evenly matched in numbers, as far as he could tell, but the Aragonese and Catalan cavalry clearly had the edge. He could still see that glorious figure in the red cross amid a sea of steel, bellowing out the Psalms as he killed and maimed with brutal efficiency. Further across the field on the left flank he could see his own lord, Berenguer de Santa Coloma, with other knights of his household, cleaving their way through the enemy, the old man still virile and strong, every bit the match of any man on the field. Silently Arnau cursed himself for having paid so much attention to that glorious Templar that he had veered off and allowed himself to become separated from his lord's men.

Another sword came from nowhere, scything round, and Arnau only managed to get his shield in the way at the last moment, the keen curved edge carving a chunk from the edge of the wooden board, a shockwave rattling up his arm from the blow. Arnau's mace rose and fell, the Moor's shield catching the blow, the metal points driving deep dents into the disc. Again and again they struggled, Arnau's breathing hot and loud in the confines of his mail coif and steel helm, the enemy's white eyes staring out from the shadows of his own helmet. The Moor's sword clattered against and bit into Arnau's black lion shield while his heavy mace battered and dented the enemy's metal disc. The man was good. There was never an opening and, with a heavy heart at being driven to do such a thing, the young warrior took the only course of action he could. His mace swung into the horse's head with a crack – a blow that would kill in moments. Had *already* killed, in fact, though it would take the beast's wrecked brain precious moments to register the fact that iron points were lodged in it. Then, as Arnau wrenched his weapon free, the horse fell, pitching forward. The surprised rider was flung from the saddle, though one of his mailed feet was still caught in a stirrup and the leg broke horribly as he fell.

Arnau ignored him and took the opportunity of the slight opening the fallen horse had created, urging his own beast back towards the flank where the company of Santa Coloma fought like demons, struggling, since it seemed the enemy had weighted that flank heavily.

The young man at arms saw the next blade coming, but had little time to react. His shield was on the other side and his mace, while brutal and deadly, was a poor parrying weapon. He leaned far to his left, yanking on the horse's reins to try and lurch out of the sword's path. The sharp edge scythed across the edge of his saddle, missing him by inches at most, but the tip scored a deep line down the horse's flesh. Arnau felt the beast's muscles and weight shifting and knew what was coming. Desperately, horribly aware of the danger posed by the man who had almost done for him, Arnau ripped his feet from the stirrups. The animal bucked, pain coursing through it, blood slicking down its flank, and the young soldier toppled gracelessly from the back, tucking into a ball as best he could. He hit the dirt and rolled painfully for a moment, then lurched backwards and tried to stand, watching the wounded horse's kicking hooves with wide, wild eyes.

Then he was up, struggling with the weight of the mail shirt, shield and mace as a spray of blood, mud and unmentionable stuff flew through the press of men, churned and lifted by jolting hooves. His world became a place of horse's legs and mail-clad feet, dancing and stamping, kicking and flailing. A battlefield of mounted men was no place for a foot soldier, for every beast carried more danger than its rider here on the ground. Arnau gripped his mace and kept his shield close and high as he pushed into the mass, dodging horses and sweeping weapons with desperation and speed as he tried to move closer and closer to the flank where his lord was fighting and where there might be more room.

They were winning. Even from Arnau's rather restricted point of view, he could identify more Christian horses and legs and surcoats than Moorish.

A figure emerged suddenly from the sea of horse flesh, the man as surprised as Arnau. A Moor with blood coating one mailed arm, his chain veil unhooked, face wild with panic as he ducked weapons and dodged hooves. His wide eyes took in the sight of Arnau in a similar predicament and for a moment they were locked there in a strange tableau, brothers in peril, sharing desperation. The spell broke and the Moor raised his shield, bringing his sword to bear even as Arnau lifted his own weapon. Then the Moor was gone, a rider plunging between them, fighting his own fight, unaware of the men struggling on foot. When the knight pressed on out of the way, hacking and slashing above, the shocked Moor was gone, disappeared somewhere in the melee, and Arnau was oddly relieved that he would not be required to kill the man who had in some way shared his fate.

A horse emerged from the press in front of him, a bay stallion of perhaps fifteen hands, its saddle empty, spatters of blood across flank and neck.

The young warrior looked about, frowning, expecting the rider to be recovering from a fall or bellowing as he fought back somewhere nearby. But the rider was gone. Just an empty saddle and a confused, milling horse. Arnau took a deep breath and let his shield drop. It was battered and missing parts now, anyway, and there was no way he would make it into the saddle with all this weight and two restricted arms.

Gritting his teeth, he grasped the saddle horn and heaved. His arms were weakening with all the swinging of the mace and absorbing blows to the shield, and the first two attempts at hauling himself up were complete failures. Finally, on the third attempt, he managed to mount the beast. Gripping the reins in his shield hand, he slipped his feet into the stirrups, slightly uncomfortably, for the animal's previous rider had clearly been a short man and the stirrups were high. Still, he was back on a horse.

Any notion of the improved safety of his position was disabused instantly as a sword came dangerously close to ending him. He lurched back, dancing the horse out of the way, and then swung his mace. The heavy bludgeon struck the sword mid-swing and the shock up both men's arms sent them dancing back as they grunted in pain and shook out aching shoulders. The sword came. Arnau ducked. His mace swung. The Moor leaned away. The sword came again and took links of chain from Arnau's elbow – a sharp Moorish blade that could penetrate mail. His mace swung. They separated once again, wheeling horses. As Arnau was contemplating how he could kill a man who seemed to leave no opening, a lance came from nowhere and emerged from the Moor's front, bursting outwards in a spray of metal rings and blood and ending the contest suddenly.

Arnau did not wait around to watch the man die. His gaze played across the fight and once again he spotted his lord, Berenguer de Santa Coloma, hacking and stabbing in the press. The number of his knights in close proximity had diminished. The army might be winning the fight overall, but the left flank was hard pressed and Arnau's master was fighting for his life. Another of the lords of Barcelona county was there beside the old man. Arnau recognised the white stars on red of the Lord della Cadeneta, minor nobility who owed fealty to Santa Coloma, just as he himself did.

The young man at arms was close now, and drove the horse on through the press, pausing occasionally to swing his mace, ducking

the Templar was here and more roaring knights in his wake to put an end to it. The Moors, previously unaware that their comrades across the field were already fleeing, suddenly realised their peril and turned, racing from the battle. Three died as they wheeled their mounts, and Arnau watched as the last strains of the symphony of death were played upon the strings of two dozen bows.

Newly arrived archers loosed from the hillside at the fleeing riders, having been deployed during the struggle by some thoughtful captain, though unable to release until now due to the confused press of friend and foe alike. Now, with clear targets, the archers were lethal. The arrows flew in wave after wave, bodkin points punching easily through the mail shirts to rip the life from the fleeing Moors, others plunging into the horses, which bucked, sending their dazed riders to the dirt with broken bones, where they were at the mercy of the Christians.

Arnau sat astride his horse, his heart hollow. The Templar nodded at him in recognition of his clear contribution, given the damage to his helm and armour, his bloodied mace and missing shield. Any other time, he would have felt an unparalleled thrill at such a moment.

Not today.

Berenguer de Santa Coloma was still in his saddle, flopping this way and that, arms trailing, chest and legs and horse all soaked in his blood. Ferrer della Cadeneta had dismounted, as had other knights across the field, removing his helm as he went about administering the *coup de grâce* to the fallen of both forces. There was no need, in Arnau's opinion, for the look of glee the man wore in this grisly task, his black hair soaked with sweat and plastered to his head. Arnau could feel his own scalp pouring out perspiration in the steel confines of his dented helmet beneath the steaming Iberian sun. Sweat and blood. Blood and sweat. The twin elements that formed the land of Iberia.

Before he realised what he was doing, Arnau had dropped from his horse and ripped his own helm free, letting it fall to the blood-soaked, hoof-churned mud. He was storming across the gore-strewn field towards della Cadeneta, fury rising with every step. He pulled the chain coif from his head and threw it aside angrily, along with the woollen cap within. His own hair ran with sweat, but he felt not the cool of the air upon his face, for hot rage filled him.

'*Bastard*,' he spat as he closed on Don Ferrer, the Lord della Cadeneta. The man was unaware of his approach and busily rifled through the clothing of a fallen Moorish noble.

'You let him die, you stinking shit,' snarled Arnau. His fingers tightened on the mace. Still, della Cadeneta had not seen or heard him.

'Santa Coloma!' the young man bellowed, beginning to raise the mace, unable to stop what had to be done. He would be executed for it, of course, but it would not be hell that awaited him for the death of a fellow Christian, for this was the administration of justice, not murder.

The mace reached its apex and suddenly, before Arnau could swing it and put an end to the cowardly bastard, his world became crimson. He stopped suddenly, stunned, as the Templar's horse filled his vision, hiding the figure of della Cadeneta from sight. The young man blinked as his eyes slid up across the blood-slicked beast, past the blood-slicked mail and into that angelic, bearded, blood-slicked face.

'"From the fruit of a man's mouth he enjoys good, but the desire of the treacherous is violence," so the Book of Proverbs tells us,' the Templar said, eying the raised mace. 'We are done with death now this day. Put down your hand.'

Arnau did so. It was almost impossible to resist that imposing, authoritative tone, especially as it cast the word of God at him like a weapon. The mace slumped to his side and the Templar nodded. 'You have done the Lord's work today. Glory in your success, for the raiders we sought are vanquished. Rejoice.'

And then he was gone, steering his mount onwards to raise the spirits of other men across the battlefield. Arnau shook his head, almost breaking the spell of peace the Templar had laid upon him. He felt the burning desire to lift his mace once more as he saw in the great warrior's place Ferrer della Cadeneta watching him with narrowed eyes, misericorde dagger in hand, soaked in the blood of both Christian and Moor.

'See to your lord,' della Cadeneta barked at him, waving a cursory hand towards the lolling body of Berenguer de Santa Coloma. Arnau almost argued. Almost refused. Santa Coloma was *that* man's lord too. Yes, della Cadeneta was a knight who outranked Arnau in society as a swan outranks a pigeon, but nevertheless the swine was not Arnau's master to order him about so. His fingers tightened on the mace once more, but the sound of the Templar's voice singing quiet songs of peace and glory robbed him of intent. Casting daggers with his eyes, he turned his back on della Cadeneta and walked over to where two other men were reaching up to try and lift the body from the saddle. Arnau went to their aid and another soldier joined them a heartbeat later. The four men lifted the body of the nobleman down and laid him upon the blood-soaked grass.

He half-expected the Templar to be there again, but as they folded Santa Coloma's arms across his ruined chest, instead the priest who had blessed them at the column before the battle appeared, standing in front of the body and administering the *De profundis* in a clear, musical tone, along with a single splash of holy water. One of the men laid out three cloaks atop one another, and with care and respect they waited until the priest had finished his rites and moved on, then lifted the body onto the cloaks and used them as a form of stretcher to lift the lord and bear him from the field.

Half a mile from here, close to the great Ebro River, the wagons waited, along with the camp followers and the infantry. Back at the wagons, the Lord de Santa Coloma would be tended by the women, who would anoint the body and wrap it in one of the many shrouds awaiting the dead. There was little point in washing the lord yet, with a hundred miles of travel to go between here and Santa Coloma, but at least properly anointed and shrouded the body might retain some dignity along the journey. Burial would have to take place at the lord's home, of course.

Hefting the burden and slowly carrying Santa Coloma from the field of battle, Arnau's gaze wandered across the grisly remains of Christian and Moor alike, all brothers in death. Now, as the heat of battle drained from him like the rapidly cooling bodies, those heretics lying mangled on the grass once more became a thing to be pitied. Especially with the knowledge that this particular personal tragedy could have been avoided but for the negligence – or even deliberate wickedness – of a Christian.

Della Cadeneta.

The man had better keep both eyes open from now on…

CHAPTER TWO

Arnau climbed the chapel steps with a sombre expression to the accompaniment of dirge-like chanting from the ornate room ahead. Each step seemed to him to be a position in the hierarchy of Aragon. This heavy, worn stone was Arnau and the house of Vallbona, a small, struggling and poor fiefdom near Barcelona. The second step with the groove from some careless spur-wearer was the chapel's owner, the Lord Berenguer Cervelló, who was currently being carried over it on a rich, fine funerary pall, wrapped tightly in white linen and smelling of strong, sweet spices to disguise the stench of a body brought a hundred miles under the Iberian sun. The third step, slightly less worn and with an ancient mason's mark visible in the corner, was the Lord Bernat d'Entenza, to whom Santa Colona himself had owed fealty and who was a close confidante of the fourth and final step: Pedro the Second, Count of Barcelona and King of Aragon. The nearest thing on the Iberian peninsula to God himself. Steps to power, and sometimes to grief.

Pedro the Second was not present, of course, for the funeral of his loyal knight Berenguer, who had died at the hand of the Moor in the service of his king. Pedro himself was far too busy establishing himself and his new rule, having succeeded only two years previously. Pedro, pious and in close league with the Pope, had enough on his plate, formulating plans to extend Christian control over Iberia, unlike his fellow monarchs Phillip and Richard who fought endlessly for control over their contested lands in France. Instead of the Aragonese king his favourite, and distant, cousin Bernat d'Entenza had travelled to the castle from his own fortress in Fraga. Arguably the most important and influential nobleman in the king's court, it would be seen as a mark of the regard in which Santa Coloma was held that such a noble might attend, even without the presence of the king. One might also point out a loose familial connection between the great, departed Berenguer lying tight-wrapped and pungent on the bier and the bored-looking Lord d'Entenza, who would likely be the man to administer the estate of Santa Coloma now, with only a daughter to inherit, regardless of how shrewd and impressive that young woman might be.

The bier reached the top step and was placed in the heart of the chapel while the various nobles, knights and men at arms took their places. The common folk stood outside in the courtyard, silently standing vigil for their lord. The chapel felt cold after the searing Catalan sun, and even in his heavy, fur-lined mantle displaying the rather obscure lion of Vallbona, Arnau shivered. His gaze played across the figures. Most were solemn, their faces downcast. Only five were not. Six, Arnau realised, if he counted himself.

The priest, of course, busy eulogising the great lord, had an upturned face, eyes upon heaven, where Berenguer's soul now resided, as his delicate voice drifted up in haunting tones to coalesce around the vaulted ceiling like smoke. Bernat d'Entenza, rather callously, had his scribe with him and was carrying out some unnamed business in whispered tones during the proceedings. Neither of them looked particularly sombre. Ferrer della Cadeneta, may the Lord send him rot within, had not once shown an iota of respect, his gaze repeatedly flicking between the preoccupied Lord d'Entenza and the last figure whose eyes had not once touched the ground.

Titborga Cervelló, daughter of Berenguer and heiress of his estate.

The lady of Santa Coloma had reached fifteen years of age only the week before her father's death, though it would have been a blind and short-sighted man who considered her but a girl. Something of an enigma and a prize at once, she was already a year past the age when one would have expected her to marry, and yet, surprisingly, remained untrothed. Arnau had watched Titborga grow over the seven years he had served Santa Coloma, watching the young woman advance in leaps and bounds with every visit from his home in barren Vallbona. Possessed of the same wit and will as her father, she was a voracious reader and orator, able to talk rings around the most loquacious courtier. She had been an able administrator even by twelve, handling the estate in conjunction with her father after her mother's passing. She was a mistress of the board at both backgammon and chess, as Arnau himself could attest. Blessed with smooth, pale skin and lustrous dark hair that fell in waves, she was a picture of beauty. And now she was the inheritor of the entire Santa Coloma estate. Her suitors would be queuing at the door once a respectful period of mourning had passed, probably sooner.

Arnau realised after a moment that he had been looking at the lady of the castle for longer than was truly respectable and glanced away only as her gaze touched his. He felt the heat of embarrassment rise in his cheeks and lowered his face until the redness faded. When he looked up again, she had her attention elsewhere.

Whatever the Lord d'Entenza decided was to happen with Titborga and the estate, it was the business of great men, not minor landowners such as Arnau. Vallbona was little more than a grand farmhouse with a tower, its inheritance an old coat of arms with barely the land and finances to support it. He would need to spend more time at Vallbona when he left Santa Coloma, attempting to improve the estate's farms alongside his old, boss-eyed steward if they were to be able to meet requirements from his liege over the next few years. Hard times had lain ahead in Vallbona even before the death of Berenguer.

The funeral droned to a close slowly, a mass reminding all of their own mortality and the need to follow the example of the man being eulogised, a small choir singing the praises of Berenguer and his line and exhorting the Lord God to watch over those he left behind. The body was removed and taken to the place of burial where a heavy stone coffin awaited, and finally the attendees dispersed with dour faces.

Ignored by the more powerful lords, Arnau spent some time with three of the other minor men at arms, drinking rich wine from the Santa Coloma vineyards and eating bread and slices of juicy lamb with local goat's cheese. They played dice – Arnau lost – and chess – Arnau won – and passed the day in quiet obscurity. Finally, as evening came on and the melodic strains of vespers rolled across the castle from the chapel, Arnau made his way to the small room in the gatehouse that he habitually used upon his visits. The heat had been stifling during the day, but the wind had changed at sunset, bringing an odd chill off the sea. Men who had stood atop the walls running with sweat only hours earlier were now wrapping up in cloaks and complaining about the breeze. Fires had been lit.

Arnau lay stretched out on his pallet, still in his funeral garb and now smelling of strong wine, pondering all the potential changes facing Santa Coloma and therefore also Vallbona. It was said that even so early in his reign the new pious King of Aragon sought a grand push south against the Almohads of Valencia. Since the enemy victory at Alarcos over the might of Castile, the reconquest of the peninsula had stalled and the Moors were becoming more confident and stronger with every passing month. And if Pedro the Second announced a new campaign, especially if the Pope were to throw in his support, all the God-fearing nobles of the country would be required to join the Crusade, bringing their men at arms with them. What then for Santa Coloma and its lesser knights? What then for parched Vallbona, which needed every hand to the plough to make it through the year?

He drifted into a near-slumber, half aware of the crackling fire in the corner of the room and the distant barking of a dog. Rosin burned in cressets, giving the room a glow of dark amber and a smell like torched pine trees. As had so often happened since the events at the Ebro days earlier, the first image to fill his wandering mind was that of blood and horses, of men and death, of Berenguer de Santa Coloma lolling, dead, in his saddle. He stirred uncomfortably at the thought, as though there might have been some way he could have prevented it.

He turned over, his mind picking out new images of blood and of death, of a man on a horse with a red cross on white, singing songs of joy in the midst of hell.

A knock at the door disturbed his reflections and Arnau rose, rubbing his weary eyes, and crossed to the door, pulling it open. The sudden draught the movement caused flared the fire in the hearth and smoke leaped up inside the room around the chimney breast. A diminutive figure stood in the passage outside, a young woman in drab dress and unimpressive wimple. He recognised her as one of the castle's maids – the personal maid of the Lady Titborga, in fact. His eyes narrowed.

'Yes?'

'Begging your pardon, my Lord de Vallbona, but the Doña Titborga requests your presence in the antechamber of the great hall with some urgency.'

Still frowning, Arnau nodded. He contemplated changing into something more appropriate than the dull grey of the funeral that he was still wearing now, but the summons had been an urgent one and so he simply threw over his shoulders a fur-lined mantle graced with his family's black lion, threadbare and darned in several places.

'Lead on.'

The maid, a pretty and voluptuous girl, led the way from the room, down through the tower and across to the hall. There, in an antechamber of ancient stone, beneath an elegantly vaulted ceiling, stood Titborga Cervelló de Santa Coloma in her mourning dress of purest white. The sound of loud conversation emerged from the great hall beyond the thick, heavy wooden doors and, though the details of the discussion could not quite be made out, they sounded purposeful and combative.

Arnau dropped to a knee and bowed his head in respect.

'My lady.'

'Rise, Señor de Vallbona,' she said in an odd, worried tone.

'How may I be of service?' he asked, climbing to his feet once more and adjusting his grey bliaut swiftly.

Something about the way the lady's eyes scoured the dim surroundings put him on edge, and when she spoke, her voice was quiet and suspicious. 'You are one of Santa Coloma's most trusted men, Arnau of Vallbona.'

'I have striven in my time to serve your father appropriately,' he replied, brow creased more than ever.

'My father spoke of you often, and well. I have seen you with him. He held you in esteem, perhaps more than one might expect for your somewhat minor rank.'

Arnau stifled the disappointment and irritation he felt at the rather blunt remark. Keeping his expression carefully neutral, he nodded. 'Your father was a great man. I looked up to him. Even at the end, I—'

'I need your help. Your *oath*, Señor de Vallbona.'

Now Arnau felt alarm. These were careful words spoken in a dangerous tone. What was happening? The evening of her father's funeral was no time for intrigues. The possibility of what might be asked of him should he give his oath so freely made him nervous, for certain, but he could not refuse such a request and live in good conscience. He had been oath-sworn to her family his whole adult life, after all. How poor it would be to honour the great Berenguer's memory by refusing to serve his daughter.

And there were other reasons, too, of course. What would Vallbona be without Santa Coloma? A poor farming fiefdom with no power, verging on bankruptcy. To refuse her would be to condemn himself and his lands anyway.

'I am yours to command, my lady.'

'So are many men,' she replied flatly. 'But most see me only as a chattel or a chit of a girl hanging on the surcoat of my father. I am the last of the direct line of Santa Coloma though, and the estate is mine, along with the authority and duty it carries. The Lord d'Entenza will almost certainly attempt to separate me from my inheritance and claim it for himself before my father's body is even cold. Santa Coloma is a wealthy title with a great deal of land – a serious prize even for a high nobleman. Were he not already wed, I would see d'Entenza's marriage bed in my future, and while that will not be my fate, I am certain that I am not to be left unchallenged as heiress. I am prepared to see the case for my father's estate argued in the royal court if need be, but many of my father's former supporters will side with the Lord d'Entenza, seeing endless possibilities there. I can rely on none of them. Only Maria here has my confidence. Maria… and a man my father trusted even with his life. I would have your oath, Master of Vallbona.'

A tinge of worry ran through Arnau. While he had the greatest respect for the lady and her house, and had devoted his life to

Santa Coloma, the very idea of standing against d'Entenza, a cousin of the king himself, was bone-chilling. A man does not pit himself against a king or his cousin lightly. Yet before he realised he was doing it, his knee hit the stone floor once again.

'I give you my oath as lord of Vallbona and vassal of the house of Santa Coloma that I will serve the Lady Titborga and no other until released by her word, or by my death.'

Titborga nodded and Arnau was surprised to hear a sigh of relief from her perfect lips.

'Then stay by my side. I may have need of your strength in the coming hours and days.'

Arnau bowed his head again and rose, moving to stand by the outer door. All was quiet and he, the lady, and her maid stood silently. What were they waiting for, he wondered, as he tried to catch snippets of conversation from beyond the door. It was impossible to make out anything useful with the roaring of the fire in that room and the gentle strumming of a vielle somewhere beyond, playing a current popular melody.

A sudden loud snort of disdain and a barked call from the hall within leaked through the door, and Arnau felt his blood chill a little. The name was *Cadeneta*, and that villain was almost certainly the source of the snort. The voice naming him had to be the Lord d'Entenza. The two men being together in the hall boded ill for the small group in the antechamber, and Arnau was about to suggest that they retire to somewhere more comfortable when he heard footsteps approaching the far side of the door. He straightened and tried to look important as the door to the great hall opened.

The Santa Coloma steward, an old man with an aquiline face and long, greying hair, stood in the doorway, silhouetted by the light of the roaring fire and of many candles. He bowed respectfully to the lady without and gestured with a sweep of the hand, stepping aside.

'Your presence is requested, my lady.'

Titborga strode into the hall of her father with a pride and assurance that belied her age and, as she approached her father's grand chair on the dais at the end – currently occupied by the Lord d'Entenza – she showed little sign of deference, her back straight and chin high. Despite his position as her vassal, Arnau felt an odd thrill of pride at the sight, as though *he* were her father. Consequently, despite the danger in the room and the power wielded by the man they approached, he found himself walking tall in her shadow and with a dignity of his own. He was Arnau de Vallbona, bearer of the black lion and knight of Santa Coloma.

His composure almost shattered as his eyes slid sideways from the king's cousin and took in the figure of Ferrer della Cadeneta standing close by, smug and oily. Arnau was suddenly very grateful that he'd not spent time changing and arming with his sword belt. Had he been able to put hand to steel right now, he would have found the urge almost irresistible. Perhaps he should tell the lady what he knew? She certainly had a right to know that her father had died through the wilful negligence of that serpent in red.

'I presume you have *summoned* me to confirm my inheritance of the estate of Santa Coloma?' Titborga said, her tone almost challenging and certainly lacking in any meekness or deference. Arnau felt his skin prickle at the aura of tension and danger that suddenly filled the room. The Lord d'Entenza's expression moved through a variety of emotions, settling into a furrow of disapproval.

'Santa Coloma has long been a bastion of Christian pride in the north,' d'Entenza replied coldly. 'The sword of Santa Coloma has been raised against the enemies of the Crown of Aragon since the days of your great grandfather. And that is where the problem lies. We live in uncertain times, with the Moor in control of Valencia and hammering on our gates to the south, Castile offering only threat and disfavour to the west as they flounder and recover from the disaster at Alarcos, and the attention of our foreign allies still riveted to the Holy Land, the kingdom of Outremer and the infidel who defiles our holy places.'

Arnau saw Titborga's hand grip into a tight fist. She knew what was coming. So did Arnau.

'I am the lady of Santa Coloma, my lord,' she said in a firm tone. 'My father raised me to understand the estate and with the ability to manage it in his absence as my mother had done before me. No one knows Santa Coloma better than I.'

'Lady—'

'You doubt me?' she snapped. 'Santa Coloma, an estate worth almost two hundred thousand gold *maravedi*, including nine farms, four wineries, six fiefdoms and two castles, with fealty from a further eight fiefdoms. I could provide you with a breakdown of the details if you wish, including the number of men at arms the estate can furnish at the king's call, how many cavalry, bowmen, crossbowmen.'

'Your intellect and administrative abilities are not in doubt, my lady,' d'Entenza said coldly. 'But a powerful estate should be led by a strong sword arm.'

'*Your* sword arm, I presume,' spat the young woman, and Arnau marvelled at her nerve.

'Hardly,' snapped d'Entenza, becoming angry. 'You are presumptuous, Titborga. Your father was soft on you. He spared the rod all too often, it appears, for you seem to forget your station.'

The young heiress wisely remained silent at that, though Arnau could see how her fingers had gone white with her powerful clenched grip.

'No,' d'Entenza said, sitting back in the old lord's seat. 'As your father's liege lord, it is my duty to see to the disposal of the estate. I have come to an arrangement with Señor della Cadeneta.'

Titborga said nothing still, but Arnau could almost sense the blood draining from her face.

'I have agreed that Don Ferrer will take your hand in marriage, joining the estates of Santa Coloma and Cadeneta under a strong military hand, as is appropriate in these dangerous times.'

'Never.'

'Do not test me, Titborga,' d'Entenza snapped. 'I held your father in great esteem and as such I seek the best interests of all concerned. You are too old for a virginal girl. You need a husband.'

'I need *no* husband.'

'The alternative is to hie yourself to a nunnery and I will acquire your estate on the authority of the crown.'

Arnau could see his lady beginning to tremble. With rage, he realised, not fear.

'I will contest the disposition in the court of the king.'

'My cousin will know where the good of the kingdom lies,' snarled the lord from the chair.

'You cannot marry me without my consent. I will seek an annulment from the crown on those grounds immediately.'

D'Entenza shot upright from his seat pointing at her with an angry, wavering finger. 'By *God*, girl, you will do as you are told! The marriage is a fair deal. You will be entitled to one third of della Cadeneta's estate in return.'

'And while he takes the opportunity to sell off my family's lands to adorn himself in gold, what am I supposed to do with a third of a chicken shed, two pigsties, and half an acre of mouldy turnips?' she snapped back at him. Arnau felt himself tremble. The sheer purple rage rising in the lord's face was matched by the impossible smugness of della Cadeneta.

'Enough!' d'Entenza roared. 'The match is made. You will give your consent or I will dispossess you on grounds of a vassal refusing her lord's command. That, as I am sure you are aware, would go to the court of my own direct superior, Pedro the Second, and the king would look rather disfavourably upon your presumption, I can assure you. You will consent to the marriage, you will go to Cadeneta and you will accept my judgement on the matter. Now begone.'

'Yes, my *lord*,' Titborga hissed, fitting more bile and spite into the title than Arnau would previously have thought possible. She turned, and Arnau started at the almost demonic expression she wore. The lady of Santa Coloma strode proudly from the hall, Maria the maid scurrying along behind. Arnau cast a last glance of utter hatred at della Cadeneta. It seemed that by the most unexpected and unfortunate turn of events he had just given his unbreakable oath to serve a woman who would shortly be della Cadeneta's wife. Would he have to kneel to that red-coated bastard?

He bowed curtly to d'Entenza, ignoring della Cadeneta completely, and then followed the lady from the room. She was surprisingly fast, given that she was not overly tall, and Arnau had to hurry as she swept from the building and made for the living quarters nearby. All the way to her apartments she said nothing, though Arnau could hear her angry breathing even above the sounds of castle life. Finally, as she entered her rooms, she spun angrily, Maria hurrying to shut the door and close the shutters of the window before even lighting the candles.

'I will *not* submit,' Titborga growled.

Arnau held up both hands. 'I understand, my lady. I hold personal grievances against della Cadeneta myself, and he is not to be trusted. But you have been left with little choice. D'Entenza effectively wields the power of the Crown of Aragon.'

Titborga pursed her lips and narrowed her eyes. 'How many times have you seen me lose a game of chess, Señor de Vallbona?'

'Rarely, if ever, my lady,' Arnau replied truthfully, 'but this is no game.'

'On the contrary. This is *very much* a game, just with the highest of stakes. Ferrer della Cadeneta is an animal. I have seen him with the women of my father's estate when he believed he could get away with it. He is the very epitome of a devil in a codpiece. My father overlooked his less savoury habits for the value of his sword arm.'

Should I tell her? Arnau wondered, but decided against it once more. She had enough to deal with right now, and was already vehement enough about della Cadeneta. She would need no further incentive to hate him.

'He simply desires the estates of Santa Coloma for their monetary value,' she went on. 'Lord d'Entenza does not realise how little he can expect from della Cadeneta in return for securing him my fortune and my chastity. The oaf will deflower me and seize my lands. The king would have no issue with that, but I can see della Cadeneta's plan as though it were threaded out in tapestry before me. He will not want lands removed from his own fief by more than fifty miles, and he will have no intention of occupying *this* castle in person and transferring his estate here, for he knows that many of his peers here despise him. So the lands, as they are, can be of little use to him except as coin. He will sell off my estates, hoard the payments and then accept an annulment from the king, allowing him to marry again and leaving me with nothing – ruined, both financially and physically. No. I will not accept this. Before he touches my flesh I will put a rondel dagger through his heart. And before he could sell one acre of my land, I would give it all to the Church.'

Arnau nodded. He could hardly fault her. 'Do nothing precipitous, though, my lady,' he cautioned her. 'There will be much to be put in order and, despite your careful accounting, the Lord d'Entenza will want a full inventory made of the estate for his own satisfaction. Added to that the need for an appropriate period of mourning and the time it will take for a betrothal and the organisation of a wedding, and you have some weeks' grace. Perhaps during that time we can find a way to circumvent this, to prevent it happening somehow without simply disobeying the king's cousin.'

Titborga paused for a time, eyes narrowing, deep in thought, and finally she nodded. 'You speak sense, Señor de Vallbona. We shall seek the wisdom of Church and state. Find me men versed in law. Priest or esquire, they will be found in Barcelona. We will scour the minds of the best men in the kingdom.'

'I will serve as best I may, Doña,' Arnau said quietly. 'But mind that your father has just this day been laid to rest. A period of mourning is appropriate, and during that time you should withdraw from civil life. It will not help your case in any way to be seen as disrespectful to your father's memory.'

The lady of Santa Coloma nodded. 'Then find the men we need and bring them here. We will consult them in privacy.'

Arnau bowed. Personally, he could see no solution. Standing against d'Entenza was tantamount to standing against the king himself, and no power in Iberia would do that easily. In counselling caution, he had bought time, but what they could achieve with such time, he could not guess.

Would that court life was as straightforward as battle.

CHAPTER THREE

Finding learned men with a good working knowledge of law and a sharp mind did not prove difficult. In fact, Barcelona seemed to be overflowing with such men, mainly priests, a few mendicants and even some lay practitioners. Finding a man who would consider aiding a young unmarried woman build a case against the greatest landowner in the region and cousin to the king proved to be a different matter entirely.

After three days of living in a pestilent inn on the city's outskirts, Arnau had found almost a round dozen men who claimed they could argue the case right up to the king's court, but who suddenly seemed either to doubt their abilities or to be far too busy to try the moment the name d'Entenza came into the conversation. Arnau had even tried to hoodwink one or two into coming with him without revealing too much detail, but those learned men pressed him until he revealed that which he had kept purposefully hidden, and the men soon lost interest in pursuing the case.

What's more, once or twice as he'd scurried around the streets of Barcelona, Arnau had felt eyes upon him, and had become certain that someone dogged his steps. He had seen the same cloaked figure – he was sure it was the same one, for no one sensible wore such a heavy mantle beneath the Catalan sun of a hot summer afternoon – several times. And by the morning of the third day the remaining lawyers he could find would no longer open their doors to him. Word, it seemed, had got round.

Thus it was that late in the afternoon three days after the Lord de Santa Coloma had been interred, Arnau de Vallbona rode into the castle, dejected and sour. Time was running out for the young Doña of Santa Coloma, and Arnau's only true hope of a solution had lain with seeking out the opinions of the sharp-minded practitioners of law. With the failure of that course, he had been wracking his brain for another direction to take, but had come up with nothing useable.

Legal recourse was going nowhere. Simple refusal of the betrothal would do no good, as had been made abundantly clear. Flight was idiotic. One potential solution had popped into Arnau's head and had sat there for some time, tempting him, before he'd dismissed it with a sigh. He could challenge della Cadeneta over his part in the death of Berenguer. A duel, sanctioned in law and public. But there were too many variables in such a plan. Firstly, though Arnau was no novice with a blade, della Cadeneta was a noted swordsman. Any duel was at least as likely to go his way as Arnau's, and that would only leave Titborga in yet deeper trouble. And even if he won, it would only buy a little time and further uncertainty. He felt sure that Lord d'Entenza would take such a course of action rather personally, and a new suitor would quickly appear on the horizon, chosen by the lord. No, satisfactory though it might be to try and put a blade through della Cadeneta's heart, it would not necessarily solve anything.

And so, his mind full of unacceptable plans and failed notions, Arnau dismounted in the courtyard and heaved his pack from the horse before leading her to the stables. The lad took the reins and went off with the beast and Arnau dropped his gear in his room before stomping across to the nobles' quarters with a heavy heart. He climbed the stairs and entered the corridor, forming in his head the approach he would take to delivering the bad news.

He stopped at the top of the stairs.

Ferrer della Cadeneta was at the far end of the corridor, rifling in the pouch at his belt, outside the door of Titborga's chamber. In the shadowy corridor, the cur looked truly furtive. He had not noticed the young man climb the stairs yet and, on instinct, Arnau slipped behind the door jamb at the stair top, peering around the edge with narrowed eyes.

Finally finding whatever it was he was looking for – it gleamed with a golden sheen in the torchlight – della Cadeneta replaced his pouch and straightened. He knocked at the door. Arnau held his breath, his fingers making their way down to the pommel of his sword where they danced, tensely. The door opened after a few moments and Arnau recognised the shape of the maid, Maria, in the opening.

'My lady is indisposed,' Maria said in tones loaded with careful respect.

Without so much as a by your leave, della Cadeneta simply grasped Maria by the shoulders and hauled her out into the corridor. The oily lord made to enter and simultaneously Arnau slipped out of the shadows, hand dropping from pommel to leather-bound hilt, ready to draw the sword, though there would be little room to wield it effectively in the narrow confines of the corridor.

He halted when he saw Titborga suddenly appear in the doorway in a simple white gown that clung to her in a most improper yet fascinating manner. Arnau could almost feel the lust emanating from the lord at the far end of the corridor, but there was so much assuredness in the lady's face he felt less fear for her than he'd expected.

'I am aghast at your interruption, good sir knight,' Titborga said in a withering, superior tone. 'Are you not mindful that I am a grieving daughter and that you are in the home of the great father I so recently lost? This is most unseemly.'

Arnau almost smiled at her manner. Most men would have shrunk before the force of her words, but della Cadeneta simply rolled his shoulders and cleared his throat.

'Come now, Titborga. We are to be entwined as man and wife in the coming days. Is it not my duty as a loving betrothed to comfort you in your time of grief? And I can be most… comforting. I can comfort all night if I must.'

The man had his back to Arnau, but the younger knight could picture the leering grin on della Cadeneta's face. Arnau's knuckles paled as his hand tightened on the hilt of his sword. He still had a knife on his other hip. Such a blade would be much more use in this place, though a knife in the back was the way of an assassin, not a Christian and a man of honour.

'If you defile my flesh with even a trace of your sickly finger,' Titborga replied in icy tones, 'then you will have dishonoured me and you will be granting me arrows for my legal bow. I shall save any impropriety from you and deliver it in my case for an annulment. It is in your best interest to leave me alone, della Cadeneta, lest in your impatience you lose me forever.'

But the lord was not so easily dissuaded. His arm reached out and, even as the lady recoiled, his index finger touched her chin, tracing a line along it towards her ear and then suddenly back across her throat in a meaningful way. Arnau heard himself utter a low growl. Titborga had stepped back, and della Cadeneta's other hand came up, opening as it did so. A gold locket in the shape of a heart dropped and then bounced upon the end of a delicate chain hanging from his fingers.

'A token of my undying affection,' the man said.

'A gilded offering,' Titborga countered, 'in a sordid attempt to buy my honour. Take your bauble and drop it in the privy.'

Della Cadeneta let out a sharp, unpleasant laugh. 'Oh, Lady of Santa Coloma, you ever display such *spirit*. I look forward to breaking you.'

Arnau felt his arm hairs bristling as the man turned to Maria, who was trapped in the corridor on the other side of the lord. The man's hands shot out and grasped the maid's breasts as he leered. 'Then I shall have a taste of what is to come,' he laughed, grabbing Maria by the shoulders and steering her towards the privy at the end of the corridor. Arnau felt the hatred within him peak, and Titborga stepped out of the doorway. Della Cadeneta paused for a moment, turning to the lady. 'Choose, Titborga Cervelló. Tonight I ride a Santa Coloma horse. It can still be the wild filly.'

Arnau started to pace forward angrily, but with a laugh, della Cadeneta disappeared into the privy with the maid. Titborga stood in the doorway, ashen faced.

'Go inside,' he told the lady as he stomped along the corridor, pointing back behind her with his left hand as he drew his blade with his right.

'You cannot,' she said, eying the sword.

'I cannot wait for God to visit him with a just reward. I shall do it for him.'

Titborga stepped out into Arnau's path. 'If you attack him, my Lord d'Entenza will see your head roll for such a thing.'

Arnau's fingers flexed on the sword hilt, but he knew the truth when he heard it. No matter his motivation, no good would come of such an act. If he were to kill della Cadeneta it would have to be in the open with no doubt as to the reason and motivation. In fair combat. And that brought him right back to the problem with the uncertainty of such a course.

'I will keep watch on your door, milady.'

'Do not do anything rash, Vallbona.'

'You have my word.'

She locked him with a long, steady, piercing gaze and then, satisfied, nodded and retreated to her chamber, clicking shut the door behind her. Arnau spent an uncomfortable few minutes then, standing outside her door, beset by the dual tortures of his lady weeping in her rooms, and the grunting and whimpering from the privy. Finally, the small wooden door at the end of the corridor was thrust open and della Cadeneta emerged, smoothing down his under tunic and pulling his bliaut back down into place. The waft of a hundred years of piss and shit billowed around him, and yet he remained the most unsavoury thing in the corridor to Arnau.

The lord paused as he stepped out into the passage, looking Arnau up and down. The younger knight suddenly realised he had not sheathed his sword, and the gleaming blade remained gripped tight in his right hand.

'If you intend to use that, Vallbona, you had better be sure of yourself. I have killed more men than the ague.'

For just a moment, Arnau wondered if he could somehow provoke della Cadeneta into launching an attack. Perhaps, if he were simply defending himself…? He swept aside the idea. Foolish. And della Cadeneta was unarmed. He would look the thug, while the oily lord would be the wronged man. No. Arnau sheathed his sword.

'I simply stand ready to preserve my lady's honour.'

'And take it at the first opportunity, I'd wager,' sniffed the lord. 'Do not ride that pony, young knight. I wish to break her myself and I would like her untouched.'

Arnau felt himself trembling with anger and clamped his hands on his sword belt in an attempt to resist the urge to gut the man there and then. Della Cadeneta simply laughed a horrible laugh. 'Oh, the certainty of youth,' he snorted as he stepped past Arnau through the narrow gap beside the corridor's wall. Maria emerged from the privy, flushed and not looking as distressed as Arnau might have expected. He was about to tell her to return to her mistress when there was a flurry of fabric and a whisper of air and a knife blade was suddenly at his throat.

Arnau flinched and even that tiny movement drew a bead of crimson. He held himself perfectly still as della Cadeneta moved around in front of him, the knife remaining perfectly still despite the movement, as though on gimbals. The lord grinned, hot breath carrying the stink of strong ale washing over Arnau, who almost recoiled before remembering the presence of the knife. One twitch of those fingers and the younger man would be breathing through his neck for the rest of his very short life. The knife was as sharp a blade as Arnau had ever encountered.

The man was so steady, so fast. Like a cobra in striking.

'Your place is standing by a door looking bored or throwing yourself into the press against the Moor, Vallbona. Do not think to try the patience of your betters. The next time you hold a naked blade in my presence I will slit your throat before you realise I'm even there.'

The knife was gone a moment later and della Cadeneta was sauntering off down the corridor towards the stairs, whistling a jaunty tune.

Maria stood before him, eyes bulging in shock. Arnau reached up and wiped away the drops of blood from his throat with a forefinger. 'Inside,' he said, gesturing to the door. The maid knocked politely and, at an acknowledgement from her mistress, disappeared inside, leaving the open door behind her. Arnau entered.

'Saints above,' Titborga whispered and, realising she was looking at his neck, Arnau reached up and wiped away a few fresh beads of blood.

''Tis nothing,' he said dismissively, though in truth he was still reeling from the speed of the man with his hidden knife. 'The low trick of a villain.'

'Your arrival was timely,' she said. 'I thank you.'

Arnau shook his head. 'You had the situation firmly in hand, my lady. I saw the ease with which you disarmed him. He went after easier pickings,' he said, earning a black look from Maria.

'Still, the presence of the only man of arms in whom I can trust relieves me of a great burden,' Titborga sighed. 'Though from the bleakness of your expression, I assume you met with little success in the city?'

Arnau slumped a little in the shoulders. 'I regret that it is so, my lady. It has become clear to me through my investigations that your case is a strong one. Many a good man said he could successfully mount such a case.' He noted the hope building in Titborga's eyes and regretted that he must dash it. 'Sadly, it appears that there is no lawyer, be he priest or layman, who is willing to prosecute even the surest case against the might of the d'Entenza family. And though your true enemy is della Cadeneta, you will I am sure appreciate that it is d'Entenza who we would face in the event.'

Titborga nodded. 'Then we must find a new plan of attack. You are a military man, Vallbona. Think of this betrothal as an ambush of which you have been warned. Apply your tactics and your strategies. Find a way around it. A way to outflank our ambushers.'

'If only it were so easy, Doña. More than once these past few days have I wished that life was as simple as the battlefield. That I had the direction and simplicity of a warrior at all times. How straightforward it is to be a warrior, or how pleasant to be a priest, charged with only a simple task.' His mind furnished him once more with a picture of that grand, proud man bearing the red cross as he hewed and sang, sang and hewed. Some men were both, of course.

Titborga strode over to the window and threw back the shutters. There, glowering purple in the afternoon gloom, the peaks of the hills behind the Santa Coloma lands watched over them. 'Somewhere out there, de Vallbona, is the answer.'

Arnau paced across the room to the window, uncomfortable standing beside the virginal young noblewoman in only a simple nightgown. His own gaze played across those peaks, then down to the tower where his own room lay, and finally to the courtyard. His breath caught in his throat. There, in the open, a cloaked figure crossed the courtyard and entered the great hall. Of course, evening was pulling in now and, while it was still warm, men going on duty for the night might well don a cloak against the chill later. But the coincidence was too great, and something about the figure told Arnau it was the same man he'd seen in Barcelona.

'It seems to me that we are carefully observed, my lady. Our every move is noted. My actions in Barcelona are even now being reported to the high lords in residence.'

Titborga frowned. 'How do you conclude this?'

'I was followed in the city, Doña. I could not prove it and did not see the man's face, but he just crossed the courtyard below us. I would stake my life upon it.'

'Then we are undone,' the lady sighed.

'The game is not over yet, my lady,' Arnau said suddenly. 'I have lost many a game of chess against you in my time. Sometimes with only a queen and a tower, a mate can still be achieved.'

'Can one be avoided?' Titborga asked archly.

'That remains to be seen,' Arnau replied, watching with nervous interest as the great hall doors opened once more and one of the castle's numerous servants appeared at a hurry. Moments later he reappeared from the periphery of the courtyard with della Cadeneta in tow.

'I think you should dress swiftly, my lady. Important dealings are afoot.'

Titborga regarded him for a moment, and then nodded. Arnau crossed to the door and exited the room, standing impatiently in the corridor for some time. Finally, the lady emerged dressed in a rich gown of claret hue with long, draping sleeves. Her belt was gold and intricately knotted. She had forgone a wimple and wore her hair long and braided with a simple unadorned gold circlet.

'Lead on, de Vallbona.'

Arnau bowed and, hand resting lightly on the pommel of his sword, he strode along the passage and down the steps, the light padding of Titborga and the maid close behind. They emerged into the pleasant evening air, the oppressive heat of the day now gone but the chill of night yet to arrive. A few folk remained in the courtyard and they bowed and tugged forelocks as their lady passed with her servant and man at arms. As Arnau approached the ornate, rounded arch of the great hall, one of his peers stepped out into the space.

'Stand aside.'

The man at arms, in his mail shirt but without helm or shield, shook his head. 'The Lord d'Entenza is in conference and does not wish to be disturbed.'

Arnau felt the rustle of fabric at his side and suddenly Titborga was stepping in front of him.

'The lord may be in conference, but he is in conference in *my* hall. You owe fealty to me, not d'Entenza. Step aside, lest I decide I am done with leniency for today.'

Again, as Arnau had heard in her exchange with the lord on the day of the funeral, there was a steeliness in Titborga's voice that was almost impossible to refuse and, though the man looked distinctly unsure and uncomfortable for a moment, he stepped aside with a bowed head.

'My lady.'

Titborga swept past him like a wave of nobility and into the hallway. A young serf stood beside the inner door, rooting around his nostril with gusto, straightening in a minor panic at the sight of the lady and her entourage bearing down on him.

'My… my lady, the Lord d'Entenza—'

'Get out of my way.'

She motioned to Arnau, who increased his pace, advancing ahead of her and pushing the serf out of her path. She paused for a moment, while the poor serf floundered on the floor in a panic, and Arnau opened the doors. As she stepped up, she hissed, 'Announce me.'

Arnau stepped inside and cleared his throat.

Bernat d'Entenza and Ferrer della Cadeneta were deep in conversation at the far end of the room – heated conversation, judging by their faces. There was no sign of a cloaked figure, but three men he did not recognise stood by the wall.

'The Doña Titborga Cervelló de Santa Coloma,' Arnau announced in a deep tone, 'mistress of this castle and daughter of the late Lord Berenguer Cervelló.'

He stepped aside and his lady swept past him like an unstoppable tide, Maria scurrying behind. Marvelling at her spirit and just a little nervous over the potential consequences, he marched down the hall behind her and came to rest as she did, facing the gentlemen, slightly behind his lady, at her shoulder.

'Am I to be so disrespected that clandestine meetings are held in my own hall without my knowledge?'

Della Cadeneta threw an unpleasant sneer at her, then turned to the Lord d'Entenza, indicating the new arrivals with a cursory sweep of his arm. 'You see the problem, my lord. Elegantly illustrated by the young lady and her hired thug.'

Arnau bristled, but kept carefully quiet.

'I am a problem?' she asked, her voice dangerous.

Lord d'Entenza sighed. For the first time, Arnau noted signs of strain about the man. He genuinely believed he was doing the best thing for a spoiled brat of a girl. Arnau knew at that moment that there would be no shifting d'Entenza.

'My lady, if you would kindly be calm,' the senior lord sighed, 'I will explain.'

'Explanations be damned,' Titborga snapped. 'This snake pries into my every affair and now he seeks to undermine what little authority I have been allowed to retain.'

'You see, my lord?' della Cadeneta sighed. 'There is no caging her.'

D'Entenza shot him a hard look. 'I have no intention of *caging* the Doña de Santa Coloma, della Cadeneta, and you would be wise to watch both your words and your tone.' He turned back to Titborga. 'Is it true that you sent your man to Barcelona?'

'There would seem little point in denying it,' Titborga replied acidly. 'But then I fail to see why I *should* deny such a thing. I am still the lady of these lands and it is my perfect right to send a man into the city should I wish. You would deny me that?'

D'Entenza rubbed his eyes wearily. 'Why must you all test me at every turn? I can hardly wait to return to Fraga.' Titborga opened her mouth to say something regrettable, but did not have the chance as the lord continued. 'I have been informed that you seek legal counsel to overturn my decisions and lock horns with me before the king. I have told you before that I will not have you defying me, no matter how proud your lineage or how much I respected your father. I was somewhat undecided with regard to della Cadeneta's request but, by God, lady, you have made the decision easy. Have your maid pack your essentials. I will have the rest taken care of.'

'My lord?' Titborga said, and her voice sounded for the first time uncertain, wavering.

Arnau felt the crevasse of failure opening beneath them.

'You will leave Santa Coloma on the morrow and travel to Cadeneta where you will await the arrival of your husband-to-be.'

Titborga's eyes bulged. 'That is impossible. Unseemly. Unacceptable. You *cannot* farm me off into some dungeon where this rapist will dishonour me each day before and after a wedding.'

Della Cadeneta took an angry step forward, hand going to his bliaut where Arnau presumed the hidden knife lay concealed. Lord d'Entenza threw out an angry arm towards the man. 'Hold, della Cadeneta. If you lay one finger upon her now, I will presume she is not far from the mark with her accusation, and I will act accordingly.' He straightened. 'The death of my dear friend Berenguer was a wretched and sobering event and we should be mourning his passing with all appropriate gravitas. Instead I find myself mediating amid a group of squabbling children.'

He pointed at Titborga.

'You, Doña, have lands and money and a good, old name. Moreover you have the spirit of your father and a mind to match the shrewdest philosopher. But you also have an unseemly stubborn streak of which I do not approve. We live in a dangerous age, Titborga de Santa Coloma. God and the king both require that we do what we must to pursue the cause of right, to drive the heretic from our shores and to let peace and prosperity settle once more upon the land. This cannot be done with hot words and able administration. Good lands need a strong knight to lead them, and there are plenty of strong swords in the service of Aragon who could achieve great things for the kingdom had they your advantages. Della Cadeneta, current childishness notwithstanding, is one such lord. With his sword arm and your resources, you will make a powerful asset for the king. It is my duty to see that happen. You *will* go to Cadeneta as I command, and you *will* marry Don Ferrer as I order. There will be no further argument on the matter.'

As Titborga's mouth opened in an 'O' of astonished fury, ready to unleash a fresh tirade, Arnau bridled at the insufferably smug face of della Cadeneta.

'And *you*,' snapped d'Entenza, rounding on the leering noble. 'You will not touch the woman until you are wed. You will not even breathe near her, because if I learn from any source that you have deflowered this virginal daughter of the great Berenguer de Santa Coloma I will have you riding the Judas cradle before the sun lowers. Do you understand me?'

Della Cadeneta gave his lord a sullen nod.

'Good. Have some of your men join a party from Santa Coloma and prepare to escort the lady to your home. While there she will be accorded every honour that her rank and sex demand. The same penalty awaits you if I hear my instructions have not been followed.'

Della Cadeneta's eyes closed to slits and he glared through them at the trio in the hall. D'Entenza threw out a finger towards Titborga. 'I see you nocking a new arrow to your verbal bow, young lady. Do *not* try my patience further lest I be tempted to let your husband do as he wishes.'

Arnau tensed, waiting, but a moment later Titborga turned without another word or a bow and stormed from the room. Arnau caught just a moment of the sheer sense of victory upon della Cadeneta's face before he too turned and followed his lady from the hall.

CHAPTER FOUR

The journey to Cadeneta, a village nestled in the forested hills of the Prades range, was some sixty miles through the Catalan hinterland, totalling three days of slogging through the heat of the day. Not for Titborga, of course, who rode in a covered carriage with Maria. But Arnau rode with the rest of the company, the horses raising a cloying dust cloud in the dry Iberian summer.

Every mile that brought them closer to Cadeneta and brutal matrimony made the young Doña of Santa Coloma slightly more obstinate and troublesome, and made Arnau a little more desperate and twitchy. All three of them, lady, maid and guard, knew that once they were ensconced in the Lord della Cadeneta's home there would be little chance of freedom. They knew that, given Titborga's currently weak position and d'Entenza's temporary support of her would-be husband, there would be no recourse. The lady would be little more than a prisoner, or a prize, the maid ignored and Arnau essentially enrolled into the service of a man he hated.

There was precious little opportunity for the three of them to discuss options during the journey, with the lady and her maid in the vehicle and Arnau following on with his horse. The rest of the column had been carefully constructed of della Cadeneta's men, ever watchful. The cur had limited Titborga's own entourage to one maid and one man and had simultaneously managed to persuade the Lord d'Entenza that his involvement was entirely unnecessary. The high lord had been only too happy to leave the arrangements in della Cadeneta's blood-stained hands and thus, apart from the three of them, the entire caravan of wagons, horses and carriage belonged to the corrupt maggot. The only bright aspect of the journey was that della Cadeneta himself was not among them. The man had been detained by d'Entenza on a number of matters and would follow on in days, allowing Titborga a little breathing space as he left the journey in the hands of his captain.

The first night they had stopped in some backwater of which Arnau had never heard, in an inn that smelled of sweat and burned meat. The young man had sat at a table in the corner with the two women and eaten a wholesome, if somewhat plain and boring, meal. Titborga had asked quietly how they could perhaps cause the column to halt and turn around, but even a whispered comment had been enough to draw a few looks from their escort, and Arnau had been forced to caution the lady to silence while in the company of della Cadeneta's men. At the end of the meal, while most of the Cadeneta soldiers caroused in the bar, the captain of the company had the ladies escorted to a room and guards put on the door. Arnau had made his way up but had been forbidden from entering the ladies' room on the grounds of 'propriety'. He had spent an impotent and frustrating night in the bunk room with half a dozen drunken soldiers instead.

The second day had dragged them ever closer to the Muntanyes de Prades and the village of Cadeneta. The Ordal Hills through which they had travelled much of the first day were now left behind, and they moved along a wide valley, then across another small hilly range and back down towards the plains.

That was where disaster – or more properly, a blessing – struck. The captain had been content that they were making good time and would reach Cadeneta easily by the evening of the third day. Then, rattling down through a landscape of brown and grey slopes, the carriage had struck a rock jutting from the verge and the wheel had broken. Though the iron band around the wheel's circumference remained intact, two spokes had snapped. The captain had tutted irritably but refused to let such minor damage slow them. The driver had warned him that the wheel would not bear the vehicle's weight like that, but the captain had been adamant – he wanted to reach Cadeneta, and would not allow such a thing to cost them precious time. They had set off once more and gone less than a hundred yards when the wheel rim had cracked and two more spokes snapped. The wheel broke entirely and the carriage crashed to one side, terrifying the horse pulling it and almost jerking the animal from its hooves. The ladies inside had screamed in panic as the whole column halted and men rode back and forth, shouting commands and queries.

It had been so farcical that it drew a laugh from Arnau. Amid the chaos of shouting men there were several distinct voices. The captain, snapping angrily at everyone and laying the blame squarely with the carriage's driver. The driver, reacting with ire and blaming the captain for not heeding his opinion. Maria the maid crying and nursing bruises where she had been thrown against the side of the carriage. Titborga demanding that the captain do something about her discomfort. Utter chaos.

Finally a man was dispatched to the nearest village, and returned an hour later with a wheelwright, who looked the damage and the carriage over and announced that he had a wheel he could fit to the carriage in his store, but it would take an hour to get there and back with the replacement, and then at least an hour to fit it. The captain had demanded that the local do it in half that time, and the wheelwright had responded that he'd be happy to do so, if the captain would just move his village a little closer. The captain had fumed and ranted. Arnau had laughed.

In the event, it took a little over four and a half hours from the initial break to get the carriage back safely on the road. Arnau had watched the craftsman work and had swiftly formed the opinion that the man was being deliberately slow just to irritate the captain. When he had finished and waited for his payment, the captain had passed over only two thirds of the sum requested, holding some back for what he termed 'deliberate delays and troubles'. Arnau had chuckled into his glove as the wheelwright simply took up a great heavy hammer and held it over the spokes of the replacement wheel threateningly. Bellowing his displeasure, but in no position to argue, the captain had paid over the rest of the sum and the wheelwright went on his way. As he left, Arnau had flicked a couple of extra coins to the man for the entertainment.

The effect of the accident on the journey was profound. That night they stayed in another grotty inn somewhere a good ten miles short of their goal for the day. The captain had been so irate by the end of the day that he had retreated to his room with two bottles of local wine and not emerged even for food. Consequently, not having been given orders to the contrary, the guards allowed Arnau into Titborga's room that evening, where they discussed their options in subdued tones.

'We can clearly rule out damage to the carriage as a cause to turn back,' sighed Titborga.

'There will be no turning back, I'm afraid, my lady,' Arnau replied. 'We have covered thirty miles or so already. We are somewhere around halfway, and it would be as easy now for the captain to plough on than to return. I regret to say that this column is now irrevocably bound for Cadeneta. And if there were ever a chance that the captain might consider a diversion or an alternative, I think we can confirm that after today there is precious little chance of that.'

'Will we make it to Cadeneta tomorrow?'

Arnau shook his head. 'The captain will push for it, but he will not succeed. Cadeneta is some five miles up in the Prades hills, if I remember the maps correctly, and we still have thirty miles to go. We might reach the edge of the hills if he is determined enough, but no sane carriage driver would risk the hill roads in failing light. No, we will have another night in an inn like this, and then press on the next morning, arriving at around noon, by my estimate.'

'Then I have just one day of liberty remaining,' Titborga huffed. 'I task you, then, Arnau de Vallbona, with effecting my escape in the little time we have left.'

Arnau's frown was deep. 'Doña?'

'I will not submit and meekly enter the house of a man who will rape me and steal my family's lands. My father, God preserve his soul, would disown me for such a thing. I will not reach Cadeneta.'

'My lady, what other option is there?'

Titborga straightened in her seat. 'Before we left Santa Coloma I completed a set of documents that will see all the lands of my family donated to the Church. Perhaps even a life of service to Our Lord might suit me? I have often considered it, and increasingly so these past few days. And should there be no other way, I shall die without feeling that loathsome touch, and my estate will go to God and not to that lout.'

Arnau felt his flesh chill at the thought. 'My lady, you *cannot* take your own life. The fires of hell await anyone who stoops to such a thing. Besides, the Church might refuse the lands of a suicide on principle. This is foolish.'

'If the worst comes to the worst, Vallbona, I shall not take my own life. *You* will.'

'Doña—'

'You will put a blade through my heart as you would a critically injured comrade on the battlefield. I shall not be denied heaven, and you will have released me. You will then take the documentation and ride for Barcelona, where you will lodge it with the cathedral there.'

'Doña, this is too much to ask.'

'Do not baulk at this, Vallbona, for it is too important. But fear not, for I do not intend to shuffle off the mortal coil so easily. I intend yet to live and thwart della Cadeneta.'

'Now *that* I will drink to,' Arnau said with feeling, and took a swig of wine from his cup. 'But how?'

'Tomorrow eve will be our last chance,' she repeated. 'Unless something unexpected occurs during the journey, we must be prepared. We will flee tomorrow night. You must have horses ready for the three of us. Saddled and harnessed and somewhere in the open.'

'My lady,' Maria said in breathless worry, 'I cannot ride.'

'With angry soldiers intent on harm behind you, I suspect you will learn fast,' Titborga responded.

Arnau was shaking his head. 'It is madness, Lady. Where will we go? None of us knows this area well. To the south somewhere is Tarragona, but none of us has a connection there. Our only allies lie back at Vallbona and Santa Coloma, and that would just be walking into the lion's mouth once more. Flight with no planned destination is foolhardy, my lady.'

'Better to be a fugitive than the wife of della Cadeneta. Better to be a *corpse* than that.'

There would be no turning her from such a path, Arnau could see even now. He sighed. 'Then we ride for Tarragona. At least there we will find civilisation. Perhaps we can seek the aid of the bishop there. Sanctuary is still an option, if nothing else. Even della Cadeneta would never stoop to breaking into a cathedral to retrieve you.'

A short while later, driven from the room by the guards so that the ladies could enjoy a respectable night's sleep, Arnau returned to his own room and began to ponder on how to best effect a safe flight. Sleep came slowly that night, and was troubled when it arrived.

He rose early with the dawn light and disappeared into the village with his spare saddlebag. With loose coin he purchased smoked sausage, hard cheese, a loaf of bread and other provisions. He was just making his way back to the inn when he passed a smith at his forge, already into his day's work as the dawn mist cleared from the hills. The craftsman's activity attracted Arnau's attention as something went wrong and the bearded young man spat a curse. Arnau paused, his eyes straying across the man's work. He was fashioning curved iron brackets for some reason, but had hammered too hard on one. It had bent back further than intended and was now wrapped around another. Arnau's shrewd gaze took in the mistake and a slow smile spread across his face.

'Can you bend the other one, so that it interlocks?' he asked the smith.

The man frowned at his mistake and then looked up. 'Like a caltrop?'

'Precisely like a caltrop. How long would it take you to do that with all of these?'

'Not more than a quarter-hour,' the smith replied, 'but I *need* these.'

'I'll pay you well.'

The smith smiled. 'Twelve caltrops, then?'

Arnau nodded and dropped what he believed to be a generous price on the table. The smith's grin suggested he'd been correct, and he added more coins. 'These and four spare horseshoes, each with a four-inch span. Can you deliver them to the inn?'

The man nodded and went back to work, and Arnau returned to the inn to find the rest of the party beginning to break their fast and look to their travelling gear. As he also went about his business, Titborga and the maid both put in an appearance, the lady throwing a silent questioning glance at him from across the room. Arnau gave her a subtle, barely perceptible nod.

The captain emerged a few minutes later in, if anything, a worse mood than the previous day. A hangover added to his irritation and made him waspish and unapproachable. There was a sullen and angry atmosphere as the last of them ate and began to make ready the horses and carriage. The blacksmith appeared in a timely fashion, seeking Arnau, and the captain demanded to know what he was doing. The young soldier fished in the bag the man had brought and produced a horseshoe, waving it at the angry, flush-cheeked officer.

'After the carriage yesterday, I do not intend to be slowed by such misfortune. A spare shoe or four is a sensible precaution.'

The captain huffed, but nodded. Deprived of a reason to take out his anger on Arnau, he turned to his men. 'Why do none of *you* think ahead like that?' he snapped.

The party forged on in the morning sunlight as the heat of the day gradually began to assert itself. They travelled hard and at an uncomfortable pace set by the captain, who was determined to try for the unattainable and reach Cadeneta by nightfall. Arnau had cause to smile when one of the escort's horses threw a shoe and the captain, steaming with irritation, was forced to come to him, cap in hand, for one of his replacement shoes. One of the serfs travelling with them did a passable job of removing the loose, broken shoe and nailing on the new one, but the incident cost them another half an hour, adding to the captain's constant simmering ire.

They moved across the flat farmland, pausing for a late lunch break at a small walled village called Puigpelat and then forging on past the city of Valls, the Prades range beginning to loom ahead as a dusky blue ribbon of hills. As the sun dipped towards that line ahead of them and the town of Valls began to flicker with torches and lamps against the coming evening, so the captain's mood deteriorated even further. From passing comments, Arnau surmised that the man had been given appropriate moneys to see them through three days of travel to Cadeneta, and no more. The captain was already personally out of pocket from the replacement wheel, and an extra night of inn accommodation for the entire party would seriously eat into the man's purse. Arnau could imagine how difficult and dangerous a matter it might be to solicit a reimbursement from the Lord Ferrer della Cadeneta, and that looming necessity would only make the captain all the more unhappy.

The man finally gave up on their chances of reaching their destination as the sun slid behind the hills and the light took on an indigo tint. Even then he lobbied to continue into the evening but, as Arnau had predicted, the carriage's driver flatly refused to try the hill roads in the gathering gloom. That way, he announced, lay both broken axles and broken necks.

They stopped for the night at some grand farming estate, where the captain negotiated with a hard-nosed landowner for space for them all. The captain most certainly paid over the odds for what they secured, though he still saved on what a proper inn would have cost them. As the entire party settled in, Arnau exchanged glances a number of times with the lady, each of them taking in everything around them, attempting to work out what was possible and what was not.

There were ten soldiers in the group and five serfs, as well as the captain, the carriage driver and the three of them. With the three spare horses they had brought, there were fifteen beasts now being stabled in the farm's facilities on the far side of the yard. The landowner had steadfastly refused to let anyone stay in his own house, but had temporarily evicted some of his workers and the overseer to allow them a small stone house and a sizeable bunkhouse. The ladies, Arnau and the captain were to have the house, while the rest would share the bunk room. Moreover there was to be a guard on the house and one on the stables at all times, partly to maintain a watch over the lady, but mostly because the captain did not trust these rural provincials further than he could throw them and wanted a constant watch on the safety of all of them and their gear.

The place's owner had grudgingly agreed to feed them all, and three of the estate's workers visited their bunk room and house an hour after arrival with a huge cauldron of unidentifiable spiced meat and turnip stew and bread, along with cheap, cracked bowls for all. Arnau and the ladies ate with the rest, silent and watchful. He knew Titborga was right: they had to go tonight if they were to go at all. But how best to be about it? They would have to make it out of the house in which the captain also resided, past the guard on the door, past another guard on the stables, and then leave in a manner that discouraged pursuit.

They finished their meal and sat for a moment in silence as two of the soldiers complained about the lack of wine or beer since they were not in an inn. The captain, clearly an angry and contrary man by nature, began by snapping at the two men and calling them dullards and drunkards – somewhat unfairly given that he himself had been the only one today sporting a hangover – but by the end of his tirade he had joined in the moaning about the absence of alcohol. When the serfs came to collect the cauldron and bowls, the captain enquired of them were they might acquire wine, and the drudges informed him that the town of Picamoixons was but two miles away, though there was a winery only half a mile from the farm if they could persuade the owner to open of an evening.

Arnau felt an opportunity opening up before him and prayed hard and silently as he listened to the exchange unfold. The two men who'd bemoaned the lack of beverages volunteered to ride to the winery and procure drink for them all. Sixteen men down to fourteen – that would help. The captain snorted that the two men were moonstruck if they thought for a moment he would let them loose in a winery with his money. He would personally supervise and assure they were not cheated and that all the wine made it back. Arnau's heart leaped. Sixteen down to *thirteen*, losing the captain and two of his men.

The soldiers escorted Arnau and the ladies back to the house and then, with a guard on the door, the young man set to scouring the place. Sure enough, there was a servants' door at the rear of the kitchen, barred from the inside. He quietly slid open the bolt and peered out into the evening light. He could just see the stables across open ground. The bunkhouse was on the other side of this building and completely hidden from view. Arrogance and carelessness go hand in hand, and the captain was so sure of himself now that no one had bothered to check for another exit from the building. Thus the servants' exit was unguarded. He shut the door once more and, pausing at the kitchen fire, perused the log basket and selected a length of timber from it. He then returned to the front of the house and watched from the window, waiting for the captain and his men, who were currently arguing, as seemed the norm, to leave. Arnau focused on the three men, ear twitching. At times like this, every ounce of information could be vital.

'… much better,' one of the soldiers finished.

'I don't care how far it is, I am not buying wine from *there*.'

'But it's good, Captain. I've had it before and it's only three miles south of here.'

'That place is a pox on the world,' the captain snapped. 'If there's anything less trustworthy than a man who gives his cock to God, then it's a *woman* who takes the vows.'

'The Templars are—'

'The Templars are *trouble*,' snapped the captain, 'and none more so than the bitch of Rourell. We will try the local winery. Even if it tastes like piss, it won't taste like conceit and chastity.'

They departed a moment later and Arnau, mind racing, heart pounding, turned to the two women in the room.

'There's a chance. A *real* chance.'

'With the captain gone?'

Arnau smiled. 'Better than that. Better even than the cathedral in Tarragona. There are Templars nearby, at a place called Rourell. Just three miles south, the captain said. He doesn't trust them, or the "bitch of Rourell" in particular. Perhaps it is a nunnery? If so it would be the safest place for you right now. Even if the captain hates the Templars, and I know that they're not always the nobles' favourites, few would dare challenge the order. The Pope takes a dim view of soldiers invading the houses of God.'

Titborga leaned back, a concerned expression on her face. 'The Templars do not have nuns, Vallbona. Would that they did.'

'Oh they do, my lady. Maybe they're not *supposed* to, but I've come across them occasionally.'

She smiled a calculating smile. 'Then my destiny, I fear, lies with the sisters of the Temple. Can you get us from this place and into their reach?'

'I think so, if we go while the captain is not here. The men are full of food and tired from the day. Few will be alert. There is a servants' door from the kitchen that looks out to the stables. Watch for me from that door. When you see me signal, hurry towards me as quietly as you can, hunched low. We need to leave this place unobserved if at all possible. Watch for the sign and be ready to go at any moment.'

Without further discussion, Arnau hurried across and collected their bags, slinging them all over his shoulder with a grunt at the extreme weight. He would have to brazen this out. They needed all their gear with the horses and, with Arnau's armour and various heavy items contained within, he could not risk sneaking from the servants' exit. If he were heard, which was likely, his discovery would reveal the existence of the other exit. Hurrying down the stairs, he emerged through the front door to the surprise of the man guarding it. The soldier gripped the sword at his side as Arnau appeared, and he stepped back, holding up his other hand in a challenge.

'Where are you going?'

'Stables,' Arnau replied in an offhand tone. 'Setting things ready for the morning.'

'You're not supposed to leave.'

'I'm not leaving. I'm going to the stables to do a few chores and then returning. Anyway, I suspect that if you think back you'll realise that it's the lady of Santa Coloma you are guarding, and not me. Not unless your lord intends to bed me too.'

This drew a smirk from the soldier, and Arnau was more than a little relieved to see the man's hand on the sword hilt relax. Time to add some subtle reassurances that nothing was amiss.

'Will there be wine made available for us, you think?'

The soldier snorted. 'The way Captain Ruiz is wading through the stuff at the moment, I doubt *any* of us will get a look in.' The man's smile slipped as he remembered he was talking to the lady of Santa Coloma's man and not one of his own compatriots. 'Be quick.'

Arnau nodded. 'I intend to. Nice warm bed in there.'

Before the man could reply Arnau hurried off, adjusting the bags as he went to redistribute the weight a little more evenly. As he walked his head remained low, yet his eyes searched out everything. Two more men stood in front of the bunkhouse engaged in a relatively friendly argument, though neither of them paid him any attention. He glanced up towards the window at which he had so recently stood and saw no sign of the women. Good. They must be at the servants' door already. He rounded the corner of the house swiftly, dropping out of sight of both the guard on the front door and the bunkhouse with its denizens. Still, he needed to be brazen. Sneaking would draw so much more attention if he were spotted. He sauntered slowly towards the stables, still sweating beneath the heavy load, and as he reached the archway into the timber building that remained gloomy and dark even with three torches in sconces, he spotted the two occupants. One was the guard who had been set to watching the stable, and the other was one of the serfs, who was busy filling a nosebag. The guard was scratching his nethers with a bored look on his face and had yet to spot Arnau in the gathering gloom. Trusting to luck, the young man slowed and was rewarded for his patience as the serf boy slipped from sight to attach the feedbag to one of the horses. Faced now with only one witness, the young soldier entered the stable and let the bag containing his mail shirt slip slightly from his shoulder.

As the guard suddenly noticed the new arrival and the commotion, Arnau put on a desperate face and visibly struggled to keep the bulky and heavy load on his shoulders. Staggering a little, he looked imploringly at the guard and hissed, 'Help?'

The man paused for a moment, clearly struggling to decide between blissful inactivity, watching this buffoon struggle, or helping the man like a good Christian. Charity eventually won out and the man scurried over and grabbed the slipping bag of mail, grunting with the weight.

'Thanks,' Arnau said with heartfelt gratitude as his hand reached up to the other bags. As the guard struggled to help haul the armour bag back onto his shoulder, he failed to see Arnau producing a stout wooden stick from another. The guard squawked with alarm as he suddenly took the weight of the whole bag when Arnau let go and, suffering and struggling, he was utterly unprepared for the blow that connected behind his ear, driving his wits from him and his eyes up into his head.

This was it. The deed was done and there was no going back now. They had to move. If they were stopped and the captain discovered what had happened, Arnau would be cut to pieces, Maria probably handed round the men until she was broken, and Titborga bound and gagged and delivered to her new husband thus. So he breathed deeply, hefted the log from the fire basket, dropped the bags and hurried along to the stall where the serf had been feeding the horse. The lad rounded the edge of the stall just as Arnau arrived, his eyes wide in surprise. The boy's gaze slipped past Arnau to the guard near the arch, and he opened his mouth to shout. The log smacked into his forehead rudely, and the serf folded into a heap, unconscious in a single blow.

Hurrying now, against the time the captain and his men returned or some random Cadeneta soldier happened to visit the stable, Arnau moved up and down the stalls. He located his own horse quickly enough, as well as the two upon whom he'd had an eye all day – the pair he'd judged to be a combination of speedy, obedient, and steady. Maria could not ride at all, and he could hardly imagine Titborga being a *great* horsewoman, so forgiving beasts were of paramount importance. Locating the three, he unhitched them, removed their nosebags, and brought them out towards the arch. There, he swiftly attached the saddlebags to them, pausing with his own to remove his mail shirt, shield and sword. As quickly as he could, struggling a little, he slipped into the armour, then fastened his bags and shield to the horse, buckling his sword at his side. Shushing metallically with every movement now, he hurried across to the small door at the far end of the stable from the main arch and ducked outside. The evening was fast settling in, and true darkness was on its way. His eyes slowly adjusted to the light and he noted with relief that the servants' door at the house's rear was ajar. He waved madly at the door where the women would be waiting and after a moment it opened, two figures emerging, running for the stable.

Satisfied that the women were safely on their way, he ducked back inside once more and grasped the reins of the three horses, leading them towards the archway. His heart skipped as he realised that the heap of the unconscious guard was moving. Slowly, the man unfolded, rising to a crouch, shaking his head. Arnau fumed. Why hadn't he hit the man twice for good measure?

Letting go of the reins once more, he ran over to the groggy guard. The man was recovering quickly now, and rising to his feet. Arnau hit him even as he tried to draw his blade, knocking him back to the floor. His mailed elbow thudded into the guard's forehead, but it was not that blow that did the damage, for he heard the crack as the man's head smacked against the stone flag below. He could do nothing about the yelp that escaped the man's lips as he fell back, and Arnau rose and hurried over to the horses.

'We go now?' Titborga asked in a hiss as she and Maria arrived.

'We do. We've minutes at most.' He helped the lady up into the saddle and then repeated the process for the nervous maid. There was an alarming moment when Maria almost slid straight off the other side of the horse onto her head, and she cried out in panic. Titborga hushed the woman, but it was too late. In the still of the evening air there was precious little chance that cry had gone unheard. Desperately, he and Titborga managed to get the maid settled in the saddle, and Arnau hauled himself up urgently.

'Go,' he said, gesturing to the arch as he rummaged in his saddlebag. The Doña de Santa Coloma needed no second urging, and walked her horse from the stables into the open, breaking into a trot immediately as she turned and angled away from the other buildings, out towards the fields to the south. The maid clattered along inexpertly behind her, and Arnau felt a moment's despair at their chances of getting away with Maria faffing uselessly, steering the horse this way and that in confusion. He paused for only a moment, letting the ladies get a little way ahead as he scattered the contents of the bag across the archway with a metallic rattle. His heart sank as he saw the first of the Cadeneta men running around the house towards them, drawing a sword as he came.

'For God and Santa Coloma,' he snarled, drawing his own sword and glancing momentarily at his fellow fugitives. Maria was not doing well, but she had managed somehow to achieve a sort of zigzag wandering trot. Titborga was already in the fields, trotting like an expert, clearly waiting to burst into a canter as soon as the others were with her. He turned his attention back to current perils.

The soldier ran towards Arnau, brandishing his sword, but he was no great warrior and was already struggling for breath as he reached the young man on the horse. Arnau simply wheeled his steed around and swung his sword, flat of the blade facing the man. The soldier's weapon lunged for Arnau but missed by a clear foot, and Arnau's own blade smashed into the man's skull like a hammer blow, sending him in a pirouette to the ground.

Others were coming now and, while Arnau had felt more than comfortable facing that one sluggish man, battling a whole crowd was an entirely different matter. He turned his horse and started to trot off after the women, sheathing his sword once more. As he caught up quickly with Maria, he reached out and grabbed her reins.

'Kick the bloody thing,' he shouted. 'Make it trot.'

She did so, belting the horse rather heavily in the side. The combination of that and Arnau's encouraging noises and guiding hand on the reins led the beast into a proper trot and then, his hand stilled gripping the reins of both horses, into a canter. Maria's eyes were wide in panic and she made worried squeaking noises. 'Leave me behind,' she offered in a small voice, but Arnau shook his head. 'Your lady needs a maid and it can't be me. I'm going to get you up to a gallop and then let go. All you need to do then is keep her pointed south, kick her if she slows, and try not to fall off.'

The maid let out another worried squawk and a moment later there was a shout of pained alarm back at the stables. Someone had found the caltrops. He wondered whether the pointed iron had been encountered by foot or hoof. Foot, he hoped. Either way the men of Cadeneta would be forced to spend time clearing the dangerous impediments and it would buy Arnau and the others precious time.

He urged both horses on until they broke into a gallop. Moments later they caught up with Titborga, who dropped in beside them, matching their pace.

'Congratulations, Maria,' she said exultantly. 'Your first ride is a success.'

Arnau cast a look at his lady that suggested perhaps this was not the appropriate time for light humour. They angled across a field towards a wide gateway and a small stand of trees that would avoid having to jump a fence and would help hide them from pursuit.

'When we round those trees, ride as though Old Nick were biting at your ankles. We need to find a road and make sure we continue south. Three miles away, they said we would find Rourell. Once we're halfway, we should be safe enough, so long as we're still lacking pursuit.'

Three miles. Three miles to the house of the Templars. What then?

But to some extent, that didn't matter. Arnau's mind drew him an image of that glorious man on the field of battle by the Ebro, killing the enemies of God with a song of praise in his heart. If anyone could help them it would be the Templars, he was sure.

CHAPTER FIVE

They joined a road less than a mile south – a main route connecting Valls and Vilallonga – and paused at a point where a side route shot off west over a bridge across the Francoli. For a few minutes Arnau had the ladies lurk in the lee of the bridge while he scouted for pursuit. It seemed they had cleared the farm's lands unobserved, for there was no sign of horsemen following them, and Arnau, with a sigh of relief, returned to the ladies, drawing them back up onto the road.

'No sign of della Cadeneta's men?' Titborga asked.

'No. We were fast enough, it seems. The ground is too dry to leave telltale hoof prints on the road, though we might still be traced if the captain is bright enough. The tracks of our passage across the fields will still be visible in the morning and then it will be clear that we made it onto the southern road. With luck they will think we have headed for Tarragona or Vilallonga and they will continue on down to the coast. But eventually they will learn there has been no sign of our passage there and they will work their way back north. Sooner or later they will track us down. And if della Cadeneta himself joins the search, I can only think it will be sooner rather than later.'

'But we will be safe with the Templars.' There was something odd about the way she said it. Not a question, certainly, and not even a statement. More like a liturgy.

Arnau nodded, eyes narrowing. 'I believe so. I pray so. But the Templars are no mere hostelry and, while aiding pilgrims in distress is the very reason for their order's existence, we cannot impose upon them forever.'

'We shall see,' was Titborga's somewhat mysterious answer, and they began to ride once more through the cool of the night, heading south. Rourell was soon signed from the road off to the east and even by the light of moon and stars, they could already see what had to be the Templars' preceptory. The village of Rourell lay a short way to the south, a few lights twinkling therein, but half a mile north of the settlement stood a small complex of buildings enclosed by a wall, with a chapel clearly visible on the edge and a belfry tower rising somewhere within.

They rode towards the complex, slowing their horses to a walk as they neared the large timber gate that filled a grand archway in the sandstone perimeter wall. The entire complex was surrounded by a ditch some eight feet deep and ten wide, a small causeway leading to the gate. Lights were present within as a glow above the wall attested, accompanied by the muted tones of a melodic chant. The night-time service, Arnau realised, at this time of the evening. A bell hung on a chain beside the gate and he hesitated before reaching for it.

'Why do you delay?' Titborga frowned.

'It is compline. It seems vulgar to interrupt the preceptory at prayer.'

'Ring the bell, Vallbona.'

Arnau chewed on his lip, but her tone was commanding, and he reached up and grasped the chain, rattling the clapper against the bell loudly and repeatedly.

'We need to seek sanctuary,' Arnau advised. 'It must be asked for in no uncertain terms if we are to find safety within God's house. Perhaps, if your ladyship will allow, I should handle the introduction?'

Titborga nodded, her face blank as they waited a long moment before hearing footsteps within, growing in volume as they approached the gate. Three sets, the hymns of praise still going strong in the distance despite the lack of three voices.

There was the clatter and thud of a wooden bar being lifted and put aside, without the curses that commonly accompanied such activity in a fortress, and the gate creaked inward. The open area within was lit by the moonlight as well as torches burning in brackets on a tall tower at the courtyard's centre and above the doorway of a stable to the right. A feeling of profound respect and awe settled through Arnau at the sight of the three figures behind the gate. The portal had been pulled open by a man roughly

Arnau's age in a black habit with a red cross on the breast. His short, curly hair was tucked into a cap and his burgeoning beard hung down across the neck of his habit. His eyes twinkled with a hazel-brown intellect. Opposite him stood a man in a similar black habit with a white mantle thrown over the top, red cross on the chest. His hair was short and straight and somewhat disordered, his beard neat and trimmed. His ageing skin was a healthy suntanned tone, his eyes blue and weirdly piercing. There was about him an odd aura that seemed composed of energy and regret in equal measures.

Yet despite the power these two men exuded, it was the central figure that caught the breath in the back of Arnau's throat. The woman wore a similar black habit and white mantle to the man, though with a white coif and wimple. She stood half a head taller than both men, her face lined with age and care, and yet somehow the authority and sheer strength she radiated almost made the two male Templars fade into the background.

Arnau found himself assessing and immediately reassessing the figures. The one in black would be a sergeant, the man in white a knight and full brother. He had no idea where a nun would fit in with the Templar hierarchy but it was immediately evident that this particular woman stood a step above both men. The words of desperate sanctuary sought died in his throat.

'What brings tired travellers to the door of God's house at such an hour?' the woman asked in a voice that made Arnau want to drop to one knee for some reason. Still, he floundered. A woman. Somehow, even though he had half-expected from the words of their escort to find a woman here, he had somehow consigned her in his head to the category of 'unimportant nun'. The fact that this woman was so very clearly far more than that still put a stranglehold on his throat.

'I am Titborga, daughter of Lord Berenguer Cervelló and heiress of the estate of Santa Coloma. This is my maid Maria and my man at arms Arnau de Vallbona.'

Arnau turned in surprise to find his lady sitting proud in the saddle and speaking in a clear and level tone as though conversing with an equal. He was suddenly struck by the notion that Iberia had never seen such a meeting of strong-willed women. Both would be able to command Arnau into Satan's maw with but a word. Both should be leading armies.

The female Templar nodded silently, then looked at the older brother at her side, who shrugged.

'This is not a hostelry,' the woman said in a tone that brooked no argument. 'This is a house of the Poor Knights of Christ and of Solomon's Temple.'

'Of that I am aware, Sister,' Titborga said quietly. 'I find myself in peril with nowhere to turn. My man here felt that the order might be relied upon for aid, given your raison d'être.'

There was a tense pause, as the two male Templars looked the travellers up and down appraisingly and the lady of Rourell drummed fingers on her forearm. Finally she took a deep breath. 'You had best enter the preceptory, then, and spin your tale, young lady.'

The gate was opened to its full extent and the figures stepped aside to allow the three visitors access. Arnau's gaze took in the complex as a whole as he entered. The southern and eastern sides of the square were filled with ranges of buildings, a second gate visible through an arch. To the north a chapel was attached to the east range by a connecting building that was almost certainly a chapter house, and this remaining north-west corner housed a tower that stood alone. It was a small complex. Compact. It smelled mainly of horses and burning torches. Straw lay about in the dirt and gravel. The stone of the walls was rough. Yet there was an odd sense of peace and of piety about the place that made young Vallbona feel like something of an intruder.

Behind them the gate clunked closed, shutting out the world, enfolding them in this house of God, and Arnau marvelled again and again at this place and the manner in which he had come here.

'Dismount,' the knight said in a deep voice accented with the more honeyed tones of western Iberia. Arnau did so, and the younger sergeant helped first Titborga and then Maria from their saddles. The reins of all three horses were then taken and the man led them into a small stable block on the right beneath the guttering torch.

'I am Ermengarda d'Oluja,' the Templar woman said, 'Preceptrix of the house of Rourell and head of this community. This is Brother Ramon de Juelle, a knight of the preceptory. Now tell me of the strange circumstances that bring you hither.'

As Titborga began slowly to relate the whole story, from the death of Berenguer to her enforced betrothal and all through their journey and flight from the farm, Arnau studied the two remaining Templars before him in astonishment. He had, as he'd told his lady, encountered a few nuns of the Temple in his time. They were commonly lay sisters or some sort of semi-sister, and rarely seemed to hold any real authority or position in the order. Never had he heard of a full sister such as this, and in command of a preceptory of knights and sergeants. This, then, had to be the captain's 'bitch of Rourell'.

His attention wandered back to the conversation just as Titborga was reaching the end of her tale, and he blinked at her closing lines.

'Thus I find myself promised to a monster, heiress to a fortune, and with no recourse from a dreadful future. How might a lady seek membership in this most august order?'

Arnau felt his skin prickle. *Membership?*

'My lady…'

Titborga turned to him with an odd smile. 'Why did you think I came so readily to such a place? Sanctuary is of little use to me, for sanctuary must one day end, and then I would find myself once more in the very same position. Did I not warn you, Vallbona, that I would promise both myself and my lands to God before I saw them fall into the hands of della Cadeneta?'

'But my lady…'

Preceptrix Ermengarda tapped her chin, apparently as uninterested in his opinions as was Titborga. 'A place in the order is not to be sought simply to escape peril or the tribulations of the world, young lady. The order welcomes chaste souls and steadfast swords, but only those who are prepared to devote their whole being to the worship of the Lord and to service within the order, which can include its own perils and most certainly presents arduous tasks each day. It is not a thing to contemplate with but half a heart.'

Titborga nodded. 'I am more than prepared, Sister. I am nary afeared of labour. I am strong of both body and will, and am a woman of letters with a command of Latin. Since I learned of Rourell, which I will grant, to my shame, is only recently, I have thought as constantly on the matter as imperilled flight would allow. It is my earnest heart's desire. My father once told me that our lands could buy us a crown if we wished it. Will they not buy us entrance into the order?'

The preceptrix steepled her fingers. 'It is not simply a matter of *purchase*, young lady. I will grant you that the order always welcomes land and finances to help support our work in the kingdom of Outremer and against the Almohads, and it is rather unfortunately true in these times of depopulation and war in Iberia that the order finds itself begging recruits in a manner seldom seen across other countries. Still, though, I would turn aside an uncommitted body before taking them to the order's bosom for mere monetary gain.'

Titborga nodded her understanding. 'I fear that the peace and the truth I seek will not be found in the temporal world, Sister. This is neither a last desperate attempt to arrest the decline of my fortune, nor a sudden and rash decision formed entirely by chance. In some ways it is a little of both, I might admit, but I feel it is more directly the result of some divine convergence of desire and opportunity. Is it not said that everything is part of the divine plan?'

This answer seemed to please the preceptrix and one eyebrow rose. 'The order cannot accept members who are in any way bound to another in the temporal world. Are you a ward of the crown? What is your age – are you of enough years to manage your own affairs? And most importantly, when your hand was promised to the Lord della Cadeneta, did you at any time confirm your consent to the match?'

Titborga smiled. 'Far from it. I denied the match at every turn. As the only surviving child of my father, I come under the nominal wardship of the Lord d'Entenza, though I am of age and more than capable of managing my own affairs.'

'And your estate is uncontested?'

Now Titborga laughed. 'Again, far from it. The Lord della Cadeneta would pull out Christ's fingernails for my lands. The Lord d'Entenza sees them as an asset with which to bind houses to the crown. I have distant cousins who bear the Cervelló name, though they have lands of their own and no legal claim upon those of my father. But the line of descent and inheritance is clear, as is my father's will. I hold title to all the Santa Coloma lands and would see them delivered into the care of the order.'

Again, the answer seemed satisfactory to the preceptrix, and she nodded. 'It is not the custom of the order to admit new members, whether they be brothers or sisters, full members, donats, associate members, knights or sergeants, in a precipitous manner. There must be a time of consideration for both the postulant and for the community considering their admittance.'

'I understand.'

'Furthermore, despite my authority within this house, any admittance must be agreed by the convent of full brothers and sisters.'

'Of course.'

'And you still wish us to consider you an applicant?'

'I do, Sister,' Titborga replied.

The preceptrix nodded again and then retreated a dozen paces, beckoning to Brother Ramon, where the two huddled into murmured conversation. Taking advantage of the momentary respite, Arnau hurried over to Titborga. 'Doña, have you taken leave of your senses?'

The lady of Santa Coloma turned a look on Arnau that would have silenced him in any circumstance. 'On the contrary, Vallbona, I may have listened to the voice of sense for the first time. As we fled the farm, it came to me as though a vision sent by the Lord. What future have I in Aragon and Barcelona? Should I somehow manage to slip the clutches of della Cadeneta, I would remain an heiress and a catch for any grasping noblemen, even were I the size and the very vision of a heifer. Even wrinkled and withered I would be sought for my lands. As long as I live I will be at best naught but a source of wealth in the eyes of men. I could donate my property and live on without them, of course, but I have seen the plight of the poor and uncared-for in this world and have no wish to be one of them. Nor have I a pressing desire to be a wife or mother. My father never instilled in me the need for such things. The only men who have ever looked upon me with a kindness born of selfless love are men of the Church. I have, since the day my mother died, considered a possible future as a bride of Christ, though I remained in the wide world for the love of my father. Now he is gone and vultures gather to pick over the bones of Santa Coloma. Is not a life in the Church to be cherished for a woman such as I, Arnau of Vallbona?'

Arnau was silent. He had no answer against such a reasoned and flawless argument. He had been unable to think of a way out for the lady because there *was* no way out. He had caught upon the idea of sanctuary, though that was but delaying the inevitable, and the unthinkable would eventually come crashing back in upon them. Despite his gainsaying, this was the clear answer to Titborga's dilemma, and the *only* answer to boot.

Moreover, the prospect was attractive. Infectious, even. Who was he to say his lady was making rash choices when he himself had nowhere to turn? Vallbona was poor. He had always known that, even before his father had drunk himself to death. But three years ago, poring over the estate accounts, it had become clear that only the affection of Don Berenguer de Santa Coloma had kept them from destitution. As such, Arnau had cleaved to his lord ever tighter. And now? Well, he'd planned after the lord's death to return home and find some way to make the estate profitable once more, but what great chance was there of that? And if the lady donated her estates to the Temple? Well then Arnau would become a tenant of Templar lands or, should she bend to the generosity of freeing him and Vallbona of fealty, then he would be free to become destitute and starve until some other lord bought out his lands and his fealty. In some ways he was every bit as desperate as the lady, for all he might appear a man of means.

He swallowed.

'Your words are wise beyond your years, my lady.'

'It is as though the Lord sent me an omen with Rourell, Arnau. There was I like Christ, lost in the wilderness and seeking a path, and God sent me not only a preceptory of the Temple but, against all odds, one commanded by a woman! Who am I to deny the *manus dei*, Vallbona?'

Indeed. And who was Arnau to do so, for that matter?

After a long interval, the two Templars returned from their private counsel.

'It is the considered opinion of Ramon, in whom I have the utmost confidence, that you have the makings of a fine sister of the Temple. That your commitment to such an undertaking is impressive and merits consideration.'

Arnau saw Titborga's knowing smile. How much of Ramon's opinion was weighed upon the vaunted Santa Coloma riches, he mused? But he instantly cast aside such unworthy thoughts. There was nothing grasping or underhand in the manner of the knight or his preceptrix. Both seemed perfectly calm and pious and reasoned.

'We will put the matter before the convent of the Temple of Rourell as a matter of some urgency, given your predicament. I daresay the *passagium* sought with the Santa Coloma lands will sway even the wariest brother,' she said wryly, throwing a knowing glance at Arnau that sent waves of shame from the soles of his boots right to his hairline. 'We will press the enrolment, in order to settle the matter of your freedom and your estate before your unwished suitor seeks you out. Please accompany me to the chapel.'

Before he realised what he was saying, Arnau had cleared his throat and gestured to them. 'How does fealty to a noble house affect a pledge to the order?'

The two Templars exchanged a strange look, and Sir Ramon beckoned to him. 'You owe fealty only to the lady of Santa Coloma?'

Arnau nodded. 'I also owe money, but only to the Santa Coloma estate. And were I to offer the lands and full value of Vallbona it would cover any debt with a clear margin.'

What the fuck am I doing? Arnau thought in the privacy of his head, his hands beginning to shake. His conscience shot back: *What you know must be done. Without the lady or the Temple you are nothing. Within a year you will be bondsman or serf. But here is a chance to be more. To be* that *man. That glorious man in white and red who led the charge at the Ebro.*

'You wish an application be made to Rourell for the name of Arnau de Vallbona?' the preceptrix asked with a totally expressionless face.

No. Lord, no. I am not made to be a monk.

'Yes, Sister.'

He wondered whether it was possible that his mouth had been cursed to somehow gainsay him.

Don't be a fool, Vallbona, his conscience pressed. *Your future is as bleak as hers. This is your path to glory. To truth. To a world of wonder.*

Damn his conscience.

Maria suddenly hurried forward from where she had been lurking at the rear and dropped to the ground beside Titborga. There were tears on her cheeks, but what drew Arnau's attention was the strange, haunted look she threw back at the gate behind them. Did Maria have such cause to be scared? But then without her lady she would be nothing, he supposed.

'My lady, please!'

'What is it, Maria?'

'I don't want to be a nun, my lady.'

'It was not my intent to give you to the order like chattel, Maria, though those who work the Santa Coloma estate will surely become tenants of the Temple. But you have been my faithful servant throughout the most trying of times. I will, if it please you, Maria, grant you both your freedom and a small stipend or sum to see to your own security.'

Again that frightened look back at the gate.

'I daren't, my lady. The Lord della Cadeneta…'

Then Arnau remembered the privy. No wonder the girl was scared.

'You may stay with us as a *consoror*,' the preceptrix said in soothing tones that sat strangely at odds with her imposing, commanding manner. 'You may enjoy the safety of the order for as long a time as you wish on the condition that you agree to follow the rules of the house and perform such duties as are allocated to you by myself or the brothers. Is that acceptable?'

A flood of relief flowed visibly through the maid.

'Then come. I shall convene an extraordinary convent of the brothers and sisters.'

They strode across the compound towards the chapel, arriving as a single voice rang out in an ancient melody across the congregation. At the doors, the preceptrix held up her hand to halt them, and Arnau listened to the haunting sound within. Compline was almost done. The lesson must have been given before they arrived, and they had been at the gate during the Kyrie eleison. Now the unseen priest was completing his benediction. Finally, the voice dropped to a lower tone and the preceptrix opened the door and stepped inside. Ramon filled the door to prevent anyone else entering, and Arnau caught only snatches of conversation. The commander of Rourell had interrupted compline only at the very end when the dismissal was being given, begging the priest's indulgence. She was clearly informing the inhabitants of the preceptory of the sudden need for a convent of admission. After long moments some sort of affirmative was clearly given, and Ramon stepped aside.

'Speak only when questioned. Answer truthfully and from the heart. Give no offence. Remember that this is a house of God and the Lord is listening to you, both word and soul.'

With that he motioned for them to enter.

Arnau allowed the lady to enter first and then waited for Maria, but Sir Ramon de Juelle shook his head. 'This is not for visitors. The maid shall wait here.'

The knight of Vallbona stepped inside. The chapel was not a grand one, but was graceful and large enough to house the preceptory's denizens, which seemed to number almost a score. The interior was plain sandstone, with a single wall painted with fascinating scenes, and the burning torches turned the warm brown stone to gold. As the two postulants entered, so did much of the congregation leave, just five remaining – the preceptrix herself, three men with the white mantles of knights and the priest in his long white robes, also bearing the red cross at the breast.

Fascinated, Arnau watched the men leave, mostly bearded and wearing the black garments of sergeants. A young boy in peasant garb went with them, as did four women in white nuns' robes. Brother Ramon he already knew, or felt he did. As the knight took a seat between two peers, Arnau studied them closely. One was clearly of more advanced years than the others, his hair and beard white and bushy, his eyes as grey as a winter sea, hard and suspicious. The other was shorter and paler than any man Arnau had yet seen, his dark hair and salt-and-pepper beard both trimmed neatly, his face settled into a sour frown from which it appeared unable to lift, a scar running from his right eye, down across his cheek and carving a pink path through his beard to his chin. They were an imposing trio, if still not exuding the impressive gravitas of the house's mistress. The priest was ancient – possibly the oldest man Arnau had ever laid eyes upon. His hair and beard were wild like the fabled Norsemen and grey as a corpse. His eyes bulged like a fanatic and yellow teeth lurked within the grey hair. The sight of him made Arnau shudder.

'These are Titborga, former lady of Santa Coloma,' the preceptrix announced, 'and her man at arms, the knight Arnau of Vallbona. I know some of you are aware of the exploits of the lady's father on the battlefield. She comes to us seeking a place as a sister of the Temple.'

'What *passagium* does she offer?' asked the one with the scar, in the sharpest voice imaginable with a thick, foreign accent, like a knife being drawn across mail. A German, Arnau suspected. Perhaps even English?

'Always with you Swabians it's about the money,' snorted the older, white-bearded knight. 'The money or the poetry anyway. The *endless* poetry.'

The scarred knight shot a hard look at his peer, and Ramon, between them, sighed and pushed them apart a little. 'Brothers, be so kind as to at least allow the girl to answer.'

Titborga glanced at the preceptrix, who nodded. 'I offer to the Temple Santa Coloma, an estate worth two hundred thousand gold *maravedi*, including nine farms, four wineries, six fiefdoms and two castles, plus sundry other assets. I have full listings in my saddlebags.'

'One thousand seven hundred?' laughed the older, white-bearded knight. 'Then welcome to the *Poor* Knights of Christ!'

Ramon chuckled at the centre, both of them earning yet another acidic look from Scar-face.

'Can you confirm that you belong to no man, nor to woman or lord?' the priest suddenly put in, in a lilting, melodic voice that belied his appearance. 'Can you confirm that you are unmarried and debt-free? That you are not promised to a different order? That you are free to give all that you are to the Lord and to the Order of the Temple?'

Titborga nodded. 'I swear.'

'Wonderful,' scar-face rolled his eyes. '*Two* full sisters. As if Rourell was not unpopular enough.'

Ramon dealt him a warning punch to the shoulder. 'Disrespect the preceptrix like that again, Lütolf, and I might break the rule not to injure you in anger.'

'As if you could injure me,' snorted the scar-faced Lütolf in scathing tones.

'You realise that the order is not the simple life of some swan-fed bishop?' White-beard said in thoughtful tones, interrupting the altercation and addressing Titborga and Arnau once more. 'That we do not live comfortable lives, sitting fat on cushioned behinds? That we serve as brothers and sisters of the Church first and foremost, with every chore and hardship and ceremony that any monk might endure, maintaining this house of God in working condition and maintaining the daily litany as any Benedictine might, but that we are also so much more? When a monk might sit back in silent contemplation of the hardships of his day, we are instead using the little time we have to keep our sword arms strong and to practise, and to clean armour and plan for battle. There is no freedom in the order. Your private moments are not yours. They belong to God, to the order, and to the Preceptrix Ermengarda.'

'And not necessarily in that order,' laughed Ramon.

Titborga bowed her head in acquiescence.

'And in agreeing to be bound by the rules of the order, you will be agreeing to obey any command handed to you as though it came from the Pope himself?' the preceptrix added. 'And acknowledging that the punishments for infractions can be brutal?'

Another nod.

'And what of the lad?' the one called Lütolf asked suddenly.

'I understand and accept all conditions. I am Arnau de Vallbona, sole owner of two hundred and fifty acres of Catalan land, with two farms, a village and the hereditary manor of Vallbona, beholden only to the lady of Santa Coloma. All that I have, I offer the order.'

There was a considered silence as the three brothers, the preceptrix and the priest seemed to hold some sort of silent exchange using only their expressions, until it was finally broken by Titborga.

'May I address you?'

Surprised looks abounded, and one or two disapproving ones, but finally Ramon nodded.

'Though it may harm my case, I feel it is only right to warn you that Don Ferrer della Cadeneta covets both my body and my lands. I am not sure what trouble he might present to the order, but in accepting me, Rourell could earn his ire. He is not the sort of man to let a slight go, and especially not one that costs him near two hundred thousand *maravedi*.'

Lütolf frowned and turned to Ramon. 'Is della Cadeneta the short one from near Reus?'

'No. He's that runt from the hills west of Valls. The one who argues over grain prices.'

'To the devil with him,' snapped Lütolf irritably. 'He has long spoken ill of us.'

'I suspect you have your answer,' the preceptrix smiled at Titborga and Arnau. 'If even Lütolf cares not for any peril your admittance might introduce, then nor will any other. Please, step outside while the convent deliberates.'

Arnau and Titborga moved towards the door, which he opened for her. They strode back out into the cool of the evening, and the lady of Santa Coloma examined him with searching eyes.

'Why, Vallbona?'

He shrugged. 'The case you made for your own future could as easily apply to me, my lady. It seemed the clear path.'

'They will take me,' she smiled 'for the lands of Santa Coloma are too valuable to overlook. And if they take me they cannot refuse you, I think. The end of our relationship as lady and man at arms is nigh, Arnau. In a turn of events that neither of us might have predicted a single month ago, it appears that we are to become brother and sister.'

And Arnau had to laugh at that.

PART TWO:
HAVEN

CHAPTER SIX

'You are familiar with the daily routine of the monastery?'

Arnau turned to Mateu, a serious-looking man in his early twenties and with the neatest, shiniest hair Arnau had ever seen. The man's black habit, denoting the rank of sergeant, was impeccable and perfectly pressed, in direct comparison with Arnau's own crumpled garment that smelled of mice and old food. It was the new arrivals' first morning at Rourell, and it did not feel auspicious.

'A little,' Arnau admitted. 'I was a regular guest at the monastery of Santa Maria in my youth. I learned my letters there.'

'Then forget what you understand of monastic life from those days.'

'That should not be hard,' yawned Arnau, wondering how long they would have before sunrise. With the lamps lit in the courtyard, he couldn't even tell whether the sky had yet acquired the indigo glow of pre-dawn.

'While it is the duty of the order to follow a straight monastic liturgy of the hours and to devote ourselves to the traditional pursuit of prayer and learning, the reality of life in the order means that certain adjustments need to be made. Even the Rule of Order, set by the blessed Saint Bernard, is bent to fit the real world. You may find that other preceptories keep their houses in a different manner, according to their needs. There has to be a melding of Church duty and temporal realism, and the preceptrix is, perhaps, one of the less traditional in her approach.'

Arnau simply nodded and stifled another yawn.

'Thus we are heading to lauds in the hours of darkness,' Mateu continued, 'rather than to celebrate the dawn and the resurrection. The simple fact is that as men of God and also of the sword, we have more chores and tasks to fit into our day than any monk could contemplate, and consequently we begin our day more than an hour earlier to grant us as much time as possible. There is more to do in Rourell than there are hands available. While the blessed Saint Bernard drew a delightful line between squires and sergeants in his scribblings, the truth in Catalunya is that we barely have enough sergeants to fulfil the preceptory's duties, let alone lay members, so there is some doubling-up on tasks. As *confanier*, I might be expected to lead horsemen into the fray, yet I am squire to Brother Ramon as well as the bearer of the *beauséant* banner. Perhaps in Outremer they have sufficient staff to be more specialised. We do not. Every brother here has at least one role. Every sergeant too. Even the sisters and the *consorors*.'

An hour before dawn, then, Arnau sighed. Another stifled yawn, and now a grumble of hungry belly joined in, like the gentle shifting of continents.

'After lauds, we break our fast swiftly,' Mateu said, his eyes dropping to Arnau's noisy midriff. 'According to the rule there is no dawn meal, but the preceptrix believes that without a morning meal men are too sluggardly. After that repast the preceptrix will assign you duties. I suspect I know what duty you will take on, but it is not my place to say. Undoubtedly someone else will walk you through the rest of the daily duties from there. I have my own business to attend to, of course.'

The new arrival nodded again. Mateu was not only *confanier* – standard bearer for Rourell – and squire to Brother Ramon. In addition to those duties, he seemed to be the man to whom the preceptory turned for a thousand small chores and tasks, such as locating appropriate apparel for Arnau. He had not had time to wash the garment, though. Rather than the neat black of Mateu's, Arnau's habit was a sort of mottled black-grey from cobwebs and stains, though the red cross stood out clearly enough.

'Will I have time to wash this?' Arnau hazarded.

'You will *find* time, Brother. Make it if it does not occur naturally.'

Arnau eyed what he thought looked suspiciously like a bloodstain near the hem, and wondered whose garment it had previously been.

They reached the chapel as several other robed figures converged on the door, which stood open, golden light issuing forth and sending through Arnau the guilty realisation that while he was still groggy and tired at this time, someone had been up perhaps an hour earlier, preparing the lights around the preceptory among a myriad of other jobs.

It was hardly a surprise to see the congregation gathered on their feet rather than seated on the stone benches that ran along either side of the chapel where the brothers had rested the previous evening while deliberating whether to admit the new arrivals. As the figures in white and black gradually assembled, red crosses ablaze on all bar perhaps half a dozen women in white nuns' habits and a young lad in peasant grey, Arnau did a subtle head count. Twenty-two, he reckoned, including Titborga, who stood with the other women off to the side, her pristine white habit displaying the cross of a sister, and Maria, close by her in plain white and looking uncomfortable and distinctly unhappy. Twenty-three, he corrected himself as the old priest arrived through the connecting door to the chapter house.

'How's your voice?' whispered Mateu as they fell into position among the other sergeants.

Arnau opened his mouth to reply, but Brother Lütolf, standing close by, gave the pair a hard look and cleared his throat. 'Any voice lifted in prayer to God is a good voice.' His eyebrow tilted irritably, an odd look with the scar running down from it.

'Lord, open our lips,' announced the old priest in his oddly lilting tongue, then paused. Arnau felt the congregation draw breath and prepared himself.

'And we shall praise your name,' the response rang out from more than a score of throats.

'To victory, the song of the psalm. All the Earth, make ye joy heartily to God. Say ye a psalm to his name; give ye glory to his praising.' The sacred melody began without the need for warning. The congregation had observed lauds daily their entire monastic life. Arnau stumbled twice over the words. He knew the sixty-sixth Psalm well enough from many recitations in church, but this was sung at a ponderous pace. He was aware that Lütolf kept glancing across at him, but kept his own eyes on the priest, avoiding eye contact with the German.

Barely had the echoes of the chant faded before Father Diego launched them into the fiftieth Psalm. This was less well known to Arnau and he found himself mouthing emptily along to some of it with faint embarrassment. A similar issue struck with Psalm eighty-seven, but with Psalm eighty-nine he was on better ground, that having been one of his mother's favourites when he was young.

Once more the echoes died away slowly, and Father Diego spread out his arms as though beseeching the gathering.

'Blessed be the Lord, the God of Israel; He has come to His people and set them free.' Arnau closed his eyes and let the words of the canticle wash over him. It was soothing in the old man's beautiful tones, and he had to stifle yet another yawn. He didn't need to open his eyes and turn to know that the German knight was watching him with distinct disapproval.

The canticle ended, to be followed by another psalm, this time a more common *Laudate* psalm that Arnau knew well enough. He opened his eyes for that and was relieved to discover that Brother Lütolf was no longer paying him any attention. The reading from Father Diego drifted by, as did the hymn and the benediction, Arnau concentrating primarily on not yawning and on attempting to stifle the rumblings from within. Finally, he joined his voice in the paternoster and listened to Father Diego's brief prayer and dismissal.

As the closing word died away in the stone vault of the chapel, his stomach let forth a huge leonine growl into the silence, earning him a grin from several people nearby and a glare from the German brother. The congregation dispersed, though Arnau was summoned by Preceptrix Ermengarda with a wave of the hand. As he followed her through the connecting door into the chapter house, he was dismayed to realise that Lütolf was following him. The summons had been for both of them.

The chapter house was empty, barring the three of them, and the preceptrix took her seat at the room's focal point, the benches for the meetings of the community all facing her. The two doors, one back into the church and the other out into the courtyard, stood open.

'Brother Arnau,' the preceptrix began, 'we are in an unusual and complicated position. Indeed, I am somewhat in two minds as to whether your social rank alone merits a full brotherhood or your youth and what is seen by some as uncertainty of purpose make a sergeant's role more applicable. I have decided upon the latter for now. The usual routine with a new member is to slowly introduce them to the community and help them find their place in it, and even then only when their membership has been lodged with the mother house and all documentation dealt with. There must be a ceremony of admission, of course. Yet the documents are not with the mother house at this time and we simply do not have time to carry out such ceremony, even if we could legitimately do so before your entry to the order was complete. However, Rourell is a small house, and short of bodies, and we can scarce afford to spare a potential worker. Thus I have decided to throw you, as well as your former mistress and her maid, straight into work and life as members of the order regardless of your unconfirmed status. When we receive verification of your documentation back from the mother house, we will arrange appropriate ceremony for you both.'

Arnau bowed his head. He'd hardly expected to sit back with his feet up while the preceptory bustled around him.

'You will fill the position of Brother Lütolf's squire.'

Arnau felt his expression slip into miserable disappointment, and the German must have noticed, for that eyebrow arched once more.

'Lütolf's previous squire suffered an accident in training a month past and the wound became infected. He passed from the world with pain and difficulty, but is now in the hands of the Lord and beyond worldly hurt.' The possibility that the stain on his garment's hem was blood suddenly seemed a great deal more likely.

Arnau marshalled his arguments in the forefront of his mind. Chief among them was that Lütolf hated him, clearly, and almost certainly did not want Arnau as his squire any more than the young man wanted to fill that role. Also, he was a knight by virtue of his heritage, albeit a low and rather impoverished one. Even as a sergeant, should a knight be lowered to the role of a squire? But then, Mateu was a sergeant of the Temple who played squire to Brother Ramon…

He looked up and the simple authority emanating from the lady of Rourell cast aside every objection. He bowed again.

'Lütolf will walk you through your duties and show you the preceptory. I hereby grant extraordinary permissions of absence from the liturgy for the rest of the day, until compline, which you will both attend. Use this time well, for on the morrow full liturgical attendance will be required.'

Lütolf bowed and gestured for Arnau to follow, leaving through the door into the courtyard. The German stood for a moment in the gloom, where the faint purple of pre-dawn was now showing, and Arnau paused nearby, waiting quietly. His eyes took in the open space, brothers and sisters performing a few odd chores before making their way to the morning meal. As they stood, a man in the black of a sergeant led a horse out of the stable, saddled and ready for a journey. The man had also buckled on his sword, though he was unarmoured and otherwise dressed for civil work. A nun scurried over to him, one hand holding her white habit up out of the muck, the other carrying a small bag.

'Breakfast?' the sergeant asked. The nun nodded. 'Bless you, Sister,' he smiled, and hauled himself up into the saddle before reaching down and taking the food.

'Go with God, Brother Carles,' Brother Lütolf called to the man.

Carles nodded his thanks and turned his horse. The gate was opened and he disappeared out into the night. Arnau, frowning, turned to the German, who threw him a look full of unexpected reproach.

'He rides for the mother house at Barberà with the documentation of your, and your mistress's, entry into the order and the donatives you promised.'

Arnau nodded and slouched. It was done, then. Oddly, though he'd yesterday committed himself to this path, it had not felt quite real until he watched Carles ride out of the gate to tell the world that Arnau de Vallbona was now a Templar.

'Later we will discuss duties,' Lütolf said suddenly. 'First I will introduce you to Rourell and its people. I expect you to swiftly become a productive and obedient brother. Come.'

The German lurched off towards another door where several other bodies were converging. Arnau followed him inside to find the preceptory's refectory. Three long trestle tables sat in lines, each with benches alongside. Food was being placed on the tables now, and Arnau's belly gave a roar of approval. The bread was still warm, as evidenced by the steam rising from it. Butter in small pots. Hard cheese and soft cheese. Jugs of ale.

Growl.

The denizens of Rourell were moving to take seats and Arnau took only three paces before realising that the knight behind him was not moving to one of the benches. Instead, Lütolf began to indicate the people at the tables.

'You already know Ramon, Balthesar and myself. You have met the preceptrix and Father Diego and, I believe, Mateo this morning. The two sergeants at the far table who are clearly brothers also in the familial sense are Lorenç and Ferrando. They are responsible for all the masonry and carpentry here in the preceptory. They are not merely workers. They are artisans.' He pointed at the young lad in grey who was carrying food to the tables. 'Simo there is something of a general worker. He does whatever is required. His father was my squire, so now he is a ward of the Temple.'

Arnau nodded, remembering that the German's squire had died recently, sympathy for the boy rising in him even as he glanced down at the stain on his own hem. What a dreadful thing for a boy his age to go through. Arnau's eyes rose once more, straying to the food in the boy's hands, and his stomach complained and urged him to take a seat.

'You met Carles outside,' the German went on. 'He is our scribe and treasurer. The sergeant at the far end overseeing everything in the refectory is Luis, who is responsible for the proper running of the house. He is our seneschal, reporting only to

Brother Ramon and the preceptrix. Guillem over there is in charge of the stables, though you will be expected to do your fair share with the horses too. There are two brothers absent at the moment. Miquel runs the mill, and Rafael is in charge of the farms. The two sisters you can see are Carima and Joana, who maintain the household and see to its tidiness and cleanliness. The cook you cannot see is Brigida, and Catarina is the maid to the preceptrix. And that, in all, is Rourell.'

He took a step and Arnau was relieved to think that finally food was within his grasp.

'We do not have time to sit and relax, Brother Arnau. Grab yourself a hunk of bread with some butter and follow me.'

Crestfallen at the very idea of missing this repast, Arnau hurried over, took the two largest slices of warm bread he could find, liberally slathered them with butter and a little soft cheese, and then hurried back to the German knight, chewing on one of them. Lütolf contrived to look disapproving once again, and gestured to the staircase.

'Last night you slept in the guest accommodation. From now on you will be in the dormitory with the others, which runs the length of this building above. The sisters' dormitory is above the other range. In respect of the rule of the order – especially articles seventy and seventy-one – fraternisation between brothers and sisters is kept to a minimum. The seed of wicked Eve is, after all, ever at work.'

It occurred to Arnau momentarily that he might be able to make Brother Lütolf uneasy if he pointed out the inconsistencies with a female preceptrix in this situation, but the man was already moving.

He exited the refectory and stood in the growing dawn light of the courtyard. Here he turned, slowly, pointing at structures. 'The west gate, from whence you came. Next to it the stables. Then the buttery and the bake house and kitchens with the sisters' dormitory over. The sisters' necessarium projects from the walls at that side. Over the arch of the south gate are the guest quarters, of course, where you stayed last night. Then in the other range we have the refectory, library, armoury and workshop, with the brothers' dormitory above and our necessarium similarly projecting from the walls. Then there are the chapter house and the church. Other than that, the belfry is the only building in the preceptory. We are compact but very efficient. You will come to know these buildings so well that you will be able to find your way around blindfolded.'

Numerous questions leaped to Arnau's mind, from the disposal of waste in the necessaria – the communal latrines – without a local flow of water, to the location of the laundry, but one thing had popped into his head, offering the faint possibility of hope, and it was this question that therefore found voice.

'Three knights and only two squires?'

Lütolf frowned.

'Mateu is squire to Ramon,' Arnau expanded. 'Even though he is a full sergeant. If I am to be squire to you, what of Brother Balthesar?'

The German huffed. 'Balthesar d'Aixere is no typical knight, nor is he a typical monk. He *wishes* no squire. Come on.'

Arnau followed him across to the stable, where the scarred German began to saddle his horse. 'Though it is Guillem's duty to maintain the stable and its occupants, when we need our own horse and he is not here, we are expected to perform the tasks ourselves. That is, until we have able assistance. In future, should we be riding, I will expect you to secure the horses ready.'

Arnau felt the tiniest flicker of annoyance at the manner of the older brother, but he fought it down. This was neither the time nor the place for an argument. Instead he hurried over and saddled his own horse. Moments later they were leading the animals out into the courtyard. Lütolf motioned to the north gate and Simo, the young lad in grey, scurried over and struggled to lift the bar. Arnau was about to dismount and help the poor lad when the locking timber finally groaned up and the boy heaved the gate open.

'Leave it open for now,' the German said to the boy as he walked his horse out of the preceptory. Arnau took care to thank Simo warmly, which did not elicit the expected gratitude, but more a frown of bafflement.

They rode out just as the first golden arc appeared above the low wooded rise to the east.

'There are three estates owned and operated by Rourell,' Lütolf announced as they rode. 'None of the land to the west of the preceptory and its immediate environs belongs to the Temple. To the north is a farming estate with olive groves and wheat fields. Vegetables are also grown there. To the east, stretching as far as the flow of the Francoli, is another farm, largely given to livestock. South, reaching as far as the village of Rourell itself and extending past it to the east, is the winery and its vineyards. All three estates are largely worked and overseen by Moorish tenants who have, nominally at least, taken the cross. Overall control lies in the hands of Brother Rafael, who will almost certainly already be somewhere out here.'

Arnau remembered the conversation of their della Cadeneta escort back at the farmhouse lodgings. 'I heard tell that your wine was good. But is it perhaps not always popular with the locals?'

Lütolf threw a look of narrow-eyed suspicion at him, but sucked on a lip and then answered.

'The order is not always popular among the nobles of the region. We are tolerated because we supply a strong arm for the king in his struggles with the Almohads. The Christian lords know they can rely upon our swords when the need is there. But when the border is peaceful and no blade need be drawn, the nobles sometimes forget our value and jealousy reigns over our acquisition of lands and moneys.'

'And…' Arnau was not sure how to express the thought in any politic way. 'And Rourell being run by a preceptrix does little to improve matters, I suspect?'

Again, that suspicious, narrow-eyed glare from the German, but eventually he nodded. 'There are men who think it unnatural for Sister Ermengarda to wield such influence and power, yes. And we are also regarded warily for our dealings with Moors and Jews. But we remain strong and pious and resistant to the influence of devious and snide temporal lords.'

They were riding east now, and the German knight reined in close to a low, arched bridge over the river, indicating a grey stone complex nearby. 'This is the mill. It is operated by a Moor and his family, assisted by two young men and overseen by Brother

Miquel. Thus is grain from the farms turned into flour for Brigida to bake into her fresh bread. In truth we have little need to purchase any goods from outside sources.'

The scarred brother leaned back in his saddle. 'I expect you to be familiar with every trail, tree, stone and body on these estates within the month. I need to know that if I ask you to find someone or go somewhere, you can be relied upon to do so without fuss or question. As such, I will permit you one hour each day after the consuming of the midday meal to explore the land and complex of Rourell and meet and speak to each and every occupant. Once you are familiar with all you will be using that time instead to train, exercise and maintain your equipment.'

Arnau nodded his understanding.

'On all days you will attend every meal and service. We do not have matins, since an unbroken sleep maintains a more healthy physique for a soldier of God. Instead, Father Diego will hold matins alone, or with any member of the preceptory who wishes to join him. Our liturgical day begins in general with lauds an hour before dawn. Then we break our fast. We then have almost two hours to deal with as many of our daily chores as we can manage before the call to prime. Many days there will follow a general convent in the chapter house to discuss any matters of import. Otherwise we continue to perform our chores until terce. The bulk of tasks should be done by then and the brothers and sisters are permitted the rest of thc morning until sext to read, study, meditate or attend in silent prayer. After sext is the midday meal, following which every man is expected to tend to his equipment and animals. This means more than simply washing your clothing and cleaning your armour. It means helping to check over the tents we use on campaign, repair farm equipment, make tent pegs, sluice out the channels beneath the necessaria, oil hinges, create new candles and torches, and so on. There is always something that needs attention. Early afternoon is when it is done.'

Arnau sighed. He'd hardly expected an easy time here, but the more the German explained, the more tired the young man felt just thinking about it all.

'The nones service follows, after which all those who wield a sword take to the courtyard or the fields in training. There is no set training regime. Each man is expected to keep himself at the peak of fitness and skill, though it is understood that squires will train with the full brothers, and often the other sergeants will join us. During that time the non-martial denizens will be preparing the refectory and the chapel and working in the kitchens. Our training time ends with nightfall and vespers, following which we meet for the evening meal. We are then given two hours of rest to pray, read or discuss matters with the other brothers and sisters until compline, following which we will often partake of wine before retiring for the night.'

'A busy routine,' Arnau said, with feeling.

Brother Lütolf frowned as though Arnau had said something idiotic. 'This is a quiet routine. Sometimes there will be extra work or visits from the mother house, and then we need to fit our daily routine around new tasks. And there are periodic times of campaigning when the king calls upon us to aid him in the south. Although we lie within the demesne of the Crown of Aragon, and it is currently the Castilian monarch who locks horns with Ya'qūb al-Manṣūr, rarely does a season pass without a call to support the king's men in some minor clash with the Almohads. In the past three years I have looked upon the walls of Moorish Valencia five times while wearing another man's blood as a shroud. A time of campaigning is arduous, for each day wears on the body and soul, and a man is additionally weighed down by the knowledge that upon his return to the preceptory there will be weeks of work to catch up on.'

Arnau sighed again and realised that the German was watching him in an appraising manner. He straightened.

'You, I think, are not made for this life,' Lütolf said flatly.

'Try my sword at practice, Brother, and I shall prove that to be an error of judgement.'

Lütolf said nothing in answer, but moved on, kicking his horse's flanks into movement once more. They spent the rest of the morning and the early afternoon touring the mill and the lands, as far as the village. Arnau was relieved to be offered samples of the foods grown on the farms and even a cup of heavy wine in the winery, so the fact that they missed the midday meal did not distress him too much, and the regular small morsels mollified his grumbling stomach.

In the mid-afternoon, they paused by a copse of trees half a mile from the preceptory and Lütolf dismounted, gesturing for Arnau to do the same.

'You are skilled with one of these?' he asked, unhooking his sheathed sword from behind the saddle and drawing it. Arnau shrugged. 'A mace is my weapon of choice, but yes, I can wield a sword.'

The German nodded as though he were listening to a delusion or a lie. He flicked the sword into the air and caught it by the blade just beneath the crossbar, proffering it to Arnau, hilt first.

'Brother?'

'Take it. Show me.'

'Swinging wildly at the air is going to prove nothing,' Arnau said.

'Later you can cross swords with me, and then we will see. For now, show me your form.'

Arnau huffed. 'No amount of training with lunges and swipes makes a grand difference in war, Brother Lütolf. You know that. Then it is about strength, will and determination. Any man can swing a blade or stab with it. It is the willingness to put that point through a man's gullet that separates a warrior from a dancer.'

'It is much as you say,' agreed the German, 'but gaining that strength and a certain level of accuracy is a matter of rote drilling and perseverance. And practice brings speed and reaction too. A man becomes a master of the blade by using it as often as possible in whatever circumstances he can. Show me.'

Feeling rather foolish, Arnau gripped the sword and began to leap about in the dry dust, thrusting and swinging, stabbing and slashing. Lütolf stood to the side, inscrutable, watching every flick of the blade and twitch of muscle.

'You fight like a girl wielding a mop,' the man said eventually in hard tones, as though stating fact rather than denigrating a brother. Arnau bridled.

'If you would care to cross swords properly with me, I will give you a scar to suggest otherwise.'

Lütolf's eyes narrowed. 'We are forbidden from causing deliberate injury during training. In fact, any mishap is brought to the preceptrix's attention and she can be very… fearsome. All training should be carried out carefully. Later, you can show me that you handle a mace better than you do a blade and I will try not to be quite so disappointed.'

Arnau felt his lip twitching as the German took back his sword and sheathed it before mounting once more. They rode back to the preceptory in uncomfortable silence. There, Lütolf announced that he had shown Arnau everything of import for a first day, and that Arnau had shown him everything he needed too. The German went off with his nose in the air and Arnau went to prepare for vespers, grumbling under his breath about miserable bastards from the north.

After vespers, they congregated for the evening meal. Arnau had hoped to speak to Titborga, but it seemed that she was to sit with the women, and had been singled out for conversation by the preceptrix. Instead, as they sat down to their repast, Arnau found himself sitting next to Ramon's squire, Mateu, and the previously unseen Miquel, who ran the mill. They talked of a squire's duties, of the mill and its workings, the estate and the preceptory in general. When Arnau, perhaps unwisely, began to talk about his German knight master, grumbling about the man's manners, the other two fell silent and turned away from the conversation.

The meal done with, Arnau was about to wander off and find someone to complain at, when Mateu located him in the courtyard with a request that he present himself before the preceptrix in the chapter house. Worried that his attempted conversations about Lütolf had been overheard and disapproved of, he swallowed nervously as he attended upon the woman who ran this place with a fist of iron. His worry increased as he stepped through the door and bowed to find the German knight also in attendance.

'I am concerned,' Preceptrix Ermengarda said by way of introduction. 'Carles rode north to Barberà with the documents of grants and acceptance for the mother house at dawn. He has now been gone from the preceptory for sixteen hours, and Barberà is less than fifteen miles from here. While there is always the possibility that he has been given some cause for delay by the preceptor at Barberà, I consider that unlikely. Carles had told me in no uncertain terms that he would return in time for vespers, and even riding slowly and allowing for time spent at Barberà lodging the documents, he should have arrived by now.'

Frowning, Arnau glanced across at Lütolf. There was none of the usual arrogant aloofness about the German now, just a brow furrowed in concern. Lütolf apparently thought this unlikely too.

'Don your armour and gather your swords. Ride north,' the preceptrix said. 'I realise that it is dark, but find out what has happened to Carles and return safely.'

The German brother bowed from the waist and gestured to Arnau, marching from the chapter house. The young man dithered for only a moment, concerned at the worried expression of Sister Ermengarda, before following.

North. Back towards the farm where they'd fled della Cadeneta's men. Somehow, he thought, nothing good will come of this.

CHAPTER SEVEN

'How can we trace where he went?' Arnau said breathlessly as they turned from the dusty track that led to the preceptory and onto the wider metalled surface of the north–south route. 'It has been dry for weeks and the road surface is hard. He'll have left no tracks.'

'We establish where he did *not* go,' Lütolf replied, as though stating the obvious

'What?'

'If Carles remained on the road, then he will have reached Barberà, and when we get there we will either find him or discover the reason for the delay. If he did not remain on the road, then we should be able to identify where he left it.'

'I still don't understand. This is a main road. Plenty of people could have moved off the road.'

'Use that mind,' snapped Lütolf, tapping his forehead. 'We are looking for tracks that veer off the road from the southern direction. They need to be fresh, not more than a few hours old. They will be horse tracks, and only one animal. It will be shod. There cannot be many such tracks. I would wager that if we find them we find Carles.'

'Or some farmer in his field.'

'Farmers are not wealthy enough to shoe horses. The hoof prints will be different.'

'It's dark,' Arnau pointed out with a sweep of his arm.'

'The moonlight is bright. Use your eyes and trust in the Lord.'

Arnau fell silent. In truth the moonlight was almost a silvery reflection of a summer's day and his gaze dropped to the dusty turf beside the road. Still, he would have to be very lucky to spot hoof prints under these conditions.

'This is a fool's errand,' he grumbled as the German brother moved to the far side of the road and walked slowly north, peering down at the ground. Arnau mirrored the action on his side and slowly, at a snail's pace, they moved north.

'The preceptrix commanded us to find Carles,' Lütolf snarled. 'A prime tenet of our order is obedience. Blessed Saint Bernard's forty-first rule: "No brother should fight or rest according to his own will, but according to the orders of the master, to whom all should submit." The preceptrix orders us. We obey without argument or question. You are too argumentative. I would rather *no* squire than a troublesome one.'

'A situation that would suit me fine,' barked Arnau in reply.

They fell into a sullen silence, moving slowly north, eyes never leaving the verge, taking in every furrow and burrow as they went. Finally, the hush becoming so oppressive that Arnau could feel it seeping into him and chilling his bones, he cleared his throat.

'Why are you set against me so, Brother Lütolf?'

The German replied swiftly, without even looking up. 'Because you committed to the order on a whim, with little or no contemplation. I do not trust that. I do not trust your motives. I fear you are running from the world and that there is no reason you are with us other than that you simply have nowhere better to be. Such a man is not made for the Poor Knights of Christ. The order demands utter commitment.'

Arnau felt the silence fall once more. He found he could not reply, for the brother had come so close to the mark it had fired an arrow of guilt into his soul. In the ensuing quiet, he found himself wondering, not for the first time, what brought a man from the cold highlands of Germany to the parched land of Iberia. Yes, members of the order could be found moving between monasteries, but still there had to be a reason for it, and the notion dug at Arnau.

Finally, Lütolf spoke again, this time in slightly more forgiving tones. 'Every man has his reason for retreating from the world. Few do so purely for the love of the Church and of monastic solitude. Few do so for the joy of protecting the good from the wicked. There are tarnished souls even among the order. Some come to us seeking redemption, such as Brother Ramon. Some come to forget, such as Brother Balthesar. Neither came to Rourell the true stuff of the order, but both have put aside their past and

The German nodded. ‘Cadeneta is seven miles west of here. Not far.’

Arnau’s eyes scoured the landscape. He felt his lips moving in prayer. He hadn’t realised he was doing it, but was already beseeching the Lord to help him to the best possible outcome: that his suspicions were wrong or unfounded, though he was now filled with a leaden certainty. Carles had not gone further than the farm. Arnau knew it. And he knew why.

There.

It was chance. Pure chance. Or was it the working of the Lord?

Something gleamed for just a moment amid the shadowy undergrowth and low trees at the edge of the farmland. Something metallic. A single moment of reflected moonlight between the leaves, and then lost in the darkness once more.

Arnau felt a shiver take him, and pointed to the trees.

‘There.’

Lütolf did not indulge in questions, just followed Arnau as he left the road and walked his horse down across the verge and through the grass towards those trees. He drew his sword, heard the rasp as the German did the same.

The evidence was a small thing in the end. It could have been anyone’s knife. A gleaming blade lying in the grass in the shadows of the trees that had for one brief moment caught a stray moonbeam and betrayed its presence to Arnau. People lost knives. And certainly there was no identifying mark on a Templar’s blade. But there was no doubt in Arnau’s mind, and he slid from the saddle, landing with a metallic shush of mail, and crept towards the knife.

Sure enough, there were tracks in the mud here. Not hooves, shod or unshod, but tracks that told their own unpleasant tale. Two booted men, dragging something that had left twin furrows in the mud between the grass. He picked up the knife. It was clean.

‘Through there,’ he said to the German knight, pointing into the trees. Lütolf dismounted and the pair tied their reins to a branch, then picked their way on foot into the trees, Arnau in the lead, both with blades ready.

given over their heart and soul to God and the cause. Thus I agreed in convent to accept your application, for every man deserves a chance to prove himself. But you are not filling me with confidence thus far, and until you do so I will continue to doubt your motives. Now look at the grass and find me the tracks Carles left.’

Arnau went back to examining the ground, turning over this new information in his mind. The more he thought on what the German had said the more he felt a strange surge of emotion. Partly guilt, yes, but also determination. When Arnau de Vallbona took an oath, he kept it. He had taken such an oath to look after his father when his mother had died and, though the old man slowly drank himself into the tomb, he had done so with a son trying to support him and turn him from that path all his last days. Arnau had then taken another oath, in place of his father, of fealty to Santa Coloma, and had been Lord Berenguer’s man to the end. He had taken an oath to the Lady Titborga and had clung to that oath through all the dangers of the past week, and that had in turn brought him to a new oath. An oath not just to the preceptrix and the brothers and sisters of Rourell, but an oath to God above. He had not yet been inducted in ceremony, but he was living the life now of a Templar, dressed as a Templar, riding through the night on an impossible mission for the Temple. He would honour his oath for, whatever his reason for blurting out his desire to join them, he loved and trusted the Lord, and the more he thought about it, the more it seemed that this path was the result of divine providence.

Arnau de Vallbona was a Templar now.

The road continued north, the wide farmland of Rourell stretching off east towards the Francoli River, the low, flat, dry fields providing a clear view in the argent moonlight. To the far side, where the German moved with head constantly bowed as though in prayer, a grove of olive trees spread out towards the line of the hills.

Arnau shuddered at the thought of those hills. The Prades range, harbouring the village of Cadeneta.

Just half a mile north of the Rourell preceptory road, he spotted the river coiling back towards them, the Francoli then running parallel with their route, rarely more than two or three hundred yards from the road. They ploughed on slowly, eyes locked on the verges, ever seeking a sign that reason said they would never find. Less than a mile further north, they reached the bridge that crossed the river and passed across it. Arnau was letting his eyes rest for a moment, looking up in the knowledge that there was momentarily no verge, when Lütolf let out a huff of satisfaction.

'He came this far. We have missed nothing yet.'

'How can you tell?' Arnau asked, his eyes dropping again and scouring the road. At the far side of the bridge, a farmer's track led off and the mud from his fields had been thrown across the road. Many hoof prints and wheel ruts carved a path through the muck, and it took Arnau a moment to spot them: the tracks of a single well-shod horse, quite fresh, through the midst of it. He sat back in the saddle, breathing heavily. Lütolf had been right. Perhaps it *was* possible.

They returned to their task, moving slowly, ever watchful.

Something occurred suddenly to Arnau, and his gaze came up, scouring the land just beyond the verge. His eyes fell upon a small stand of trees some distance away and confirmed his suspicion. This was where he and the ladies had joined the road yesterday, having crossed the farmland from their caravan.

Cadeneta in the hills. The farm. A missing Templar. Arnau felt a frisson creep across him, making the hairs on his arms stand proud.

'I have a feeling.'

The German turned a frown upon him. 'What is it?'

'I don't know quite yet. Just… a feeling.' He slowed his horse and then came to a halt. Lütolf did the same, still watching Arnau with interest.

'There. That gateway. That's where my lady de Santa Coloma and I, and Maria too, reached the road. Half a mile across those fields is the farm where we were staying with the captain and his men. This is too much of a coincidence.'

They found Carles on the other side of the small thicket. It took some time in the shadows, for he lay in the undergrowth covered with his black habit, the red cross folded inside.

'The insolent knaves,' Lütolf hissed.

Carefully, Arnau crouched and lifted the black cloak. The body of Carles lay face down and the young sergeant gently rolled him onto his back, feeling slightly sick at the thought of what he and his lady had apparently visited upon Rourell. Carles was dead, clearly. He had taken two arrows to the chest, both of which had been snapped off later, though the heads and a small section of shaft remained lodged between his ribs, the man's tunic sticky and viscous with congealed blood. Even mortally wounded, it seemed that Carles had tried to fight, for he had also taken a sword cut to the arm, which had broken it so that it flopped and almost came away separate when the body was turned. Finally, a dagger had been driven through the heart, probably after he was already dead, just to be sure.

'Too much to hope this was stray Moors on a raid,' Brother Lütolf said, no question in the sentence.

'No,' agreed Arnau. 'The sword was a long, straight Christian one, not a curved Almohad blade. And the blow that dispatched him was from a knife with a triangular section. A misericorde dagger carried by a Christian.'

He sat back on his heels and breathed deeply. 'I would like to think that this is the work of bandits. I do not believe as much even for one moment, but I would like to.'

'There is a simple way to check,' the German prompted him.

'What?'

'The documents.'

Nodding, Arnau set to searching the body. 'They would probably have been in his saddlebag, I think. There's no sign of them on his person. But his purse is still here, as well as a ring. If they did not take his purse, then these were no bandits.'

He rose and turned to Lütolf. 'It seems to me very unlikely that this is the work of anyone other than the men of della Cadeneta.'

'It would appear that you have unearthed a hive of villainy,' the German whispered. 'Men that will kill a brother of the Temple like murderers in the night are low indeed. And fearless, for I will not allow such wickedness to go unpunished.'

For the first time since his arrival, Arnau actually felt in concord with the German knight.

Lütolf straightened and turned slowly in a circle.

'Wherever you are, heed my call, you base churls,' he bellowed into the night. 'Ezekiel, chapter twenty-five: "And I will strike down upon thee with great vengeance and furious anger those who would attempt to poison and destroy my brothers. And you will know my name is the Lord when I lay my vengeance upon thee." With the death of a brother you have set in motion events that you will live to regret for the rest of your short and violent life.'

His words echoed away into the darkness without receiving a reply. Arnau felt a chill again, but the guilt and the determination were back in waves. Stooping, he gathered up the body of Carles and straightened, adjusting his grip with a grunt. The German knight led the way back to the horses and together they tied the body over the back of Lütolf's horse. Mounting, they began to make their way south once more, towards Rourell.

'This is my doing,' Arnau said quietly.

'Yes.'

He flashed a momentary glance of irritation at the scarred knight, for he'd expected the man to deny it and assuage his feeling of guilt.

'But it is also the fault of your lady, and in her plight she must be considered blameless, so the same applies to you. The true guilty party here is the villainous cur who would cut down a man of God for mere temporal gain. Come. Back to Rourell.'

It was a short return journey, given that they now had no need to move slowly and examine the verges as they passed. They reached the turn-off and left the main road, heading for the looming walls of the preceptory. Arnau turned to the German brother and opened his mouth to say something, but instead his eyes widened, looking past Lütolf and into the olive grove. Two figures were moving beneath the trees.

'Hold,' he bellowed, ripping his sword from its scabbard. Lütolf, surprised, spun to look and Arnau watched in horror as one of the two lurking figures raised a crossbow, already loaded and ready, aiming it at the knight. The German clearly saw it at the same time and tried to lurch out of the way. There was a twang and a thud as the bolt was released and through Lütolf's sharp reaction alone he was saved, though the missile instead thudded into the neck of his horse.

The animal reared in agonised panic and its rider was tipped unceremoniously from the saddle, dislodging the body of Carles in the process, both Templars, live and dead, landing in a tangled heap. The horse lurched, bucked, kicked and then fell, writhing and shrieking. Lütolf backed away desperately from the flailing hooves, dragging the body of Carles as he went.

Arnau bellowed in rage and kicked his horse into motion, thundering towards the olive grove. The two men, seeing the black-clad Templar coming for them, their crossbow discharged and temporarily useless, turned tail and fled into the trees. Arnau made to follow them, roaring his anger, but even as he left the small road, the reality of the situation insisted itself. There was simply no way he was going to forge on through those twisted, ancient branches on horseback. The two men were running fast, ducked low for safety. Arnau slid from his horse, sword in hand, and started after them, but a cry of pain drew his attention and he turned.

Lütolf was dragging himself across the gravel, clutching his shoulder where a flailing hoof had caught him a glancing blow. Torn between the desire to race off after the fleeing men and rushing to help his brother Templar, Arnau dithered. His roving eye picked out the two men just as they disappeared from sight among the trees. One had his shield strapped to his back, and Arnau knew the shield, knew the design all too well. If he'd been in any doubt as to who had been behind all this, that doubt was now completely destroyed.

The shield held the white stars on a field of red that labelled him one of della Cadeneta's men.

He hurried back towards the German, who was now out of danger from the dying horse, clutching the body of Carles to him as he sat in the dust and rubbed his painful shoulder.

'What are you doing?' Lütolf demanded.

'You needed help.'

'Nonsense. Get after them.'

'I'll never catch them now. Wouldn't have done before. They had a head start through the trees on foot.'

The German snorted his opinion of that, and slowly, hissing, pulled himself upright. Arnau helped him to his feet despite the snarled order not to, then crouched and lifted Carles, draping him over Arnau's own horse now.

With Lütolf plodding along beside him and clutching his shoulder, Arnau led his own horse past the now-still body of the other beast, the three of them making for the preceptory a short distance down the track.

'Such audacity. To attack a man of the Temple within sight of Rourell's walls,' the German said, shaking his head.

Two Templars, thought Arnau irritably, though he kept that to himself.

'They were della Cadeneta's men?' Lütolf prompted.

'They were. I saw the shield of one.'

'Then they are hunting your Lady Titborga.'

Arnau nodded. 'I suspect they followed our tracks to the main road and then lost us there. If it was only seven miles back to Cadeneta, the captain probably sent for more men. They will have combed the landscape for signs of us over the night and this morning. It will have been sheer bad timing that Carles rode north through the middle of their search. Perhaps they saw him coming, put two and two together with the preceptory so close offering the chance of sanctuary, and made to stop him.'

Lütolf hissed. 'Whether they challenged him or not, Carles was aware of how they fit into your tale. He was bearing those documents and would not have stopped for them. So they put two arrows in him to halt him, and then finished him off, robbed him and left him in a ditch. Such men have no fear of God or the

Church. And if they were watching from the road, then they are now convinced Rourell is where the lady went.'

'I am sorry we brought this to your doorstep, Brother Lütolf.'

The German brushed aside the apology. 'Blame is a dangerous thing. It festers and corrupts. Guilt the same. Neither will do us any credit now. The fact is that a base villain, intent on harming and robbing a virginal noblewoman, has set his sights upon Rourell and does not baulk at the thought of slipping a blade into a warrior of Christ. We need to speak to the preceptrix urgently. When we get through the gate, hand the reins to Guillem and tell him to see to Carles. I will go ahead to see the preceptrix. Follow on as soon as you are done.'

The gate to the complex was opened upon their approach, and Arnau was momentarily surprised at the lack of activity until he realised that they had been long enough on the road that they had missed compline altogether and the preceptory had settled in for the night. Young Simo struggled with the gate and the bar but this time Arnau was too preoccupied to consider helping the lad. He led the horse and body off to the stables, though Guillem was nowhere to be seen. As the gates were barred behind him, he heeded the German's earlier words and set to removing the saddle and harness and stabling the horse himself. He had just filled the hay rack for the beast and closed the stall gate when Guillem arrived at a rush.

'Simo told me you were back.' His eyes slid to the body and he blanched. 'Carles.'

'Yes,' Arnau answered darkly. 'I have to see the preceptrix with Brother Lütolf. Could you manage to deal with Carles for me?'

Guillem nodded and stooped over the body. Arnau thanked him hurriedly and then scurried out of the stables and across the courtyard to the chapter house. At the door he paused, assuming this was where the others would be found, and knocked politely. The door was opened by the German knight a moment later and he motioned for Arnau to join them, then closed it once more.

The preceptrix sat upon her chair, and the two men hurried over to her.

'Brother Lütolf has explained what you found. You are sure these are della Cadeneta's men?'

Arnau bowed his head. 'There is no doubt, Sister. I saw the shields. They are watching Rourell and it was almost certainly they who killed Carles.'

The preceptrix drummed her fingers on the chair arm. 'Two hundred thousand gold *maravedi* could turn many a heart dark and make them consider otherwise unthinkable courses of action. And without wishing to cast calumnies at the lords of Catalunya, della Cadeneta has ever harboured such a dark heart. He is known to me as a man of little moral fibre. That he would kill a soldier of Christ for such a sum is hardly a surprise, though it does sadden me.'

Arnau nodded. *Sadden* was hardly the word he would have used. Anger, perhaps…

'And it seems unlikely that this is the end of the matter,' the preceptrix added. 'I would wager that this is the desperate work of the captain of whom you spoke, who escorted you from Santa Coloma. Afeared of how his lord would react, he is desperately attempting to recapture our dear sister before della Cadeneta arrives. He was, I believe you said, following on a few days behind.'

Arnau nodded. 'Though he is eager and despicable. I suspect he will already be well on the way.'

'Then we can likely expect an escalation,' Lütolf put in. 'For now, they watch the preceptory. I would recommend that we make regular armoured tours of the properties surrounding and try to keep this wicked rabble away from our doors.'

Preceptrix Ermengarda looked unsure for a moment, an expression that seemed odd on that certain, commanding face. 'Perhaps, though I fear for my people if we are gathering an enemy who does not baulk at the murder of a Templar sergeant. We must be careful. Life should go on as it is for now, but yes, we must remain ever vigilant. I am tempted to send word to Barberà but am beset with twin worries. I have no wish to send another brother to the grave in the manner of Carles, and we are lacking proof of della Cadeneta's complicity in the affair, for all that his men attacked you on the road. There could be an argument suggesting that his men acted alone and without their lord's consent in his absence. If I take charges against him to the mother house, charges that will then likely reach the king, we must be certain that he is the villain beyond all doubt. Since he is as yet not even in our vicinity, such an accusation would be foolishly made.'

Arnau and Lütolf both nodded at the truth of this.

'But the documents' Arnau sighed. 'If the documents pertaining to Santa Coloma lands are already in the captain's hands, as well as those confirming the applications of myself and the lady into the order, then those applications are yet to be lodged legally. We are still not members of the order, and those lands are still fair game. Possibly, holding those documents, della Cadeneta can even lay claim to them in Titborga's absence? I'm no student of law, but it seems to me…'

The preceptrix was waving him to silence with a curious smile. 'I am nothing if not cautious, young Vallbona, though the death of our beloved brother might suggest otherwise. Knowing the men of Cadeneta to be at large, and the value of such documents, I had Carles make copies. At this stage legal title to lands and fortune do not need to be confirmed, just the details of the proposed donation and of the brother or sister to be admitted. This is simply the initial lodging of records. Thus Carles was carrying only copies of our Templar records, rather than any document which might be legally binding outside our order. The lady de Santa Coloma's lands remain hers safely for now. Those records will have to be lodged in due course, but I am loath to risk another messenger until we are more informed as to the situation in the world outside.'

'What is our next step then, Sister?' Lütolf asked quietly.

The preceptrix's expression hardened. 'We prepare for any eventuality. We continue on with our lives as servants of God and of the Temple, we trust in the Lord and we take our cue from the Book of Exodus and not the Book of Matthew.'

The scarred German nodded his approval and Arnau frowned in incomprehension.

Lütolf turned to him. 'Put aside all Matthew's thoughts of turning the other cheek, de Vallbona. "If there is serious injury, you are to take life for life, eye for eye, tooth for tooth, hand for hand, foot for foot, burn for burn, wound for wound, bruise for bruise." The word of the Lord demands vengeance upon della Cadeneta.'

CHAPTER EIGHT

Arnau stood in the clear area of dry, dusty brown earth and eyed his opponent warily. The walls of the preceptory rose nearby, at once imposing and comforting, the sounds of hammer on anvil, of horses and men, of daily life rising across the surroundings in the afternoon sun.

Brother Lütolf stood immobile and emotionless, a Germanic statue to order and control. His sword tip barely moved, while Arnau's wavered like a snake hypnotising its prey. The younger man, his sergeant's robe now finally clean and neatly pressed, but already gathering dust from the surroundings, swallowed as he changed his footing.

'Whenever you are ready,' the scarred brother said in the offhand tone of a disapproving tutor.

Arnau forbore to reply, instead keeping his eyes on the German. The younger knight had learned from good sword teachers in his days at Vallbona. He was no dunce with a blade, even though it was not his chosen weapon, but the main thing his teacher had drummed into him during those hot tiring days of training was that no amount of skill could replace wit. If a man could anticipate his opponent, then the actual strike or parry would be a simple thing. It was advice that had served Arnau well in his time. Every opponent had at least one tell if you studied him enough. Of course, in the heat of battle, that was not often possible, but in a duel such as this, it could mean the difference between failure and success. A man might always take an involuntary glance in the direction he was planning to move. A knee might twitch before a step. One memorable opponent had always rubbed his thumb on his sword's guard before a lunge.

Lütolf of Ehingen was unreadable. It was baffling. Every man Arnau had faced had at least given *something* away, but the German might as well have been carved from alabaster. Arnau would hate to play the man at dice. Not that such a thing would be approved of in the order, of course, he thought with a tinge of regret.

Well, if Lütolf could play the man with no tell – a thing of which Arnau knew he himself was incapable – then he would take the contrary path. He would be the man with *every* tell. He knew that he himself would have something that gave him away, though he knew not what it was, and that the German would be watching for it in exactly the same manner, so instead, Arnau would play the fool.

He began to move. Stepping back and forth, left and right in a haphazard manner, shifting his fingers on the hilt, eyes darting this way and that, arms rolling. He would be unpredictable. Lütolf would not see him coming. He readied himself mentally even as his dance of distraction continued.

'Are you ill?' asked his opponent in an acidic tone.

Arnau lunged. In the midst of a strange sidestep, he suddenly leaped forward, sword sweeping unstoppably for the padded chest of the German standing motionless in the dust.

A moment later, Arnau was on the ground in a beige cloud with the blunted tip of a practice sword hovering, immobile, an inch from his windpipe. All he'd experienced was the thrill of a strike the man couldn't possibly have anticipated and then a rushing feeling as he fell past the sidestepping Lütolf and collapsed to the ground, almost doing himself an injury with his own sword.

'Rise,' the German said in that same aloof teacher's tone.

Arnau, who would love to be angry but was currently too astonished, did so as his opponent stepped back and removed the weapon from his throat.

'Incredible,' the young knight breathed.

'*Quite* credible,' Lütolf said dismissively. 'especially given your strange Saint Vitus's dance.'

'You moved so *fast*.' And with a black-purple shoulder, bruised from a flailing hoof too!

'All I needed to do was pivot on one foot. You made such a show of moving about that I reasoned it was to distract me from a coming blow. The only blow you could strike at such speed from that position was a lunge. All I needed was to anticipate which foot you would lunge with, so I kept my stance even, ready to pivot on either foot. All very simple. As, I am beginning to fear, are you.'

Arnau felt his lip twitch at the insult.

'Come. Stop this crazed dancing and face me properly. If you have a tell you are trying to hide, then let me find it and I can explain how to nullify it, though there is a simple way to smooth out all such wrinkles in one's martial actions.'

'Oh?' snapped Arnau, still irritated, but curious nonetheless.

'The peace of the Lord. I am at perfect peace while I wait, for the word of God fills my veins and animates every sinew. My trust in Him is so complete that I am motionless and prepared. You are still too full of the vices and wiles of the temporal world, like Ramon. He also cannot stand still. But it is in the act of giving one's entire being to the order that a man can achieve such control and peace. Perhaps when you are ready you will not need to dance like a leper's bell, clanging this way and that.'

Arnau sighed and stepped back, making a futile attempt to dust himself off.

'Very well. Let's go again,' he said to the German. 'Perhaps you would care to try me?'

Lütolf shrugged and fell into his usual motionless stance. Arnau prepared himself, sword tip up, dancing just a little. He stood as still as he could, though there was an ache in his left knee from where he'd hit a cobble when he fell, and he momentarily changed stance to relieve the pressure.

The German was on him like the wrath of God. The practice blade in Lütolf's hand swept through the air and halted an inch from Arnau's neck once more. The younger man had had only moments to react, had managed to lift his own sword perhaps halfway to a decent parry, before the German, like a bolt of lightning, struck.

'You are slow and sloppy,' Lütolf said, removing his sword and stepping back. 'Your knee was slowly giving. All I had to do was wait until you changed leg and catch you while your balance was uncertain. You move with the indecisiveness and clumsiness of a Hohenstaufen.'

Arnau sighed and stepped back. He'd always considered himself a good swordsman. He'd killed efficiently in that battle by the Ebro, for sure. Yet next to Lütolf of Ehingen he felt like a novice. And what was that about a Hohenstaufen? What had the emperors to do with anything?

'What is your psalm of choice?' the German asked.

Arnau frowned. 'I would say the learning of Ethan the Ezrahite – eighty-nine – for it was my mother's favourite.'

'Recite it. Not out loud. In your head.'

Arnau, still frowning, concentrated, forming the words.

'You look like you are trying to defecate,' Lütolf noted. 'Do not force yourself. Just relax into the psalm. You know it. You do not need to concentrate so.'

He was right, Arnau realised. He stood calmly, allowing himself to watch his opponent while the words of the psalm rolled through his mind.

I shall sing without end the mercies of the Lord.

In generation and into generation, I shall tell thy truth with my mouth.

I shall sing of the Lord's constant love forever. To all generations, I shall tell out thy faithfulness with my mouth.

For thou sayest: without end mercy shall be builded in heavens and thy truth shall be made ready in those.

I disposed a testament to chosen men; I swore to David, my servant…

The German struck once more like a bolt of lightning, that blunted sword coming this time not for the neck, but for the gut. He was so fast it was barely credible. Yet somehow at the last moment, Arnau's sword was there, turning the blow aside, only partly, but it was impressive it had reached the position at all, given the man's speed.

Lütolf stepped back, nodding in satisfaction. 'Better. See how in the peace of the Lord you focus your instincts so much more easily? You did not plan to counter my strike, but because you were not overthinking your predicament, you were able to react so much more readily to my attack. Admittedly, while you avoided a belly wound that would mean slow and agonising death, a real blade would have cut into your liver and you would even now be going grey as dark blood pooled about your feet, but the reaction was still an improvement.'

Arnau blinked in surprise. He was unable to react or respond, partly through surprise, and partly through the remarkable pain that had built in his side and was even now attempting to fold him in two and drop him to the ground. He gasped.

'There is still a long way to go,' the German added. 'You have adequate skill, and more than some I have seen in our order, but your concentration and your control is pitiful. You must learn control and peace if you are to be truly effective with that blade.'

Arnau gasped again.

'We will take a few minutes for you to recover.'

Gasp. Arnau stood motionless, trying to override the pain in his side that he knew would already be blossoming into a good bruise. Gradually it moved from debilitating pain to dull, insistent ache, which rippled out into the surrounding flesh. They were wearing mail hauberks over specially thick padded arming tunics for practice work, and he dreaded to think what that blow might have felt like without the extra protection.

Slowly, quietly, the pain began to dissipate. He attempted to change his footing finally, and found that he could do so without too much discomfort. He rolled his shoulders. He was all right. The pain would be intense that evening, along with the aches in all his muscles, but right now, he was controlling it. A notion came to him.

He struck like an asp. One moment, he was standing like an invalid, gasping in breath that he no longer quite needed, recovery more or less complete. The next, his sword had flicked up and was moving for Lütolf's own gut.

He missed the German knight by perhaps a finger's width, staggering on into the dust before he finally turned, wide-eyed.

Lütolf shrugged. 'You have tells for sure, but that was simple to anticipate. You were testing your readiness when you shifted position. I could see that, so I had an inkling that you would come. Still, it was well played and reasonably fast. There is hope for you.'

He continued on with rather backhanded compliments and dissections of Arnau's lunge, but the young knight was no longer paying him any attention. His gaze was, instead, locked on the middle distance. As he'd staggered to a halt, he'd seen something flash momentarily, off in the fields surrounding Rourell. Sun on metal or glass, but what would glass be doing in a field? His eyes scoured that landscape. There it was again. A series of flashes. Definitely sun on metal. He could make out the shape of one of the farmers trudging along behind an ox-drawn plough, and the gleaming was beyond him yet by some distance. Half a mile away or more. At the edge of a small stand of trees.

He blinked as something smacked into the back of his head and he turned to see Brother Lütolf glaring at him with disapproval, his gauntlet swinging in his fingertips from the slap.

'It is courtesy to pay attention to an instructor, not to mention the potential for saving your life.'

Arnau brushed aside the comment, gesturing out towards the trees. The flashing had stopped. 'I saw something out there, by the trees. Could have been someone in armour. Maybe even two or more. Metal flashing in the sun.'

The German knight seemed entirely unimpressed by this. 'Or a farmer with his tools. Or a travelling tinker. Or a boy with a bucket.'

'I don't think so,' Arnau said, doubtfully.

'Both Ramon and Mateu are circling through the estates. If there is trouble, they will find it. Tomorrow, you and I shall take on that task, but for today, leave such matters to Brother Ramon and his squire and concentrate upon the matter at hand. If the enemy is to be chastised for their wickedness it would behove you to know one end of a sword from the other.'

Arnau nodded absently, less than certain and ignoring the unsubtle jibe, fighting the urge to climb onto his horse and ride out to investigate the flashing. Finally, dragging his eyes from the middle distance, he focused instead on the irritated German.

'Come for me again,' Lütolf ordered, tapping his chest as he settled into a relaxed stance with his sword tip in the dust.

Arnau looked the man up and down. Lütolf could read Arnau like a psalter, clearly, and could anticipate his moves. Could he be distracted? Arnau remembered that battle by the Ebro. The Templar who had led the charge, singing his psalms of glory as he slew the heathen. Arnau had become so wrapped up in the man that he had let himself drift away from the Santa Coloma company, with disastrous results. Could such a thing distract the German brother? Not the glory of the Psalms, for that was bread and butter to Brother Lütolf. But perhaps there was a different way to have just such an effect.

He readied himself, sword in both hands, bent slightly at the waist and rocking gently from side to side.

'We shall speak the praises of the Lord and His strength, and His power,' Arnau sang suddenly. The German frowned in incomprehension. Why was the young man bleating out the seventy-eighth Psalm and not simply keeping it in his head as he had been instructed?

Arnau continued to sway gently. 'And the marvellous deeds which He did. And He raised witnessing in Isaac…'

There it was. Just through the veneer of frowning disapproval, he saw Lütolf's eyelid twitch at the misquote. The psalm called upon Jacob, not Isaac. The mistake cut deep into the German, down to his pious bones. Arnau had to force himself not to smile. He would make an opening.

'And He set law in Israel. How great things commanded He to our fathers, to make those known to their sons.'

He managed to maintain a good musical tone as he continued, watching the German, waiting for the moment.

'He smote a stone and waters flowed, and streams issued in abundance. Whether also he may give bread or make ready a board to his people? Therefore the Lord heard, and delayed, and fire was kindled in Isaac, and the ire of God ascended on Israel.'

Lütolf's eyelid twitched and danced again at the transposition of Isaac for Jacob.

Arnau struck.

Once again, the German danced nimbly aside, but this time Arnau had been so close. He heard Lütolf's indrawn hiss of pain as the younger man's practice sword caught him a glancing blow on the hip as he moved away.

'Clever,' the German said in a voice dripping with disdain and disapproval. 'But one must remember that *Satan* is clever. Some things are beneath a pious man.'

Typical, Arnau thought as he moved back into position. When he finally landed a blow on the man, Lütolf managed to make it Arnau's fault for being ungodly. He was about to launch into a defensive diatribe on the value of using wit and guile against an enemy and the differences between that and the influence of Satan, when he was momentarily distracted by a flash once more. His gaze strayed up to the fields in the distance again, and he scoured that treeline, looking for the armoured figure he was sure was behind the glinting.

He staggered in shock as the blow landed. Brother Lütolf's practice sword slammed into Arnau's fist. The younger man's sword fell to the ground from agonised fingers, one of which had broken with a loud crack.

'Pay attention, Vallbona,' snapped the German.

Arnau stared at him, then down at his hand and the sword lying in the dust. Ignoring Lütolf momentarily, he gently removed his mailed gauntlet, with some difficulty, for his little finger stuck out at an angle and was already swelling and red. With a hiss, he tried to push it back into line with the others and the pain that lanced through his hand made him yelp loudly.

'Practice is over for now,' the German said in neutral tones, and started to walk towards the preceptory. Arnau stared after him. Lütolf had not yet acquired a replacement horse for the one that had been killed beneath him, but Arnau had his mount with him. He bent, picking up his sword with his undamaged hand, and slid it into the scabbard, then grasped the reins and began to lead the beast back in the wake of the German. As they trudged through the hot arid dirt, Arnau three times shot glances back to those trees, each time failing to catch a reflection of a sunbeam.

Finally, he reached the gate as Lütolf entered. The German spotted the preceptrix with Titborga, striding across the courtyard towards the chapter house.

'Sister,' Lütolf called and made to intercept them. The two ladies stopped, the preceptrix's eyebrow arching.

'I have to report an incident,' the German said. 'Vallbona was distracted repeatedly during training and my irritation got the better of me. I sought to regain his attention, but in doing so have damaged his hand.'

Arnau was there now and he and his horse came to a halt.

'Show me,' commanded Preceptrix Ermengarda. Arnau did so, raising his deformed sword hand. The preceptrix's already arched eyebrow arched even more, impossibly so. Even Arnau began to wither under her gaze and, since it was directed at the German, he couldn't imagine how contrite Brother Lütolf must feel.

'This is unacceptable, Brother. You know the rules better than most. Injuries during training are to be avoided. Deliberate injuries all the more so. You must not strike a brother Christian in anger. It is not our way. Remember the 235th rule. Had Vallbona been a full brother, I would now have that habit from your back.'

Lütolf bowed his head in penitence and Arnau almost jumped as the preceptrix turned to him. 'Rarely, though, is there smoke without a flame. The rule also forbids brothers to incite anger in one another. You are new and yet to be granted full ceremony, so it would be unseemly to discipline you for such, but be aware that good conduct begets good conduct.'

Arnau blinked at the chastisement that seemed so unfair, but the preceptrix had already turned back to the German. 'Brother Lütolf, you will do vigil in the chapel this night once compline is done. This will be your penance.'

The scarred knight bowed his head a little lower and then moved away without looking at Arnau. The younger knight was glad. There was a good chance some of the harsh words rattling around in his head might have crept out had the man looked at him.

'Come, Brother Arnau,' the preceptrix said, and then swept off towards the chapter house. Titborga threw a look of concerned interest at Arnau and then hurried away in the preceptrix's wake, lifting the hem of her white habit from the detritus of the courtyard, Oddly, and also typically, the preceptrix's habit remained down and yet had managed to stay pristine.

Perhaps noting the look on his face, the preceptrix cleared her throat and interjected. 'Brother Balthesar is quite correct. Let me distract you from these uncomfortable ministrations with a tale. It is an old tale, especially for those here who have endured it before, but I am aware of the unusual nature of my command here, and the intrigue it inspires within those who hear of it. Perhaps the story of how I come to be preceptrix of Rourell will turn your thoughts from the pain of your hand?'

Arnau, his interest piqued over a question he had asked in the silence of his head many times, nodded, noting that Titborga similarly leaned forward in her seat with curiosity.

'It is, however, a sad tale.' She poured herself another cup of wine without offering it to the others and then set to with her story. 'My husband Gombau and I were travelling from Tàrrega to Perpignan to visit the king. Our lineage, you see, was of the highest pedigree and our estate sizeable. My husband was sought by clerics and kings alike for his support. On the journey, close to the Pyrenees near Figueres, our retinue was set upon by bandits – a ragtag force of escaped Moorish slaves who had banded together to prey upon the Christians of the region. My husband fought them off, along with the men at arms, of course, but several of them, on departure, loosed arrows from their horses in the manner of the Persians of old. Most were harmless, but one pierced the window of my carriage and took the life of our daughter Maria. She died in my arms in a welter of blood.'

Arnau felt a cold chill run through him. Suddenly, he was not sure he wanted to know the rest of the story. Titborga's face was also an open-mouthed 'O' of horror, and the young knight could see from the preceptrix's eyes how hard it was for her to relive the tale. He wondered why she had volunteered to do so, and considered perhaps that in the telling she somehow managed to numb the pain a little. He opened his mouth to ask her to stop, but at that moment Carima pulled a bandage tight and instead Arnau bit deep into the leather, catching his tongue painfully.

'I was filled with fury,' the preceptrix said. 'First with sorrow, of course, but then swiftly with fury. And when Gombau came and found what had happened, he vowed such terribly ungodly things

Carima finished with the bandages and began to pack away her kit. Arnau thanked her in a rather embarrassed voice and was grateful when she smiled and told him not to worry. He felt he could learn a thing or two about compassion from the young Jewess. Things in the Order of the Poor Knights of Christ and the Temple of Solomon were not as simple as he had assumed, watching that glorious knight in red and white leading the charge at the Ebro.

in his rage. We travelled on to the king, and my husband beseeched him – this was Alfons, of course, not the current king. He demanded the king hunt the bandits that so infested the region and bring them to justice. I was with him, rabid in my support. But the king was not well. His health was failing – he died within the month – and waved aside our plea, considering bandits a minor irritation in the face of his own mortality and his rush to complete his Pyrenean unity.'

Arnau nodded. He remembered that *minor irritation* in practice. The escaped slave bandits had caused trouble across the region, as far west and south as Vallbona's own door. They became something of a force to be reckoned with before they were finally put down.

'In rage and hollow desperation, Gombau and I pledged to the Templar order all our lands and wealth, seeking only to do precisely that for which the Poor Knights were created: securing the safety of travellers and pilgrims. Gombau was sent to Castile where he was enrolled in the latest push of reconquest. He died on the field of battle against the Moor. I had been serving as a sister in Barberà, doing my best to influence the preceptor there to deal with the bandits who slayed our daughter. It astounds me how my lineage and influence survived both my entry into the order and the death of my beloved Gombau, for I was able to call in a number of debts and favours and secured for myself this preceptory. As such I had considerable say in the region's Templar activity. Within the year the combined might of the Temple in Catalunya, along with a small force from the new pious King Pedro, put an end to the roving bandits. I have been the mistress of Rourell since then.'

'And proved the match of any preceptor I have encountered, I might add,' Balthesar put in.

The preceptrix gestured to the wall the building shared with the chapel, and Arnau turned to see what she was indicating. A sword was hanging there, gleaming and strong. A fine sword, too, but solid. A soldier's sword, for all its decoration.

'My husband's blade. I keep it to serve as a reminder of what I am: a commander of the Poor Knights of Christ and the Temple of Solomon. No, I have never wielded the blade, before you ask. I may command here with a fist of iron, but I am a woman, and that fist has never held a sword. Yet it remains important as a symbol. Never forget what you are or why you are here.'

Arnau nodded. 'To protect the Christian from the heathen,' he replied with confidence. The look he received in return made him shrink back into himself.

Balthesar's quiet tone cut through the suddenly heavy air.

'We protect the innocent and the God-fearing from the wicked, Brother Arnau. We live in turbulent times, but the order is not about the Christian and the Moor. Or the Jew,' he added, gesturing at Carima and sending a wave of guilt flooding through Arnau as he realised she was glaring at him. 'It is simply about the good and the wicked,' the old knight continued. 'It does not do to see the world in such a basic manner as good Christians and bad everyone else. Sometimes, Vallbona, the wicked wear a cross. Sometimes the innocent do not.'

Preceptrix Ermengarda was nodding. 'Your encounters with the Don della Cadeneta should have clarified that point for you. Though the order's work with non-Christian associates is not universally welcomed, there are certain realities to be accepted in this world. Without the ministrations of good Carima here, herself a daughter of Solomon's seed, you would probably have lived out the rest of your life with nine fingers. Thanks to her, you will simply have a bent digit. Without the simple honesty and agricultural understanding of our Moorish labourers, our fields would not thrive. Without the expertise of our Moorish overseer, the millstones would not turn to make our flour. If it is righteous reconquest you seek, you should hitch your wagon to the King of Castile's horse, not to the order.'

Brother Balthesar smiled, and Arnau nodded with a faint sense of humiliation. Why had he espoused such an ardent viewpoint in the first place? Had he not himself always seen the Moor in a relatively sympathetic light?

A possible answer struck him suddenly. Perhaps it was the influence of the hard-edged, overly pious Lütolf. Perhaps the German's inflexible attitude had begun to inform his own?

CHAPTER NINE

Arnau exited the dormitory doorway and emerged into the warm night. He could hear the hum of conversation from the refectory where the various brothers, sisters and sergeants had gathered for wine and conversation, the only relaxing moment of the day for the order. To some extent he'd been tempted to join them, but he knew that Lütolf would be there with his Germanic nose raised so that he could look down it at those he considered less pious. Since the training incident, he had gone out of his way to spend as little time as possible with the scarred knight. Not an easy thing to do for his squire, and they had continued to train, regardless of the growing wall between them and the pain in Arnau's hand. But the young sergeant simply could not find it within himself to spend what little free time he had in the man's presence.

Instead, Arnau crossed to the stables to check up on his horse. Regardless of the role Guillem played in the care of the preceptory's animals, it was still expected of every member of the community to maintain his tack and animal and, though Guillem was quite thorough, there was always more to do. The courtyard was empty in the golden glow of the lamps and Arnau paused in the doorway of the stable before he went in, savouring the night air before inhaling the heady aroma of many horses in a small space.

His attention was caught by movement across the way and his eyes focused on the doorway to the sisters' dormitory, from which a figure in white had just emerged. One of the smaller women, from the size of her stride, though it was impossible to tell who at this distance and in this light, especially as she was largely covered by wimple and coif.

The figure was carrying a small wicker basket and a lamp, which bobbed and twisted as she walked towards the south gate beneath the arch. Curious, Arnau left the stables again and shuffled over to the arch's entrance just in time to see the nun open the small door inset into the heavy wooden gate and pass through it. He heard it shut and lock with a click from the far side and frowned. What would a nun be doing leaving the preceptory at this time of night? Still, she had clearly been on some recognised business or other, and had been walking quite openly. There is a strange habit of those attempting subterfuge to slink as though they are about suspicious business. The small nun had not exuded such an aura. She had walked. She had even been humming quietly. Plus, of course, she had a key. The only three keys to that door belonged to the preceptrix, the seneschal of the preceptory, Luis, and Brigida the cook, so she was certainly about the business of one of those three.

Shrugging, Arnau returned to the stables. He found the hay rack for his horse and topped it up, trying to keep his bound and throbbing fingers from knocking painfully against anything, then filling the rack for Lütolf's new beast while he was about it. He spent some time carefully brushing the mane and polishing his saddle with eight fingers, then, some quarter of an hour having passed, he emerged once more into the sultry Iberian night air and paused, drawing a deep breath. Somewhat invigorated, he decided that a little time maintaining his sword and armour might be in order, despite having spent time at it earlier in the day. Then, he had been in Brother Lütolf's company and had done a poor job of polishing, immersed in disgruntlement as he had been.

A little vigorous rubbing of pitted steel might allow him to work out some of his frustrations, and he made for the small armoury, listening to the evening symphony of crickets across the countryside, the hum of conversation from the refectory, the sounds of the animals in the stables, Father Diego singing hymns in the chapel in a low murmur.

And an unexpected thread. A sound that was almost buried beneath all the others, but was so out of place that it leaped to Arnau's ears like a trumpet call.

The sound of scuffling. A struggle.

Even as he frowned and tried to work out where the sound was coming from, there was a brief squeak of a scream that was instantly muffled as someone clamped a hand over a mouth. Without having yet identified the precise location, its significance was so clear that Arnau was hurrying for the south gate before he'd realised it. It had to be the nun. *Had* to be.

He grasped the handle of the inset door with his good left hand and turned, but the wooden portal simply clonked and rattled, refusing to open. Of course, the nun had locked it as she exited. He could hear a gruff voice now somewhere out there, so low the words were not audible, and then the clopping of hooves. Urgently, he scurried across to the heavy bar. Simo had lifted the one on the west gate, and Arnau had assumed this would be as easy. It proved not to be. Having the inset door and the west gate, no one had bothered fully opening the south gate for some time, and the bar was almost welded into place with grime and rust.

The young knight gritted his teeth and heaved, positioning his grip on it to spare the damaged finger. It moved little more than an inch and then dropped back into place, Arnau's hands sore, his arms screaming in pain, his finger throbbing worryingly. He tried again, panting. It moved a little more and then dropped back. As he heaved in a breath he could hear whimpering outside and two men's voices as they argued quietly.

Bending back to it, he prepared for a third try when suddenly a figure appeared beside him. Brother Ramon was there now, lending his strength. Together, they heaved the bar up and dropped it to one side. The doors opened with difficulty and a tortured groan.

Arnau and Brother Ramon burst out onto the causeway that crossed the ditch outside the preceptory, looking this way and that in the silvery moonlight. They spotted the nun in but a moment, a heap of white on the dark, dusty ground, a broken lamp lying nearby, still burning and lighting mostly dry earth.

The two men ran over to the shape and, as Ramon dropped into a crouch, Arnau scanned the area. For a moment, he thought perhaps he saw riders a few hundred yards from the road, but a blink later there was nothing, and he couldn't be sure. His gaze dropped.

The figure, heaving in sobbing breaths, was Maria, Titborga's maid. As Ramon moved her into a seated position checked what he could within the bounds of modesty, Arnau took in her situation. She had been beaten. There were burgeoning bruises on her face that would later be colourful and cover most of the skin. One eye was pressed shut under a red welt. For a moment, as she held up her hands, he thought they were also wounded from the gore on them, but then he realised the blood was someone else's. She had scratched with her nails like a hunting cat. But perhaps the thing that shocked him, and certainly the thing that started a simmering rage building within him was the torn white habit. Certain damage would be consistent with a physical attack, but someone had torn Maria's habit from the bottom hem, ripping it open to display her womanhood. Some despicable monster had seemingly attempted to rape a *nun*.

His memory corrected him. She was only dressed in the habit as a *consoror* – a temporary resident, and not a full sister. Maria was not a nun. He dismissed the distinction as an unworthy thought. Still, the savagery and wickedness made his blood boil. He caught sight of Ramon's eyes and recognised two things in them. Firstly, that the knight felt that same fury. Secondly, that Brother Ramon was, in fact, in his cups in a manner that broke at least one of the order's rules concerning moderation.

'Where were you?' he asked the knight.

'Buttery. Checking the wine.'

That figured. But in the event it had been a good thing, for the buttery was next to the arch and hence Ramon had been able to hear the commotion outside almost as well as Arnau.

'Are there tracks?' the older knight asked as he rocked Maria gently.

Arnau peered at the ground, lit gold by the fallen lamp and silver by the moon in the clear sky. 'Yes. Three horses, I would say.'

'What were you doing out here?' Ramon asked the wounded girl.

Between sobs and through a painful split lip, Maria murmured her story.

'The Doña – *Sister* Titborga – had smelled the bouquets we had put together for the preceptrix's bedclothes and had asked if I could do the same for her.'

Arnau frowned and Ramon looked across at him and shrugged. 'A small indulgence. The sharpness of the order's rules can sometimes be dulled with such tiny allowances. The sisters often have scented sheets.'

'I checked with the preceptrix and with Brother Luis,' Maria said in a worried voice. 'I was looking for lavender and evening stock to dry in a posy. Neither grows within the walls, but I know there are patches without.'

That explained her having the key, at least.

'Who attacked you?' Ramon pressed, not without sympathy, as the thud of boots announced more people arriving from the preceptory. Arnau turned to see Brothers Lütolf, Balthesar and Mateu crossing the causeway at a run.

'Don't know,' Maria said. 'Couldn't see. I was bent over, gathering stock.' She pointed at a half-filled basket that seemed to corroborate as much. 'They attacked me from behind. One tried... he tried to...' She broke down into a fit of sobbing once more and Ramon consoled her again as the new arrivals checked the ground hereabouts and gathered up the broken lamp and the basket.

'Three lots of horse tracks,' Balthesar confirmed. 'All well-shod, so knights and soldiers. Not just thugs. Could be bandits.'

'Bandits would not dare come so close to the preceptory,' Lütolf said, shaking his head.

'Not *ordinarily*, my friend,' Balthesar countered. 'But these are not ordinary times. It may be that a hostile don in the vicinity watches Rourell with wicked intent. That this young maid was part of that same don's wedding caravan can hardly be coincidence.'

Arnau nodded. There had to be a connection. He leaned closer to the beaten girl. 'You did not see a face?'

Again, Maria fought back her sobs, shaking her head. 'They held me from behind. They were going... Then they heard the gate. Heard someone coming. I think that changed their plan. Two ran off to their horses and the other... he spun me, but I only saw a

'Stay there, Brother Arnau. Stoop and gather night broom, if you will.'

The others shuffled off and Arnau, feeling supremely foolish, lamp trembling in his hand, bent over and began to uproot flowers, dropping them in the basket. He could hear the myriad crickets at work, a grey nightjar chirring, two owls in the distance. He could hear the muted noise of the preceptory. He could hear the fibrous tearing noises as the plants came free from the dusty earth. Mostly, what he could hear was the three men reaching a point some yards away and then turning and moving back towards him.

Still uncertain what was next expected of him, he continued to gather plants.

Suddenly arms were around him. Despite the fact that his conscious mind knew damn well who the arms belonged to and that there was nothing to fear, still instinct took over and he began to fight and struggle, ignoring the pain in his finger. They had trouble holding him. He stopped short of scratching and biting, and finally tore himself from the grip of two of the men, spinning in the hand of the other. He had a brief flash of Balthesar's face before a hand came rushing at him. He simply couldn't believe they were going to punch him. He recoiled, readying himself to strike back, but the old, white-haired brother halted the blow just before it landed, instead clamping it over Arnau's eyes. He was suddenly grabbed again and held tight.

'What have you seen?' Brother Balthesar asked quietly.

Arnau continued to struggle for a moment, but then fell still as he realised they were only mock-containing him, with no real force.

'I heard you coming. I mean, I knew you were coming, but still I heard you clearly. Maria cannot have missed it. She cannot have been taken by surprise.'

'Bear in mind, Brother,' Mateu put in, 'that she does not have unimpeded hearing as you and I do. She wore a wimple and coif. I have not donned such garments myself, clearly, but it occurs to me that they cover the ears and must at least partially dull the hearing. On occasion I have to shout to Sisters Carima and Joana to engage their attention.'

Arnau nodded. It was possible, he supposed, that intent on her task and beneath her monastic apparel, she had not been able to hear what he had, especially given that he had been expecting to hear something.

'So what did you see?' Brother Balthesar said again.

'I saw the three of you. Only for a moment, but all of you.'

'You are thinking like Arnau, who was expecting us. Think like Maria, who was not. Do not tell me *who* you saw. Tell me *what* you saw.'

Arnau frowned and thought hard. Now that he replayed events in his mind's eye – the hand still clamped over his face helped a lot there – he had actually seen rather little. The shapes he had known to be the two knights and the sergeant, but he had not actually *seen* more than a flash of them. Had it been anyone else, he wondered how many details he would have retained.

'I saw enough to know you were in white. I don't think I actually saw a cross, and I don't remember registering Mateu's black habit. I saw mail. Someone's mail. That and a flash of grey hair. That's all.'

'None of us is wearing mail tonight,' Lütolf noted. 'Your mind is adding details from what you *expected* to see.'

Balthesar's voice cut in. 'Now, Brother Arnau, keep your eyes closed for, let's say the count of fifteen, and then open them.'

The hands were withdrawn, leaving Arnau with an oddly lonely and nervous feeling as he stood, sightless in the night, counting steadily. Finally, at fifteen, he opened his eyes and looked around. The other three were some way across the field and running. He shouted after them and they stopped.

'What can you see?' Brother Balthesar shouted across the field.

'Three men,' he called back. 'Two in white and one in black.'

'Can you make out any detail?'

'None that I'm not simply expecting to see,' Arnau admitted, and the three men strolled back towards him across the field. Together once more, they fell into deep thought.

Brother Balthesar finally straightened. 'What we can deduce, here, is that though Brother Arnau was aware of our approach, we cannot say for certain that Maria would have been. The flashes of detail she provided are consistent with what our young brother saw himself. Essentially, Sister Maria's tale rings true in every way we can determine. The only questions that remain are why the men were here and whether they had singled out Maria specifically or whether they would have attacked any lone figure outside these walls. We cannot be certain the men belonged to della Cadeneta, though it does seem likely.'

Arnau nodded with a sigh. It was much vaguer than he'd hoped. Somehow he'd imagined Brother Balthesar's odd reconstruction would supply them with some pertinent piece of information rather than simply making everything possible and nothing certain.

'Would della Cadeneta really bring violence against the Temple?' Mateu asked with a hint of disbelief. 'I mean, the order responds strongly to threat. We all know that.'

Lütolf turned to him. 'There are rats who despise us among the nobles of every country, Brother Mateu. Nobles see us as a threat and an opponent. The crown sees us as a useful resource, but laments the fact that lands and fortunes that the king could use for his own purposes are instead donated to the order. As long as we are useful against the Moor, we are free from interference, but the time will come when we are too big to be ignored and too strong to be accepted. And even now there are men who would see us fall if they had half the chance of doing so without bringing down the wrath of the Church and the Pope upon their heads. But if della Cadeneta decides to stand against us I doubt he will do so alone. He will find support among the greedy and the disaffected, whether they be high lords or low bandits. Della Cadeneta, I suspect, does not fear us.'

'I will change that,' Arnau said quietly.

'Not until it is definitively confirmed that he is behind all this,' Balthesar warned him. 'And even then, not without the instruction of the preceptrix. You are a brother of the Temple now, Arnau. Not some lone avenging knight.'

Arnau cast his eyes down as he nodded, not through embarrassment or fear, but to prevent the passion and defiance in them being seen by the others. Oddly, as he mastered his emotions and lifted his head again, he noted a similar look in Brother Lütolf. The man was prepared for trouble. Good. At least there was one thing that the two of them might agree upon.

Half an hour later they were in the chapter house with the preceptrix, Ramon and Father Diego.

'The time may have come for us to send word to the mother house,' Preceptrix Ermengarda said in emotionless tones. 'There is a rising feeling of danger at Rourell. We have already lost a sergeant and almost Brother Lütolf, and now base villains stoop to attacking a woman of God within sight of our own church. This is unacceptable. I would seek the advice of the preceptor of Barberà and perhaps his support. If we can secure Barberà's backing we might be able to play host to a few of their brothers for a while, increasing our strength considerably. Moreover, Barberà can pass on the details that we do have, and our suspicions, to the higher authorities – maybe even the master of the Temple in Iberia. Mayhap with such strength and recognition of our position, the petty ambitions of a nobleman might melt away.'

Arnau somehow doubted as much, but the idea of having perhaps half a dozen extra knights around Rourell had a certain appeal, there was no denying it.

'Brother Lütolf, you and Brother Arnau will ride at first light. Arm yourself and be cautious. Remember what happened to poor Brother Carles. Be wary, but ride north for Barberà. I will give you a sealed document that you may present to the master there on my behalf.'

The German knight bowed his head and stepped back. He turned to Arnau. 'See to the horses and our equipment. We must be ready at dawn.'

CHAPTER TEN

They left the preceptory while the sun was still a fireball eating the horizon, a huge red glow across the world's edge with a glowing yellow heart, the sky above still black though now streaked with a mackerel skin of gold. The world was eerie by such light, as though they left a house of God and rode into the maw of hell itself.

The track stretched out from the causeway towards the main road, and despite the lack of movement anywhere around them, Arnau could not drive from his mind memories of the German brother fighting for control of a rearing horse as crossbow bolts thudded into flesh from the shadows of the trees. Or of Maria hunched over, gathering flowers for her former mistress as three thugs intent on rape and violence crept up behind her.

It felt as though a thousand unseen eyes followed their every step. The skin between Arnau's shoulder blades itched with that feeling of being observed. There was no reason to believe they were, beyond previous encounters anyway, and yet Arnau would bet his entire estate on the fact that they were being watched. If he hadn't donated it to the order, that is.

Brother Lütolf seemed unaffected. He rode straight-backed and sure, the mail hauberk and leggings shushing with every movement of his steed. Every other hoof beat brought the clonk of the knight's shield against his hard leather saddle. Arnau could even swear he heard the man breathing through the grill in his closed helmet. Arnau wore only a kettle hat of dulled steel, favouring the feel of fresh air on his face to the protection of a metal mask.

They moved over a small wood-plank bridge, across an irrigation channel, and then passed the small knot of trees where the German had almost died mere days ago. Arnau's eyes raked the shadowed boles, searching for the shapes of men of ill intent.

Nothing moved, but the young sergeant's eyes remained locked on that place of ambush until they were past it and onto the main road.

Finally on a wider track, the two men fell into double file for the first time since leaving the preceptory. Arnau, as thrilled as ever with the company, remained quiet, musing on the situation, and was somewhat surprised when Brother Lütolf broke the silence.

'You feel it, Vallbona?'

Arnau frowned, wondering for a moment what the German meant, but then nodded. Lütolf was not quite so confident and aloof as he appeared, then.

'Yet I see no one,' Arnau breathed. 'No sign of movement.'

'God is with us, for we are *manus dei*. Our observers may be well hidden, but the Lord sees all. There may be nothing to see from the road, but they are there nonetheless.'

Arnau nodded. It was precisely how he felt, though he'd not have thought to pin his preternatural feelings on the presence of the Lord. Did that make him a bad brother, he wondered? Not to have such unshakable trust in the support of the Lord in every endeavour?

'Why are they not attacking us, then?' Arnau said quietly, in little more than a whisper. Then, when there was no reply, he realised that the heavy enclosed helm was stifling the German's hearing, just as Maria's coif had done last night, so he repeated himself, slightly louder.

'Prudence, I think,' Brother Lütolf replied.

Arnau waited for more and presently the knight turned to him. 'The first time they attacked us it was desperate instinct. We had spotted them and they reacted precipitously. I very much doubt their master would have commanded them to begin a war with the order, not yet at least. It was the short-sighted reaction of two low knaves. And last night was an attack on an unarmed and defenceless woman, from which they desisted the moment the preceptory stirred and men came to her aid.'

'They are being careful?'

'That, and probably your friend della Cadeneta is now arrived and in control. He will be circumspect in his approach. He will not tangle with us directly unless he has either considerable backing of import or no other choice. They watch us now, for they are not at all sure what we are about. We are still within Templar land here. Perhaps a mile up the road we will leave our demesne and then it will become clear that we are riding north. I suspect that then they will decide that we are too important to leave in peace.'

Arnau felt a chill run through him. Images of the body of Carles lying in a ditch beneath the trees assailed him.

'I know,' Lütolf said, as though looking directly into his mind. 'But remember that Brother Carles was on a simple courier mission with no expectation of trouble. He was unarmoured and unaware of the danger. We are not. You have your sword loose?'

Arnau frowned. 'What?'

'Draw your blade a couple of inches and work it back and forth, then leave the guard perhaps half an inch from the mouth of the scabbard. Then when we run into trouble, your sword will come free quickly and with ease. I have seen more than one man die because he was too slow in drawing his blade.'

Arnau did so and was surprised he'd never thought of it before. The first time he pulled it free it took a little effort, as though the scabbard sucked at the blade, but the second and third time it eased, and was then sliding in and out with grace.

When we run into trouble…

'You are expecting a fight, then, Brother Lütolf?'

'I fear it is inevitable. They will assume that we are on the same mission as Carles, lodging the deeds of Santa Coloma with the mother house. Whether that be their guess, or the truth, either way they will not allow us to reach Barberà. Now they wait, for we are still on our land, but the moment we pass from Rourell's land and they guess what we are about, they will have little choice but to try and stop us.'

'I know della Cadeneta to be a snake, but I find it hard to countenance him raising a blade against the Templars,' Arnau shivered. 'Would they really try and stop you? Me, yes. But you?'

The German's expression remained stony. 'He has already committed himself, whether he likes it or not. When his men killed Carles, they set him on a road from which he cannot deviate. His men began a conflict, and if he backs out now, not only does he lose all hope of Sister Titborga and her lands, but he will be liable to defend himself against accusations of the murder of a holy man. Now he is committed, for good or ill. He has to see it through. Besides, taking arms against the order is not unknown. Even now our brothers in the Amanus March are in conflict with the King of Armenia over property occupied by him that rightfully belongs to us. The world is never simple, Vallbona.'

Arnau nodded glumly. 'I prefer the mace, mind.'

The German looked around at him. 'The mace has its uses. When facing a heavily armoured opponent, its crushing weight can help nullify the enemy's iron cote and helm. But when facing lightly armoured or unarmoured men, the sword is a far more versatile weapon. The lunge, which you cannot achieve with a mace, gives you a reach that a clubbing swipe will not. A mace might break bone, but your eye for a target has to be good to guarantee incapacitation or death. A sword blow to most places will cripple if delivered with enough power. The one to the arm renders either shield or weapon useless. The leg puts them down on the ground, helpless. The gut is agonising and will put them from the fight. The torso is death. The neck or head is death. The sword is the better weapon. Use your sword.'

Arnau pursed his lips. In his experience he'd been doing quite well enough with the mace, but whether he agreed with the German or not, the man had many years more experience of combat than him, and part of the rule of the order was obedience, after all.

His fingers danced on the head of the mace that hung from the pommel, tied to the saddle with the thin leather thong loop that in battle would go around his wrist to prevent loss.

They rode on for some time, the feeling of being watched never leaving them, pushing the hairs on Arnau's neck erect even beneath the habit and the mail. They had travelled less than a mile along the road when the increasing light, now beginning to throw the world into sharp contrasts of golden glow and black shadow, picked out the shape of the bridge across the Francoli. Here, a few days ago, they had found the body of Carles.

But the light illuminated more than a bridge. Or perhaps more accurately *less*.

The bridge across the River Francoli had been demolished. A single arch rose from the near bank, and a matching one at the far side, but the main span at the centre was gone, and with it any chance of an easy crossing on the road.

As they neared, gradually slowing the horses, Arnau scanned the area. The rubble from the broken bridge lay to the west of the crossing by a few feet and had gone some way to damming the small seasonal flow. Consequently, the river to the east, upstream, had widened and deepened considerably. There would be no crossing there. On the downstream side, the water had narrowed to a mere stream, but the riverbed glistened with the telltale sign of thick mud. It would be feet deep and harbour treacherous stones that could easily make a horse lame. Additionally, the banks there were steep and could be dangerous.

'What do we do?'

Lütolf was looking this way and that in the same manner as Arnau, but the young man realised with a start that the German was not examining the river and potential crossings. He was scanning the far bank and the trees near them.

'Ready yourself,' the knight said quietly. 'This bridge was no accident.'

As the German unhooked his shield and lifted it into position, Arnau did the same. For a moment he was torn between the sword and the mace and, uncertain even at the last moment which he would wield, he untied the leather thong with difficulty, given his two bound fingers, and made the heavy iron club ready.

The attack came without warning, but thanks to their growing sense of anticipation neither of the men were taken by surprise. Eight men, Arnau surmised at first glance, four on each side of the road, and each group containing one man with a loaded crossbow. His attention locked on the four men coming from the right side of the road; he completely ignored the German and left him to his own fight. Four men was going to be a struggle, for certain. He had automatically selected the mace, since he'd been fiddling with it when they emerged with a yell, and he lifted it and realised in an instant that he was a dead man. The crossbow swung to face him and began to rise, aiming for his heart. He would not fall foul of the footmen, for that bolt would pick him out of the saddle and kill him outright.

Instinct kicking in over both thought and training, Arnau swung his arm, ignoring the throbbing finger, and let go. He'd not had time to loop the thong around his wrist to maintain his control over the weapon, and that simple fact saved him from impalement. The mace, let go at full swing, shot through the air, spinning end over end, and hit the crossbowman full in the face, ending his life in a grisly mash of pink and white and spurting blood.

The bolt twanged from the bow under spasming fingers and dug deep into the rough surface of the road only a few feet from the agonised, dying archer.

Arnau ripped his sword from its scabbard, grateful for Lütolf's earlier advice as it whispered free with ease just in time to find itself in the way of a swung blade gripped by a man who more resembled a mastiff than a man, face contorted with ripples of flesh and scraggy beard with a flattened, ugly nose. Arnau silently thanked the German knight. Had he not previously loosened the blade in the scabbard, it would never have freed in time, and the mastiff's blade would now be carving through Arnau's mail leggings rather than grating along his own sword with a metallic rasp.

He turned the blade with sheer effort and the ugly fellow stepped back and came in for another swing. From the corner of his eye, Arnau spotted a tall and surprisingly young, willowy fellow coming in with a sword at the other side. There was nothing he could do. He lifted the shield and thrust it in the way, praying the hardened board with its simple black and white design would take the blow and absorb it. As the tall, lithe youth landed a harmless strike on the shield and recoiled with the reverberation up his arm, Arnau concentrated on the mastiff.

The ugly squat fellow in the dusty brown tunic came at him again, and this time Arnau readied his sword, but shifted his weight in the saddle. As the man swung, Arnau kicked out. His mailed foot caught the man at the meeting of collarbones and there was a chorus of bony cracks that was audible even over the noise of the fight. The hideous man's eyes widened in shock and his sword went astray, failing to connect. As the man slipped to the side, for good measure Arnau twisted his foot, ripping the jagged spike of his spur across his neck and opening the flesh in a welter of blood.

Even as the mastiff went to join the crossbowman in the Devil's parlour, the tall, willowy one landed another blow on Arnau's shield, though this one was considerably harder and the reverberation that shot up the young man's arm numbed the limb. He spun in the saddle, trying to bring his sword to bear on the young fellow, but then, finally, he succumbed to the weight of numbers. The fourth man, as yet unseen in the scuffle, had managed to get close enough to slam a blade into the horse's middle, ripping into the soft flesh of the underbelly. Agonised, the beast reared and Arnau had to cling on desperately not to fall, knees locked tight around the animal's girth, feet still in the stirrups, reins gathered tight and short in the now-numb shield arm.

The beast leaped and thrashed in pain, and through sheer chance a flashing hoof connected with the willowy youth, breaking an arm and sending him yelling back to the ground.

Arnau had to get off. The beast was dying on its feet and its mad dance would soon end, at which point it would fall and probably roll, pinning Arnau beneath it and breaking his leg at best. With some difficulty as the animal leaped and bucked, he pulled his mailed boots free from the stirrups. He was just in time. The animal lurched and fell, and Arnau, arm still unfeeling, could not tell whether he'd let go of the reins or not until he passed the point of balance and leaped free.

He hit the ground badly, some distance from the agonised horse, and lay there for precious moments, dazed and winded, unable to focus.

Once more, Arnau almost died. Lying on his back and rocking gently this way and that, trying to regain his wits, he almost took the falling blade full in the chest. It was pure fluke that he did not; his shield arm, gradually recovering feeling, flopped over him as he rolled and happened to be covering him as the man's sword descended. The tip of the blade – unusually pointed for a Christian weapon – hit the rawhide of the shield and ripped through it into the linden boards behind, but the thick wood robbed the blow of sufficient strength to punch right through and, instead, the sword tip carved a thick line across the surface and then slid into Arnau's side, ripping links of mail free and scoring a painful line along his ribs before thudding into the ground.

Dazed, winded and now in pain, with the numbness of his arm returning, Arnau stared up at his last opponent, who seemed both determined and destined to finish him off. Arnau tried to bring his own sword up, shield arm useless once more, but he simply couldn't do it in time, especially with only three fully working fingers.

His eyes widened in shock as the heavy-set man above him suddenly jerked and the tip of a sword emerged from his chest in a rush of blood that sprayed out, filling Arnau's eyes and mouth, clogging his nose and almost choking him. He grunted in further pain as the man landed heavily on him and then rolled off to the dirt.

There was a horrible moment when the young knight was in pain and discomfort, unable to raise sword or shield, blinded with blood and almost unable to breathe. Then suddenly he sat up and coughed out another man's blood, choking and gagging, the line of hot pain burning across his ribs beneath the wrecked armour. He let his sword go, presuming the fight to be over, and wiped the gore from his eyes, blinking until the world finally came back into focus.

'You are welcome,' the German in front of him said in a tone that dripped with sarcasm.

Arnau blinked in surprise.

'I will not always be there to save you, Vallbona. You must improve. You must practise.'

Arnau's brow folded in irritation. He'd killed three men on his own. Three! The fact that Lütolf must have killed five rankled deep down, but he clung to the knowledge that he'd fought off and dispatched three assailants, and with a broken finger to boot, which was a feat to be reckoned with.

Slowly, painfully, he gathered up his sword and tried to rise, staggering in the process and almost falling over. Still blinking, eyes slicked with blood, he looked about. Lütolf wandered casually across to the willowy lad who was rolling around on the ground crying and clutching his broken arm, and punched his sword down through the lad's chest, transfixing the heart. As he did so, Arnau could faintly hear the German murmuring under his breath, a prayer for the boy's soul. For a long moment, Arnau concentrated on his sword, wiping down the blade with the sleeve of his black habit until the gore was gone and the metal gleamed, then sheathing it. He then looked about him again.

They were all down. All eight. They had done it.

The German gestured at his own horse, which was lying not far from Arnau's, a crossbow bolt jutting from its neck.

'Twice. *Two* horses smacks of carelessness, does it not?'

Arnau blinked. If he were more inclined to believe in miracles in the everyday world, he would have sworn that Brother Lütolf had just made a joke.

'What now?'

The German shrugged and hissed. He had apparently taken some injury, then.

'It would appear that we are beset once more. The preceptrix will need to hear of this.'

Arnau frowned. 'But the way is clear now. We can go on to Barberà as ordered. I mean, we'll need to find another place to cross, but there's bound to be one.'

Lütolf removed his helmet and shook his head. 'Once we cross the river here, we are far from Temple lands and moving into an area likely under the watchful eye of your hill-dwelling noble friend. We have no horses. It would take too long to walk, and we would be at increased risk of renewed attack the further we got. No, going on would be foolish and wasteful. We return to the preceptory.'

'But—'

'I don't know about you,' the German said meaningfully, 'but I am hardly equipped to weather that same storm twice.'

As if to illustrate his point, the knight held up what was left of his shield – little more than two white pieces of linden board, held together with a scrap of rawhide and half a strap. He was right. Arnau hated to admit it, but the German was absolutely correct. The state they were in, they would never survive another attack like that, and north of this bridge they would have to travel several miles through lands that della Cadeneta and his men would likely have watched and manned. The oily nobleman was determined to acquire the Santa Coloma riches and lands.

'We are assuming this was della Cadeneta, of course?' he said.

Lütolf cast away his broken shield and spread his hands. 'Once more there is not a single shred of evidence against him. He is coy and wily. These men could so easily be just another gang of rogues on the road seeking to waylay unwary travellers, taking advantage of a fallen bridge to ply their ungodly trade.'

He folded his arms. 'But we know that is not true, do we not, Vallbona? Two crossbows among such a rabble? The crossbow is an expensive weapon and not all that common among outlaws. Two in one small group? And a bridge that happened to collapse? There has been no storm and floodwater, no shifting of the earth. No, that bridge was deliberately demolished to prevent a rider from Rourell carrying documents to Barberà. As long as the papers are not lodged with the Temple officially, the lady of Santa Colona and the fortune she represents are still fair game. A good student of the law would find a way to put them in della Cadeneta's hands. But not when those records are lodged. Then he has lost both woman and estate to the Temple.'

'This is bold, though,' Arnau said as he took a step forward. The stretching of skin sent an agonising pain through his side and he reached down to the wound to find blood on his hands.

'How does it look?' he asked, gesturing to his side.

The German bent and hooked a finger through the black Templar habit into the broken mail hauberk, lifting it outwards and parting it, the arming garment beneath and the tunic below them all. He peered at the wound inside.

'If you were old enough to shave, you would have encountered worse wounds.'

Arnau almost laughed. It may have been at his expense, but that was, he was sure, the second joke the German had told in as many minutes. If the man kept going like this, Arnau might even have to admit that Brother Lütolf was human.

In response, as the German knight let go, Arnau reached in and prodded his wound. It was extremely painful, but a little exploration with gritted teeth confirmed that Lütolf had been correct in his conclusion that the wound was relatively minor. The cut was long, but thin and not deep. It had only just broken the flesh, really.

'Should we search them? Just in case?'

The German shook his head. 'They will have nothing incriminating, you can be sure. Beyond that, it would simply be looting.'

As Lütolf went over to the horses and said a farewell to his latest doomed beast, Arnau scoured the ground until he found his discarded mace not far from the crossbowman with the imploded face. He picked it up, hissing at the pain in his side as he did so, and cleaned the head as best he could on the dead man's tunic. He then tied the mace to his belt with the thong and tucked it beneath so that it would not swing about. Finally, he collected up his shield, which would be repairable with a little work and, pulling a carrying strap from the saddlebags of his fallen horse, slung it over his back.

'It would appear we are to be beasts of burden,' he sighed, unfastening the saddlebags and pulling them out from the dead horse with some difficulty.

'A little hard work is no penance,' said the German knight in his usual infuriatingly holier-than-anyone manner. Arnau simply grunted and forbore to rise to the bait this time. Instead, he slung the heavy bags over his shoulder and settled them into position, grunting at the twin pains in his side and his finger.

He strode to the edge of the fight and waited there, feeling the burden already, but with a mile or so yet to carry it.

'Where do you think you're going?' Lütolf asked archly.

'What?'

'You forgot something.'

Arnau frowned, and the German pointed to the younger man's horse as he went over to his own and began to unfasten the saddle and tack.

'You jest,' Arnau said in surprise.

'The rule specifically forbids us from incurring loss to the order.'

'I hardly think that *this* was what the great Saint Bernard of Clairvaux had in mind.'

'Rules are rules, Arnau of Vallbona. If you still intend to be *Brother* Arnau, then you must learn humility, obedience and the simple value of labour.'

Arnau glared at the German knight, but stepped across to his fallen horse and removed the saddle with some difficulty and a lot of small yelps of pain. Finally, he pulled it free with Lütolf's help and the two men lifted saddlebags over one shoulder and saddle over the other and began to make their weary and painful way slowly back to Rourell.

Arnau couldn't help but note with irritation that because the German had lost his shield, at least he didn't have the weight of that added to his burden as Arnau did. Mind you, Lütolf did have the weight of several extra decades to carry with him, the younger man reminded himself. Still, the German was not visibly wounded, while Arnau's finger still throbbed and the blood from the thin cut at his side oozed out into the tunic and mail.

The sun was still low enough above the horizon that the shadows cast by trees left black stripes across the road. Little past sunup and already they'd killed eight men and determined that they were cut off from the mother house at Barberà. Arnau staggered along for a while grumbling in the privacy of his head, trying not to ponder on the idea that God heard everything he said even there.

Finally, discomfited by the endless silence, he cleared his throat to ask a question that had been nagging at him for some time.

'What brings a German to Iberia, Brother Lütolf?'

The scarred knight grimaced for just a moment, which interested Arnau.

'I am a brother of the Temple. I go where I am sent. Where the enemies of the righteous are to be found.'

That was half an answer at best.

'But Germany?'

Lütolf turned an irritated face to him. 'Why do you persist in calling me "German"? I am from the Duchy of Swabia. I am Swabian. I am no more German than you are Iberian.'

Arnau thought he could spot a way to make the mile pass much faster looming in the indignation on the other man's face.

'I *am* Iberian,' he replied with feigned confusion.

Lütolf huffed irritably. 'You are from the *peninsula* of Iberia, but the nation of your birth would be the Crown of Aragon. Or perhaps, if you are old fashioned and cling to your region's history, Catalunya. Either way, you are only Iberian by dint of grand geography.'

Arnau smiled to himself. This was more fun.

'So you are Swabian by nationality but German by geography?'

Brother Lütolf growled and turned to him. 'Swabia is part of the *Holy Roman Empire*.'

Something about the emphasis the knight placed on those last three words spoke of ill feeling, and Arnau suddenly remembered the man's reference to the Hohenstaufens, the very Swabian family that provided the imperial crowned heads, during that painful training session. Some history lay there, just beyond clarity, infuriatingly tantalising. Someday, he would unravel that mystery.

'And is Germany not part of the Holy Roman Empire?' he taunted.

Lütolf exploded in irritation. 'Germany does not *exist*, Vallbona. Germany was a place imagined by the Romans in their pagan delusion. Now, for the love of all the saints, will you drop this subject?'

Arnau nodded. This was the most animated he had ever seen Brother Lütolf. Even being shot at with crossbow bolts had not elicited this kind of emotion.

'Who rules the empire at the moment?' he asked in a voice serene with the calm of innocence, while inside his gut churned with laughter at the sight of the expressions marching across Lütolf's face. The subject was, in fact, quite the talking point in many courtly circles at the moment: how the old emperor had died last September and now everyone with even a vague claim to the throne was crawling out of the woodwork and proclaiming himself prince of somewhere.

Lütolf's lip twitched a couple of times and he picked up his stride slightly, stepping ahead.

'Save your breath for the walk, Vallbona.'

Arnau struggled on to catch up, but was smiling as he did so. He had found a chink in the German's mental armour at last.

PART THREE: ENEMY

CHAPTER ELEVEN

'There is trouble at the Granja de la Selva,' Brother Rafael said, reining in his sweating horse as Simo made to close the west gate behind him.

'Leave it open,' Brother Lütolf waved to the boy, then turned back to the sergeant on his horse. 'What sort of trouble?'

Arnau noted other figures converging on them now in the morning sun. He closed his eyes for a moment, picturing the Granja de la Selva, trying to remember which of the farms it was. The northern one, he was fairly sure. Olives and wheat. Low, flat fields of gold and ordered orchards of ancient, gnarled trees. Quite an area, dotted with sheds and miscellaneous farming structures. He remembered the farmhouse – a long, extended affair with a bunkhouse attached – a well and an olive press in a separate building, a long arcade of wide arches in a stone and rubble wall.

He had met the farmer and his family, along with a few of the workers on that first day when the German knight had taken him on a tour. He'd tried some of the olive oil from the farm on fresh bread. The farmer had been a Moor, his family tending the land for more than a century, long before the area was recaptured and ceded to the Templars. He'd been a chubby-faced man with an easy smile, his wife a homely but engaging sort from Lleida. The children had been noisy and full of life. What trouble had befallen them, Arnau wondered.

Preceptrix Ermengarda was one of those figures now gathering around Brother Rafael, her expression neutral, but her bearing tense within her white wool armour.

'Preceptrix,' the black-clad brother said, inclining his head. 'Mujahid and his family are beset by their own field hands. They are shut up in the house with the field hands battering angrily on the windows and doors. I tried to ask what the problem was, but the moment I came within speaking distance, the workers began tearing cobbles from the ground and hurling them at me. Rather than risk provoking the situation further, I rode straight here.'

The preceptrix nodded. 'You did well. Guillem? Fetch me my horse.'

Brother Rafael looked uncomfortable; torn, Arnau realised, between the desire to see his mistress resolve whatever issue had arisen and worry about the danger to her should she ride to confront the trouble. 'Sister, they are very agitated. A cobble almost unhorsed and brained me.'

Ermengarda d'Oluja turned a fierce expression on the sergeant. 'I will not have unrest. Mujahid and his family are under the care of the order. Luis? Rourell is yours until my return.'

The seneschal nodded his understanding and old Balthesar waved. 'I shall stay with Brother Luis to be certain of the security of the preceptory, but take good men with you, Sister. This could be dangerous.'

Preceptrix Ermengarda nodded and gestured to the other knights. Moments later Arnau and Mateu were in the stables, hurriedly helping Guillem ready the horses, including the new piebald that had been granted to Arnau and the bay to replace Lütolf's latest loss. Presently they rode from the west gate, the preceptrix and Rafael, the agricultural overseer, with Brothers Lütolf and Ramon and their squires close behind. The six of them made their way along the dusty track through the fields. After a quarter of a mile, Arnau complaining silently about the pain in his side with every step of the horse, they rounded a large olive grove and the picturesque farmhouse came into sight. Arnau's breath caught in his throat. He'd not realised how many field workers there must be in a farm this size, but quite a crowd had gathered outside the building. As they neared, he could see that the few windows in evidence had all had their shutters pulled closed.

At a nod from Brother Ramon, Mateu moved ahead, falling in beside the preceptrix, raising high the imposing black and white banner of the Temple. Not as imposing as the preceptrix, in Arnau's opinion, but as their approach was noticed by the gathering, he saw a number of arms fall to their owners' sides and cobbles drop to the ground. Not all, though. There was anger here, unassuaged.

The small party reined in and the white-clad sister of the Temple at the head, beside the great banner, rose in her saddle as though preparing to couch a lance and lean forward over the beast's shoulders.

'What is the meaning of this unprincipled, unruly display?' she demanded in a tone that could drag an answer from a stone. Yet there was no reply. Not one figure among the crowd spoke. No one even moved.

'This feels dangerous,' Brother Ramon said quietly. 'Be careful, Sister.'

'Care be damned. This is insurrection and I will not have it.' The preceptrix extended her hand and thrust a digit out, sweeping it across the faces in the crowd. It stopped on a reedy, middle-aged Moor with thinning hair and a yellow tunic. He flinched as though struck.

'I know you, Wasil al-Hafiz. You are a kind man. You make straw dolls for the girls. You even made one for me this Easter past. I would never have thought to see you acting in anger, armed with a rock. You *know* the man in that house and his family. Mujahid is a good man. You are prepared to stone him like some biblical execution?'

The cobble dropped from the man's fingers and clattered on the ground.

'*All* of you are better than this. There are those in Aragon and Catalunya who despise the fact that you remain in our lands as anything other than slaves, and do not believe that you can be trusted, for all your acceptance of the cross or your oath of service to the order. Many a lord in this region would like nothing more than to chain you or send you south to the vile Almohads whom even good Moors such as you despise. Yet the order treats you well. You have all you need and more than many. You have the protection of the Temple. Whatever the cause of your dismay, I cannot imagine there is any foundation to it.'

More cobbles fell from loose fingers and Arnau marvelled at the sheer power and command the preceptrix exuded. He could picture Brother Lütolf attempting such a thing. It would likely have ended in bloodshed. But the authority of Sister Ermengarda was absolute.

'Disband and go back to your duties and we shall speak no more of this,' she announced.

There was a long pause, and then, as though the crowd had burst from the centre, they dispersed, heading into the outbuildings or out into the fields. As soon as the mob had gone, the only evidence of the event the scattered fallen rocks, Sister Ermengarda slid from the saddle, the others joining her. Arnau and Mateu took the reins and tied all the beasts to the hitching rail, then joined their superiors at the farmhouse's entrance. There was a click, and the door opened.

Arnau noted with shock the huge welt on the farmer's head where he had been struck, presumably with one of the rocks. The man stepped aside and gestured for the visitors to enter. As his wife and daughter went about opening the shutters and flooding the building with light, Mujahid stood with his head bowed, and gestured to a seat. The preceptrix took the offered chair and sank into it, folding her arms. Without needing to be ordered the five men gathered in a small group, standing behind her.

'Now, Mujahid, what is this about?'

The man's young son ran in then, paused to bow to the preceptrix, and then carried his dampened cloth to his father. Mujahid took the ball of wet material and pressed it to the injury on his head.

'I have never seen anything like it, Sister.'

'I have,' his wife snapped. 'In Lleida, back when the Christian conquest was still raw.'

'*Re*conquest,' corrected Brother Lütolf, earning himself a warning glance from the preceptrix.

The Moorish woman glared at the German for a moment, then returned to her tale. 'When there were still sons of Allah all across the land and matters were being settled, there were men who would not accept that our world was gone. They stirred up hatred and bile among even the best of people and aimed it at our new overlords.'

Mujahid nodded sadly. 'It is an unfortunate fact that many still bristle at the coming of the cross. Many see it only as a temporary measure before the Christian lords are driven out once more and the *taifas* return. Among these men it is easy to stir up trouble. And when part of a group succumbs to such bile, it spreads like wound-rot, infecting even the good flesh.'

'You are saying that someone has been stirring up the Moorish workers?' Brother Ramon prompted.

'I believe so. They accused me of betraying my history and our people. Of living fat off the profits of Christian conquerors while they languish in indentured servitude.'

'To some extent they are correct, of course,' the man's wife said savagely, still glaring at Lütolf.

'Aisha!' barked her husband in a sharp warning.

'Please, let us have concord and peace here,' the preceptrix said quietly, and eventually, as the farmer's wife nodded her agreement, she continued. 'I have never stinted on our care for the workers on Rourell's estates. We take only our tithe and leave you all to profit as you can from what is left. We do not actively pursue your oath to the cross, as some masters might, for in this cracked and broken world of ours we must seek to bind things together once more, not widen those cracks. So tell me, given that I have been as lenient as it is possible for a preceptor to be, what I can do to counteract the work of any unseen rabble-rouser?'

A thought suddenly sprang into Arnau's head. A memory from the day the German knight had broken his finger. Men in armour, he was sure, glinting in the fields to the north. And within days the workers of those fields were rebelling? Too much coincidence there. He filed that away to point out later.

Mujahid looked uncomfortable now. His voice cracked a little as he spoke.

'That, I fear, is a large part of the problem, Preceptrix.'

'Explain?'

'The very idea of a woman wielding such temporal and spiritual power is… not universally accepted, Preceptrix.'

'Not even among Christian lords, Mujahid,' she replied earnestly. 'Are you saying that my position is becoming a matter of contention among the workers on the Templar estates?'

'It would seem to be the case, Sister.'

Preceptrix Ermengarda steepled her fingers. 'In two years commanding Rourell we have had no trouble. Once the initial shock of my sex and position wore off and I settled into the role, we have had peace and understanding among all the estates, to a level I cannot even claim among my own peers.'

The farmer nodded solemnly. 'And the suddenness of this change of spirit among my people is what leads me to suspect someone has been stirring them up. When they met this morning and refused to work to support a – if you'll pardon my repeating their words – a *Christian witch*, I harangued them. I reminded them of your care and diligence and of their oaths. They hit me with a rock and then started to threaten my children. I came inside and hid.'

The preceptrix was nodding.

'If there is any repeat of this sort of behaviour among the workers, do not confront them, Mujahid. You are too good a man to suffer such wounds. Send to Rourell. We will come and resolve the issue. With good fortune and God's will, after our little chat just now they will return to their normal lives and all will be well.'

The farmer nodded, though Arnau could not see it being that easy. Wishing Mujahid and his family well and telling the man to call upon the preceptory if he needed any help or there was a complication with his injury, the small party exited the building once more into the morning sun. Figures were moving in the fields and the distinctive sound of the olive press at work suggested that all had returned to normal at the farm, yet as they remounted and made their way back to Rourell, all eyes were downcast, and the few times Arnau managed to glimpse a face before it turned away, the only word he could use to describe their expression was 'hostile'.

After sext, and the midday meal that followed swiftly on, Arnau found himself waiting for Brother Lütolf and their training session, but he decided that he would use some of the time as the

German had initially suggested, becoming familiar with Rourell's lands. He saddled his piebald mare and left by the west gate.

First he toured north through the wheat fields and by the olive groves, mail hauberk hot in the sun but affording him just a crumb of confidence, given recent events, black habit with red cross marking him unmistakably as a Templar sergeant. He spent a good twenty minutes around the Granja de la Selva, nodding his greeting to Mujahid as he passed, and to Rafael when he bumped into him at one of the olive groves. What struck him was the general sense of anger and unease that permeated the land, rising from every toiling body in those fields or orchards. This, he decided, was not going to go away quickly. Near the perimeter of the estates, his eyes repeatedly strayed to the surrounding countryside, half-expecting to see the sun glint off armour beneath the trees somewhere. That he didn't see it made him feel no easier.

He called by the mill and met Brother Miquel there. He'd hoped, on a whim, to gauge the atmosphere there too, but only the miller and the brother overseer were present, the bulk of the workers out with the cart and the beasts of burden, delivering flour to the preceptory, the village of Rourell and the town of Vilallonga del Camp a little further south. The miller seemed content enough, but then he would not be the one a rabble-rouser targeted.

Riding on, he checked out the Granja de Moli with its smaller area of cultivated fields, but with herds of goats, sheep and cattle. Also, this farm bred horses and oxen for the preceptory. Consequently there were a great number of workers in the fields, pens and paddocks, but even more in the complex of farm buildings, which included a butchery. Despite everything, Arnau felt tense and nervous moving among the Moorish workers hefting cleavers and knives. Though there was not the simmering undercurrent of barely tamed rebellion here that he'd felt at the other farm, there was still a sense of disquiet and discontent that was almost palpable.

Starting to feel more and more concerned by what he was seeing, Arnau moved on to the Granja del Camp with its vineyards and winery. Despite it being early in the season, the vines were already laden with burgeoning bunches of heavy blue-black grapes, and workers moved among them, tending the plants, weeding, removing pests and performing the myriad other tasks of viniculture. Not one met Arnau's gaze, which worried him further. At the winery, he discovered that the vintner and his helpers were off with a few cases of wine, seeking potential new merchants in Reus. Uncomfortably aware that he was alone on an entire estate of potentially rebellious Moorish workers, Arnau picked up his pace and rode back to Rourell, looking forward to dismounting. The pain from the cut to his side was barely noticeable the rest of the time, but riding made it ache badly.

Brother Lütolf was outside the west gate, swinging his sword in wide circles, loosening muscles. Each time the blade was in his left hand and reached the apex, the German grunted, and Arnau realised that the damage from the horse kick days ago was still affecting him, despite his best efforts to hide or overcome it.

'When I suggested you ride out alone to familiarise yourself with the estate,' the German announced, 'that was before we knew that there were hostile folk out there with bloody intent. You were foolish to do so.'

'Yet I live still, Brother Lütolf,' Arnau said, rather grouchily. 'Given what we saw this morning, I found myself wondering if it was the La Selva farm alone that had suffered such unrest.'

The German paused, his head cocked to one side. 'The same thought had occurred to me. And was this the case?'

'I don't think so,' Arnau replied, dismounting and tethering his steed. 'I suspect our rabble-rousers have been at work throughout Rourell's lands. I would be willing to wager that the glint I saw in the fields the other day when you tried to maim me was connected to this whole situation.'

'Perhaps,' Lütolf agreed, completely ignoring the jibe over the broken finger. 'When Rafael goes out on his rounds tomorrow morning, I think we should go with him. Have our horses readied at dawn and we will accompany him on his visits. And make sure you are fully armed and armoured at the time. For now, though, I want you to forget entirely about that overgrown club to which you are so attached and work on concealing your tells. Come.'

The following hour consisted of yet another series of painful and humiliating lessons, having every flicker of an eyelid analysed for its potential power to betray his intentions. With every blow and parry, Arnau expected the stitches in his side to open beneath the wrappings, though it seemed Carima truly knew her business and he remained intact despite his exertions. Indeed, for some time they put aside their weapons entirely and played a ridiculous game in which Brother Lütolf gave him four options to choose from mentally and then attempted to ascertain which one he had selected purely from his manner and stance. Irritatingly the man had been correct the lion's share of the time. Finally, they returned to the preceptory and the horse was stabled. Life fell once more into monastic monotony, though Arnau was beginning to find the routine of prayer and praise, work and practice to be soothing in an odd way. When compline was done and the male contingent of Rourell retired to the refectory to partake of wine while the women congregated in the chapter house, Arnau wandered in, scanning the trestles for somewhere to sit and socialise, and against all expectations, it was the German knight who beckoned and pushed back a chair.

'Brother,' Arnau said, nodding his head and sinking into the seat with a weary sigh.

'Sometimes I forget to credit someone when they deserve it,' Brother Lütolf said. 'I am quick to correct and scold, for there seems so much in this world that requires that attention, but I am aware that a lack of empathy is a fault in my character. It is not intentional. You did well today, Brother Arnau, in your eager attention to the situation in the Rourell lands that had not spurred any of the rest of us into investigation, and you also did exceptionally well with your training. You are mastering your movement and controlling yourself well. Soon you will be inscrutable, and a dangerous opponent. Though I still wish you would consign the mace to the role of a secondary weapon, as it really should be.'

Arnau smiled. Even in recognising his faults and attempting to offer praise, the German was incapable of doing so without some sort of backhanded verbal slap. On this occasion, Arnau found it oddly endearing. He reached out and poured himself a cup of wine, then offered Lütolf a top-up. The scarred knight dithered for a moment and then, with a shrug, nodded. He clacked his cup against Arnau's and drank quietly.

Then the German turned. 'Brother Balthesar? You rode picket duty this afternoon and evening. I presume you still found nothing worrying, else you would have mentioned it?'

The white-haired knight placed his wine cup on the table and stretched. 'I found several sites of burned-out campfires around the periphery of the lands. They could potentially be a source of worry, but they might just as easily have been youths, trysting lovers, farmhands or even travellers stopping for the night. I have seen no sign of men with crossbows or with red shields, certainly.'

'And what of the atmosphere in the surroundings?' Lütolf added.

'Sullen, I would say,' Balthesar noted. 'Not rebellious, but clearly unhappy.'

Arnau nodded. 'That was my impression. All is not right within the Rourell estates. Trouble is building, of that I am certain.'

There was a chorus of silent nods at this and the atmosphere in the room descended into a tense, muted worry for the rest of the evening before the brothers decided in unison to clear away and move up to the dormitory. Arnau there suffered an unpleasant, largely sleepless night, surrounded by the cloying warm night air and a symphony of snores.

He rose with the other brothers the next morning, still uncertain how the first person awake knew when to rise before even the cock realised it was a new day. It was a mystery he was determined to get to the bottom of without having to ask the question directly and rather foolishly. He had earlier dismissed the notion that Father Diego simply did not sleep at all, since he had never seen the man when he wasn't moving, but the fact that the priest did not seem to have a bed in the dormitory was making the idea attractive once more.

Lauds passed with a sense of anticipation and impatience for Arnau, and it was clear that Brother Lütolf was suffering a similar eagerness to move on the day. As soon as the service ended, the young squire was arming and preparing himself and then, as the German arrived in the armoury and began to equip himself, Arnau hurried to the stables and made ready their horses.

'Do you think you two can manage to get through a day without getting your horses shot or stabbed?' Guillem asked archly. 'It's just that we breed our own horses and try not to buy them in, and you and Brother Lütolf have cost us more steeds in a week than we'd lost in the last two years.'

Arnau felt a glow reach his cheeks, and reminded himself that he had lost only one, and in the service of the preceptrix. The German had now lost two. With a rolling of his eyes at the stableman, he finished preparing the horses just as Rafael came in for his.

'Brother Lütolf and I were planning to join you this morning,' he told the sergeant in charge of the farms.

Rafael nodded. 'After yesterday's trouble, I shall welcome the company.'

Outside, a few minutes later, the two sergeants in their black habits pulled themselves up into their saddles, Arnau grunting with discomfort as he shuffled in place, while Brother Lütolf did the same, white cloak settled over his horse's flanks. Arnau was interested to note that Rafael was fully turned out in mail hauberk, helm, shield and sword, just as they were, which was not his common manner for overseeing the farms.

'Expecting trouble?' Arnau asked, gesturing to the mailed sleeve.

Rafael shrugged with a shush of steel rings. 'Expecting? No. Prepared for? Yes.'

They rode out of the west gate and curved off to the north. The Granja de la Selva lay half a mile away across fields and olive orchards but they all knew that something was wrong the moment they moved away from the preceptory walls. There was not a single figure to be seen in the fields. The same story unfolded as they moved north through field and orchard with still no sign of human life.

'I do not like this one little bit,' Brother Rafael said quietly as they rounded the corner of the orchard to find the farmhouse still and silent, windows and door open. Arnau could not agree more. The hairs on his neck were standing proud again and he could feel the tension building in the air.

They dismounted at the farm and tied up the horses, each loosening the sword in his sheath and settling his shield into place before they moved towards the farmhouse's door. Brother Lütolf moved through first, the two sergeants close on his heel. The German passed across the threshold and stopped just inside the house. Rafael and Arnau stepped to the side to look around him, and the young sergeant's blood chilled.

Mujahid and his family were there, still in the house. He and his wife, his boy and his girl spun slowly in the cool morning air, twisting this way and that on the ropes that suspended them from the ceiling. Arnau stared. Hanged. All four. A farmer, his wife and two innocent children, all spinning slowly in the air, naked as the day they were born. Arnau fought over his rising gorge and joined the German and Rafael as they moved closer.

Each body was grey and lifeless, unmarked bar one thing: a cross carved roughly into their forehead.

'Della Cadeneta sinks to a new low,' he hissed.

'This was not your friend. Not directly, anyway,' Brother Lütolf said. 'This was done by the workers. I have seen it before. If they believe a Moor has sold out his people to us, they mark them like this. I had thought this sort of abomination over. It used to happen often a decade or two ago, when memories of the conquest were fresher, but I believed we had moved on past that now.'

'There were some as did not want to do so,' said a hollow, reedy voice from the shadows.

All three Christians' hands went to their sword hilt, preparing to draw, though the figure that emerged into the light was anything but threatening. It was the balding, middle-aged man the preceptrix had picked out yesterday. He looked haunted. Terrified, even. Wasil al-Hafiz, Arnau's memory helpfully supplied.

'Tell us.'

'The man came back last night,' Wasil said quietly. 'I watched. I listened. So did they.'

'Tell us about him.'

'I do not think he was truly one of us,' the nervous man said. 'He was dressed in the manner one might expect of an *ulama* – a scholar of Islam – and he was certainly a great speaker. He worked the crowd like an entertainer at the fair and got their blood boiling at their ruined heritage, at the wrongs he saw as done to them, at the suppression of their culture. He quoted the book. He quoted the Hadith. But he was slipshod in his quotations, and I do not think he knew them well.'

Arnau frowned. 'Could it have been a Christian masquerading as a Moor?'

The man shook his head. 'I do not think so. Or perhaps a child of two worlds. But I think he was a son of Al-Andalus who had renounced his faith. I think he was a fallen son of Allah. But he roused them all, despite his slips. Mujahid came to find out what the noise was and they… they wanted to tear him apart. In the end they brought him inside and took the woman, the children. They did this. Many would have fled, but it was clear from the mood that the mob would have killed any who turned away. I hid here and waited. They were gone an hour ago. Perhaps more. I would not be a part of it.'

Brother Lütolf nodded his understanding.

'Take them down and see to their burial,' he said rather tersely to Wasil. 'I care not whether you feel the need to bury them as Moor or Christian. Just see to them with honour. And then you must decide whether to come to Rourell and seek sanctuary or to run yourself and try to find somewhere you will be safe. I will not criticise you for either decision.'

With that, the German turned and swept from the building, beckoning to the two sergeants.

They mounted and left the farmhouse, riding for the mill and then the other estates. It was disheartening but no surprise to find that a similar thing had happened everywhere. The workers at the mill had gone. Simply melted away into the night. At least they had not taken the time to murder the Moorish miller, who was distraught and apologetic. They told him to go to the preceptory, but he insisted on staying at his mill and trying to finish the work that had been left in process.

The livestock estate was in chaos. Everyone had gone, including the farmer and his family. They had taken all the horses with them and opened the gates of every paddock and field. The livestock was mostly gone, fled into the countryside. What remained ambled happily and free. The winery was deserted, though at least the vintner and his people would still be seeking business in Reus and had therefore avoided falling foul of the rebellion.

'Rourell has just lost all viability as a house,' the German said, regarding the still, empty wine press and the silent fields. 'Without grain or oil, meat or animals, we cannot sustain ourselves. Despite the wealth donated to the order, we cannot simply buy everything we need. This is no longer to do with you and yours, Vallbona. Your enemy has now targeted the order itself. And yet they continue to do so with subterfuge and hired villains, never leaving evidence that della Cadeneta is the culprit.'

The three men rode back to the preceptory in a sullen, worried silence. This concerted campaign to ruin the monastery itself represented a new step forward in enemy strategy. At first it had been observation and casual, opportunistic violence. Then there had been direct targeting of brothers and sisters. Now they were moving against the house as a whole. None of the brothers cared to mention what the next step would likely be. There was only one move left to advance the game, after all.

They rounded the corner of the house on the approach to the west gate and immediately the three brothers reined in, staring. A column of men was waiting outside the gate, queuing for entry as a carriage made its way into the preceptory. Arnau, heart racing, counted forty men in armour on horseback, each bearing a shield with a busy design. They were not close enough to pick out the coat of arms on the shields, but the same design hung on the pennants that snapped in the warm breeze.

A red flag with a white three-towered castle below a golden crown.

'I don't recognise them,' Arnau said, quietly.

'I do,' Brother Lütolf replied darkly. 'The Baron Alberto de Castellvell. No friend of the Temple, he. A hater of men. The sort of Crusader who darkens the name of Christians everywhere. His presence can be no good thing.'

Ahead, the column of the baron's men filed into the preceptory. Memories flashed through Arnau's head, bringing back snippets of conversations and discussions at court over the years. Castellvell. A man prized by the king for his role in the Reconquista. A man who hated the Moor more than he hated Satan himself. A man with little conscience and no compassion.

A cousin of the Lord d'Entenza who had betrothed Titborga to della Cadeneta and begun this whole foul mess.

Arnau's heart sank.

CHAPTER TWELVE

Leaving Guillem to deal with the horses and pausing only to remove their shields and helmets, the three Templars marched across the courtyard towards the chapter house. Several small milling knots of men at arms in red and white got in their way and were less than gracious in making way for the three brothers passing through.

It chilled Arnau to see them here. Not so much for what they might mean, being connected tenuously to d'Entenza and therefore even more tenuously to Titborga's betrothed, but more because the force of white-and-red-clad soldiers looked so much like the oily della Cadeneta's men that Arnau kept flinching and instinctively reaching down to the hilt of his sword. The baron himself was in his coach, as they could easily ascertain from the barked orders coming from within and the small knot of officers gathered around it.

Having finally pushed their way across the open space, earning angry glances from knights as they went, the three Templars clanked through the chapter house's open doorway to find that many of the preceptory's population had already gathered there. Preceptrix Ermengarda sat upright and impressive in her chair at the end and, while most of the others sat on the stone bench that ran around the edge of the room, Sister Titborga occupied a separate chair close to the preceptrix, as though under her personal guard. To add to that level of protection – or force, perhaps – Brother Balthesar stood behind Titborga, armed and armoured. The three new arrivals moved to the bench together, standing as close to the preceptrix and Titborga as they could manage.

A single simple wooden seat sat unoccupied in the room's centre, facing Sister Ermengarda, and it almost made Arnau smile to realise it was the stunted one from the refectory that no one wanted to use. Having been shortened to level out uneven legs, it was now too short to sit in comfortably for more than a minute. It had been so placed that the person sitting in it would appear to be on trial, surrounded by Templars.

Barely had the three men settled than Brother Luis appeared in the doorway, the chink and shush and rattle of armoured men behind him. He paused and cleared his throat. 'Baron Alberto de Castellvell,' he announced, and then hurried to one side to sit on the stone bench near the door.

The man who entered sent a shiver through Arnau. Tall and impossibly thin, the baron's face was drawn and haggard. He did not look able to lift a sword, let alone win renown as a warrior in the Reconquista. Still, Arnau reminded himself, this man was a butcher, licensed by the king.

Castellvell strode into the room, his soft calfskin boots making hardly a sound, the gentle brush of fabric from his expensive clothes almost lost in the metallic din of the four soldiers who entered behind him and took up position near the door. The baron strode forward, eyed the small chair with a thunderous expression, and then, with some difficulty and rearrangement of robes, sat in the low seat, his chin rising as he was forced to look up at the preceptrix. The trial was about to begin…

'Sister Ermengarda,' he greeted her in an offhand tone, completely failing to acknowledge her formal title.

The preceptrix nodded. 'Don Alberto,' she replied in much the same tone.

'I am come bearing the olive branch, Sister, seeking to calm what appears to be an increasingly tense situation.'

'Indeed?' Preceptrix Ermengarda replied.

Castellvell pursed his lips, seemingly irritated at not receiving the deferential response he had expected. In a terse voice he went on, indicating the room and its occupants with the sweep of an arm. 'It is no secret that I do not approve of this arrangement, Sister. Your order precludes the very presence of women, let alone in such a position of authority. The Pope *himself* disapproves of Templar sisters. To find myself haggling like some low merchant with a woman sets my teeth on edge.'

'You are the very soul of grace to lower yourself so,' the preceptrix said in gentle tones and with a blank expression.

Castellvell bridled, breathing heavily. 'In your position, Ermengarda d'Oluja, you should be somewhat circumspect. You should take care not to raise your sweet face above the parapet for fear of someone putting an arrow into it, if you catch my drift.'

'You feel I ought to hide behind my skirts and not take an active part in the politics of our land,' she replied calmly.

'Quite so. You command here at the whim of men who owe your lineage much, but there are others who would happily see you hied off to some rural nunnery and a true battler of the heathen placed in that seat.'

'How lucky I am that the former outnumber the latter.'

Arnau marvelled at her cool. Her tone was calm and neutral with each verbal bolt she shot, and each missile hit home, raising the temper and irritation of the baron in his tiny seat.

'Do not mock me, woman. I will not be the subject of mirth for chattel and Moor-lovers. I have come at the behest of the Don Ferrer della Cadeneta. That I lower myself to playing negotiator in the affairs of my lessers irritates me endlessly, but the king commands that his barons keep the lands of Aragon and Barcelona peaceful and united against the true enemy. As such I am doing the best I can in such dreadful circumstances to heal the troubles between Rourell and Cadeneta. This cannot go on as it is.'

'I quite agree,' Preceptrix Ermengarda replied. 'So if you would kindly inform your friend della Cadeneta that Titborga de Santa Coloma is now a member of the order of the Poor Knights of Christ and the Temple of Solomon and has donated her estate and fortune to our coffers, I would be grateful.'

Castellvell made a strange rasping sound, but the preceptrix gave him no time to load his verbal crossbow. 'And please exhort him not to attempt to rouse our workers against us like a low knave.'

Brother Lütolf raised a hand. 'I apologise for interrupting proceedings, Preceptrix, but this morning we have visited the estates to find all our workers fled; incited, it seems, by a villain masquerading as a Moorish holy man.'

Ermengarda shot a surprised look at the German, but recovered admirably, and turned back to the baron. 'See how della Cadeneta sets himself against the order?'

'He is doing no such thing,' snapped Castellvell. 'You draw in a woman to your order, something that is expressly forbidden in your own sacred rule, you grasp her fortune for sheer greed and personal gain – the Temple does not need her lands, and you know it – and you do all this against the wishes of the great Lord d'Entenza, confidant of the king himself. In doing what you have done, you have broken your own order's rules and set yourself against the rightful temporal law of the Crown of Aragon.'

'The order has been pleased to accept the Doña de Santa Coloma as a sister. Our reasons and justifications for such are none of your business, Baron de Castellvell. Once the appropriate documents are lodged with our mother house and accepted then only the grand master could overturn such a decision. I think it rather poor taste your accusing this august order of greed in accepting a donation of lands, while supporting the claim of the grasping, acquisitive della Cadeneta to the Santa Coloma estate.'

'Enough of this sparring,' spat Castellvell. 'I did not come here to bandy words with a woman claiming high station to which she is not entitled. This visit is a courtesy and might be treated as such.'

'Then perhaps it should have been courteous?' the preceptrix shot back.

Gritting his teeth in irritation, the baron continued. 'Your course of action thus far is unwise. I have attempted to dissuade della Cadeneta from any precipitous action, and in doing so offered to attempt to persuade you to see reason. If reason you would do so, refuse sanctuary for this runaway bride, forgo any claim on her soul or her lands and turn her loose. Della Cadeneta will get his wife, d'Entenza will get his support, the king will get his peace and I will get some rest.'

'No.'

'Think again, Doña d'Oluja. The Temple's reputation in the region hangs by a thread. You would not want to be the one who snips that thread, believe me. You can still strengthen the all-too-necessary relations between your order and the nobles of Aragon, but to do so you must relinquish this woman. She is destined to be a wife. Let her be one.'

The preceptrix nodded slowly, then turned to the younger woman by her side.

'The decision is yours, Sister Titborga. Are you made for the marriage bed?'

Titborga shook her head. 'I give my body and my estate to the order and my soul to the Lord. Della Cadeneta will have none of them.'

Preceptrix Ermengarda turned back to the baron with an apologetic expression. 'It is not in the remit of the order to refuse a good Christian the chance to serve God. Sister Titborga stays at Rourell.'

Baron de Castellvell rose with a sour face.

'I have done what I can. On your own head be what follows. I detest you, Ermengarda d'Oluja, for your presumption and your harbouring of the heathen to your bosom, and I do not trust your order any further than I would trust al-Mansur himself, for you deny your own rules and are set upon a path of acquisition and opposition to God-appointed temporal rule. Regardless, I will not raise a hand against you, but know this: neither will I raise a hand in your defence when della Cadeneta comes for his bride, and come he surely will.'

'Then it would appear we have nothing further to discuss,' the preceptrix said, coldly.

Without another word, his expression speaking volumes, the baron rose with some difficulty, straightening his knees and stamping life back into his feet. He bowed curtly, then turned and stomped from the room, his four armoured men following on.

Brother Luis made to close the door behind him, but the preceptrix raised her hand. 'Leave it open. We have no secrets from him, and I want him observed until he is outside our walls.' Luis bowed his head and left the door open, moving to stand in the gap and keep one eye on the furious departing baron and the other on proceedings in the room.

'Was it wise to antagonise him so, Sister?' Ramon asked quietly from the bench.

'He was here purely to threaten,' the preceptrix replied angrily. 'I do not respond well to threats. Besides, even hating me as he does, Castellvell is not stupid enough to start a war with the order. The king would tear strips off him for it. He will be of no further harm, and he was never going to be of aid to us, so we have lost nothing of value. The message is clear, though: we stand alone against della Cadeneta, and he will come. He has already killed and assaulted, and now attempts to ruin us. He has made every move he can without direct confrontation. He has tried to proceed without overt conflict so far, but even with the aid of a powerful noble, he has failed. If he comes, what can we do, Brothers?'

Ramon shrugged. 'If he comes with his men, Sister, we will be in trouble. They amount to a sizeable force alone. But I believe he will keep his soldiers at Cadeneta and send hired men against us. That way he can deny responsibility in the aftermath and blame it all on bandits or suchlike. He is no idiot.'

'If he comes, we will beat him,' the German brother corrected him in flat tones. 'We are righteous and God will watch over us. Della Cadeneta is clearly spawn of the Serpent and shall never prevail.'

Ramon cast a sidelong glance at his brother knight. 'God can watch over us, but I will feel better knowing that we are strong in ourselves too. Luis, I want an inventory of everything of potential use in the preceptory – weapons, tools, potential blockages and supplies.'

'You sound as though you are treating this like a siege,' the German said.

'In anticipation of one, yes I am. Preparation costs nothing.'

'Return to the dormitory,' the preceptrix ordered, gesturing to Titborga and the other nuns.

Brother Balthesar moved round from behind the younger sister's chair. 'The yard is full of dangerous men. I will escort you.'

Titborga began to make her way out, Carima and Catarina alongside her, leaving just the men in the chapter house with the preceptrix.

'Do you really think della Cadeneta would attack Rourell?' Arnau asked quietly, in disbelief.

'I think a savage driven by greed and lust is capable of a great many things,' the preceptrix replied. 'It is a dangerous game to play, but he is cunning. The men he sends are not from his household. They are but rough hirelings. If he can overcome us and secure Sister Titborga then he can still claim her as a bride and inherit her estate, since we have not yet lodged the records. If he is successful, any impropriety will be smoothed over and ignored by the king and the barons, and the Temple will accept the damage in order to preserve their relationship with the Crown of Aragon. And if by some reason della Cadeneta should fail, he can disavow all knowledge of his ruffians and walk away untouched by anything more than a little suspicion.'

'He has nothing to lose,' Brother Ramon said quietly.

'What do we do?' Arnau asked. 'Send for more help?'

'Only as a last resort,' the preceptrix replied. 'Two such missions have ended in violence thus far. I would be tempted to move the entire preceptory to Barberà, but I fear that to do so would open us to twin troubles: leaving Rourell at the mercy of Cadeneta's hirelings, and exposing Titborga to potential attack on the road. No. She must remain within the walls for now, as must we all. Ramon has the right of it. We prepare for the worst, but I do not want anyone riding north unless our hand is forced. We cannot afford to lose another brother.'

Arnau was about to pose another question when the sound of an altercation drifted in through the door. Brother Luis, who had been concentrating on the conversation, turned and peered outside.

'Trouble,' he called, then rushed out into the light.

Arnau was among the gathered men as they piled out into the dazzling sun of the courtyard. His gaze swept over proceedings and he realised instantly that they were on the very brink of disaster. Baron Castellvell stood on the step of his carriage, staring with outright hostility. His men were bristling, swords half drawn in threat.

Close to the belfry, Arnau could see the shapes of Sisters Titborga and Catarina, shaking slightly. Carima was just visible as a heap of white on the filthy ground. One of the red-clad men at arms stood nearby, growling, his lip twisted in a sneer as he rubbed his knuckles with his other hand. He was snarling something at the nuns. Over the tense sounds of pending violence, Arnau couldn't quite hear what he said, but he had definitely caught the words 'filthy Jew'.

Brother Balthesar was crouched by the fallen sister as the soldier massaged his knuckles.

The man had hit a nun! In his mind, he had struck a heretic, of course, but that was immaterial. Arnau felt a moment of shame at the memory of his own reaction when he had realised her Jewish heritage and had blithely condemned her people as heretics as she mended his finger.

Lütolf and Ramon began to push the baron's soldiers aside, heaving their way towards the altercation even as the preceptrix emerged from the chapter house with a face like an avenging angel, stark and deadly.

Arnau could see the situation beginning to tip towards further violence, and his heart thundered as he saw Brother Balthesar rise from the heap of white habits that was Carima, unfolding like some dreadful Titan, his expression enough to make even the darkest demon flinch. He shouted something to the brother, an attempt to stop what he knew was coming.

He felt a tiny tinge of relief when Balthesar did not rip his sword from his scabbard, but the ageing, white-haired Templar was far from harmless even empty handed. His hand flew out and caught the baron's man on the cheek. At the resulting faintly metallic crunch, Arnau remembered that the brother was wearing his mail shirt, complete with sleeves and gauntlets. While the soldier's slap had been enough to send Carima to the ground, Balthesar's strike lifted the man at arms from his feet and sent him flying back to land on his posterior, nose broken, head ringing and blood streaming down the lower half of his face.

A dreadful silence fell across the courtyard in which the only perceptible noise was that of Ramon, Lütolf and Arnau pushing through shocked soldiers.

Balthesar was growling, a fierce sound like the throaty rumble of a wolf, and his very stance spoke of further impending violence.

'What is the meaning of this?' bellowed the Baron de Castellvell from the step of his carriage, though he received no answer.

From the ground, the fallen soldier grunted 'Bastard. I'll see you hang for that.'

'How blessed are those who keep justice, who practise righteousness at all times,' quoted the older brother, his fist tightening as if readying for a blow. The soldiers close to their fallen comrade now drew their blades with a collective rasp. Arnau made to draw his own sword in response, but was surprised as the German brother's hand fell over his own and pushed the hilt back down.

'Do not join this madness.'

Arnau came to a halt, shaking, furious at the baron's men for their conduct, furious at Lütolf for restraining his hand, furious at himself for not already being over there, ripping into these godless thugs. Ramon and Lütolf reached Balthesar a moment later as the other two nuns finally helped Carima to her feet, the young woman's face scraped and red from the slap.

The soldier with the broken nose, still uttering words that should not be said in such a holy place, rose to his feet, finger wagging angrily at his attacker.

Brother Balthesar went for him, and all that saved the soldier's life was Lütolf and Ramon grabbing hold of their friend's shoulders and physically holding him back.

'See dow de gread ad powerful Order od de Tebble,' sneered the man, his voice changed and distorted by his ruined nose. 'Jew ad boor lubbers, weak ad useless.'

He spat blood into Balthesar's face and the venerable Templar lunged for him again, Ramon and Lütolf gripping him as tight as they could.

'Rewed by a whore!' added the soldier, earning him a shocked look even from his friends. Balthesar, so stunned by the insult to his preceptrix, stopped struggling for a moment and the German brother adjusted his hold in preparation.

There was a dreadful silence.

Then Brother Ramon hit the soldier. Hard.

This was no slap, but a punch. Lucky the baron's man was that Ramon was dressed only in his church garb and his fist was bare and not mailed, for encased in steel that blow might well have killed him. As it was, it sent him reeling back and falling to the ground again, this time barely conscious. The man collapsed onto his back with a sigh.

'Enough!' bellowed the preceptrix from the chapter house step. 'Any man who does not sheathe his sword this instant I will see excommunicated for his part in defiling the Lord's house.'

Every sword snapped back into place or slid into a scabbard at that, and three men stooped and lifted their fallen companion by the shoulders, supporting the stunned, broken man.

'Leave Rourell,' Brother Ramon snarled at the men at arms. 'Now, before my friend here considers letting Brother Balthesar go.'

Several of the men flinched as they caught the eye of the older Templar, who was still struggling in his compatriot's grip.

'Forth, to Castellvell,' the baron shouted from the coach, and the soldiers, still glaring at the three Templar knights, helped their wounded friend into a saddle and then mounted themselves, leading the injured soldier's reins as they exited through the west gate and out into the countryside.

Arnau watched angrily as the men at arms filed out, banners raised as soon as they passed beneath the gate. The baron's coach, the nobleman now concealed inside, began to move out in the column's wake and, at a call from the occupant, rumbled to a halt outside the chapter house. The curtain was swept aside, and the cadaverous face of the baron emerged, expression fierce.

'You have made your bed, Ermengarda of Rourell, and those of all your people. Neither I nor any God-fearing noble of Aragon or Catalunya will raise a finger to save you from the righteous fury of a spurned husband. You have condemned your brothers and sisters.'

'I hear a lot of hot words and yet no truth, Baron de Castellvell,' the preceptrix replied in a cold voice.

'I expect your brothers to be punished for their conduct against my man. I will leave the matter to your conscience, in the hope that you have one.'

The preceptrix inclined her head only very slightly. 'Brothers Ramon and Balthesar will be dealt with in strict accordance with Templar Rule. I presume it is too much to expect that you will see to a similar disciplining of your soldier?'

The baron snorted. 'For striking a Jew? Faith, woman, but he should be *rewarded*.'

With that, he gestured for his driver to set off and the carriage rolled away through the gate, the last of his entourage following up as a rearguard.

'Get Carima into the refectory and see to her,' the preceptrix said, gesturing to Titborga and Catarina, then turned to where Lütolf had finally let go of Balthesar. The German moved back towards Arnau as the other two knights fell into position in front of their preceptrix.

'Surely she will not punish them?' Arnau breathed to Lütolf as the German came to a halt beside him.

'There must be *something* done. It is in the rule, although if I remember correctly, the text on this matter is extremely vague and open to interpretation.'

'But they were protecting Sister Carima.'

'That does not excuse injuring a Christian in anger.'

Arnau's feelings on the matter were quite to the contrary, but he remained silent as the two knights stood before Preceptrix Ermengarda, heads bowed.

'The rule of our order is complex on this matter,' she said. 'It calls for potential punishment for any blow inflicted with a sharp instrument, a stone, a stick, or anything that might kill or wound. Given that in both of your cases a simple punch can certainly wound, if not kill, a certain level of punishment is required. The rule leaves it to our discretion whether to take from you your habits.'

Arnau's eyes widened, and even the German drew a disbelieving breath. The confiscation of a brother's sacred garments was one of the worst punishments possible, a matter of extreme dishonour.

'Remove your habits,' the preceptrix ordered. A chill enveloped the courtyard as all stared in astonishment at the sister. The two men did so, ashen faced, handing the famous white robes to the preceptrix. She took them in both hands and then nodded. 'Let that be a lesson to you. Put them back on and wash the blood from your knuckles.'

There was a look of horrified disbelief in the eyes of the two brothers, but Arnau caught the preceptrix's face as she handed back the garments, turned and retreated into the chapter house. There had been a small, mischievous smile there that threatened to make Arnau laugh.

'Sainted Mary, but I almost thought she meant to do it then,' Lütolf whispered in shock. 'Though it will be some time before either of them considers landing a punch without permission, that's for certain.'

CHAPTER THIRTEEN

Two days passed in a strange limbo of tension and anticipation. The denizens of Rourell went about their tasks and duties as usual, though in a strangely muted, taciturn manner, as though contemplation of coming disaster might hasten its approach. There was a gradual gathering too, instinctively, unintentionally. None now seemed to spend their time about solitary chores or in personal contemplation. All tasks and social activities were now carried out in large groups or with the preceptory's full community involved. No one truly expected to be suddenly attacked, and yet Rourell subconsciously prepared itself.

Brother Ramon, whom Arnau now believed to be a slave of the grape, and probably had been during his entire time in the order and before, no longer spent his solitary time in the buttery feeding his personal demon, but emptied a few jugs in the refectory in front of everyone else. Arnau watched him with interest, knowing that the order's rule specifically forbade excessive indulgence. Yet at no time did Ramon seem to him drunk, his hand remaining steady, his mind sharp. Moreover, the preceptrix continued to treat him as though there was nothing noteworthy in his behaviour, though when the knight's back was turned, the young man had noted an odd sympathetic expression on her face. There was some story there, he was sure, though opening up that tale would be a task for another time, as he'd learned yesterday.

Arnau had made the mistake of trying to urge Brother Ramon into some revelation the previous night after compline, as the folk of Rourell had gathered in the refectory in their now-common muted indulgence. They sat in small groups with murmured conversation and no laughter. Ramon, as was often the case, sat on his own with a cup and a bottle, and Arnau had joined him. He had drunk beer with the knight, constantly attempting to manoeuvre the subject of their stilted mutterings, and constantly failing. As the night had ended and the brothers and sisters moved off to their dormitories, Arnau's head had been a little fuzzy. He'd climbed the stairs slowly, in expectation of a hangover the next day, something he had not had in months now. It had taken little time to fall into deep slumber.

He wasn't sure what woke him. Perhaps it had been a hooting owl. Perhaps a noise from one of the other beds where the male populace of Rourell slumbered on. But then owls were common, and he'd become used to the night-time symphony of the brothers quickly, so neither seemed likely. Perhaps it was just discomfort. Certainly, as he turned in his blankets to lie on the other side, there were unaccustomed aches and strange noises from his torso. Then the bladder pressure started. He lay for some time, willing the increasing urgency to go away, turned over again several times to see if it would ease, and then finally lay on his back in discomfort, wishing it would stop, knowing full well that he was merely delaying the inevitable.

Finally, unable to bear the increasing strain any longer, he threw back the blanket and rose from his cot on bare feet, padding across the wooden floor towards the door to the necessarium. There was a faint odour of dung that clung to that corner of the room despite the fact that waste was deposited through the holes out into the open air.

He turned the door's handle and padded into the fetid room, shutting the portal behind him to contain the smell. Compared with that of the monastery in which Arnau had spent time in his youth, this facility was a small and basic affair. The abbey of Santa Maria's latrine arrangements had been impressive: a row of toilets perhaps fifteen long in a wide room of their own, as big as Rourell's dormitories, and with a constant strong flow of water beneath carrying away waste into the river for some other poor fool to deal with further downstream. Rourell's was different. Ingenious, but small. There was no running water here, and the preceptory was surrounded by a dry ditch. Consequently there was no constant supply on hand to wash away the waste. Instead, a water tank on a raised platform at the outer corner of the preceptory above the ditch caught the meagre rainfall and stored it, augmented by buckets brought from the well if necessary. From the tank, a set of wide gutters ran at a gentle slope below both the male and female necessaria, around the walls, across the south causeway and then through a channel out into the fields, where the shit was unceremoniously deposited, aiding the growth of the olives or wheat, no doubt. The water was halted by a small sluice door which could be lifted by means of pulley and rope from within the preceptory to wash the drain clear.

Arnau stood at one of the apertures and lifted his black sleeping habit, identical to his daytime one. With a sigh of relief, and wondering whether he would find it easy enough to fall asleep again upon his return to the dormitory, he let go, peeing out through the hole and down into the warm night air outside. Above each toilet there was a slit-like window through the thick wall, acutely angled, more for additional ventilation than for viewing, and as he stood with the seemingly endless arc of urine dropping through the hole, his gaze fixed on the somewhat narrow view through that aperture.

He blinked at the momentary sight of two white figures passing by. Frowning in confusion, he clamped off the flow with a little difficulty and let his habit drop into place once more. On a whim, he hurried to the next narrow window, just in time to catch the briefest glimpse of white blur past.

Knights or nuns. At least two. He'd have questioned his eyes and his imagination in the depth of the night had he not seen that flash of white through the second window for confirmation.

Still frowning, he stumbled back through the door, allowing it to shut behind him. Straining his eyes in the gloomy interior, he scanned the beds. There was a telltale human-sized bulge in each. The figures outside were not knight brothers, then. So they had to be either nuns – or possibly not connected to Rourell at all, though that seemed unlikely. For a brief moment he considered shouting an alarm and rousing the brothers from their slumber, but instead padded across to his cot, grabbed his hose and boots, and opened the outer door, padding down the stairs. He was not sure yet what this all meant, and it would be unhelpful to deprive the entire male population of the preceptory of a good sleep without at least an idea of whether there was really any trouble.

At the bottom of the stairs, he slipped into his hose, tying them to the drawstring of his *brais* hurriedly, then slipping into his boots. He opened the next door and stepped out into the courtyard. There was no sign of movement here, but he could hear the gentle tones of Father Diego in the chapel. The man never slept, Arnau was sure. He contemplated speaking to the priest, but decided the old man could be of little use. He didn't know how to rouse the sisters without entering their dormitory, which was, of course, expressly forbidden – a rule even Preceptrix Ermengarda enforced emphatically. The west gate was barred, which meant that no one had left that way without someone inside to replace the lock. That left the south gate, which was closest to where he'd seen the figures anyway.

He hurried into the shadows of the arched corridor. The moonlit countryside beyond the preceptory showed through cracks and tiny pinpoints around the gate. He made it to the timber, blinking in the gloom, using his hands to guide him. The bar was still in place. He tried the small inset door. It opened, and Arnau's heart pounded. He'd expected it to be locked. Starting to feel rather nervous and acutely conscious of his vulnerability, he hurried back to the courtyard and opened the door to the armoury, feeling around until he found the hook on which his sword belt hung, lifting it and scurrying into the open air once more. He fastened the belt round his waist as he disappeared into the darkness of the archway once more. Once again he wondered whether he should be rousing someone else, or possibly clanging the main bell, raising an alarm.

No. He still didn't know what was going on, and if he wanted to catch up with the white figures, he was losing time. He'd already delayed too long getting dressed and equipped.

Biting down on the nerves that threatened to unman him, he passed through the door inset in the gate, closing it behind him. Somehow the fields surrounding Rourell had never seemed so open and clear to him, brightly lit by moonlight. Despite his black sergeant's habit, Arnau did not believe for one moment he was well hidden. Any hidden crossbowman could probably put a bolt in him without a great deal of effort, and the open ground provided no cover whatsoever.

Crossing the causeway over the ditch, he immediately turned to his left. As he passed the corner of the preceptory, he glanced up at the projecting shape of the necessarium and identified the slit window at which he'd stood, extrapolating from it. He turned in the direction the figures must have been moving, marvelling that he'd seen them at all from that angle. He squinted into the night and there, just below the looming distant shape of the mill, he spotted two small white shapes gleaming in the moonlight. He contemplated for a moment shouting out to them, but reasoned that drawing further attention to their presence might not be the cleverest approach. Consequently, he picked up pace and hurried on in their wake, making little noise other than the pounding of his feet, the heaving of his breath and the occasional clunk and tinkle of his sword at the belt.

They had almost reached the mill by the time Arnau was halfway from the preceptory, and he noted with concern how the pair then split up, close to the building's west wall. One white figure moved to the south corner, making for the main door, or perhaps the bridge across the Francoli that stood just beyond. The other came to a halt and both remained where they had separated. Arnau's suspicion and worry deepened, and he broke into a proper run now. There could be no good reason for this, and no good outcome, he was sure.

His eyes remained locked on the two white figures as he closed on them, and his nerves jumped a notch at the next change. The southern figure rounded the corner towards the door and bridge and, as soon as it was out of sight, the second figure, who had been standing still, turned and hurried away to the north, the opposite end of the building. The move was furtive and deliberately hidden from their companion. Arnau's breath came in rasps as the figure turned the north corner and disappeared as he closed on the mill.

What to do? Pursue the more suspicious white figure around the northern side or follow the initial person around the south? Sharply, he remembered his earlier nervousness upon exiting the preceptory door, and his eyes searched the nearby trees and the undergrowth near the river, half-expecting to spot hidden archers. Another dreadful thought struck him. What if this whole thing had been engineered to arrange for Rourell's door to be left unlocked? What if, even now, black-clad murderers were moving through the darkness, making for that unwatched door?

The notion was so alarming that even in his current predicament, Arnau turned and peered over his shoulder. Rourell was still and peaceful in the moonlight, a faint glow from the chapel rising above the walls. There was no evidence of a horde of sable killers stalking through the fields towards the monastery. For just a moment, he wondered whether to run back and alert someone in the preceptory, in case his wild notion happened to be correct. No. He was being driven to irrationality by nerves. If he left now, he would completely miss what was happening here and, being secret and hidden, it had to be important.

So who to follow? The surreptitious one who went north seemed more likely to be causing trouble, but was also calmer and more unhurried. The other could be in trouble, given the seeming innocence of their manner.

That decided him. It seemed almost certain, given the circumstances, that the figures were nuns, even though he'd not seen them close enough to be certain. And if a nun was in danger, then it was his duty as a God-fearing Christian to come to her aid, let alone as a brother of the Temple. He hurried away to the south, though his gaze kept flicking back to the northern corner in case that second figure reappeared. It did not, and he rounded the southern corner in time to witness the brink of disaster.

The figure was most definitely a nun. She was standing calmly by the door of the mill, looking off towards the south as Arnau rounded the corner. Behind her, he could see half a dozen shapes emerging from the trees and scrub bushes by the river, each a burly man and armed with clubs or lengths of rope. His eyes widened as the nun's gaze flicked round in surprise at the new arrival. Somehow, from the moment he'd seen them engaged in furtive activity near the mill, he had instantly formed the belief that it was the former maid, Maria. Given her previous escapade outside, it seemed oddly likely. So when his eyes met those of Titborga, his heart jumped.

In that moment he realised just how much trouble this meant. Half a dozen thugs closing on the heiress of Santa Coloma, and they were not armed with swords and maces and crossbows, but with weapons of subjugation and containment. They were intent on making off with her. That immediately explained who they were and who they worked for.

The attackers spotted Arnau a heartbeat later and they reacted with surprising efficiency, two of them making straight for Titborga while the other four peeled off into pairs, running to bypass her and intercept Arnau. The young sergeant drew his sword with a metallic rasp and prepared himself. He had the advantage over them in one way, given that they had only stout lengths of wood with which to fight while he wielded three feet of deadly, sharp-edged steel, but given their numerical superiority his own advantage seemed rather laughable.

He could not win out against six men – the fight at the broken bridge had taught him that. Then he had faced only four and he had been armoured and with a shield, yet still he would have fallen to the fourth had Brother Lütolf not been there to save him. Despite everything he'd privately thought about the man, he wished beyond all things that the dour German was with him now.

His immediate objective, then, was bleakly simple. He could not win in a fight with these ruffians, and to flee would be to doom Titborga to capture. He had to somehow get himself and his lady into safety. His eyes strayed to the mill door. Was it locked?

He broke into a run. All he had to do was get past them and get her to safety. Two of the men passed the nun at speed and made for Arnau, clubs raised. The young sergeant ran at them, sword above his head as though he were intent on cleaving someone straight down the middle, grunting with the pain in his side caused by the pulling on the narrow cut there. A nagging thought told him he was displaying every tell the German brother had identified during their recent training sessions, but he had neither the time nor the incentive to worry about such things now. A duel was a duel, slow and well thought out. A melee was something different and depended almost entirely on will, instinct and reflexes. At the very last moment, as the two men flinched, each wondering whether they would be the man to die by that raised sword, Arnau nimbly ducked to the right, passing both of them, sword still held high.

Sister Titborga was struggling with two men now, one of whom was gripping her right arm tightly, trying to uncoil a rope with the other. The second man had her other arm and was waving his club maniacally. The remaining two were now on the far side of the attempted kidnapping to Arnau and had scrambled to a halt, turning to come for him.

Arnau's raised sword fell, biting deep into the shoulder of the man struggling with the rope. He screamed and let go of Titborga's arm, staring in horror at the limb that hung from his body at a weird angle, held on only by muscle and sinew. Giving them no time to recover, Arnau grabbed Titborga with his empty hand and pulled so hard that she cried out in pain. Her other captor, surprised, saw the woman slip from his grip. Arnau had her now.

'The door,' he barked. 'Try the door.'

She ducked past him and ran to the mill door. Arnau felt his nerves tighten at their predicament. Very good that Titborga was behind him, hurrying to the door. But now he was facing five men who had moved into an arc around them and were closing, tightening the cordon. In moments, he would be fighting five men, and he was already sadly convinced how that would turn out.

'It's stuck,' she yelled in a panicked voice.

More likely locked, his mind shrieked at him, but there was nothing else they could do. He had committed them to the door, though there had been in truth little other choice. Now there was no way they could get away to left or right unless he succeeded in killing all five men.

They began to swing knotted ropes and flail with clubs as they closed on him.

'Force the fucking thing,' he shouted, promising to do penance later for swearing at a nun.

He pulled his arms to the left, hauling back the longsword in his hands, and then swung it in a wide arc, eyes watering at the pain in his side as he did so. The five men halted their advance in the face of the horrible injury the blade threatened. They edged forward just a step, and he brought the sword back the other way in another heavy-handed swing, using every ounce of his strength and yelping as the cut in his side burned. The sheer exertion and pain was almost too much. Spots danced before his eyes and his mind whirled for precious moments.

'Kill him,' bellowed a new voice, and Arnau's eyes flicked sideways to see another thug, presumably their leader, climbing up from the river with two more men at his side. He was the only one armed with a blade. The five men around Arnau advanced again, seemingly more afeared of their own master than of the Templar's swinging blade. Arnau whipped it back and swung again, wondering how long he could keep this up without collapsing. The next few steps and they would be within his arc.

'How's the door coming?' he asked with some urgency.

'I don't think it's locked,' the nun replied. 'I've got the latch up, but I think something's blocking it from inside.'

Wonderful.

The men were on him now. His next swing caught an extended arm. The contact robbed his arc of speed and strength, but broke the wrist of the man so badly that jagged white bone protruded from the mess. The others came at him fast now. He stepped back two paces and swung again, uncomfortably aware of the closeness of Titborga behind him. He was out of space, but the one who'd dropped from the line, screaming and nursing his ruined hand, had ripped out of the thugs the extra courage their master's words had instilled, and their advance faltered once more, the Templar's sword swinging back and forth in his horribly reduced space, threatening agony for the next man who advanced.

'I cannot move it,' Titborga yelled.

'Kill him,' snarled the man now at the top of the bank again, ripping his own sword clear of its sheath.

Arnau was out of time. The men began to move again. They knew, just as did Arnau, that one of them would be maimed in the next few moments, but that the others would have the chance to overpower the sergeant near the door. None of them wanted to be the man hit by the blade, but it was a one-in-four chance. Not bad enough odds to make them falter further.

Arnau and Titborga were about to die.

'Fuck it, move!' he bellowed again with feeling, not even bothering to feel apologetic about it this time.

He turned, sword point dropping, and threw himself at the door a mere four paces behind him. The nun saw him at the last moment out of the corner of her eye and had barely moved aside before the young sergeant hit the timber. The door flew inward and he fell into the dark, stumbling over the grain sack that had blocked the timber, rolling by instinct and keeping the sword out to the side to reduce the risk of self-injury. The pain was exquisite, and he felt as though his side were afire, his vision blurring with the agony and the effort, but he forced himself to focus despite everything. Better to feel agony than the cold embrace of death, after all…

As he leaped to his feet once more, he saw Titborga throw herself inside. He ran to the door as the thugs closed on it and grabbed the wood, heaving it closed. A club smashed through the gap and caught Arnau a glancing blow on the shoulder that would hurt badly and bruise impressively, but was far from incapacitating. The door jammed half a foot from the frame and Arnau realised why at a scream. One of the attackers had got his leg through the gap in a desperate attempt to stop the Templar shutting it.

Throwing his back against the door and wincing at the new pain in his shoulder, Arnau lifted his sword as high as he could, point dangling, and then slammed it down into the leg in the doorway. The blow was poor but effective. The blade plunged deep into the thigh, grating off the femur and carving through muscle. Its owner howled like something from a nightmare on the other side of the door, and Arnau, just for a moment, stepped forward, releasing his pressure on the door. The leg, predictably, was pulled from the gap, and before anyone else could try and stop him, Arnau slammed his back against the timber once more and pushed the door to. He floundered with his left hand, trying to grasp the latch, but from this angle it was impossible. There was a thump and the door shuddered as someone outside hit it with their shoulder. For a frightening moment, it felt like Arnau was being pushed out of the way, but he grunted and reapplied the pressure, holding the door closed.

'The latch,' he hissed. 'Titborga, the latch!'

She was there a moment later, fastening the thing. It would not bar entry, of course, and they did not have the key.

The door shuddered under another thump.

'What do we do?' she asked Arnau, all business now. The young sergeant's eyes scoured his surroundings in the minimal light, and he felt a wave of relief as his eyes fell upon the metal brackets on either side of the doorframe.

'There will be a restraining bar somewhere near the door. You need to find it and slide it through that iron loop near the latch. Then feed it through the one at the other side. *That* will hold it against them.'

As the nun started scouring the wall and floor nearby in the dark, using her hands more than her eyes, she was breathing heavily. 'It has a lock,' she said, 'why a bar too?'

Arnau felt the door budge momentarily again and changed his position, bracing his feet against the flagstones a little better and pressing the door back once more as the latch rattled, someone outside trying to deal with it. 'This mill was built at the same time as the preceptory, not long after the area was taken back by the Christians. Have you found the bar yet?'

'No, I… Wait, here it is.'

There was a sound of scraping wood, and the nun rose once more with a length of timber, trying to feed it through the loop. 'With the danger from the border,' Arnau went on, 'and with raiders everywhere, even mills and cottages and barns were equipped with ways to defend them should it become necessary. It seemed likely this place could be held against the rampaging Moor if necessary.'

He felt the bar slide past his back, beneath his shoulders, and with a little wiggling and hurrying back and forth, Titborga slid the stout timber bar home.

'Thank the dear Lord for that mercy,' she said through heaving breaths.

'That mercy and others,' Arnau added, wiping his sword on his black habit and then sheathing it. 'Find the window shutters and make sure they're secured. I'm going for the north door. If it's not being watched, maybe we can get out that way.'

As the nun hurried around the windows, securing the shutters with two thick bolts each, designed to keep out marauders every bit as much as the door, Arnau lurched through the open doorway in a dividing wall and into the other side of the mill, making for the north door, hand held to his painful side. He stopped as he approached. Male voices were audible, muffled through the timber. It seemed unfeasible that they were anything other than more of the thugs. Consequently, he grabbed the same sort of bar that stood in the dark corner of the room and lifted it, sliding it home through metal loops.

A moment later he was back in the main room of the mill.

'We need light,' Titborga suggested. She was correct. They were safe for now, inside the mill, but it was almost pitch dark in here and already Arnau had almost walked into the mill's workings and tripped over debris twice.

'There will be lamps. I remember when I came here there was one beside each door on a little shelf, along with flint and steel. As soon as it's lit get the glass closed, though. We don't want the flame burning openly in the mill.'

'Why not?' the nun puzzled as she hurried over to the door that was still resounding to the thuds of a pair of charging shoulders.

'Nearly everything in a mill burns easily, and *nothing* burns easier than flour dust.'

Leaving her to her work, he ran back to the north door, found the items precisely where he remembered and began to strike the light, praying that there was not enough flour dust in the air to combust. It *smelled* of flour overwhelmingly in here. Moments later he had the wick lit and closed the lantern for safety. As the glow increased rapidly, he carried the lamp to the doorway between the two rooms, where he placed it on the floor so that it gave adequate light to both. A similar glow dawned at the southern end, where the nun had lit the second lamp and left it on the shelf. Slowly the interior of the mill became visible in the golden glow.

'What now?'

'Now we're in trouble,' Arnau replied. 'We're surrounded and seriously outnumbered. They're outside the north door too.'

'Maria,' sighed Titborga regretfully.

'So it *was* Maria. I thought it might be.'

'How did you come to be here, Vallbona? *Brother Arnau*, I mean. Not that I am not indebted to you, but why are you here at all?'

'Providence. The Lord's workings, clearly. I was up in the night, easing my bladder, when I saw you both through the necessarium window. I hurried out after you, not sure what was going on. What *is* going on?' he prompted.

'Maria,' Titborga replied. 'She came to me in the night. Said she had word from Peter.'

'Who is Peter?' Arnau asked as his eyes did circuits of the mill's interior, searching out anything potentially useful.

'Peter is – *was*, I suppose – the seneschal at home.'

Arnau frowned, thinking back. He had vague recollections of an old man with thinning hair and a neat white beard who wore a perpetual scowl, as though the world had been made solely to annoy him. He'd spoken to the man many times over the years and it had never once occurred to him to ask his name. What he did remember was a man fiercely loyal to the Lord Berenguer and the Santa Coloma estate, as were most of the people there.

'Maria said that Peter had come with news of Santa Coloma and my inheritance. He did not wish to meet me at the preceptory, but it was important. He would meet me at the mill.'

Arnau rolled his eyes. 'You are intelligent, my lady. I know that from the many games of chess and conversations we have shared. How did you fall for such a feeble lie? As if the old man would have ridden all the way here and then lurked in a mill in the dark rather than presenting himself at the gate.'

Titborga was nodding, her face flushed with embarrassment. 'I was, I admit, not thinking clearly. It is a sad fact that sometimes blind optimism overrides common sense. The very idea that our circumstances could change for the better and eliminate all this trouble filled me with hope. I should have questioned Maria, but I have known her all my life. She is Santa Coloma like you.'

'Not like me,' grunted Arnau as he grasped the sides of the ladder and began to heave himself up towards the rafters, wincing at the searing pain each step brought. As he reached the roof, he moved across to the eaves and peered out of the gaps beneath the roof tiles. Unable to spot what he was searching for, he moved further along with some difficulty and a close shave or two.

'What are you looking for?' Titborga called up.

'There,' he replied, peering out. A squat but well-built cottage sat close by, and he squinted at it. The building, the house of the Moorish miller, was dark and silent. There was precious little chance the man was asleep, given the commotion at the mill. He had probably not fled, given that even when his workers ran away he had refused sanctuary and gone on working his business, and with all the shouting and banging at his mill mere yards away from the house, unless the man was the heaviest sleeper in the world, then likely tonight had not gone well for him.

'The miller is gone. He won't have run, but these ruffians might have dealt with him. There will be no aid from that quarter.'

There was a hiss of disappointment from below, and Arnau balanced carefully on a beam, using joists to left and right where possible, and crossed the mill like a rope-walker at a town fair. He felt the nerves rise in him at the sight of the dim mill floor so far below him, as well as the various workings, but he was soon at the far side and peering out under the eaves once more.

Infernal luck. Despite everything going on at the mill, it was just far enough from the preceptory that the noise and activity had gone unnoticed there, and there was no sign of movement. He grumbled his disappointment and leaned over the drop. 'No one in the preceptory noticed. We're on our own.'

As a series of subdued noises suggesting unladylike statements rose from the dim floor below, Arnau retrod his dangerous and acrobatic way along the beam to the ladder, where he simply grasped the sides, wrapped his insteps around the uprights and slid down in sections, wincing at his side once more and taking care not to cause friction burns to his hands. He might need his sword arm in perfect health tonight, after all.

'What now?' Titborga asked, another outing for that same question that kept leaping to her lips. Arnau held up a hand to shush her and then hurried over to the south door on light steps.

'It's gone quiet,' he whispered back to her, pointing at the door, which was no longer thumping and shaking under blows from without. He put his eye to one of the narrow gaps around the edge, being careful not to put it up too close straight away in case some enterprising villain was close to the other side with something long and pointed. Thankfully he was rewarded instead with a partial view of a confab going on some way from the mill.

'… boarded tight,' one of the men was saying. 'No door, no window.'

The boss, whom he could only partly see, nodded. 'It's old. From reconquest days. Defensible against raiders, and certainly against us.'

'So how do we get in?'

'I'm not sure we want to,' added another of the men. 'That man was a Templar sergeant. I saw the cross on his breast.'

'There are *twelve* of us,' said the boss, scathingly.

'Only till that sword starts to swing. We'll get him, obviously, but only half of us will be alive to see it.'

The boss rounded on the recalcitrant ruffian. 'Think of all that silver waiting for you. Better than standing under a bridge robbing merchants for a couple of coppers a day, eh? Now tell me: in all your opinions, have we run out of options? There's no way to take the woman?'

There was a chorus of affirmatives.

'Then you know the deal. If she can't be brought back alive, then she doesn't live at all. As long as she doesn't get back to the monastery intact.'

Arnau's heart skipped. *Capture or kill?* That seemed stupid. Not like della Cadeneta. But pondering on the problem for just a moment suggested otherwise. The unctuous lord would win all if he held both Titborga and the documents to her lands. But if he couldn't have her, and she died before she could attend the ceremony of admission to the order, then her lands were still hers and not the Temple's and she would have no heir. Disposition of her estate would be the task of the Lord Bernat d'Entenza, who almost certainly would grant them straight to della Cadeneta, thereby creating a strong sword arm backed by a sizeable estate to serve the king. Capture Titborga, the enemy wins her estate. Kill Titborga, the enemy wins her estate.

He hissed his discontent at the horrible realisation. Titborga's value had just changed. Della Cadeneta had realised that, other than losing a servile whore he could break, her death would serve him as well as her capture, and that put a whole new complexion on things.

'Fetch torches,' the ruffian boss outside told his men. 'We fire the mill.'

'Shit,' Arnau said, stepping back from the door.

'What is it?'

'They're going to burn the mill down with us inside. Della Cadeneta believes he can grab your lands anyway if you're dead before you can complete your admission to the order.'

'So we're trapped in an oven?' she said, breathlessly.

'No. An oven just gets hot, and it heats up slowly. This place is made at least half of timber. Old, dry, seasoned timber. And grain. And dust. And oil. We're not in an oven. We're in a bonfire. When this place catches, it'll be an inferno in minutes.'

Eyes wide and wild, Titborga dropped to her knees, clasping her hands in prayer. Arnau watched her, contemplated doing the same, as he was sure the German brother would advocate, but decided instead that his eyes, hand and mind were better employed scouring the mill for a solution. Did that make him a bad Templar? To put his faith in his own ability before the Lord?

Perhaps. But with luck it would make him a bad Templar rather than a pious corpse.

Chapter Fourteen

Arnau fought off the panic as he hurried around the mill, searching for any solution to their dreadful peril, taking the time to send up prayer after prayer for deliverance any moment his mind was not full to brimming with desperation and fear. The very idea of burning alive was simply the worst thing he could imagine. No death in battle could be as awful. In fact, he had quickly come to the private, silent decision that if no way out presented itself, he would put Titborga to the sword and then throw himself upon it like a Roman of old before the flames could lick at his flesh.

Titborga remained kneeling, hands folded in prayer, her faith in the Lord strong enough that such a course of action was the only one she could imagine. Now, watching her as he ran around in a panic, Arnau could see how fitted she truly was to a life married to the cross. She had been right about that all along.

Arnau checked each door and window in quick succession, but even through the tiny gaps, he could see that men had been set to watching for any attempt at escape. Futile to try such a thing. Outnumbered as they were, they would not make it far from the mill before meeting their maker. The doors and windows discounted, Arnau climbed the ladder once more into the rafters, grunting at each painful step, and then began to shuffle along the eaves of the roof this way and that, peering down. Of the dozen men that seemed to constitute the enemy force, six were watching the mill exits while the others were gathering dry scrub and piling it against the two doors.

There was little time. Even now they were finishing their foraging and preparing to light the dry tinder outside the doors. It had not rained in so long that the entire mill was like matchwood, and any flame would race around it in minutes. No windows, no doors, no time.

No one watching the riverside…

Two men to the south, two to the north and two to the west, keeping tabs on the doors and windows, but no one watching the side of the mill facing the river. Of course, there were no windows or doors there, so they probably deemed it unnecessary. It *was* unnecessary, he realised with a sigh. No real hope of escape that way either. They could probably lift a few tiles from the roof and sneak out under the eaves of the building, but what then? They would be on the top of a funeral pyre. They couldn't climb down east, west or north without being seen. They could, perhaps, have jumped into the river in the wintertime, but right now, with the low flow after so many dry months, that would be a death sentence anyway. Perhaps they could climb down that side, but Arnau was not keen on the idea. There were precious few hand holds and it was a long way down to the river. Besides, one noise and they would attract the attention of the brigands anyway, and then they would be worse off than now.

Grunting in exasperation and wincing with pain, he clambered quickly back down the ladder only to hear a distant roar, reminiscent of a waterfall. Moments later, thick grey smoke began to pour under the south door and through the small cracks in and around it.

'Titborga,' he yelled, 'grab some empty sacks and push them against the bottom of the door to stop the smoke.'

Though he had interrupted her prayers, the young nun nodded emphatically and rose swiftly, searching around for sacks and then running over to the door. Arnau grabbed more from the corner of the room and ran to the north door, which was also now admitting smoke. He stuffed the sacks against the bottom of the wooden portal, praying they did not catch fire themselves, as that might just propel the conflagration fatally forward. Smoke was still leaking in through the cracks in worrying amounts, but at least the flow of choking black had diminished a little. Arnau looked up. No point in going back up the ladder anyway, but now it was unthinkable with the black smoke pooling in the rafters like deadly fog.

Was it his imagination, or could he already feel the heat building?

His eyes raked the building desperately. Nothing. Just sacks of grain, empty bags, tools, a grain hopper, other bits and pieces that were beyond his ken and the great grindstones with the sets of wheels and pulleys to operate a sack lift. Nothing useful there, though of course, he could only see the *top* parts of the workings…

His skin prickled with a frisson. Most of the mill's actual workings were beneath the floor. The two of them could not go outside, and they could not go up. Could they go down?

'Look for a trapdoor,' he suddenly shouted, starting to hurry around the main room, peering at the floor, kicking aside sacks and piles of chaff and sweepings. Titborga joined in and moments later they were scouring the floor on their hands and knees. Now, just as Arnau had suspected earlier, they could feel the growing heat in the building. The south door was starting to burn. Once the fire was inside, it would race around the dry beams supporting roof and machinery and the whole place would be an inferno in minutes. Death was imminent. They searched harder, Arnau undoing his sword belt and laying it to one side, as the swinging scabbard interfered with his crouching.

'Here!' Titborga said.

Arnau looked up to see the young nun, white habit stained and ripped, brushing the floor with her hands, pushing the dust aside. He hurried over and nodded his relief. A square some three feet in diameter was fitted into the floor with a heavy iron ring inset. There was a bolt, but fortunately no lock. Arnau began to try and work the old rust bolt back and forth, fingers sore and aching as he did so. Moments later, the metal came loose with a scrape and a thud, and he rose to a crouch, grasping the metal ring in both hands.

With a noise like the ignition of hell itself, the south door burst into flame. The room was already full of black smoke down to almost head level and the smell was appalling. Arnau heaved on the ring, trying to ignore the pain in his little finger and the soreness of the stitches in his side as he did so.

The trapdoor had clearly not been opened in years, and the heavy timber was sealed tight with grime and age. Arnau paused, rose to take a breath and realised his mistake as he heaved in a lungful of smoke and burst into a coughing fit that threatened to turn him inside out. Rasping and choking, he scoured the area and located a small utility knife on a shelf. He ran back over to the hatch at which Titborga was now fruitlessly pulling. Still hacking and coughing, he pulled his habit up to cover his nose and mouth, motioning for the nun to do the same if she could – he had no idea how a habit, coif and wimple combination worked. Ignoring her again, he turned his attention to the hatch once more, jamming the small knife into the crack around the edge of the trapdoor, sawing it up and down with difficulty, cutting through the accumulated muck. Finally, as his eyes streamed with tears in the choking, roiling smoke that was now almost down to ground level, filling the building, he jabbed and stabbed at the barely visible hinges, trying to free them a little, each blow reminding him of the pain in his side.

The knife blade snapped suddenly, and Arnau narrowly avoided slashing his own wrist badly in the process. Throwing the broken hilt off into the hot smoke, sweating and crying, Arnau reached down and grabbed the iron ring once more, heaving upwards.

'Hurry,' Titborga said, her voice muffled by the fabric over her mouth and nose. A somewhat redundant suggestion, in Arnau's opinion. What did she *think* he was doing? Flames were now licking up beams and rippling across sacks. Arnau heaved again and there was a deep grating noise, like the snoring of some subterranean giant.

An explosion off at the far side of the workings sent a wave of black smoke and searing heat across them, and Arnau was knocked flat for a moment, his ears whistling at the noise, Titborga floundering alongside him. Flour. More explosions would come yet, and each one would increase the speed and power of the conflagration. Rising to a crouch once more, Arnau set to. Gritting his teeth and grunting with effort, he heaved and pulled.

The trapdoor came free so suddenly that as it sprang open, Arnau was hurled backwards into the hot black fog. It took him precious moments to rise and get his bearings in the smoke and he almost walked into the fire by the door before turning and hurrying back towards the nun's urgent shouts.

Gagging and coughing, eyes moving from one dreadful orange fireball to another all about them, Arnau reached the trapdoor. What lay beneath was shrouded in pitch-black mystery. Momentarily he considered trying to fetch one of the lamps, but quickly decided the idea was idiotic. Even if he could find them in this they would either have exploded or would be far too hot to hold. Instead, he nodded at Titborga and sat on the edge, dangling his feet into the darkness. He reached out and picked up his sword and belt from the floor nearby.

'Lord preserve me,' he said with feeling, and dropped into the hole.

He was surprised to hit stone only perhaps eight feet below, and fell painfully onto his backside. His hands felt around. The ground was thick with muck and unpleasantly slimy. He rose and blinked repeatedly. The cool and the fetid damp air were something of a shock after the superheated, parched world above, and he found that he was coughing uncontrollably again.

'Is it safe?' a voice called from above.

Arnau turned slowly, still coughing. Now that he was beginning to get used to it, there was a faint light to this underground world. It took him but moments to spot the source. Moonlight shone in from the waterwheel fixings. He grinned in the darkness and waved up to the hatch.

'Come down.'

Titborga landed considerably lighter than he had, with a lot more grace, and nimbly stretched and turned to take in her new surroundings. Smoke was beginning to drift down through the hatch, and Arnau tried to reach through it to the lid, though there was clearly no chance of closing it. Ah well.

Here lay the truly arcane workings of the mill – strange cogs and shafts that transferred the vertical turn of the axle into the horizontal turn needed to drive the grindstones above. Somewhere in the mill proper there must be a sort of brake the owner used to disconnect some shaft and stop the querns above turning, for the waterwheel spun at a ponderous pace, driven by the river's flow even as low as it was, while the workings leading upward were still and silent.

'Can we get out this way?' Titborga asked, then broke into a fit of coughing.

'I think so. Let's hope, as it's our only chance now.'

He hurried over towards the light, taking care not to touch the turning axle or any other part of machinery. The last thing he wanted was to be trapped in the mechanism while the mill burned down above him. With some relief, he reached the outer wall.

The water wheel was quite a large example, and Arnau could see that the water was a good six feet below, driving the great circle of timber round. The hole in the outer wall was not large, just a little wider than the axle, really, which was anchored in place with age-old timbers. Could he get through there? The only answer that leaped to mind was 'maybe'.

'We have to be quiet now,' he hissed at Titborga. 'Don't want to attract attention. You'll have to pass me my sword when I'm through,' he added, handing her the sword and the rolled belt to which it was attached.

He peered at the slowly turning great wooden axle, imagining what it would be like to be caught beneath it and ground like flour. Taking a breath of fetid, horrible air, he pulled up the sagging hem of his filthy habit and tucked it into the drawstring of his *brais*, flushing slightly at displaying his underwear in front of a nun. Still, better the impropriety than to have flowing black robes get caught in the machinery. He was sure God would not punish him for such a thing in these circumstances. He would say the paternoster a few times later in personal penance.

Preparing himself, Arnau heaved in several deep breaths and then forced all the air from his lungs and pulled himself into the narrow gap. The discomfort was intense. The axle turning against his back was a horrible sensation as he pulled on the stonework, heaving his bulk towards the air and freedom. There was a terrifying moment when he felt his chest wedge between the spinning wooden beam and cold stone, but a little grunting and heaving, and he managed to unjam himself. A stray waft of his habit caught the beam and was pulled beneath it. His garment tore with a dreadful noise and one of his hose ties snapped, the woollen stocking rolling down a little.

Finally, as he was beginning to wonder if it was at all possible, he was free of the aperture and immediately launched into a whole new hell as he fell into cold shallow water six feet below, hitting the submerged timber of the wheel with a dull thud and a splash. He was then sickeningly lifted with the turning of the wheel until he was almost lying vertically, before falling back in a ball and beginning the process again. Slowly, stomach churning with the constant movement, he managed to get to his feet and walk against the turning of the wheel so that he remained in place. He looked up.

His sword suddenly plunged from the gap above and dropped into the water, almost taking off his nose in passing. No scabbard or belt was attached. He crouched, still keeping pace with some difficulty, and retrieved the soaking blade. He then looked up again.

Titborga was emerging from the hole with remarkable ease. Unlike his own unceremonious fall, she turned and dropped, landing lightly on her feet. Arnau tried not to look too closely at her, since her habit had been pulled up and knotted at the waist. He was fairly sure that would require some lengthy penance. More than just a few paternosters, for certain.

'My sword belt?' he said, his voice little more than a whisper. 'Scabbard?'

The nun gave him a look that suggested he had asked for something insane. 'If *you* couldn't get through there with the thing, why would *I*?' she hissed back.

She ignored his frown and danced across the turning timbers to the water. There, with no ceremony, she dropped into the Francoli River with a gentle splash. Her surprise at the shallowness was palpable as she stood straight, the water only coming up to her midriff. Judging the turn of the wheel carefully, Arnau dropped into the water beside her. The two then stood for a moment, unfastening their habits so that they dropped back into place more respectably. Arnau could feel his one leg of hose flapping around his ankle underwater. Now was not the time for messing with that, though.

The mill was truly ablaze now, great tongues of orange emerging through the eaves, smoke pouring up into the night sky in a thick roiling column. Arnau gestured to the north and they began the slow, difficult slog upstream against the current. Once past the turning wheel, he moved closer to the bank and finally managed to find an area where the water became much shallower. A tile dropped from the roof and hit the water just a foot from him with a loud splash, and his heart thundered at the realisation that he could yet be killed simply by falling debris. Eyes constantly darting back and forth between the ruined roof above and the dark banks of the river, he gradually climbed until he left the water altogether and was away from the wall of the mill. There, he moved slowly through the undergrowth up to ground level. His eyes scoured the area. There were no longer ruffians watching the north door. There would be little point now, of course. Had he and Titborga still been inside they would have been dead for some time.

Breathing in relief, he hurried out with Titborga at his back. On an odd instinct, he turned and looked back along the river. He could just see the shapes of a dozen men walking across the bridge. One of the departing figures stopped for a moment to look back at the mill and his eyes fell on the two shapes on the riverbank, illuminated by the blazing building. There was a brief kerfuffle on the bridge and the men started to run back, but quickly halted their return and sped across the bridge once more. Arnau stood still and watched them find horses in the trees, mounting quickly and riding away south.

His attention returned to his immediate surroundings. A small heap lay not far from the glowing rectangle that had once been the mill's north door, now an inferno churning out black smoke. He hurried over, shying away from the intense heat of the doorway. The heap was composed of two bodies: one a nun, the other a dark, swarthy man in nightwear. He knew it was Maria and the miller before he turned the bodies over and saw the wounds, hers a vicious blow to the forehead that had cracked her skull and broken her head, his blue-black ligature marks where he had been garrotted with a rope.

'Whatever Maria's motives for any of this, she has paid the ultimate price,' Arnau breathed.

'I shall grieve for her, Vallbona. No matter how she has fallen I will pray for her soul.'

He nodded. 'We will have to come back for them in the morning. I cannot carry them to the preceptory.'

The pair moved off, rounding the mill's corner and staying a safe distance from it as more tiles and timber began to fall from the collapsing roof.

His tired eyes caught movement nearby, and he was as thankful as a man could be to see the white and black habits of Templar knights, nuns and sergeants hurrying from the monastery to the mill. Almost certainly it was their approach that had driven the arsonists and kidnappers to flee before their work was complete.

Arnau was standing, exhausted, stained black and yet soaking wet with Titborga leaning on his arm, in danger of collapse, when the preceptrix and the others arrived.

'Della Cadeneta?' Preceptrix Ermengarda asked quietly, her eyes still on the burning mill.

'Again, no evidence,' Arnau coughed. 'They were bandits, I think, but clearly hired by someone. They tried to kidnap Titborga. *Sister* Titborga,' he corrected himself quickly. 'But when I managed to get her into the mill and bar it, I overheard them let slip that their mission was to capture her or, if not, to kill her before she could return to the preceptory. I fear della Cadeneta has decided that he can pass up possession of the sister and still get his hands on her estate.'

'He is correct. But if he is convinced that our good sister expired in the blaze, perhaps his attention will no longer be so riveted on Rourell and we will be free to deal with the issue at leisure.'

'I fear not, Preceptrix,' Arnau sighed. 'The brigands spotted us climbing the riverbank. I believe they were coming back for us when they saw you all approach and had to flee. Della Cadeneta will hear of their failure soon enough, may he be damned to hell.'

Brother Ramon noted the heap of bodies behind them near the burning mill.

'Maria?' he asked, pointing.

Arnau nodded. 'And the miller.'

'What were you all doing out here?' Brother Lütolf asked suspiciously.

'Maria tricked me into believing an old friend was here with an important message,' Titborga replied. 'Brother Arnau happened to see us leave the preceptory and came to investigate. Were it not for his timely arrival, I would now be in their hands.'

Though the preceptrix nodded her approval at Arnau, the German brother's expression was less sympathetic. 'And it did not occur to you to raise an alarm? Then perhaps those two would not be in God's hands and the mill would not have burned.'

The preceptrix turned on Lütolf. 'You are being uncharitable, Brother. A warning to the rest of us would not have saved Maria or the miller. Nor, I suspect, the mill. Had he delayed, Brother Arnau would have been too late to be of aid. All is as the good Lord designed. Come. Let us return to the preceptory. There is nothing to be done here until the blaze dies away, and there is no chance of catching those men now. Brothers Luis and Mateu, would you bring the bodies of the unfortunate pair? They must be dealt with before the scavengers can get to them.'

With that, the preceptrix began to stride back towards the monastery, the others keeping pace. Arnau and Titborga fell in with the group, leaving the bodies to the two other sergeants. All the way back, the German knight studied them, his expression unreadable, and Arnau's irritation grew. At the monastery's south gate, Simo let them all through, helped the brothers with the bodies and then pulled it shut.

'Search Maria's body,' the preceptrix said. 'Find the gate door key. If it is not there and has been lost we must stop using that door, for it is entirely possible that the enemy has acquired the key. If so, nail it shut and bar it until we can arrange a new lock.'

Catarina was hurrying across the courtyard in their direction, her face full of concern, and Preceptrix Ermengarda gestured to her. 'Please go to the sisters' dormitory and bring all Maria's things to the chapter house, Catarina.'

The nun bowed her head and scurried off. The knights and sergeants, the preceptrix and the two drenched and filthy survivors moved into the chapter house, where lamps had now been lit.

'This is a very worrying turn of events,' the preceptrix announced as she sank into her chair, motioning for the rest to do the same. 'It represents, I believe, a change in the mindset of our opponent. Evidence notwithstanding, I presume we are all in concord that this can only be the work of the Don Ferrer della Cadeneta?'

There was a chorus of murmured agreement and nods all round.

'Then della Cadeneta has now moved on from cajoling and threatening, even via powerful nobles, and through attempted kidnap. But the next step seems clear. He has abandoned such thoughts now and has resigned himself to an attempt to appropriate Sister Titborga's lands following her demise. Since we continue to grant shelter and succour to the dear sister, we therefore place ourselves beside her in the sight of his crossbow. I fear the sand in Rourell's hourglass runs low, brothers and sisters.'

At this bleak appraisal all remained silent, thoughtful and uncomfortable, and a few moments later Catarina entered with a half bow, struggling to hold a blanket-wrapped bundle. At a nod from the preceptrix, she placed the bundle on the floor before them all and unwrapped it. All Maria's possessions, brought with her from Santa Coloma and on horseback from the farmhouse, lay in that pile.

'If Maria has been in contact with someone from outside the preceptory, which now seems likely,' the preceptrix said, 'then she must have been doing so for some time. Perhaps there is a clue in her belongings?'

Catarina began to go through them, removing one item at a time and holding them up for the brothers and sisters to observe. It was sad, watching the life of a girl – a woman, really – reduced merely to a display of a few tatty possessions. There was little of note in there and nothing of particular value, and soon the pile was reduced to just a heap of crumpled garments, most of which had not been worn since her arrival and her donning of the white habit. Still, Catarina continued to hold up the clothing and then, suddenly, as she lifted a pleated bliaut skirt that had been rolled into a ball, something chinked and rattled and fell to the blanket below.

They all peered at it.

A heart-shaped gold locket on a long and delicate chain.

All faces in the room folded into frowns at at the seeming incongruity of this expensive item among a poor maid's belongings. All but two. Arnau and Titborga stared at the locket, then exchanged stunned looks. The last time Arnau had seen that piece of jewellery it had been hanging from the hand of Ferrer della Cadeneta as he stood outside Titborga's room in Santa Coloma. The night he had tried to buy her chastity with a bauble. The night Arnau had almost killed him, and he had almost killed Arnau. The night, he remembered with a shock, that della Cadeneta had raped the maid in the garderobe. Or had that been strictly true? *Had* he forced her? Had he *needed* to? Arnau remembered Maria's face that night as she re-emerged. Not a look of horror or shame as he'd expected. Had she become della Cadeneta's that night? Had she perhaps been his even before? Either way, the locket confirmed the connection.

'She has been della Cadeneta's accomplice,' Titborga said, sadly. 'Don Ferrer tried to give me that locket upon a time, and I refused it. That he gave it to Maria is all the proof I need.'

The preceptrix nodded. 'Pass me it, please, Sister Catarina.' The nun did as she was requested, and Preceptrix Ermengarda clicked open the heart and peered inside. 'A likeness of della Cadeneta,' she confirmed. 'Not a particularly *good* likeness, for it does not exude wickedness like the real thing, but enough for me to be sure. Whether this is enough proof beyond your story or not is a question for better legal minds than mine, though, I think.'

'Preceptrix,' Brother Ramon said quietly, 'I believe the time has come. Della Cadeneta's hirelings have proved themselves men of no conscience, intent on rape, kidnap, incitement, arson and even murder. We all know what comes next. If we are going to send for aid, it must be now. This will be our last opportunity. The forces of the wicked are gathering and Rourell is an island of sanctity amid them. I have the fastest horse at Rourell, and Mateu the second fastest. Give me the papers and the locket and we will ride for Barberà.'

The preceptrix was nodding. 'I fear you are correct, Brother. The moment of decision is upon us, and I do not think we can delay further.'

Lütolf half-rose from his seat. 'Begging your indulgence, Sister, but I would request the opportunity to make this ride. My horse might not be as fast as Brother Ramon's – indeed, I am not sure I even *have* a horse right now – but I owe Cadeneta's men a debt of vengeance.'

'Vengeance is not part of our creed, Brother.'

'Was it not you who told us to take our lead from Exodus and not Matthew, Preceptrix? An eye for an eye over the turning of cheeks? We all know I am the best swordsman in Rourell, and this is simple truth, not unseemly pride. And my squire, Brother Arnau, is intimately involved in the matter. He can bear witness and vouch for the truth as both a secular noble and a man of God. He and I are the clear choice to bear this news and fetch help from Barberà. Please do not deny us this.'

Arnau had initially felt shock and then some nervousness at the idea of leaving the dubious safety of Rourell and riding for the mother house, but as the German spoke, the truth and clarity of his words hit home. They *were* the two who should go.

'I concur,' he said, rising. 'I can stand for Vallbona and Santa Coloma in this matter just as Brother Lütolf can stand for the order.'

There was an uncertain stillness in the room for a moment. The preceptrix turned first to Brother Ramon, who looked unconvinced but shrugged and then nodded, then to Brother Balthesar, who added his own consent with a nod.

'Very well, then.'

'Do we wait for morning?' Arnau asked quietly.

'No,' Lütolf replied. 'Time is now short and things move apace to a cataclysm. With the preceptrix's permission, we will take a quick bite of bread and butter, then arm, saddle up and ride for Barberà.'

He turned to Arnau with a wrinkling of his nose. 'Via somewhere you can wash.'

CHAPTER FIFTEEN

The map had been laid out upon the refectory table, and Arnau studied it with interest. He'd ridden the fields and estates of Rourell several times now over the days he'd been here and not once had it occurred to him to enquire whether there was a map. It was interesting to see how it all fitted together.

Rourell preceptory sat at the heart of the map, a square of fortified piety. It was passed by two roads, one on the western side, running from Vilallonga further south, up through the ridge of hills to the mother house of Barberà and beyond. The other, on the far side of the river to the east, past the burned mill, running south to Tarragona and north to Valls. Twin lines that bound the Rourell estates. And about that map wove the somewhat seasonal Francoli River from the coast, running up the east side of the estate beside the mill, curving around to the north, past the La Selva farmhouse where the trouble had begun, and then off towards the hills north-west where Cadeneta lay.

'There are two crossings,' Brother Lütolf was saying. 'The one on the Barberà road we know has been destroyed. It is possible to work round that and continue north by following the river into the hills and through La Riba, crossing at Montblanc, but that means tackling dangerous hilly regions at night and means we will be circling around Cadeneta for much of that time. I think we can all agree that this would be a foolhardy course to take.'

Arnau nodded, as did Brothers Ramon and Balthesar and the preceptrix.

'Which leaves the longer route. Past the mill, across the river there and north to Valls, then cutting across to the west. This adds perhaps two miles to our journey but has the benefit of taking us further from the area we know della Cadeneta's men have been watching.'

'Although we also know that some of his men were at the mill,' Ramon reminded them.

'True, although that was for a specific purpose.' The German rumbled deep in his throat and tapped his lips thoughtfully before tracing the line of the river north from the mill bridge to the broken one, then back. Partway along, his finger came to rest and he tapped the map. 'There.'

They all peered at the chart, frowning. 'There's no crossing there.'

'No,' the German admitted, 'but there, just beyond the La Selva farm, the river is wide and subject to banks of gravel and reeds. At this time of year a rider can cross the Francoli in most places anyway, so long as he's watchful of what might lie beneath the water to lame a horse. Near the farm there is nothing hidden. The crossing would be easy and shallow. Both bridges have been the focus of della Cadeneta's attention. If we want to make it north without following Carles into paradise, an unknown crossing might be the best choice.'

Arnau nodded. The sense of it was clear, and that seemed to have struck the others too, as they all confirmed their agreement.

'Vallbona, see if Brother Guillem has made the horses ready.'

Arnau, who at less tense times might have bridled at the knight's terse and haughty manner, simply nodded and hurried out to the stables. On the way, he adjusted the hang of the fresh black habit – his daywear one – over his damp skin. He'd not had time for a real bath, given how long it took to fill the wooden tub, but a quick dip in the horse trough had rid him of the soot, at least.

Guillem had saddled Arnau's horse and made her ready, checking the shoes and stirrups. Another mare stood ready, a white one with a thick mane. Arnau helped settle the saddlebags into place and then led the animals out into the night air. It was odd, seeing the preceptory in the deepest night with all the bustle and activity of daytime, and he prayed it stayed safely this way for some time as he stood holding the reins and waiting for the German knight.

Lütolf appeared a moment later, emerging from the refectory fastening his helmet into place and checking the sword at his side.

His mail shushed and chinked as he strode across the ground to the animals and the two sergeants. Approaching them, he reached down to his belt and untied a drawstring bag passing it over to Arnau. The young sergeant took it with a puzzled frown.

'The pendant, the documents and the money for our journey,' the German explained as he hauled himself up into the saddle.

'Me?'

'If we run into trouble, I will be the target of choice, Vallbona, as a full knight. They will assume, correctly, that I am the more dangerous, and they will assume that I hold anything of value, with my sergeant-squire along for support. If the worst happens, you can ride on for Barberà while I buy you time. Understand?'

Arnau did so, and nodded, tucking the container into one of his saddlebags and then pulling himself up into the saddle. 'We can't afford to run into trouble,' he said with a sly smile. 'You'll be for it if you lose another horse.'

The black look he earned from Brother Lütolf made the barbed joke worthwhile, and Arnau was still grinning to himself as they approached the gate and Simo and Guillem removed the bar and let them out into the dark world beyond the preceptory walls. The night felt truly oppressive out here, far from any notion of safety. Arnau had that same tremor of nerves he had felt before the mill, when he'd stepped out alone and decided that he was easy prey for any crossbowman in the area.

'Ride steady,' the German told him, 'not fast. Save the beast's energy for when we might need it.'

The two men trotted lightly across the fields towards the farmhouse where only days ago they had found the grisly scene of the hanged family. The moonlight cast a bright, silver light over everything, and the farmhouse loomed large ahead of them just as the monastery dwindled to a small shape behind. Stark in the bright glow, the farmhouse's arrangement of windows and door suddenly looked oddly skull-like to Arnau, especially given that they lay open and black rather than shuttered as they had been when people still lived there. The place sent shivers through him, partly for the image he had formed in his head and partly through the memories of what had happened there.

He turned his eyes from the place and instead peered off ahead towards the river he knew was perhaps three or four hundred yards beyond, invisible in its shallow valley, hidden by the thick green growth. His eyes rose from that to the distant hills beyond, a blacker line beneath the black sky. Somewhere beyond them lay the mother house. What would happen at Barberà, he wondered? Would they be believed? Supported? Would the master there send knights to aid them? Would he agree to petition the grand master, or the king even, against the villainy of della Cadeneta? This was something of an unknown. Even the German knight did not seem at all sure of what reception to expect, but both men – *all* of Rourell, in fact – had agreed that there was no real alternative. They had come to a time for decisions, and had made one, for good or ill.

Fifteen miles through field and forest, hill and valley, across rivers and past towns. On other days it might have been a pleasant ride.

The young sergeant's eyes were inevitably drawn back to that looming shape ahead and to the left. Eye-socket windows staring at them, dark and lifeless. He shuddered and turned away again.

His heart jumped as Brother Lütolf's horse suddenly screamed and reared. The German knight, caught completely by surprise, tumbled from the back of the beast, his ankle twisting, caught in the stirrup. Arnau watched in horror as the animal dropped back to the ground and Lütolf fell, bouncing on the earth painfully. There was an unpleasant crack from his leg and then the horse was off, running, dragging its rider by the leg.

Arnau panicked. What to do? Why had the horse reared?

He ripped the sword from his scabbard on instinct alone and felt for the shield attached to his saddlebags, his eyes all the time on his companion. By some miracle, despite what had to be a broken leg, the German managed to get his foot from the stirrup and collapsed in a heap on the ground as his latest horse ran off into the darkness, screeching.

Arnau kicked his beast into life and raced towards the German as Lütolf tried to stand. He managed to get to his feet for moments, but then fell with a cry, his ankle giving way beneath him, turned at an unnatural angle. Damn it. A broken ankle not only put the German out of action, it might easily kill him, or at the least end his career as a man of the sword.

Panicking, Arnau reached him and dropped from his horse, running over.

Lütolf turned, seeing the black-clad sergeant hurrying to him, and his face blanched.

'What are you doing?'

'You're injured. You need help.'

'Ride for Barberà, idiot!'

It was then that Arnau realised his mistake. That was precisely what he should have done: as soon as the German was unhorsed, he should have kicked his mount into speed and raced north. Instead, he had dismounted. But there had been no sign of danger. Just a horse that—

He heard the crossbow bolt thrumming through the air and had only the blink of an eye to wonder what dying would feel like before the missile whispered past him and thudded into his horse's head. The beast perished on its feet, with no time even to cry out, slumping to the ground, silent. Arnau stared.

'Run, you fool,' the German snapped, waving a desperate arm.

No. He couldn't run. He couldn't leave Lütolf to his fate. Instead, he reached down and grasped the German's shoulder and helped him upright. Lütolf struggled to push him away, but Arnau held tight.

'You'll get us *both* killed. Run.'

'No.'

The German cried out as they took a step towards the olive press shed, and Arnau changed his footing to ease the pressure.

'I'm done, Vallbona. Get away from here.'

'I can't.' Could he? There was certainly no point in going on without a horse. He could run for Rourell once more, though how long he would last in open ground in bright moonlight he could not guess.

With Brother Lütolf repeatedly berating him for his continued presence and rhythmically whimpering as any pressure was applied to his right foot, the two men shuffled towards the dubious safety of the press house.

Arnau's eyes rose once more to that skull-face of stone and timber.

There was a thud. Lütolf pushed Arnau away from him, and the younger man staggered to one side, almost falling, as the bolt thudded into the German. Roaring with pain, Lütolf lurched forward a pace, sword rasping free of his scabbard as he reeled. Arnau could see the shaft of the bolt, an ash shaft with bright white flights, jutting from his chest, just below the left shoulder. His mind calculated what their positions would be had he not been pushed out of the way, and came to the instant and unpleasant conclusion that Lütolf had saved his life, and that he would otherwise have taken that missile full in the face.

'God's blood!' bellowed the German as he lurched and hopped forward.

There was a horrible silence, and Arnau realised that there was only one crossbowman and he was having to reload between shots.

He ran. For the looming arch of the press shed, and for the German knight, who was between him and it, snarling and shouting as he limped and hopped forward. He reached Lütolf a moment later and could almost feel the unseen archer preparing to shoot once more. Without stopping, he hit the German full pelt, knocking the man forward as he fell, taking care to hold his sword out to one side to prevent injury, keeping his shield between the two of them and those skull windows as much as possible.

The bolt thudded into this shield a heartbeat after they hit the ground, and he felt a searing pain as the tip punched through the linden boards and carved a small nick from his forearm. The German was howling in pain as he tried to get to his feet. In another heartbeat, Arnau went through the last few shots in his mind. The crossbowman had to jam his foot in the stirrup, haul back the string – something that took strength and effort, probably with a hook for the job judging by the power of the bolts – and fish another missile from his quiver, drop it in place, lift and aim. Another count of ten, and the man would be ready again, he reckoned.

Ticking off the seconds in his head, he rose to a crouch, and passed Lütolf, sheathing his sword.

Five.

He grabbed hold of the German's arms and began to pull him unceremoniously through the dirt towards the press shed.

'What are you doing, you fool? Run!' Lütolf said again.

Two.

One.

More. Either he'd mistimed it or the man was slower this time.

Two.

Three.

Thud. The bolt slammed into the prone German's already ruined leg, punching straight through muscle and bone and drawing a cry of agony from his lips. But then they were disappearing into the shelter of the shed, the welcoming darkness defying any archer's eye. He rattled out apologies as he dragged the knight, the fresh bolt head catching repeatedly on the ground as they moved, making his shattered leg bounce and dance about, bringing him fresh and constant agony.

'We're safe,' he breathed with relief.

'We are not safe, you idiot.'

Arnau could hear them then. More than one voice and the clatter of armour and weapons. There was more than a lone crossbowman, then. They had simply not come out into the open for fear of getting between the archer and his prey. But now the two Templars were hidden from missiles, it would be the turn of the footmen.

Damn it.

'Where is the bag?' Lütolf hissed, tears of pain running down his face. Arnau's heart chilled. He'd been so busy worrying about the wounded German he'd not given a moment's thought to the bag of documents and evidence. Now those all-important records were still in the saddlebags of his dead horse, out in the open and in full view of the crossbowman.

'Shit.'

'You left them with your horse?' the German said, wide-eyed in disbelief. 'You reach new heights of foolishness, Vallbona.'

He would have liked to take offence at that, but the simple fact was that Brother Lütolf was absolutely correct. Since the moment the German's horse had bucked, Arnau had made a string of utterly idiotic decisions. And now they were trapped in a shed awaiting death at the hand of bandits, while the documents they needed to protect above all sat on a dead horse far from here.

'Shit, shit, shit, shit.'

'Get the documents and go to the preceptory.'

'I—'

'If you argue with me on this, Vallbona, when I pass the gates of blessed Saint Peter I shall have them locked against you for all time. Get the bag and get back to Rourell. I care not how you do it. Just go.'

Arnau stared helplessly at the wounded German. His white habit with the red cross was now mostly crimson across the torso from the chest wound. Between that and the pulverised leg, Lütolf was done for, and they both knew it. Still, despite the vast differences between the two of them, Arnau felt a tearing at his heartstrings at the thought of losing the overly pious German. He hated the man in a way, but by God he would miss hating the man.

'There,' Lütolf said, pointing across the dark interior of the shed. At the far side, a small square of silvery light denoted an opening in the wall. 'Go, and God go with you, for there is no place for him here.'

Arnau stared, still unable to pull himself away.

'Go,' commanded the German in a compelling voice.

Arnau scampered away through the darkness, snapping off the white-flighted bolt jutting from his shield as he went. He reached the wall moments later. It was an egress for water. Gathered in a large tank outside, it was channelled through the wall into a smaller container inside, presumably part of the processing of the oil. He could see moonlight reflecting off the liquid surface and, for the second time that night, dropped into cold water. As he stooped to pull his way through, he heard a cry of pain and looked back to see Lütolf upright, leaning on the doorframe with his sword drawn. The man was shouting now, in his native tongue.

'Herr, höre meine Stimme! Im Blut der Gottlosen gebadet, werde ich meinen Beistand im Haus Gottes finden – also gewähre mir Rache!'

Arnau, regret cascading through his soul, pushed his way through the wall, losing sight of the German and emerging once more into the open, out of sight of the farmhouse frontage. In the distance, across the shed, he could still hear the German bellowing, though now he had reverted from his native language.

'The Lord governeth me, and nothing shall fail to me; in the place of pasture there he hath set me. He nourished me on the water of refreshing.'

Arnau blinked back tears. Never had he heard the beautiful, powerful twenty-third Psalm spoken thus, as a lament in the face of death, and it pulled yet more of his heartstrings free. Trying not to picture the scene, and entirely failing, he moved to the corner of the shed. He would be in view of the windows for long moments as he went for the horse. He could see the saddlebags from here.

'He converted my soul,' Brother Lütolf's voice went on. 'He led me forth on the paths of rightfulness; for his name. For why though I shall go in the midst of shadow of death; I shall not dread evils, for thou art with me.'

The last strain of his voice was lost beneath a metallic clang as swords met. Arnau, heart in his throat, peered around the corner. Four men were pressing into the doorway of the shed. Even as he watched, one of them staggered backwards, crying out, clutching his belly where, in the moonlight, Arnau could just make out his guts sliding free like coils of rope. Mortally wounded and leaning on a wall for support, still the German was formidable.

They were busy. The crossbowman might not be. Perhaps he was even now running to join them, bow discarded, rondel dagger in hand. Whatever the case, the Templars were out of time, and whatever grace the dying German was buying him would soon dissipate.

He ran. As he emerged into the open, knowing that it would be moments only before those fighting men realised he was there, he began to swerve this way and that, zigzagging wildly. His caution paid off as a crossbow bolt hummed through the air and thudded into the ground where he had been a moment earlier. *Shit*. He began to count through the reload once more.

Twenty-two…

He reached the horse and dived over it, shield held safely to the side. There, with the dead beast between him and the farmhouse, he reached over the bulky corpse, pulling his shield back in the way, and began to open the saddlebag.

Eleven…

Fishing inside, he found the bag and tried to pull it free, though it caught on something. Desperately, he pulled, cursing the bag and begging the good Lord.

Four…

It ripped free a moment later and as he hauled on it the sack tore, the money and the locket falling back into the saddlebag, lost from sight. He cursed like the worst sinner.

The next crossbow bolt thudded into his shield, narrowly missed impaling Arnau's hand in the process, and instead punched deep into the dead meat of the horse, pinning his shield to it.

Twenty-two…

With difficulty, he slid his grip free of the pinned shield and used both hands to grasp the leather-bound document wallet that was even now falling out of the bag.

Twelve…

He dropped back behind the horse's body and breathed heavily. What now?

He could hear furious fighting at the shed door, but the screaming was all coming from one throat.

Six…

He lifted his head to look across the beast and could see that the three men at the shed were now hacking and stabbing at a figure prone on the floor in the doorway, their companion sitting on the ground nearby and staring down at his own intestines in horror.

Lütolf of Ehingen was no more.

Arnau was on foot and without a shield, enough open ground around him that it would be difficult to cross without taking a bolt in the back. As if to confirm that, another missile thudded into the saddle inches above his head.

The Francoli. The river was the only answer. It was low-lying, below the level of the farmland, filled with reeds, bushes, trees and dense undergrowth. If he could get to it, he would be able to stay out of sight all the way back, or at least until he was close enough that he could make a last short dash to safety.

Twenty-two…

He rose and ran. The man on the ground clutching his belly was far too preoccupied to care. The other three footmen were busy hacking apart the body of the Templar in the olive press shed's doorway. The archer was probably yelling a warning to his fellows, but with all the noise of their furious butchering and the screaming and wailing of the gut-wounded man, he would be hard to hear. Arnau ran like he had never run before, barely daring to breathe. He was past the shed and hurtling off away from the farmhouse, heading north, before he even realised he was out of sight of them all and temporarily safe.

Still, he did not break his stride. He could see the line of the river just ahead, a wide, shallow depression filled with grass and undergrowth, a few banks of shale and a pitiful flow of water at the centre. In the late winter with the thaw-water from the lower foothills of the Pyrenees, this river would be both wide and deep. Not so now.

Something hissed past his ear and his eyes bulged as the crossbow bolt thudded into the bark of a tree just ahead. The archer had moved to one of the building's rear windows. Why had Arnau not anticipated that? Damn it.

Once more he broke into a zigzag run, counting off seconds as he did so. As the next bolt came, he reached the bank and half-ran, half-fell down it into the vegetation.

Wasting no time, he immediately rose and turned to his right, pushing past an ancient tree and stumbling along the turf close to the water. The world of the farm was lost to sight, which meant he was now safe from the constant missiles at least. Likely the footmen were coming, but he had a good head start. Breathing heavily, he pounded off to the south-east, following the course downstream, back towards the burned-out mill almost a mile away.

He had gone some distance when he heard the shouts of men at the riverbank, arguing about where he had gone. He worried for a moment that they might hear him, but quickly dismissed the concern. All he could hear of them was angry raised voices. The only sound he was making was the thud of feet on turf and mud, and those would not be audible that far back. Out of sight around the wide curve and through endless greenery, he was as good as clear as long as he kept running and made sure not to stray onto the gravel that would betray his footsteps.

Breath coming in heaved gasps, feet weary and sore as they pounded along, he counted off the paces as he ran. Once, as he moved around the huge curving course of the river, he rose along the bankside a little to avoid an area of pooled water and gravel, and caught a momentary glimpse of the walls of Rourell, rising like the gates of heaven in the darkness.

It felt as though he'd been running forever, though it could not in truth have been more than fifteen or twenty minutes, even given the difficult terrain, but his heart eased and relief flooded him at the sight of the burned-out shell of the mill rising on the riverbank ahead, smoke still pouring from the charring ruin into the sky. Here, he clambered up the slope, fearing to come too close to the mill in case others awaited action there. Heart pounding, he cut directly across the farmland in between, making for the welcoming glow of the preceptory.

He reached the south gate and pounded on it only twice before the large portal swung open. The inset door, he noted as he staggered inside, was now barred and nailed since the loss of one of the keys. Simo shut the gate behind him and barred it, and Guillem hurried to help as Arnau fell to his knees, exhausted, in the courtyard. Moments later, doors were opening and men and women in black and white were hurtling out towards him.

Ramon was there, and Balthesar, Mateu was trying to help him up. Then, as he started to recover and looked up, there was the concerned face of Preceptrix Ermengarda.

'Brother Lütolf?'

Arnau shook his head sadly. Finally finding his breath, he proffered the documents in shaking hands. 'Crossbowman at the Granja de la Selva, along with other brigands. Lütolf and his horse took the first two bolts, my own horse the third. I reached safety with Brother Lütolf but it was too late. He couldn't walk and had been struck in the chest.'

'Lord above,' Ramon breathed in shock.

Arnau flinched, knowing that he'd not told all the tale yet and realising that he would be due plenty of penance for not revealing how his own stupidity had cost him the horse and the chance to ride on to Barberà. He would pay for that, no doubt, in due course.

'I managed to save the papers, but everything else was lost. They had men in the farmhouse. Brother Lütolf took one with him, even mortally wounded. Bought time for me to flee along the river back here.'

The preceptrix smacked her hands together angrily. 'This is my fault.'

'No, Sister,' Ramon began, but she held up a hand to cut him off.

'Mea culpa, Brother. I sent the two of you on this doomed errand, despite knowing what had happened on previous attempts to leave Rourell and make it to Barberà. I should have taken my warning from the precedent, and yet like a fool I still sent you. Barberà is cut off from us. We are alone, I think.'

Any further conversation was cut short by the dinging of the bell atop the tower. All looked up to see Luis leaning over the parapet.

'A fire!' he bellowed, pointing off to the north.

'Come,' the preceptrix said, gesturing to Arnau and the two white-clad knights, then hurried over to the belfry, pulled open the door and began to climb the stairs within. Arnau was immediately behind her, and the others following as they climbed. It was the first time Arnau had been up the tower, and as they emerged at the top he had a moment of vertigo at the view, head reeling, stomach flipping as his knees turned to liquid. This was worse than being in the mill's rafters by some stretch.

'Show me,' the preceptrix said to Brother Luis, scanning the dark countryside around them, but as Arnau's senses recovered and he also looked about himself, gripping the parapet for support, he had no need for Luis to point it out. A campfire had burst into life at the farmhouse of La Selva.

'But look,' Luis breathed in anguished tones, pointing east now. There, another blaze had begun close to the burned-out mill – on the bridge itself, by Arnau's estimation. He spun, and his stomach lurched again. Another fire was sparking into life where Rourell's access track met the main road. With sinking spirits, he turned slowly. More fires were bursting into life here and there. Within another minute there were a score of them all around, circling the preceptory – on the road, by the river, in the fields and farmhouses. Arnau felt a chill fill him from the floor up despite the warmth of the summer night air.

'Brothers,' the preceptrix said, her voice a troubled whisper, 'I fear we are under siege.'

PART FOUR: TEMPLE

CHAPTER SIXTEEN

How much time had passed, Arnau couldn't say. The preceptory had exploded into a flurry of activity following the revelation at the tower top, and Arnau had expected to be given immediate and important tasks, but as a new arrival with no specific remit he seemed to be temporarily overlooked, no one asking anything of him. Consequently he hurried around, lending a hand when anyone shouted. He was immensely grateful when the preceptrix called a *consejo de guerra sagrada* – a council of war – in the chapter house and he suddenly had something official to do.

'We are in a weak position,' Ermengarda d'Oluja said with that same gravitas as any king or noble planning a Crusade against the infidel. 'Rourell was briefly a house of twenty-one souls, though since we have lost Brothers Carles and Lütolf, and poor deluded Maria, we are now eighteen. We cannot know how many there are of the enemy, but there are more of their campfires than we are people, which suggests a dreadful math.'

All nodded at this. In recent encounters,the thugs of della Cadeneta had numbered anywhere from four to a dozen. That suggested perhaps two hundred men facing them in all.

'Moreover,' the preceptrix added, 'eight of us are women, children, or old men. And do not be mistaken – I run this house as any general commands an army, and I will not be disobeyed or bargained with, but my arms are simply not made by God for the swinging of a sword.'

Arnau's impression was rather different, and he noted the way the preceptrix's eyes fell upon her husband's blade hanging on the wall while she spoke, even as she openly dismissed the notion of wielding it.

'Nor,' she continued, 'are Simo's, or any of the sisters – the *consorors*. Even Father Diego's time to swing a sword is now sadly passed. We are hopelessly undermanned. I have planned my last throw of the dice and, while I will not tell you what I roll or where, we cannot rely upon its efficacy. Therefore while eight of us are not made for rude war, we must needs be prepared to raise what arms we can against the enemy. We must fight to the last – man, woman and child, we will defend Rourell, for we are sons and daughters of the Lord God and of Saint Mary and we will *not* submit to the wiles of the wicked. It might be that very stance which has brought this upon us, and some might have turned away those who brought trouble to Rourell. Not us. We are the Poor Knights of Christ and the Temple of Solomon, and we SHALL PREVAIL!'

This last was shouted like a war cry, and even in the desperate circumstances, Arnau felt the power and pull of it.

'Brother Balthesar, you will see to the fortification and preparation of the preceptory against attack. Luis will see to the arms and equipment. Those of us who cannot supply a sword arm can surely lend our strength and our will in other ways. Everyone will deal with their usual roles, but must place themselves at the disposal of Balthesar and Luis, should they require us for anything. Brother Guillem, I would like you to remain behind for now. Everyone else, be about your work. Prepare for battle.'

Arnau stepped out and looked up into the indigo vault of heaven. The night was almost past and dawn close. It was hard to imagine anything other than a lazy summer's day was coming to Rourell. He sighed.

'Regrets, Brother?'

He looked around to see Mateu standing beside him, stretching.

'Always. And in droves. But not about coming here, other than for bringing this to your doorstep. To save one girl, we may have condemned a whole monastery.'

'That is not the way to think of it, Arnau de Vallbona. Had we been uneasy at the idea of taking you in and standing against the wicked, we could easily have turned you away. But that is not the way of the order. Our very function is to protect the innocent from the wicked. It was for that purpose the great Hugues de Payens sought the *creation* of the Templars. Who would we be if we turned away a stricken woman for our own safety?'

Arnau nodded. 'Still the guilt rides me.' The silence suggested that Mateu had no answer for guilt.

'Guillem is busy with the preceptrix,' Brother Ramon said suddenly, right behind them. 'So I want you two to go to the stables and prepare your horses, as well as mine and Miquel's. Then go to the armoury and get yourself armed for battle. Meet me back by the west gate as soon as you are done.'

Arnau frowned at the knight. 'What are you planning, Brother?'

'I intend to put the fear of God into the enemy, Vallbona. I, you two and Miquel. The rest will be busy.'

'The preceptrix wants us to be on hand for Brother Balthesar,' Mateu reminded him.

'Balthesar has enough people to move carts and lift sacks without us. We will not be long, but I want to give the enemy something to think on. Get moving. Horses and armour.'

Sharing a worried look, the two sergeants hurried over to the stables, found their steeds, as well as those of Miquel and Ramon, and began to tack them up.

'Is this a good idea?' Arnau murmured as he adjusted his saddle. 'I mean, Brother Ramon hasn't checked with the preceptrix, has he? And the rule of Rourell is hers entirely.'

Mateu shrugged. 'You'll get used to Brother Ramon. He's a little… unpredictable… sometimes, but he's shrewd, and the preceptrix trusts him utterly. If he believes we should rile the enemy a little, he's almost certainly correct.'

Arnau wasn't so sure. In his opinion, when you were wielding only a pointy stick and surrounded by a pack of hungry wolves, the *last* thing you did was leap at one and poke it in the face. Still, he had been given instructions by a brother of the Temple, and was not about to shirk his duty. Plus, despite his worries, there was a deep, parched thirst for revenge in his soul that needed assuaging. These men had killed Brother Lütolf, and little would give Arnau more pleasure than gutting the man responsible.

The horses ready and tethered near the stable doorway, Arnau and Mateu hurried across to the armoury. Miquel was already there, his sandy hair soaked with sweat where it poked out from the mail coif around the side of his face. Together they armoured and then fastened on their sword belts, took their maces, shields and lances.

'You won't need the sticks,' Brother Ramon said as he hurried through the door, already armoured and ready, and grabbed his shield. 'We need to be quick and precise but also flexible and prepared for anything. Hard to be flexible with ten feet of wood tucked under your arm. Come on. We need to be fast. Dawn is upon us and I want to strike while we still have the poor light on our side.'

They were out in the courtyard a moment later and hurrying across to their horses, attracting surprised glances from the other occupants of Rourell as they passed. Arnau hurried inside the stable and grasped the reins, preparing to lead the horses out into the pre-dawn air. He noted with interest the empty stall nearby where Guillem's own horse was kept, as the man in charge of the place. With a shrug, he dismissed the absence and led the beasts out of the stable.

Mounting swiftly, they walked their mounts out towards the west gate where Simo and Lorenç were busy gathering timber and nails and mallets, preparing, presumably, to seal the great timber portal.

'Where are you lot going?' demanded an authoritative voice, and they turned to see Brother Balthesar crossing the yard towards them.

'Leave one gate for a little longer, Balthesar,' Ramon said.

'What are you planning?' the white-haired knight asked, eyes narrowed suspiciously.

'To put a pin beneath the enemy's backside, Balthesar. They are altogether too confident right now, and that worries me. I would like to shake their faith in easy victory.'

The older brother stood for a moment, scratching his chin, then finally nodded. 'Perhaps you're right, Ramon. We'll hold the gate until you return, but mind that you do so. No foolish heroics. Put the fear of Jesu into them and then get back here straight away. We've lost Lütolf. I will not relish holding vespers and vigil for another departed brother.'

The older man nodded to Simo, who pulled open the gate. The four men, one in glorious white, the other three in the black habits of sergeants, emerged into the gloom. There was a growing mauve tint to the darkness as the sun's appearance neared, but the enemy campfires still burned low, almost extinguished, marking out the camps' positions.

'We need to be Odysseus and Diomedes,' Ramon said, 'attacking Dolon and the Thracians tonight. Or Brennus leading the Gauls into unsuspecting Rome, perhaps. But we should take more care. I do not want to be thwarted by geese like the Gauls or mess around duelling heroically like Odysseus. Straight in, kill like a laughing butcher, then straight out.'

They all nodded. 'Do you have a plan, Brother?' Miquel asked as they started to pick up pace a little, heading for the twinkling light where the track met the main road.

'Ride in, kill villains, ride out,' Ramon said, simply. 'Be flexible. Be careful. Do not land yourself in danger and do not get yourself entangled or trapped. Ride through their camp and cut and kill, then turn and ride back doing the same. If by the time we have made two sweeps they are getting themselves together, we ride for Rourell. If they are still disorganised, we might try another strike. No singing or shouting, though. Stay silent. A silent enemy is a frightening one, for they cannot as easily be identified and numbered. And we do not want other camps rushing to cut off our escape due to the noise. Are we all clear?'

There was an affirmative chorus.

'Good, because we need to go now. The sun is almost here, and they will hear and see us coming shortly. Put hoof to stone at speed. Ride.'

The four men kicked their horses into a faster pace, breaking from a trot into a canter. Then, as they covered half the distance to the main road and their objective, they moved up to a gallop. Ramon, Miquel and Mateu drew their swords, shields settled in place with those hands also holding the reins. Remembering Lütolf's scathing remarks, Arnau almost followed suit, but still found himself unhooking the mace from his saddle and looping the leather thong around his wrist. Old habits were hard to break, and he wasn't wholly sure he really *wanted* to break this one.

The enemy camp was sheltered by the dotted trees of a disorderly olive grove with thick grass beneath, just to the far side of the junction. Even in the dim glow of pre-dawn, Arnau could see the shapes of their tents cast into stark shadow by the low golden glow of the dying fire. There was not a sign of movement, though it would be a foolish force who had not left even one pair of eyes on the night landscape beyond the fire. Arnau found himself praying to the good Lord that the brigands in the pay of della Cadeneta were so sure of themselves in their overwhelming numbers that they could not envisage danger and had left insufficient guard.

Brother Ramon directed the attack in silence, beneath just the drum of sixteen hooves. His sword jabbed towards Mateu and then out left. Towards Miquel and right. Towards Arnau and forward.

The lookout was asleep.

Arnau grinned and threw his thanks up to God. The man in the drab brown tunic, his shield propped against the rock upon which he sat and his sword still sheathed, blinked awake in shock at the thunder of hooves so close. He rose, wide-eyed and desperate, hand going to the hilt of his sword as he opened his mouth to yell a warning to his fellows.

He got as far as 'Ah— urk,' as Ramon's sword took him in the side of the neck, robbing him of life and cutting through windpipe and gullet in the process, ending his warning before it began. The man fell in a heap, hand still on the undrawn sword.

Mateu and Miquel disappeared now on the other side of the nearest tents, and Arnau followed the knight as he passed between two more and into the ring by the campfire. Their luck had been astonishing for its element of surprise, but before they could begin to cause havoc, a second picket, sitting on the far side, somewhere in the olive grove, began to yell.

The commotion kicked in an instant later. Voices called from the tents in a panic, accompanied by the distinctive sounds of people arming themselves in a hurry. Ramon glanced over his shoulder at Arnau and used his sword to indicate the second watchman out in the field.

'Kill that one.'

As Arnau nodded and galloped past the knight, skirting the glowing remains of the night's fire, Brother Ramon began God's work. A bandit, drawn by the commotion, emerged from his tent, sword in hand, and barely had time to straighten and look up before his face sprouted three feet of gleaming steel. Ramon reined in his horse, wrenching his blade back from the brigand's head, twisting it as he did to ease its withdrawal. The man, dead before he could land a blow, toppled back into his tent doorway, earning a cry of shock from a fellow within. Ramon, sharp-eared, estimated the location of the voice, drove his mount three steps around the tent and slammed his blade through the canvas. He was rewarded with a meaty thud and a scream as the man whose shout had betrayed his location even in the gloom died without even leaving his tent.

Arnau watched all this in the blink of an eye as he passed through the camp, making an almost cursory swipe at a body emerging from a tent and being rewarded with a grunt of pain. He'd not killed the brigand, but had left a mark the man would remember him by if he lived.

Then he was in the trees.

The second lookout had been watching the dreadful events unfold in his camp, trembling. He'd picked up his shield and drawn his own sword, standing beside a gnarled log upon which he'd been sitting, but the sounds of butchery and death, and the sudden sight of a black-clad Templar on a horse bearing down on him was too much.

He ran.

Arnau, briefly, considered turning and riding back, leaving the man. He was only one cowardly thug, after all. But somehow the memory of having let those two red-tunicked men of della Cadeneta flee into another treeline so many days ago robbed him of the will to abandon pursuit. He charged, picking up speed once more.

The man hurtled between the olive trees, casting away his shield as an unnecessary encumbrance and trying to put as many twisted ancient trunks between him and his black-clad pursuer as possible. Arnau was having none of it this time. He'd let those men go that once. He'd not had the chance to strike the men who attacked Maria. He'd had to flee the farmhouse and leave the men who'd killed the German knight to their wicked victory. Not this time.

Ignoring the whipping of branches against his mail, habit and skin, he ducked low to reduce the chances of being unhorsed and bore down on the terrified lookout, who as he ran was beseeching God at the top of his voice to help him.

'God has no mercy for the wicked,' Arnau snarled as he rounded an ancient bole and found himself less than ten paces from the desperate bandit.

'Please,' the man begged, head turning to implore Arnau for mercy even as his legs carried him onwards.

The Lord was with the Templar, needless to say. Without his eyes on the path ahead, the man's foot caught a half-buried root and he stumbled. He did not fall, for all his momentum and desperation, but slipped into a strange circling lope as he tried to retain his footing, even unbalanced as he was.

Arnau's mace swung out and struck the back of the man's head.

The result was appalling even to the young horseman. The villain was bare-headed, and the mace's iron points smashed through the skull as though it were little more than eggshell, mashing the brain within and peppering it with shards of broken white bone.

The body continued loping forward for a moment, conscious will ripped away but maintaining momentum. Then, in a graceless tangle, the figure slumped to the ground, spilling brain and mush and blood out onto the dark grass.

Arnau felt his gorge rise at the sight, turned his head away from the twitching, spasming corpse with half a head. Hardening himself, he remembered how these men and their devious master were responsible not only for this mess as a whole, but also specifically for the death of two brothers of the Temple.

Wheeling his horse and leaving the dreadful shaking mess in the grass, Arnau put heel to flank and rode back for the camp.

The sun suddenly put in its first appearance, a blade of bright light cutting across the world.

Moving at a slightly more careful pace now, swerving around trees, Arnau reached the camp to find the job all but done. As he emerged from the trees, he could see that a few of the brigands had managed to arm and gather in a small group, backs to one another. Seemingly Ramon had deemed it sensible to continue the fight after their first sweep, since all three of them were there, two men in black and one in white, hacking and slashing at the small group of desperate defenders, all that remained of a camp taken horribly unawares in the dark.

Arnau saw it from his vantage point away from the fight, and his blood ran cold.

Not again.

Almost a repeat of the death of his lord Berenguer. Ramon and Mateu were busy smashing steel into desperate flesh, and Miquel was with them in the fight, but from here Arnau could see death closing in on the sergeant in charge of the mill. One of the fallen, presumed dead, was rising unsteadily to his feet, clutching at a wound, but with wicked blade in hand, right behind the Templar.

'Miquel!' Arnau bellowed at the top of his voice, urgently, once more kicking his steed into a thundering pace, desperate to stop what he could see coming.

The sergeant heard the shout, turned in surprise, looking for the source of his called name. The fallen bandit struck, his blade slamming into Miquel's unprepared side. Arnau felt a tiny thrill of hope. He'd seen such sword wounds plenty of times, and even from a distance, it looked as though the armour had repelled the blow. At least, if the blade had penetrated Miquel's mail hauberk, it had not been the deep and direct killing blow the bandit had intended. With God's grace, Miquel would survive the attack.

The sergeant, taken completely off guard by the stab, yelped in pain, suggesting that the blow had been at least partly successful.

Miquel turned, attempting to bring his own sword down on the already wounded thug, but the pain in his side was too much and he cried out, and instead tried to dance his horse around. But Arnau was there. Leaping two fallen bodies and a planted spear, he leaned left in the saddle, grunting at the ache this brought in his own stitched cut there, and swept out with his mace. The iron head, still coated in the hair and gore of the watchman, slammed into the bandit's arm just below the shoulder, snapping it like dry, brittle kindling. The man screamed, sword falling from his hand, and collapsed to the ground.

'Time to go,' shouted Brother Ramon, his concerned gaze levelled at this latest incident. Arnau, ignoring the howling man he'd just ruined, pulled in next to Miquel as the four of them made to depart the camp. The black habit at the man's side was ripped, and Arnau could see the shattered links of the broken mail beneath, turned gleaming red with the man's blood. His heart skipped but, as the man hissed in pain, Arnau noted the brightness of the blood, which gave him hope. A damaged liver produced dark blood, and the blade would be unlikely to have cut the bowel so close to the sergeant's side.

They broke from the villains' camp and hurtled back along the access track at breakneck pace on rapidly tiring horses, making for the walls of Rourell, which now glowed a welcoming golden brown in the dawn sun amid the still-dark fields below.

They were perhaps halfway back to the preceptory when the alarms began to sound throughout the surrounding camps in response to their raid. Enveloped in the din, they reached the walls of the preceptory just as Simo and Lorenç wrenched the gate wide open. The four men rode in and came to a halt. Simo and Lorenç slipped the locking bar in place and then began, with the latter's twin brother helping, to move barrels and tables in front of the timber, blocking it and bolstering it against damage.

Preceptrix Ermengarda had two of the sisters with her in the centre of the courtyard, both struggling under the weight of quivers of quarrels. Titborga and Carima. The four men slid from their saddles, and as he did so Miquel squawked at the pain in his side and dropped his shield to clutch his ribs. The preceptrix, eyes suddenly sharp and concerned, moved towards them, beckoning to Carima.

'How is it?' she asked, approaching Miquel, who carefully, gingerly, lifted the habit out from the wound, tearing the black cloth to make the hole larger and display the broken mail and torn flesh beneath. There was quite a bit of blood.

'Carima?'

The Jewish-blooded sister hurried to the sergeant's side, dropping the quivers to the ground in the process, and started to wipe away blood carefully with her white habit. She frowned at the wound beneath.

'Worse than Vallbona's, I'm afraid. Debilitating for now. I will need to clean out the wound, as there are metal and cloth fragments inside that will fester and cause rot. Then he must be stitched and bound. But I believe his organs to be intact. As long as fever does not take him Brother Miquel should recover, but he will be of no use in the coming days.' She turned from the preceptrix to the wounded Brother. 'We will go to your dormitory. I will stitch you there and settle you for the time being. You must not stand or even rise to a seated position without consulting me first. Do you understand?'

Arnau marvelled at the authority in the sister's voice. What was it about the women of Rourell that made them more fearsome and more commanding than any Crusader lord surrounded by men at arms?

The young sister turned to her mistress for confirmation, and Ermengarda nodded. It was, of course, as forbidden for a nun to enter the male dormitory as it was the other way around, but when it came to the practical application of medical care, the preceptrix was not about to let a man suffer for a simple rule. Besides, the chances of any of the men spending time in there with her at the moment were rather small.

Miquel and Carima made their way across the courtyard, the former grunting with every step, the latter fussing over him and sending Simo for her medical bag. The preceptrix took two more steps and stopped in front of Brother Ramon.

'Tell me it was worth it.'

'It is never worth seeing a comrade wounded, Sister,' Ramon replied seriously.

'Quite. But since there is nothing we can do about that, did you achieve success in your endeavour?'

Brother Ramon nodded. 'I believe so. We killed more than twelve of them and put the fear of God in them. You can hear the alarm going around their camps even now.'

'You are aware that this act might precipitate an attack earlier than we might otherwise expect?'

'Yes, Preceptrix. But it is a calculated risk. We may have spurred things on and brought forward the coming cataclysm, but in doing so we have made several subtle changes to the enemy. Their confidence will be shaken. They have lost a dozen men, which means a dozen fewer to climb these walls. They will no longer be calm and confident. They will be watchful and alert, which means they are not getting as much rest and preparation as they were. And we have got the measure of them. They may be numerous, but they are not soldiers. I do not fear their approach as I would the men at arms of Cadeneta. In being forced to rely upon mercenaries for appearances' sake, he has by necessity scraped the bottom of the barrel.'

'And I have cast my dice,' the preceptrix said mysteriously. 'I hope you are right.'

'And those?' Ramon asked, gesturing at Carima's quivers of bolts that Titborga was struggling to gather up with her own burden.

'Yes?'

'The crossbows are meant to be used against the Moor when in battle, Sister. You know the laws. The Pope banned their use against Christians decades ago.'

Preceptrix Ermengarda levelled a look at Ramon that brooked no argument. 'I find that I could, with ease of conscience, argue that the men against whom we stand can make no claim to Christianity. The murder of ordained knights, a woman in the habit of a nun, and converted Moorish workers. These are not the acts of a Christian. And given that they are preparing to lay siege to a house of the Lord, I doubt there is a lawyer across Iberia, be he priest or squire, who would deny me their use.'

Ramon nodded slowly. 'I concur. These men represent the sendings of the Devil. They are no servants of the Lord.' His expression was suddenly businesslike. 'How many do we have, again?'

'Eight bows. Plenty of bolts.'

'Balthesar and I can deploy them effectively. Where is he?'

The preceptrix turned and lifted her gaze to the top of the belfry.

'Let's join him, Sister,' Ramon said, then added 'The horses. I don't see Guillem. Mateu, get them stabled for me.'

Mateu nodded, grasped the reins of all four horses, two in each hand, and began to lead them towards the stables. The knight and the preceptrix wandered off towards the tower, and Titborga, having abandoned her attempt to carry everything at once, disappeared with half the quivers. Arnau found himself standing alone in the courtyard, free of orders and with everyone else busy. He'd not been given specific instructions, and though he was certain Ramon had meant him to help Mateu stable the horses, since the command had not been given he struggled for a moment with his conscience. Curiosity won out over duty and he hurried off in the wake of Ramon and the preceptrix, entering the dark stairwell of the tower and following them up.

When he emerged at the top, he found Balthesar with Luis as well as the two he had followed. The older knight and the squire had placed two crates by the west and north parapets, a crossbow lying on each. Beside each crate stood two quivers, each with near a dozen bolts.

'How long have we got?' the preceptrix asked, and Arnau's gaze rose from the deadly weapons and their ammunition to look out across Rourell's landscape.

'Not long,' Balthesar said in a breathy whisper. 'See, they amass already.'

Arnau squinted. Sure enough, he could see a camp out in the fields towards the farmhouse, and the men – perhaps a score of them or more – were gathering at the near edge of the camp while a companion doused the remains of their fire. The same scene was playing out all about them as they moved around the parapet.

'Where have you placed the other crossbows?' Ramon asked his fellow knight.

'One in the window above the south gate. There is not room for more than one man to shoot there. One by the west gate on a platform we have made of crates and barrels. One on the roof of the chapter house. One in each necessarium. The windows there have limited visibility, but there are plenty of them. The other I have not yet placed.'

Ramon shook his head. 'The necessaria are a poor choice, Brother. Place a second at each gate. If there is inadequate room for two men to shoot simultaneously, then they can take turns and stagger their shots, speeding up the barrage. And, though it might be sacrilege, have one of the smaller windows knocked out in the chapel's north end. There will be a good field of view from there. Other than that you've got it covered well, I think. I especially like this vantage point.'

Brother Balthesar nodded. 'Good, since I have you placed here.' Arnau thought the knight might argue, preferring to be somewhere he could put his sword arm to use. Certainly Lütolf would have done so. Instead, the younger of the two knights nodded. 'Agreed. Mateu with me?'

'No. Only three men are experienced with the weapon: you, Mateu and Father Diego.'

Arnau blinked, trying to imagine the ancient, mad-looking priest wielding a crossbow. Even in his head the image was laughable. Brother Ramon must have read something in his expression, for he turned with a smile. 'Father Diego was once a knight too, you know. More deadly than any of us. He was one of the victors at Santarem over a dozen years ago, before he settled for a more peaceful life. But he will wield one of these in each hand before he will let the dirty boot of those curs out there sully the floor of his church.' He turned back to Balthesar. 'So where?'

'Given your decisions, Mateu at the south gate and Father Diego at the west, each of them with a less trained man they can support. And Lorenç and Ferrando at the other positions – they may not be experienced, but both men have a good eye and a steady hand.'

'And here?'

Balthesar pointed past Ramon, at Arnau.

'Me?'

'I presume you've no experience with a crossbow?'

'I've never even held one.'

'Then you're going to have to learn fast,' Ramon said with that same smile. 'Because you and I are in the eyrie, Brother Arnau. We have the best seats at the whole performace.'

Around them, the camps having disgorged their denizens, the mercenary army of Ferrer della Cadeneta began to close in on the monastery.

CHAPTER SEVENTEEN

Arnau's heart thundered. How could there be so many low-life mercenaries and bandits in Iberia? Certainly della Cadeneta must have recruited every thug, drunk and outlaw across Catalunya and Aragon, for the forces of the enemy flooded across the fields towards Rourell like a tide of unwashed and hostile humanity. Admittedly, they were more of a shapeless mob than an organised army, running wild, brandishing weapons of all varieties, dressed in drab and colourless garments and with little in the way of armour. But the sheer *number* of them was daunting.

The young sergeant lifted his crossbow and weighed it. It was heavier than he'd expected. For some reason, since it was constructed of wood and not iron like his sword and mace, he'd expected it to be lighter. If anything it was *more* weighty.

He waited nervously, watching the enemy closing on the walls. Still, Brother Ramon had not readied himself. Then, out of the corner of his eye, he spotted movement from his companion at the north side, and he turned to watch. Instead of preparing his bow as Arnau had expected, the knight dug into a large pouch at his belt and withdrew a flask. Surely not now? Arnau knew that no small quantity of wine would seriously affect Ramon, but surely it would at least *slightly* influence his aim?

He frowned as the knight unstoppered the flask and stood it on the crate before him. His brow furrowed further at the realisation that the flask bore a cross upon it, and that there was no cup. He'd seen similar bottles in the buttery below, stored for church use. Sacramental wine.

'Here they come,' Ramon said quietly. 'Be conservative with your shots. Make each one count.'

Arnau nodded nervously and watched as the knight reached out for a strange wooden apparatus on the box and then, gripping the crossbow in the other hand, dropped the tip to the floor. Jamming his foot in the stirrup of the machine, he put the twin hooks of the wooden mechanism against the string and settled the weapon into place. He then pressed the contraption flat, grunting with effort, and by some marvellous means the wooden hooks pulled back the string until it clicked into place. The knight then dropped the wooden thing back to the crate and selected a bolt.

Realising that he was watching, yet remaining inactive, Arnau grabbed the wooden machine on his own crate, grasped the bow and mimicked the knight's routine, marvelling anew as the wooden mechanism clicked the string into place with ease and just a little effort. As he reached for a bolt, he heard an odd tinkling noise and glanced across in surprise to see that Brother Ramon had dipped the point of the bolt into the sacramental wine and waggled it around before withdrawing it and placing it into the groove on the weapon. Not having a jar of the wine himself, and baffled by the knight's action, Arnau simply inserted the bolt dry into his own crossbow.

'Let them have it the moment you're sure of a shot,' Ramon said, leaving Arnau as clueless as before. He'd never fired one of these in his life. How could he possibly be sure of a shot?

He was further taken aback as Brother Ramon lifted the crossbow into position, training the weapon on one of the brown-clad bandits hurtling across the last stretch of field towards the ditch surrounding the preceptory, for the knight began to chant quietly.

'This is the Lamb of God who takes away the sins of the world. Happy are those who are called to his supper.'

He fell silent as the figure upon whom Ramon had set his sights reached the edge of the ditch and paused, trying to decide how best to cross. The weapon discharged with a click and a thud and the bolt struck the man dead centre, where his collarbones met, punching deep into him and knocking him back to the soil.

'May the Lord Jesus protect you and lead you to eternal life,' Brother Ramon said quietly as he reached for the wooden apparatus and began to reload the bow. Arnau stared. It might be an oddly abbreviated version, but the young sergeant recognised some of the wording of the viaticum, the prayer for the dying. Strange.

Trying not to ponder on yet another oddity of this place, he lifted his crossbow, nestled the stock against his shoulder and weaved the point among the many possible targets, selecting a howling fellow in grey waving a sword. He tracked the man's movement and then twitched the trigger.

The shot had three unexpected effects. The first was that the bolt missed its target by a huge margin, and Arnau could only count himself fortunate that completely by chance it plunged into the thigh of a man further back, sending him spinning to the ground in the press of men. The second was that he only saw part of that, for the weapon's string snapping back into place actually pulled the whole thing forward rather than the kickback he'd been expecting, and he staggered forward a pace, almost falling across the crate. The third was that he'd been trying to sight along the groove, and the weapon snapping forward had grazed the skin of his cheek and chin in the process, leaving a fiery pain in his jaw.

'Keep the stock away from your shoulder, cheek and chin,' advised Brother Ramon without even looking around, then, having settled his second bolt, wine-coated, into place, began to intone the viaticum once more. 'This is the Lamb of God who takes away the sins of the world…'

Still shaken, wincing at what he knew would be a horribly bruised jaw, Arnau dropped the tip of his crossbow, inserted his foot in the stirrup, and used the wooden mechanism to pull back the string. Lifting it once more, he inserted his second bolt and looked around. The sounds of battle suddenly became apparent to him. He'd been so intent on his first shot he'd not heard the shouts and screams, and the thuds of the other weapons being discharged around the preceptory. Men were falling here and there, but there were hundreds of them, and the difference the crossbows were making was negligible.

He scanned the bodies and, quite by chance, found that same man in grey who'd escaped his first shot, making for the causeway to the west gate. Frowning, he lowered the tip a little, assuming that the shot would go high as the first had.

He released, and felt chagrin as the shot this time fell slightly short, punching into the earth by the man's foot, entirely unnoticed as Grey-tunic hurtled forward to pound on the gate. Behind him, Brother Ramon was busy readying his third shot, intoning his prayer of salvation for the man he was about to kill. Arnau readied his own weapon once more, settling the thing into place. He chose a tall fellow and tracked him, keeping the point aiming at the centre of the man's torso. He came closer. Closer. Onto the causeway. Close to the walls.

Arnau released.

The bolt was perfectly on target. Unfortunately, the man disappeared behind the wall as the bolt was in flight, and the tip struck the parapet, sending it ricocheting off high into the air. He did not see where it came down, but Rafael, who was busy pushing yet more benches and barrels against the gate directly below the misfire, turned and glared momentarily up at the belfry. Arnau felt the flush in his cheeks, and bent to reload.

'Stop overthinking it,' Ramon said, again without looking. 'Every time you pause to check whether you're still on target, you're increasing the chances of missing because you are allowing the target to move more. Pick your target, estimate in your head how far he moves in the count of three, move that far ahead of him and release. Do it swiftly and all in one movement, and you'll be much closer.'

Arnau frowned, but lifted the stock, aiming his second bolt at the tall man. One… two… three… He twitched the bow forward by his estimated distance and pulled the trigger. The shot missed once more, but was close enough that its passage by the man's hip as it thudded into the ground made him stumble to a halt in shock. Arnau would have wagered good money, if he'd had any, that the man had pissed himself.

Feeling more confident, Arnau dropped the tip once more, pulled back the string and inserted another bolt. His loading had become much speedier already. He lifted it, found a target with ease among the men running at the walls and shifted it ahead by the estimated distance. He released, and the bolt thumped into the man's shoulder, sending him flying backwards to the ground.

Grinning in a most unseemly way for a man thieving life from another human, Arnau reloaded, taking the briefest moment to count the remaining bolts while he jacked the string back. Thirteen, including the one he'd just picked up and dropped into the groove.

Select. Aim. Snick.

Another man spiralled into the ditch, shrieking.

'How has della Cadeneta managed to hire so many men?' he breathed as he reloaded.

'He's had a week or so,' Ramon reminded him. 'The disaffected, the poor, the greedy, they live in every corner of this land. Centuries of warfare have ravaged Iberia, my friend, and left her broken. Finding a man who will kill for money or food is far from difficult, and many still see the Temple as something foreign, not part of the Church they understand. Many will not baulk at standing against us in the same way they would against a Benedictine or an Augustinian. Della Cadeneta will have offered rich rewards. If he wins, whatever he's paid will be worth it. And he only has to pay the survivors, after all.'

Still, it seemed unbelievable to Arnau. How from one small conflict over a potential marriage, in little more than a week they had come to defending holy ground against a veritable army of outlaws.

He shouldered his weapon once more and took down another man.

The next shot missed, and the one after, though he was becoming more consistent with his aim and no shot now was falling too short or too long, any misses more down to the enemy's unpredictable movements or sheer ill fortune. Load. Shoot. Load. Shoot. Swiftly, the supply of bolts beside him dwindled. He listened, and could hear others now falling silent too, where their own supply of missiles had run dry. What would they do then, he wondered? He felt an odd flash of irritation when Brother Ramon reached across and plucked one of his three remaining bolts from the quiver and loaded with it. Taking the penultimate missile, he nocked, shouldered, and loosed, watching the bolt thud into a man's neck. He reached for the last one, but the knight beside him had already claimed and loaded it.

Moments later, the last bolt released, Ramon straightened and removed a knife from his belt. Steadying himself with his foot in the stirrup once more, he sawed through the bow's string until it gave with a sharp snap, the arms of the bow twanging straight.

'What are you doing?' boggled Arnau.

'No use to us now, but *they* might have ammunition.'

Arnau nodded, imagining the bandits laying hands on his crossbow and loading it to aim at him. Swiftly, he found his own knife and cut through the string of his weapon. Leaving the two ruined bows, they hurried back to the stairs.

'What now?'

'Now we stop them at the gates, if we can.'

They took the stairs two steps at a time, hurtling back to the ground, where they emerged, blinking, into the courtyard while all around them were screams and thuds and angry shouts.

Lorenç and Ferrando were still atop the roofs, he could see, moving around, peering over the edge here and there to make sure the enemy were not managing to scale the walls. Fortunately this was no true besieging army, and they had no catapults, rams or siege ladders as one might expect. Here and there men would try to climb the walls of the preceptory, but Arnau had seen the outside of the place several times now, and could not imagine any ordinary man succeeding in scaling them. Their only true hope of ingress was the west gate or its southerly companion. Still, the twin sergeants moved around the parapet across both ranges and the chapter house, making sure no one reached the top, casting down tiles or small rocks whenever they found someone making an attempt. Even as Arnau watched, heart in throat, Ferrando had to throw himself to the rooftop bodily as an arrow whirred through the air above him. Their work was fraught with peril.

As Arnau looked this way and that, wondering where to go, he saw the preceptrix and her maid Catarina carrying a pew out of the church to aid in the blocking of the west gate. Young Simo and Sister Joana emerged from the armoury carrying swords and hammers, looking wide-eyed and panicked. As the two youngsters ran past, Brother Ramon waved them to a stop and grabbed the weapons from them, slipping them all into the same bag.

'Get up the belfry. Once you're inside, lock the door, then head up to the top and stay silent. Don't show yourselves.'

Grateful for the chance to move to relative safety, the pair ran in through the tower doorway, slamming the heavy wooden door behind them and bolting it shut with a heavy clonk of iron.

'Come on,' the knight said to Arnau, then raced off into the shadowed archway that contained the south gate. In the gloom of the arched passage, Arnau could see Brothers Balthesar and Mateu. The sergeant was pushing furniture and barrels harder against the gates, wedging them as best he could, while the knight, his agility belying his age, was crouched atop the barricade, his sword lancing out through the narrow gaps between the gate's leaves or below the hinge, driving into bodies unseen outside, as Arnau could tell from the yelps of pain that echoed through the gate and along the passage.

Even as Ramon hurried over and found a similar position to join in, the whole gate suddenly shook from a bang that sounded as though the vaults of hell had opened beneath them.

Brother Ramon leaned forward and put an eye to a gap in the gate.

'They've made a ram. A tree trunk.'

'Will the gate hold?' Arnau asked, nerves starting to rise once more.

'Not for long against that,' Balthesar replied as the whole gate shuddered once more under a second blow. Arnau felt his heart skip as a similar bang echoed across the courtyard behind them.

'The west gate,' Ramon shouted. Balthesar glanced at his fellow knight, who nodded. The older of the pair leaped down from the barricade and ran out of the passageway, heading to check the other gate. Arnau began to climb carefully up towards the blocked gate, but Ramon waved him back even as the gates shuddered once more and there was an audible crack.

'The walls are safe, but the gates could fall. Get up to the roof and bring Lorenç and Ferrando back down where they can be more use.'

Arnau dithered for a moment. He didn't like the idea of leaving Ramon here and running off on an errand, but duty was duty, and

Ramon's squire Mateu was here, pushing the blocking furniture and bits and pieces back into position where they were shaken out of place with each blow of the ram. As the squire continually repaired the blockage, Ramon was stabbing through the gaps, trying to wound anyone without, though they had clearly largely drawn back to make room for the ram.

'Go,' snapped the knight, and Arnau turned and ran. Beside the armoury, he dived into the stairway that led up to the male dormitory. He burst out into the bed-lined room to see Carima leaning over the still form of Miquel in his cot. The sergeant hissed with pain with each movement of the sister's hands as she bound him with care and some difficulty. Ignoring the ministrations, Arnau ran over to the ladder, clambering up through the opening and onto the roof of Rourell. He could not see Lorenç from here, somewhere at the far side of the roof's low pitch. Ferrando, however, was crouched nearby, arrows clattering against stone and tile.

'Get down,' the sergeant yelled at Arnau, who had just emerged into the open. As if to add weight to the man's words, an arrow clattered against the roof tiles a pace away from Arnau.

'The gates are being rammed. Brother Ramon wants you back downstairs.'

Ferrando nodded and turned, cupping his hands around his mouth. 'Lorenç!'

There was no reply. Arnau watched the colour drain from the sergeant's face as he rose despite the sporadic hail of arrows and scurried along the edge of the roof. Arnau ran after him, flinching as another missile clacked against tile next to him. He rounded the corner to the northern side and almost knocked Ferrando from the wall top. The sergeant had stopped. Arnau looked over his shoulder and was saddened, if not entirely surprised, to see the shape of Lorenç slumped over the parapet with arrow shafts jutting from his back.

'Come on,' he said, tugging at Ferrando. The man did not move.

'He's gone, come *on*.'

Still, Ferrando stood, staring at the body of his twin brother. An arrow thrummed through the air past them, then another. Arnau's eyes drifted to the crowd of men besieging them below. Behind the men in the ditch, who were now largely moving along the walls, heading for the weak points of the two gates, several archers and crossbowmen were busy loading or aiming. He could see one crossbowman levelling his weapon and, unable to move Ferrando with words, Arnau threw himself bodily at his fellow sergeant. The two men hit the tiled roof just as the shot was taken, the bolt whipping through the air where the man had stood a heartbeat earlier and smashing through the roof tiles. For a sickening moment, Arnau thought they were both going to go over the edge and plummet to their doom in the ditch outside, but at the last moment he managed to jam a foot against the stonework of the low parapet and prevent the fall. Ferrando did little to prevent it.

'We have to go. If you don't, you'll die too.'

From the lack of response, Arnau was fairly certain that such things no longer mattered a great deal to Ferrando, and he grabbed hold of the man and began to heave him along the rooftop as arrows and bolts clattered into the building above and below them, their bodies almost covered by the low parapet. Finally, after what felt like hours, Arnau reached the hatch. He bundled the silent, pale, almost catatonic brother into the hole.

'Climb the damned ladder,' he snapped, horribly aware that every heartbeat spent on this roof threatened death from a dozen barbed arrow heads. Ferrando's head turned, the eyes glazed and uncomprehending. 'Down!' snapped Arnau, pointing into the gloomy interior. An arrow passed above them so close he felt the air vibrate. Ferrando, still dumbstruck but spurred into mechanical action by the sight, grasped the ladder and half-climbed, half-slid down it into the dormitory. Arnau dropped in after him, thanking God that they were both still unharmed despite a number of close shaves.

'What happens if the gates fall?' he asked Ferrando as they stood at the bottom of the ladder. His eyes were on Carima as she completed her ministrations of Miquel. Ferrando remained silent, staring blankly at him.

'Are the gates in danger?' Miquel called across from his bed, then hissed in pain.

'Probably. They're being hit with rams.'

'There's only two safe places to fall back, then,' Miquel said. 'The belfry and the chapel. Can't fit many in the belfry, though. The chapel can be closed off, along with the chapter house. If the gates fall, that'll be where the preceptrix rallies us.'

'And then the dormitories will be open to them. You can't stay here.'

'He shouldn't exert himself,' Carima said quietly.

'If he doesn't, and the gates fall, he'll be hacked to pieces,' Arnau replied flatly.

'Help me with him,' the nun said, and Arnau rushed over and helped gently lift Miquel from the bed. With his grunts and squeals of pain, they helped the wounded sergeant over to the stairs and then down them into the courtyard. There, Arnau left the pair to it as they lurched and hobbled over to the chapel, while he hurried back towards the south gate in the passageway.

He felt a chill of panic as he took in the situation. The gates were still taking a battering, but the heap of tables and crates had largely tumbled away and been pushed inward, and Mateu could do little to stop it now. The gates were about to go; that he could tell even with his limited experience of sieges.

'Where are the brothers?' Ramon bellowed urgently from the gate.

'Lorenç is gone. Ferrando is useless.'

No further explanation was necessary, and Ramon nodded his head, resigned. 'This is becoming desperate.'

'I've sent Carima and Miquel to the chapel in case the gates fall.'

'Good man.'

His words were punctuated with a huge ligneous *crack* as the entire barricade slid inward across the flagstones with a low rumble. The locking bar had given way, and a gap a foot wide had opened between the leaves of the gate. As Ramon began to jab his blade in and out of the gap, holding back the mass of men outside, Mateu clambered through the pile of timber and put his shoulder to one leaf of the gate, putting all his weight into an attempt to push it back home. It was futile, and Arnau could see that, though perhaps his fellow sergeant felt he should make one last attempt to hold the portal.

'No,' bellowed Brother Ramon, waving his free hand at Mateu as he stabbed once more.

'We can hold it,' grunted Mateu, feet braced, back against the gate, pushing hard. Remarkably, Arnau watched the gate slide back a little, the gap narrowing. 'Help me,' Mateu yelled at Arnau, and the young sergeant ran towards the blockage and the contested gate, but once more Ramon waved him back. 'The gate's lost. Get back. Mateu, go!'

Still the black-clad squire-sergeant grunted and heaved. 'We can—'

His words were cut short as a great, heavy axe blade crashed through the timber of the gate and deep into Mateu's back, smashing through ribs and spine as easily as the wood they were pressed against. Mateu spasmed for a moment, then grinned, and dark blood poured from his mouth. He gave a deep sigh and expired, still pinned to the wood until the man outside heaved back his axe with difficulty and the sergeant slumped to the ground. Brother Ramon stared down at his squire for a moment, and then gave a savage roar and redoubled his flurry of blows through the gap in the gate, dealing steely murder to anyone who dared come close.

'The gates are falling,' called a voice from behind Arnau. 'Fall back. To the chapel!'

Arnau turned, eyes wide, to see Preceptrix Ermengarda standing in the courtyard, her husband's sword belted at her side like some warrior queen of old. His astonished eyes turned back from the preceptrix to Ramon, who was stabbing and thrusting and cutting through the narrow gap in the gate like a man possessed, roaring his anger as he did so. Arnau watched in horror the blades of axes smashing through the timber of the gates and beginning to tear apart the leaves.

'Ramon!' he bellowed. The knight paid him no heed, killing and maiming.

'Brother Ramon!' he yelled again. Finally, the knight stopped slamming his sword out and paused for a moment. A blade whipped in through the gap and almost took Ramon's life until he fell backwards into the pile of chairs, tables and crates. He tumbled painfully and gracelessly down the barricade, stumbling to a halt next to Arnau. The sergeant flinched at the sight of the knight. Ramon was unwounded, but pale as a ghost beneath the layer of blood and filth of battle.

'Mateu—'

'Mateu is dead,' Arnau said, sharply. He turned to see that the preceptrix had gone, hurtling over towards the west gate. Across the courtyard, Luis had closed the doors of the chapter house and was standing by the chapel door, waving people inside.

'Come on,' Brother Ramon said, sanity finally settling back into his eyes. With Arnau close by, he ran back out of the passageway and into the open. Arnau's heart sank as he glanced across to his left once they had emerged into the light. Others were retreating from the preceptory's west gate, led by Brother Balthesar, but the old knight was limping and staggering, one leg barely able to support him, drenched in crimson. His sword was nowhere to be seen, nor his shield, as he used his left arm to cradle his broken right. His skin, where it could be seen through the gore of his victims, was a worrying grey through loss of blood.

The preceptrix was standing before the chapel, waving him on. She turned to shout back inside over her shoulder. 'Carima, prepare yourself for more wounded. Catarina and Titborga, lend a hand with the injured. Everyone else inside and secure the perimeter.'

There was something powerful about the sight of the preceptrix with a sword strapped to her, and for a moment he understood how the powerful male nobles of Aragon might take against such a woman, threatened by the sheer strength of a woman of God, who they felt should be meek and obedient. There was certainly nothing meek about the Amazon standing at the heart of Rourell and bellowing out commands even as her monastery fell around her.

With a crash, the south gate's destruction was complete, the barrier of furniture pushed aside. A similar tale was being played out at the west, and men were beginning to pour through. Almost all the denizens of Rourell were in the church now, and as Balthesar limped through the doorway, helped by Brother Rafael, Arnau and Ramon dived inside with the preceptrix, Luis hauling the door shut and heaving the bar into place to seal it.

The interior of the chapel was dim, but Father Diego appeared a moment later through the adjoining door to the chapter house with a burning taper, which he used to light the candles around the church.

'Should we not bar that door?' Arnau asked.

'The chapter house door is also sealed,' Ramon replied. 'Should they break in there, *then* we will seal this one. Better not to confine ourselves more than we must.'

Arnau looked around. Carima had set up a small hospital area near the altar, using pews. Upon one lay Miquel, moaning softly. On another rested Balthesar, silent as the nun worked on his wounds. Catarina and Titborga were helping as much they could. Brigida stood close by the preceptrix, eyes wide with panic. Luis and Rafael were checking the windows while Father Diego, having now lit the candles, sat with Ferrando and talked quietly to him, trying to heal the mental hurt the sergeant clearly suffered.

That was it. That was what remained of Rourell in addition to Arnau. Discounting the two wounded men, and Ferrando who, it seemed likely, would be of little help in the coming hours, they numbered nine in total. Three sergeants, one knight, three nuns, a priest and the preceptrix.

His heart suddenly turned to ice. And Joana. And Simo. Trapped in the belfry and separated from the rest.

Never had Arnau felt more in need of courage and guidance than right now. The world faded around him, the noise and the desperation, the panic and the smell of blood. Arnau walked through the midst of it all, past the makeshift hospital and to the altar with its image of Saint Mary, where he dropped to a knee and began to pray for the deliverance of so many innocents whose lives had been overturned by the arrival of the three desperate fugitives from Santa Coloma.

CHAPTER EIGHTEEN

The muted sounds of victorious savagery were clearly audible through the church door. Preceptrix Ermengarda and Brother Ramon were involved in a muttered council of war in the corner, the three nuns were hard at work dealing with injuries, and the rest were checking weapons or praying as they deemed fit. Arnau, however, had neither the patience nor the will for either right now, and so he stood at a narrow slit window to one side of the church door, peering out, wishing the window was of coloured, decorative glass rather than being plain and clear, and therefore making him horribly visible should some enemy crossbowman decide to take a shot.

The enemy had flooded into the courtyard from both gates, crashing like the tide against the interior walls. The sight was stomach-clenching, though the one small mercy Arnau could identify was that the entire mob seemed to fit in the courtyard, which surely had not been possible when all this started, and pointed to the serious depletion the Templar crossbows and swords had wreaked on the enemy. They must have almost halved. Of course, that still meant they were hopelessly outnumbered and trapped in a church awaiting death, but still, it was something.

As soon as the rough thugs filled the yard, they began to spread out and search. Men pushed through every doorway and disappeared inside. Arnau watched with anger through the narrow window as all the meagre goods belonging to Rourell were dragged from their places and fought over by snarling mercenaries, like a hungry wolf pack with a fresh carcass. Anything that took no one's fancy was simply discarded and trodden on. Bedclothes dropped from high windows to be torn apart, horses brought from the stables and taken away with saddles and tack, the few spare items from the armoury distributed among the attackers. Fortunately, the preceptrix had had the foresight to have the armoury largely emptied, and its contents were here, in the north end of the church. They may be trapped in a chapel but at least they were well armed.

Arnau's eyes had repeatedly shifted to the top of the belfry, where he knew innocent Joana and young Simo hid. Briefly, once or twice, he saw a head appear at the parapet to check what was happening and then disappear once more. He willed the pair to stay hidden and not draw attention to themselves. His heart had thundered in his throat as he watched three of the enemy work at the tower door, trying to force a way in, but the timber was too thick and too well sealed, and they soon gave up, especially as it became apparent that the defenders of Rourell were holed up in the church and chapter house.

Soon they would turn their attention to these buildings, but for now they were content to loot and destroy with wanton abandon. Arnau watched sadly as the last few possessions of his former secular life were dragged from the stores and fought over. His shield, with the black lion of Vallbona, disappeared in the hands of a toothless bandit with lank hair and a wicked grin. He would not have been able to keep the equipment anyway, mind. In due course the shield would have been repainted plain Templar black and white and added to the armoury. His fancy clothes would have been distributed among the poor, which, oddly, was exactly what was happening now, though not in the way he'd envisaged. Somewhere, Titborga's possessions would be being ravaged too. Since neither had attended the ceremony that would see them officially part of the order and the records were not yet lodged with the mother house, they remained officially secular nobles, and it was not yet the place of the preceptrix to divest them of the trappings of their former life.

There would *be* no trappings now.

A shout of anger and alarm somewhere in the centre of the courtyard drew Arnau's attention, and he focused on a small knot of shouting men. It seemed from the commotion that someone was wounded. He watched the gathered figures help a man to his feet, his head covered in blood, his feet unsteady. What was happening?

His blood chilled as a second man suddenly screamed, his head half-caved in, blood and brains spattering his closest comrades. Arnau's gaze travelled up the stone wall to the top of the tower in perfect unison with a score of eyes at the yard's centre. Joana was leaning over the parapet, having just dropped something heavy into the crowd.

No, Arnau thought, unable to shout, unwilling to bring this nightmare scene to the attention of the others, for there was nothing any of them could do about it. His gaze remained riveted on the parapet of the belfry even when Joana disappeared from it. There had been no sign of Simo, which could be good, or bad. He began to wonder what had happened to the young nun when she reappeared suddenly, casting the heavy bronze bell she had removed from its beam over the parapet. The bell fell and shouts of warning saved a man's life when he leaped out of the way as the deadly falling missile thudded into the ground, breaking the flagstone. In the tower, Joana cursed them all, imploring almighty God to strike them down for their villainy. It was all bravely done, but while she had removed two more of the enemy from the fight, she had also made them aware of her presence.

Arnau watched, heart in mouth, as one of those rams that had been used to break the outer gates was brought into the yard and ferried through the press to the tower. The ram was settled in place in the grip of a dozen burly men and the mob moved back to allow room. It began to swing, slamming into the tower door so hard that dust and fragments of mortar tumbled from the walls of the belfry into the crowd below.

'What's happening?' Rafael asked, scurrying over towards him.

'They're going for the belfry,' Arnau replied quietly so that his words would not carry across the church.

'Lord!'

'Quite. They'd given up on it, but Joana started throwing things down on them, so now they're breaking down the door.'

Rafael leaned against the wall. 'It will go bad for Sister Joana. For Simo too, but we all know what this sort of rabble will do when they capture a girl.'

Arnau nodded, bleakly. It did not bear thinking about. He wished they still had a crossbow. Even one bolt would be enough to end it for Joana before the worst happened, but it seemed she was to be denied even that. There was no way to help her, or Simo. He wondered where Simo was. He had to be in the tower, after all. Joana continued to rain rubble down on the heads of the crowd. She had used everything truly heavy now, even dropping the broken crossbows out, and had cast down bits of wood and boxes. Arnau watched her using a knife to try and prise a stone from the parapet. It would be fruitless. On the somewhat tenuous bright side, she had seriously injured at least three more people with her constant barrage.

On the twelfth blow the tower door cracked and burst inwards and, roaring their victory, men began to pour into the stairwell. Arnau prayed that the good Lord would be merciful and grant Joana a quick and clean exit from this world.

'*Pater noster qui in coelis est, sanctificetur nomen tuum…*'

The voice was clear, light, feminine and almost musical, and somehow managed to cut through the commotion outside. Almost every figure in the yard came to a halt and looked up. Those inside the tower continued to move, as evidenced by the echoing sound of pounding feet.

'*Adveniat regnum tuum, fiat voluntas tua et in terra sicut in coelo…*'

The paternoster – the Lord's Prayer – intoned in such a sweet manner. Arnau looked up to see Joana leaning over the parapet. Rafael muscled in next to him, with difficulty, finding a way to peer out of the window. They both watched, ice cold.

'*Panem nostrum quotidianum da nobis hodie et dimitte nobis debita nostra…*'

The crowd were silent, as though at mass, as riveted to the clear prayer of the young nun as were her comrades at the church window. Arnau's already heavy heart took another blow as he watched Joana climb up onto the narrow wall and stand straight, steadying herself with a hand on the stonework.

'God, no,' Arnau whispered.

'*Sicut et dimittemus debitoribus nostris et ne nos inducas in tentationem, sed libera nos a malo…*'

The crowd was spellbound. Rafael, wide-eyed, choked. 'She cannot. Not that. She will be denied heaven for eternity. Better to be *raped.*'

Arnau wasn't sure he agreed with that, which probably made him a bad Christian, but still. He shook his head, eyes still on the girl. 'Heaven awaits her, Rafael.'

'But…'

'This is not suicide, Brother. This is a nun striking a blow in holy war with the only weapon she has left.'

They watched, shivering, as Joana pulled her hands back from the stone, teetering on the parapet. Behind her, they could hear the attackers emerging from the stairwell.

'Amen,' Joana said, and fell.

Arnau could not look away. Even as she toppled outward, one of the men who'd climbed the tower ran over and grabbed at her arm, trying to stop her. The young sergeant couldn't see the nun's face, but he could quite imagine the ferocious determination on it as Joana grabbed hold of the man and pulled him over with her, toppling out into the open air.

The crowd below had been mesmerised by the scene, watching Joana, immobile. Only as she fell did desperate activity explode among the men in the courtyard, for they were still tightly pressed and there was little chance of everyone getting out of the way.

Sister Joana and her unfortunate attacker hit the gathered crowd at speed and the whole group disappeared with a roar and a number of stony, bony cracks. It was impossible to tell from the chapel window who had died, but it seemed more than likely the death toll exceeded the two falling figures alone. Filled with grief for the young nun, still Arnau's eyes rose to the top. There was yet no sign of Simo. He peered, frowning, at the door below, and the men who'd broken in emerged, looking shaken and dispirited. Still no Simo. Arnau prayed the boy was all right, wherever he was.

He only became aware of the presence of his superiors when the preceptrix spoke close to his shoulder. 'Joana?'

Arnau nodded. 'She is with God now.'

'Better that than with *them*,' the mistress of Rourell said, with feeling, drawing a nod from both the sergeants.

'And Simo?' Ramon added. Arnau turned to see the pale face of the knight and the haunted look to his eyes. This would be torturing Ramon, for it had been he who had consigned the young pair to the tower, believing it to be a place of safety for them. He would feel entirely responsible.

'No sign of Simo.'

'Let us pray for him, then,' Ermengarda said.

'Still they do not come,' Brother Ramon said. 'They ravage and loot both ranges, take the tower, but still they do not come for us.'

The preceptrix nodded. 'It is a rare man, even among the villainous, who will willingly bring violence against a church. Remember the vengeance the Lord wreaks on such men.' Arnau remembered it all too well. He had been part of that vengeance, in the army of Santa Coloma at the battle by the Ebro, where they had trapped and butchered an Almohad raiding party. Those Moors had had the temerity to burn a church with a priest inside, and the full weight of God's wrath had been brought down upon them at spear point. These men would fear similar reprisals.

'Diego,' the preceptrix said quietly. The venerable priest wandered over towards them.

'Yes?'

'How is your haranguing voice? It would appear that even amid the wreckage of our monastery, the enemy are reluctant to attack a house of the Lord.'

Father Diego gave a wild yellow-toothed grin, his eyes bulging more than usual. 'Stand back, Brothers.'

Arnau and Rafael retreated from the window, and the old priest reached up and unlatched it, opening it outwards so that he could be seen clearly, if only from a narrow viewpoint. The slit was too narrow for a person to fit through, but an arrow could pass within easily, and Arnau held his breath.

'Behold, godless heathens!' Diego bellowed through the window, and once more everything outside fell silent, bar the agonised wailing of a couple of men who'd lived through the falling bodies and wreckage to suffer the ongoing pain of their wounds. Arnau flinched. He wasn't entirely sure that calling them *godless heathens* was the best way to appeal to them, but the words were out now, and all anyone could do was follow.

'This,' Diego bellowed, his voice strong and clear despite his appearance, 'is the house of God. "How fearful and worshipful is this place? Here is none other thing but the house of God, and the gate of heaven." Genesis twenty-eight, for those of you who care for their immortal soul. Because, and make no mistake out there among the filth of impious human refuse, the man that crossed this threshold with anything other than devout prayer in mind damns his soul to an eternity of fiery torment in the pit of the Great Adversary. Begone with you, lest the Lord strike down his wrath upon you.'

With that, he stepped back and slammed shut the window. Arnau stared at him. There was absolute silence. Even the wounded and dying outside had fallen quiet in the face of the old priest's threat of damnation. It had been well said, Arnau had to admit. More confrontational and accusatory than Arnau might have thought safe, but still, it had struck into the heart of every man out there, and the silence was that of each man examining his soul.

The silence ended suddenly with a bang that shook the very walls. Arnau started in shock at the sound, wondering what it was. The second crash, though, carrying with it the sound of splintering timber, made the source clear.

'The chapter house,' Luis said, running through the door from the church. Preceptrix Ermengarda was at his heel, Catarina running to join her mistress.

'Stay in the church,' bellowed Brother Ramon after them. 'Sister, stay here and close the door!'

But the others had gone into the chapter house. Ramon turned to Arnau and Rafael. 'Get the bar ready to seal that door,' he barked, pointing at the heavy portal that connected church and chapter house. Arnau nodded and the pair of sergeants ran over to the door, locating the bar and lifting it. Arnau noted gloomily that the old loquacious priest had threatened damnation on any man who entered the church, but he'd not mentioned the chapter house.

Readying the bar, they waited by the door and Arnau peered through it, immediately wishing he hadn't. That second blow from the ram had cracked open the chapter house door and, even as the preceptrix had entered her place of council with Luis and Catarina, brigands had been pouring through it. Ramon, sword in hand, grabbed Luis and physically propelled him back towards the church even as he prepared to fight the tide of villainy flowing towards him. The preceptrix, immediately realising her mistake and the peril in which she'd placed herself, ran into the room and skittered to a halt, backing up and rather inexpertly drawing her husband's heavy blade from her side. Catarina spun to flee also, but fortune was not with her, and she slipped, turning her ankle and collapsing to the floor with a yelp.

'No!' the preceptrix bellowed and made to go after her, but Ramon was there, waving her back towards the door. Arnau watched in cold fear as Luis and Ermengarda retreated hurriedly towards them, while Brother Ramon ran towards the approaching mercenaries, where Catarina was struggling to rise, whimpering at the pain in her ankle.

'Get up, girl!' Ramon shouted at her. He stepped beside her and caught the swinging sword of a brigand with his own, knocking it aside. 'Get up!'

But she did not. Whether she could not, or had simply frozen in panic, Arnau could not tell, but she remained on the flagged floor of the chapter house. Luis and the preceptrix pushed past the doorway into the church, and Arnau willed the girl to rise. Still she did not.

Ramon caught another lancing blade and delivered a riposte, drawing blood from an unseen figure in the crowd. The enemy slowed their advance, wary of that bloodied dancing blade and the white-clad knight who wielded it. Another man took a step forward and jabbed with his sword. Ramon spun and hacked down with his own blade, taking the hand off at the wrist and then falling into a prepared stance, sword at the ready for the next man.

'Get up,' he hissed urgently at the young nun. Still Catarina did not move, sobbing as she held her ankle. Arnau knew what was coming. They all did. There was a tension building. The men facing Ramon were nervous about pressing their attack, well aware of the deadly skill of their opponent, but soon something would snap, and they would come at the Templar en masse. When that happened, Ramon was dead. There was simply no way he could hold off that many adversaries.

Another sword. Another parry. Another warning wound.

The tension was almost at breaking point. Arnau felt his fingertips drop to the hilt of the sword at his side even as his other hand maintained his grip on the locking bar. The preceptrix, standing close by, cleared her throat. 'Ready yourself to seal the door, Brother Arnau. Nothing more.'

His fingers left the weapon and he gripped the bar, though his gaze remained locked on Ramon.

A man slashed with his sword and caught the Templar knight's habit, ripping a wide hole in it and sliding with a nerve-jangling sound across the mail beneath without penetrating. Ramon grunted and delivered a response with gusto, his blade cutting the man just above the thigh, sending him falling back with a cry of pain. The mood was ugly. Any moment now…

Ramon reached down with his free hand and tried to grasp Catarina.

'Take my hand,' he hissed. She looked up, eyes rolling in terror, but someone in the crowd must have grabbed her good foot, for the shape of the young nun suddenly jerked away across the floor and disappeared, screaming, into the crowd.

Ramon bellowed his fury, desperately reaching, trying to grab the white habit as she was yanked away from him, but she was gone. The knight howled like a wounded beast and swung his sword in a mighty arc, biting deep into flesh and raising screams of pain from the mob. The preceptrix called for him, but Ramon was deaf to all but the song of battle. He leaped forward, sword biting, cleaving, slashing, stabbing, a fine mizzle of red rising to fill the air of the chapter house like fog. Cries of agony rose above the sounds of swordplay, and Arnau almost lost sight of the knight for a moment as the enemy made to surround him and cut him down, but even in such blind fury, the Templar was good. He back-stepped twice, keeping the enemy from cutting him off. There was a new cry as one of the mercenaries landed a blow on Ramon, and he bellowed something for which he'd need to do penance later, but still he was up, still fighting.

Luis suddenly ran past Arnau, ripping his sword from its scabbard and leaping into the fray even as the preceptrix ordered him to hold back. Arnau lost track. He saw swords swinging and flashes of white and black habits amid the brown and grey, and then suddenly a miracle occurred. Ramon and Luis emerged from the chaos, backing towards the door, staggering but intact. Their swords, running with blood, coated with hair and gore, wavered threateningly at the press of men who slowly advanced at the same pace as the pair backing away.

Arnau prepared himself, nodding at Rafael. The two men, white and black together like pieces from a chess board, fell back through the door and, even as the brigands roared and rushed for the church, the two waiting sergeants slammed the portal shut and pushed the bar home into the metal brackets.

'Will that hold?' Arnau whispered, listening to the fists thumping on the far side.

'For a while at least,' Rafael replied as the two sergeants backed away from the door, trembling.

Arnau turned to the survivors, eyes wide. The preceptrix was busy upbraiding Luis for disobedience even as her eyes thanked him for his timely action. There was no doubt among them that Ramon would now be gone had it not been for Brother Luis's blessed insubordination. Even then, Luis was limping and his shield arm was drenched in blood. Ramon seemed intact barring one wound, though that injury was bad and was to his sword arm. He'd managed to hold the blade up threateningly as they backed through the doorway, but as soon as the door was closed and locked, his arm had dropped, shaking, the sword falling from his trembling fingers. The cut to his upper arm was so deep and long that Arnau could see the white of bone. The muscle had been badly damaged. There was simply no way Ramon would lift a sword with that hand for some time, if ever again.

'We cannot win against these odds,' the preceptrix said, suddenly.

'That's nothing new, Sister,' called Balthesar from his makeshift hospital bed. 'We always knew there would be too many of them, from the moment the campfires lit.'

'True. But we have fought back to our last redoubt. If the church falls, so does Rourell and every soul therein. There is still one chance, but for it work we need to shake the attackers off. To make them doubt and reconsider their course. To harry the snake's tail until it shows its head. Faith will be our weapon now.'

Arnau frowned. How faith could help them, he could not imagine. 'Would that I could turn back time,' he murmured.

'What was that, Brother?' the preceptrix asked, and Arnau flinched. He'd not meant it to be heard. He turned to the powerful mistress of Rourell, feeling chastened and sad.

'I wish I could turn back time. To the night we fled the farm and came here. I would urge my lady to ride on for Tarragona and not bring this terror to your door.'

Ermengarda fixed him with a look that made him feel extremely uneasy. 'Young man, feel not regret nor guilt. Remember that the protection of the innocent is the very purpose of our order. Forget the farms and the reconquest and the maintenance of the monastery and focus on the fact that without that very simple vow – to protect those in need – we would not be *here* to help. And the situation may appear dire, but we are yet far from lost.' She turned back to the others. 'Father Diego, would you lead the congregation in a little reminder of the purpose of this edifice?'

'You have anything in mind, Sister?'

'Psalm thirty-seven, I think.'

Arnau stared. Sing? They were trapped, wounded and with no hope, and the preceptrix would have them sing songs at the enemy? And yet a memory rose from deep within, an image of a glorious Templar leading a charge, singing psalms as he rode down the Moorish bandits. Perhaps there *was* a place for that glorious union of song and steel together, after all.

Father Diego's voice rose in its perfect tone, and within a heartbeat every throat in the chapel joined it.

'Do not thou follow wicked men; neither love thou men doing wickedness.'

Arnau almost smiled, picturing what would be going through the mind of every man out there with even a hint of a conscience. Already there had been consternation at the thought of attacking a church, then with the death of Joana in such a violent, visible manner and the haranguing of the priest, there would be many hearts quailing at what they must do next. And now here were voices raised in song of sacred scripture, urging them not to obey a wicked master.

'For they shall wax dry swiftly as hay, and they shall fall down soon as the worts of herbs.'

The followers of the wicked shall surely desiccate and wither.

Arnau, still singing, moved back towards the window where he'd been standing earlier. The song continued and as he anticipated the lines to come, he settled his mouth near the opening, preparing to bellow out those damning words to the crowd outside.

'Cease thou of ire, and forsake strong vengeance. Do not thou follow wickedly. For they that do shall be destroyed, while they that suffer the Lord shall inherit the land.'

He put his eye to the window once more. He was sure there were fewer men in the courtyard than there had been before. Of course, they could all be moving into the chapter house, ready for a final push. But he could see doubt in many eyes as he scanned the yard.

'And yet a sinner shalt seek his place, and shalt not find it, but mild men shall inherit the land and shall delight in the multitude of peace.'

Arnau smiled at the sight of two rough-looking fellows, one with a patch over a ruined eye, sharing a look at the rear of the crowd and retreating quietly through the darkened archway, abandoning their fellows. Sometimes even a wretched sinner could be reminded of the straight path in the right circumstances. Outside, in the face of a church full of song and stout hearts, many a wicked man was suddenly discovering a buried conscience.

Feeling a growing sense of hope, Arnau remained at the window, singing the song of David and watching dangerous men melting away into the shadows, unwilling to be a further part of this. By the time Father Diego led them through the final strains of the psalm, Arnau was starting to wonder whether they might just survive this day.

There could not be more than thirty men remaining in the courtyard. It was still a lot, especially with both of the house's knights out of commission, but it was so many fewer than they had seen flooding across the fields that this felt like a victory in itself.

'But the health of just men is the Lord, and he is their defender in the time of tribulation. And the Lord shall help them, and shall make them free, and he shall deliver them from sinners, and he shall save them, for they hoped in him'

Faith, but Arnau hoped those last lines were a true reflection of the world. He felt the hairs stand proud on his neck of a sudden, and a shiver ran through him. A single figure had entered the courtyard through the west gate: a man in red and white, clean and neat and radiating arrogance.

'Ferrer della Cadeneta,' Arnau said, almost under his breath, so quietly that he was surprised he'd been heard when Ramon, busy wincing as Carima looked at his arm, rose to his feet and turned to address him.

'Cadeneta? So, the serpent shows his head at last.'

Arnau watched the nobleman pass into the centre of the courtyard, his mercenaries stepping respectfully out of the way. He stopped and turned in a slow circle, taking in the gathered faces, perhaps irritated by the sheer level of uncertainty and discontent he could see.

'Many men have fallen to reach this point,' della Cadeneta said, loudly. 'But that means two things to me. It means that those men left here are the strongest, the bravest and the luckiest. And it means that every man here is worth an extra half share over my offer.'

Some of the doubt vanished at the promise of extra pay, and Arnau cursed silently.

'All you need to do now,' the enemy lord went on, 'is break down one door and bring to heel a bunch of women, old men, children and invalids, and you will go home wealthy men. What do you say to that?'

There was a subdued wave of gratitude outside, but Arnau's attention was drawn instead to his compatriots, for the preceptrix had walked over to join Ramon among the injured, and she had the oddest smile. Arnau, eyes narrowed, hurried over.

'How long has it been since dawn, do you think?' Ermengarda asked.

Ramon pursed his lips, hissed in pain at something Carima was doing, and peered out through the north window. 'At least two hours now, I would say. Perhaps more.'

'And how far will a rider get in that time?'

'Unassailed, on open ground and with a purpose?' Ramon grinned. 'I would say he'd make ten or twelve miles. If it's the road to Barberà we're talking about. It *is* that road, is it not?'

Arnau was with them now, or so he thought. 'But how will we get a man past *them*?'

'Dear Brother Arnau, we do not need to. My rider is long gone.

Arnau blinked, and then everything fell into place. Dawn. Guillem's horse.

'You sent Brother Guillem out before dawn?'

'Of course,' the preceptrix smiled.

'But how? Why? It was—'

'Faith, Vallbona,' Ramon said with a smile. 'Do you really think I would be foolhardy enough to risk a raid on the enemy campfire just for the purpose of instilling a little fear?'

'We were a distraction?'

'Quite. We deflected all their attention while good Brother Guillem passed us in the dark, black-clad on a black horse, riding with alacrity for Barberà.

A grin broke out over Arnau's face. 'Then—'

'Yes. Della Cadeneta has already lost. Guillem will be close to Barberà now and he carries the original, and indeed *only*, documents admitting you both to the order and confirming the donation of the Santa Coloma lands. No matter what your enemy out there does now, he will not inherit the estate.'

Arnau laughed, almost hysterically.

'How's your sword arm?' Ramon asked. Arnau frowned, and the knight gestured to his own ruined arm. 'Someone will yet have to whip that dog into his place. It will not be me, nor Balthesar. But I suspect that you have as much to pay him back for as any of us. Let's see how far our dear departed German brother improved your skills.'

The preceptrix nodded and waved to Rafael. 'Open the church door.'

CHAPTER NINETEEN

The courtyard was silent as the church doors swung ponderously open, Luis and Rafael drawing them back. The small Templar party revealed by the opening portal was artfully positioned for effect. At the forefront stood Preceptrix Ermengarda, tall, serene and imperturbable, battle sword slung at her side like some Valkyrie of pagan myth. At her left shoulder was the blood-soaked, white-habited figure of Brother Ramon, his useless, tightly bound sword arm hidden by the folds of the preceptrix's own garments. To the right was Father Diego, eyes bulging, teeth bared like some savage canine. Then behind them Arnau and, once the doors were fully open, the other two black-clad sergeants fell in beside him. And to one side, in full view and yet safely behind them, stood Titborga.

Arnau could feel the intake of breath from the assembled men. Far from rushing the suddenly open church, the mercenary force of the enemy lord fell back from the doors, opening up a wide path across the courtyard to where Ferrer della Cadeneta stood, shining black hair perfectly coiffured, swarthy and confident. His garments of red and white over a fine mail hauberk were clean and neat, his sword slung at his side. The man's eyes played across the gathering in the doorway and came to rest on Titborga for some time before returning to the woman whose will kept Rourell from him.

'Quit your church and hand over the girl, and I will not be forced to do something regrettable,' he said in conciliatory tones.

'You must be aware,' the preceptrix replied, 'that you will control this building only over the bodies of everyone here.'

'Save the lives of your remaining people, woman. I have won the day and you know it.'

Arnau could feel the uncertainty in the yard. Other than the lord himself, every other figure out there was unsure which confident figure had the right of it.

'You've won nothing, della Cadeneta. To carry today, you must storm a house of God and murder priests and nuns. The moment you commit to that, you damn any man here who thus far has kept his hands clean of such sin. Hell awaits, Cadeneta. Eternal damnation in the next world, and excommunication and ignominy in this.'

'Yours is a heretical monastery, Ermengarda d'Oluja, defying the rule set down by Saint Bernard of Clairvaux, by the Pope and by your own order. You cannot threaten us with damnation, for you are in violation of all good Christian ordinances yourself.'

'*I* can,' hissed Father Diego from her side.

'And if you win,' the preceptrix went on, 'what is it that you win, della Cadeneta? A church full of bodies and a ravaged monastery. For no Templar will submit to you – neither knight, nor sergeant, nor sister nor donat. No one. You cannot take Sister Titborga alive, and if you could, she would be of no use to you now.'

'Idle talk,' della Cadeneta replied dismissively.

'No, Don Ferrer, it is not. The documents pledging the Santa Coloma lands to the order are now safely lodged with the Templar house at Barberà, and so are the records of the admittance of Sister Titborga and her man, now Brother Arnau.'

'Lies.'

'No, della Cadeneta. Simple truths. My sergeant rode before dawn, slipping your net of wickedness thanks to the heroic efforts of my brothers. And should you decide to try and chase him down, you are too late. It has been hours. Even now Brother Guillem will be in the chapter house of Barberà. You have lost, della Cadeneta. You can achieve nothing here but sackcloth and ashes.'

If Arnau had been in any doubt that Guillem had slipped past the mercenaries and made it to Barberà, it would have vanished in the expression that swept across Don Ferrer's face – a look of astonished disbelief gradually melting into rage. He had not known, and if he had not known, then Guillem had succeeded.

A low groan rose from the assembled mercenaries. Likely half or more of what they had been promised had been a cut of the loot when the Lord della Cadeneta inherited the Santa Coloma estate. No inheritance meant that all he could offer was his own paltry funds, and Arnau knew well that della Cadeneta was not wealthy. That was, after all, why he had so desperately pursued Titborga in the first place.

'Take the church,' snarled della Cadeneta.

Silence.

'Kill them all. I will double your pay.'

Still silence. No one moved. More than one of the gathered warriors would be wondering what the impoverished lord planned to use to double the pay they had not yet fully received anyway. Arnau almost smiled as he watched the rage crescendo in the don's expression. Then bodies began to melt away from the periphery of the group, slipping into the shadows of the arch or through the ravaged west gate, away from this awful scene.

'Take the fucking church, you dogs,' snapped della Cadeneta.

More men left. The ones who remained stood still, perhaps staying in the hope of receiving some of this mythical pay, but more likely to watch this fascinating mummer's play draw out to its conclusion.

'I will kill the bitch myself,' della Cadeneta roared, taking a step forward and ripping his sword from its scabbard menacingly.

Arnau glanced to his left to find Brother Ramon looking at him. He was uncertain whether it was Sister Titborga or Preceptrix Ermengarda to whom della Cadeneta referred, but either way, he would touch neither without facing the might of the Temple. The wounded knight nodded to Arnau, and the black-clad young sergeant stepped around the gathering of Templars, walking to the church step and trotting down it.

'No you shall not, Don Ferrer.'

Della Cadeneta took another pace forward, his expression shifting once more, through surprise and disbelief and into sardonic, dark amusement.

'Well, well. The young Lord de Vallbona. A man whose own claim to high nobility was to cling to the hem of a great lord like Berenguer de Santa Coloma.'

'Who you, by omission of action, allowed to die on the battlefield by the Ebro.'

He could almost feel the shock and horror in Titborga back in the church at the revelation. It was time, though. Time for vengeance and truth both. 'A timely warning I gave you, and still you sat and watched our lord trapped and slain when you could have warned him in turn or rushed to his aid. I wonder, did you already have designs on his daughter and his lands on the way into that battle? Were you looking for the opportunity to kill your own lord and relieved when the opportunity presented itself to let the Moor do it for you?'

'Silence, whelp.'

Close to the bone there, then. That idea had not occurred to him before, but had suddenly risen now, and seemed unpleasantly likely.

'But all your dark designs have come to nothing,' he said loudly. 'Here you stand, still poor, still hated, but now indebted to a mercenary army that you probably cannot pay, faced with the implacable Order of the Temple. How does it feel to have lost *everything*, Ferrer della Cadeneta?'

'You, Vallbona, are little more than a pup. I remember bloodying you outside your lady's apartments at Santa Coloma when you first thought to keep her from me. You are slow and inexperienced. You might be able to swing a mace on the battlefield, but you are no match for a true swordsman. Come and face me if you wish, for I will gut you and leave you to hang like a ham in a butcher's.'

Arnau stepped a few paces forward, his eyes straying over the men lining the way to his enemy. It seemed extremely unlikely that any of them would consider intervening, yet there was always a nagging doubt. He had spent so much of the last week waiting for iron-headed bolts to hiss from the undergrowth and steal his life that walking openly among these men seemed foolhardy at best.

Then his gaze fell on one thing that halted him in his tracks. He could feel the tension in the Templars at the church door as he stopped in his march against the enemy. But his eyes would not leave that one splash of colour among the drab greys and browns of the mercenaries. There were four crossbowmen he'd seen among the crowd, who'd have been at the rear of the fighting and were still hale and safe. And three of them he'd disregarded instantly. Not this one, though.

Drawing a frown of confusion from the Lord della Cadeneta, he took one step towards the archer standing in the line. The man flinched at the look in Arnau's eyes.

Would it be murder? It mattered not. The decision had been made with that first glance. If it *was* murder, he would do penance, but he would not turn away from it. His hand reached down to the quiver at the man's side. The archer tried to turn, pulling the store of ammunition out of reach, but Arnau was quick. His hand closed on the red-painted flights of the bolt and whipped it from the quiver. He lifted it to eye level, holding it halfway between his face and that of the crossbowman.

'Interesting colours. The last time I saw these bolts they were sticking out of the body of a knight of the Temple – Lütolf of Ehingen, murdered in a farmhouse a mile from here.'

The crossbowman's eyes widened in horror and recognition. To him, probably all black-clad sergeants were the same. He would not have recognised Arnau for the man he'd missed at the La Selva farmhouse. His eyes remained wide in shock as Arnau changed his grip on the bolt in a single heartbeat and, in the next, plunged it deep into the man's throat. The archer coughed and gagged, bubbles forming through the mess in his neck around the shaft of the projectile, blood rising to coat his gnashing teeth.

He half-expected a melee then. The mercenaries to react to this unexpected death of one of their own and to leap in against Arnau and butcher him en masse. But it did not happen. It is, after all, in the nature of mercenaries to look out for themselves above all, and there would be nothing to gain for them in such an act now.

The crossbowman, still coughing and gagging, touching gingerly the bolt jutting from his neck, dropped to his knees in agony. The other mercenaries nearby backed away, perhaps wondering who would be next. Arnau did not have to turn and look back to know that Ramon was nodding his approval.

Della Cadeneta stood still, sword point lowered, and as Arnau resumed his implacable march towards the man, the mercenaries drew further back, forming an open area between the church and the belfry.

'Sebastian!' barked the oily noble, watching Arnau's approach with less certainty now. Arnau's march slowed as the crowd parted to one side and a man stepped out between the Templar and his quarry. The young sergeant looked the man up and down. He was not big, nor impressive in any obvious way, but his swagger and confidence suggested he was a man of some importance among the mercenaries, whether through rank or reputation. He held a sword in his hand and narrowed his eyes.

Arnau sized him up. Nothing now was going to stop him getting to della Cadeneta. Sebastian had to be good to be that confident in this company. But was he good enough? He was a mercenary, after all.

The man struck, fast, but not unexpectedly. Arnau saw the movement coming and his own blade slipped in the way, turning the attack aside. Sebastian was fast, and there were no obvious tells in evidence, but the strike had been formulaic and bland. A man who had trained with a blade under a soldier but had never learned anything beyond his basic training. Rank, then, rather than reputation. A quick glance at the other mercenaries nearby confirmed it. Sebastian was one of their captains, a man with a history as a trained soldier, who could marshal a force and keep it together and focused in a battle. But no great swordsman.

He decided to test the man. Pulling his blade back, even as Sebastian recovered from his lunge, Arnau swung wide, a heavy, powerful blow for the midriff. Sure enough, his opponent turned with the blow so that he could take the flat of Arnau's blade with the edge of his own. A tried and tested formula. The man was predictable. He would expect Arnau now to capitalise on that, swinging back the other way, and he began to turn in order to take Arnau's next blow, but the young Templar, having his enemy's measure now, continued to turn in a full spin, slicing with his blade in the same direction as before. Sebastian, taken by surprise, suddenly found himself staring in horror at the approaching blade with his own sword on the wrong side to block it.

Arnau's edge slammed into the man's side, shearing through the meagre protection of a padded jerkin and smashing through the ribs within. Sebastian made a gagging noise, stared at his killer in shock, and fell, his side a bloody mess. The young sergeant almost lost his grip on his sword as the man collapsed, and struggled to jerk it back. Recovering, he firmed up his grip on it and straightened once more. With his gaze locked on della Cadeneta he stepped heedlessly across the shuddering body of the mercenary captain and closed on his true enemy. The pain in his side hurt more than ever after the added exertion, but determination held him steady and strong.

'This is foolish, Vallbona. You know how easily I can kill you. You throw away your life for nothing. And if by some strange trick or miracle you *did* manage to kill me, you know what doom you would bring down upon yourself and this weird sect with whom you have thrown in your lot. My death at the hands of the Templars would wash through the nobility of Aragon like a tide of disapproval. Already this preceptory and the witch who runs it are distrusted. The king ignores it, for your swords have always been of use to him against the Moor. But when your blades are turned against his own knights? Things will change, Vallbona. Baron Alberto de Castellvell and the great Lord Bernat d'Entenza would both heap blame and ignominy on you for this.'

He smiled unpleasantly. 'Though the point is moot, since you will be fertilising the fields as carrion by then.'

'Sheathe your tongue and brandish your sword instead,' Arnau said loudly, 'for it at least *that's* clean and does not reek of horse dung.'

It was a cheap jibe, but well timed, for it brought another blaze of anger into the man's eyes and turned a number of mercenary hearts further from their former master. Around the edge more of the bandits took the opportunity while unobserved to slip away through the preceptory gates and vanish.

Arnau looked della Cadeneta up and down. The man was still as a rock, waiting. No tells. No signs. He was an expert with the blade. Arnau would have to be better than he'd ever been to win this day. He had to display no tells of his own. It had been little more than a week since they had arrived at Rourell, fugitives, and yet in such a short time, so many changes had been wrought, both around and within Arnau. A week ago he had only *thought* himself strong. Now, he knew it, for he had learned from the best.

Lütolf. The German had pressed him. Annoyed him. Irritated him. Wounded him. Badgered him. Chided him. Shouted at him. Taught him…

As with the move from a secular life to the simple ways of the Poor Knights of Christ, Arnau divested himself of that which he did not need. As he'd put away a rich surcoat with the black lion of Vallbona in favour of the monochrome black of the sergeant, so he let the trials of the preceptory around him go, melting away from his cares and his consciousness. As he had put aside the sword that had been his grandfather's in favour of a plain blade from the Temple armoury, so he let his ties to Santa Coloma go, his connection with Berenguer and Titborga. As he'd given over his money and his signet and anything of the self, so he let go of Lütolf of Ehingen's death and the shuddering form of the dying crossbowman nearby. As he had pushed away the idea of nobility and succession, of family and women, so the crowd of mercenaries around him fell away into meaninglessness.

He was a Templar. That was what mattered. Ferrer della Cadeneta was the enemy, and there was nothing else in the world right now. The serenity and certainty that flooded him must have shone from his eyes, for something in della Cadeneta's demeanour changed in that moment. Doubt crept into the man.

I shall sing without end the mercies of the Lord.

In generation and into generation, I shall tell thy truth with my mouth.

His mother's favourite. Psalm eighty-nine: the learning of Ethan the Ezrahite. He came to a halt in front of della Cadeneta, a sword-and-arm reach away, mind already rattling ahead through the psalm…

I shall build thy seat; in generation and generation.

Lord, heaven shall acknowledge thy marvels and thy truth in the church of saints.

Something about his was clearly off-putting to della Cadeneta, whose lip had acquired a twitch.

Arnau was calm. He was at peace and there was nothing in him but the word of the Lord and the readiness to do His work.

Della Cadeneta broke. He was fast. God above, but he was fast. That sword came from a dipped waver to neck height, slicing forward in the blink of an eye, a cobra strike. Even the German brother would have broken a sweat facing the Lord della Cadeneta. Arnau simply leaned a hand width to his right and the blade whispered through the air above his shoulder.

Lütolf had been a good teacher. The best, in fact, for all his faults. For while the German had put him on his backside in the dust in this very position days ago, it had taught Arnau something important. It was not enough to be calm and ready to avoid or parry the enemy blow, he must be ready to return the favour.

Arnau pivoted on his right foot, the momentum from his lean adding to the speed, and spun, his blade flicking out horizontally.

He almost had the man then, in that first exchange. As he spun, so his blade would have cut deep into della Cadeneta's arm had the man not pirouetted away with the same grace and simplicity as Arnau's pivot.

Both men came to a halt, swords thrust forth, facing one another again, their positions having swapped so that della Cadeneta now faced the tower, while Arnau faced the church and the gathered Templars therein. He focused for just a moment on the figure of Brother Ramon, and that almost brought his demise. Della Cadeneta, faster than a lightning strike, swung his blade low and deadly, aiming for the legs below the hem of the mail hauberk. Arnau reacted late, and only just in time, lurching back in a clumsy manner, and even then the lord's sword tip caught on the rings of Arnau's mail leggings, close to that vulnerable spot above the mail, where the chausses were tied up. Slow. Distracted. Everything the German knight had chided him for. His attention wandering, just as it had done with that reflection across the fields.

God, who is glorified in the council of saints, is great and dreadful over all that be in his compass.

Lord God of virtues, who is like thee? Lord, thou art mighty, and thy truth is in thy compass.

Arnau felt the tension drain from him once more.

Perhaps he could use this? Use della Cadeneta's recognition of such easy distraction?

He allowed his gaze to focus on a point slightly off to the right, above his enemy's shoulder. Sure enough, della Cadeneta struck at Arnau's left, where his blind side would be had he been truly distracted, and not dissembling. In fact, his eyes had been defocused, allowing him a wide field of vision.

As della Cadeneta's sword lashed out, Arnau lightly sidestepped and slashed out with his own sword. He was rewarded with a grunt and, as they dropped into position facing one another once more, their positions reversed again so that he was now facing the tower. Arnau could see the marks in the mail of della Cadeneta's left bicep. He'd not drawn blood – the man was so fast and swords were near impossible to put through mail – but it had been a palpable hit and would have bruised badly and perhaps done more damage besides. Of course, the man was bright enough not to fall for the same trick again.

But della Cadeneta had lost all his smug certainty. He was no longer convinced of a guaranteed win and a simple victory over his young adversary. And whatever his threats that his death could bring disaster to Rourell in the form of retaliation from the Aragonese crown and its nobles, the realisation that that would be of precious little consolation to a cooling corpse was settling into him. Good. Arnau was growing more confident and calmer by the heartbeat, while della Cadeneta was sliding into uncertainty.

There was a long pause, a second of inactivity and silence that dragged out to another, and another, as the two men watched one another warily, both now well aware of the dangers they faced, both respecting the other's skill and ability no matter how little respect they may have held for the person as a whole. The birds cawed high above. Cicadas in the fields. But within the walls of

Rourell, there was no sound. It was as though every soul held their breath, waiting.

Arnau moved first. Keeping himself calm and free from distraction, he had continued with his mental recitation of the eighty-ninth Psalm, but the Lord himself seemed to have given him the moment to strike.

For mine hand shall help him, and mine arm shall confirm him.

The enemy shall nothing profit in him, and I shall slay his enemies from his face, and I shall turn into flight them that hate him.

He slashed. His blade slammed into chain links point-first, and in a moment of heaven-sent miracle he must have found a weak point, for it broke them. The tip punched into the metal and sheared through the padding and fabric below. But it was a hollow victory, for the Lord della Cadeneta had seen it coming at the last moment and leaped aside, and the blow scored only a hot line of pain across the man's side rather than being the killing blow Arnau had intended. Moreover, he was struck with a horrible challenge as he saw his enemy's response coming while his blade was still trapped in della Cadeneta's mail hauberk.

He twisted and leaped back, yanking his sword from the shirt with difficulty. He felt the muscle in his arm tearing at the dreadful effort of extricating the sword, and simultaneously sensed the enemy blade striking his other arm. The pain shot up both limbs, one from the pulled muscle in his sword arm, the other from the enemy's blow. He couldn't tell what damage della Cadeneta had done, but his arm had gone dead. It was agonising, but numb. Had it been hacked off? One look confirmed it was still there, and the mail sleeve was intact. The rings had dampened the blow, so it must be broken. Damn.

He fell into position facing della Cadeneta once more, trying not to reveal just how badly injured he was after that dreadful exchange. His sword came up and the pain in his damaged muscle was intense. He felt tears welling up in the corners of his eyes.

Give me the strength to see this through, Lord.

And I shall set his hand in the sea; and his right hand in floods.

He shall inwardly call me, saying Thou art my father; my God, and the up-taker of mine health.

That he was. God was in him, giving him the strength to go on, determination overriding all his difficulties. Once more the pair had changed places during the blow, and Arnau was facing the belfry again. He was determined not to be distracted, and yet he seemed doomed to be, for something moved behind della Cadeneta. Arnau allowed his eyes to defocus once more so that he could take in everything, foreground and back, centre and periphery, without blinding himself to any of it. A figure flashed into sight in the shadowy interior of the belfry. In the gloom it was little more than a black wraith, and no detail could be made out other than the basic shape. But that shape alone sent a songbird of joy and hope flying free in Arnau's soul, for it was a small figure, and there was only one person in all of Rourell that size.

Simo was alive.

Arnau allowed his focus to close in once more on della Cadeneta, a new strength flowing through his damaged arm, and once more something must have shown in his expression, for the wicked lord before him suddenly looked momentarily afraid.

Della Cadeneta dived, his sword swinging wide but low as the man made a brutal effort to duck beneath any potential parry of Arnau's and go up under the hauberk for a killing blow to the groin. But the young sergeant was ready. Readier than he had ever been, in fact.

And I shall set his seed into the world, and his throne as the days of heaven.

Forsooth if his sons forsake my law; and go not in my dooms.

If they make unholy my rightfulnesses and keep not my commandments.

Arnau's blade dropped, caught and turned that of della Cadeneta, and he spun and danced away with an almost cursory flick of his own sword in answer. As he came to rest once more facing the church, Arnau noted with satisfaction the line of the cut he had scored along della Cadeneta's cheek, blood sheeting down his chin and neck from the wound. The man looked shocked.

I shall visit in a rod the wickednesses of them; and in beatings the sins of them.

And in that next moment, he knew he had won.

For della Cadeneta's attention was torn from the fight momentarily as Simo emerged from the belfry, roaring his anger. A heartbeat was all it took. Ferrer della Cadeneta's eyes ducked left and focused on the source of the audible rage: the young man in the tower door.

Arnau struck.

It was not an elegant blow. He could not swing wild. His arm's strength was spent, the muscles too damaged to control such a blow. Besides, he knew how little chance there was of cutting through the mail. It had been miraculous to achieve it once. Instead, he lashed out, his sword leaping forth like a lance. He knew the chances of getting a sword tip through the links of mail were infinitesimally small, but sometimes a weapon did not need to scythe through flesh to kill. His own favoured mace was capable of killing through mail as easily as through wool, and he took his cue from that.

The blow landed in the dead centre of della Cadeneta's chest, even as the man's gaze whipped back in shock to his predicament. Arnau's arm might be tired and wounded, the blow unable to penetrate the mail. But he had leaped with it, elbow bent, putting every ounce of his strength behind it. The tip of his sword disappeared into the rings of the mail hauberk, the blow so heavy that it drove steel and padding and fabric all inwards against della Cadeneta's chest. There was a horrendous cracking sound from within, muffled by the man's clothes and armour, along with a number of lesser bony cracks.

The man's sternum had shattered.

Arnau fell back, exhausted, the last vestiges of strength falling from his arm, just as his sword fell from his fingers.

Della Cadeneta looked down in horror. His mail shirt was intact, the white and red surcoat atop it a little torn. But the damage had been done within. The lord took a deep breath, but nothing happened. Somewhere deep inside, his lungs flapped, unable to fill with anything but blood, shattered ribs sticking through them.

He heaved another desperate, experimental breath. Still no air filled his lungs. He dropped his sword, the contest forgotten.

Arnau collapsed to his knees. Simo ran over and grabbed him to stop him falling flat on his face, and the two men of Rourell watched della Cadeneta, eyes wide, desperately sucking on air that could not help him as he slowly drowned in his own blood.

It took some time, which Arnau considered part of divine justice playing out. Della Cadeneta, increasingly panicked, clawing at his throat, trying to extricate himself from his mail hauberk and failing dismally, arms shooting out imploringly to the mercenaries he had hired. Arnau's gaze roved across the courtyard, and he was interested to see how few there were left. Many more had melted away during the fight, realising the game was up and that it would profit them not at all to be the ones standing here when it was all over. Of the dozen men still there, not one moved to help the stricken lord.

In a last, desperate, attempt, della Cadeneta reached out imploringly to Arnau. The young sergeant watched him die. As his body finally gave in, he collapsed first to his knees, eyes rolling wild, then they simply slid up into his skull and he topped over to lie motionless on the ground.

'Lord, where be thine eld mercies, as thou hast sworn to David in thy truth?' Arnau said quietly, skipping to the end of the psalm as Simo helped him painfully to his feet. 'Lord, be thou mindful of the shame of thy servants, of many heathen men, which I held together in my bosom. Which thine enemies, Lord, did shamefully; for they despised the changing of thy Christ. Blessed be the Lord without end.'

He stepped carefully past the prone figure of his enemy. His eyes rose from the body to the few remaining gathered men and he motioned Simo to halt.

'Remember this,' he shouted to the few mercenaries in the yard. 'The Lord demands respect and fear, but He can be forgiving. Go home thankful and raise families in His light.'

He turned away from them once more and, with Simo helping him, shuffled back towards the church, where the preceptrix,

Ramon, Titborga and the rest stood with expressions of deepest sympathy and of great joy for the safe return of the boy.

It was over.

Rourell had prevailed.

Arnau de Vallbona was no more, but *Brother Arnau* had been born anew and baptised in blood.

And it was over.

CHAPTER TWENTY

Arnau de Vallbona, Templar sergeant, stood in the dusty ground and looked down with an air of sadness. The Rourell graveyard had been so small and unobtrusive that he'd not previously known it existed. There had only been three burials there since the preceptory's founding, and only one of those was recent: Lütolf's squire – Simo's father. Now the German knight lay beneath a blanket of dirt beside the sergeant who had served with him in life. Simo shed no tears. Perhaps this past week or more had wrung from him every drip of grief he could muster and he had been left dry, though the lad had displayed shrewdness and an instinct for survival in the tower, when he had deliberately stabbed himself in the shoulder and lay there, swathed in blood and with a knife still jutting from him, apparently dead and ignored by the bandits who walked repeatedly across him.

Lütolf and his predecessors were not alone in the small graveyard either. The brothers had been busy digging for hours. Lorenç's grave lay close by, his brother Ferrando immobile at its foot. The mason had not spoken a word since the death of his twin. Both Father Diego and Carima had proclaimed that it could be a permanent state, something broken in his mind with the loss, but both had vowed to use every hour God sent to return their brother to the fold.

Mateu lay next to Lorenç, and Brother Ramon, already frustrated at the bandages and salves and sling that held his arm tight until it healed, stood beside his grave, saying farewell to the man who had been his squire and his friend. Arnau was torn between Mateu and Lütolf's gravesides, and stood between them, for one had become, against all odds, both teacher and friend, and the other had been the first welcoming voice at Rourell, the man who had helped Arnau find his feet that first day.

Carles finally lay at peace, buried with his brothers. Joana too, beside him, and Catarina, for there was no call for chaste separation in the grave, after all. Six dead, and all because of the greed of Ferrer della Cadeneta and the desperation of Titborga and her man at arms.

The other dead lay elsewhere, of course. The graveyard of a monastery was no place for common bandits and mercenaries, nor, despite Titborga's protests, the body of Maria, never a true sister, and a proven betrayer and fool. Following the Christian value of charity, of course, the burials of all had been paid for by Rourell, though interred at the village to the south, many in a collective grave and with no headstone, for no one knew their names.

Ramon had protested at the order's paying for their burial. Indeed, he protested at such villains and godless animals being buried at all, but the preceptrix had been adamant, pointing to the dire straits into which Arnau and Titborga had been forced by events beyond their control. Perhaps there were mitigating stories behind everybody in that mercenary army. Only God should decide whether they could be redeemed. It was not the place of the preceptory to do so.

Guillem had returned from Barberà, having officially lodged all the records. His face had been ashen as he took in the evidence of what had happened in his absence, but he had not been given time to brood. The body of Ferrer della Cadeneta had been unceremoniously draped over his own horse and tied there, and Guillem was sent off again to deliver it to the lord's home and whatever family he might have, to deal with as they saw fit. Rourell would not bury the vile man. Preceptrix Ermengarda's charity only went so far.

'What happens now?' Arnau said wearily.

'We rebuild,' Ramon answered immediately. 'We repair, replace and replenish. Though what moneys we had in the coffers here were stolen, the order will distribute sufficient coin to return Rourell to its former strength. And with the donations of yourself and the good sister, no coin-pusher from here to the grand master at Acre will argue with us.'

'And the staff?'

'The field hands and millers and so on? It is quite possible they will drift back to Rourell, chastened and apologetic. After all, once the vehemence of their stance wears off, what choice will they have? Some might travel south to Valencia and seek solace among their own, though I think they will find the new Almohad lords there harsher masters than we. Otherwise they will turn to banditry and begging. Many will come back. Not those who committed atrocities, of course, for they will know what awaits them, but forgiveness is in our very nature. And there is always a supply of folk who need homes and work. Replenishing the actual brothers and sisters might be more troublesome, but it will happen. After all, we have two new members already.' He smiled.

'Will we have a ceremony?'

'Of acceptance?' Brother Balthesar cut in. 'Of course. Both you and Sister Titborga, though separately. It is unseemly for a sister and brother to attend a joint ceremony. I feel, though, that we should ask you once more. Your application was accepted in haste and in principle when you were both under a great deal of strain and pressure, with an enemy dogging your heels and threatening your future. He is gone. All is in flux, but should you feel the need to reconsider your path, now is the time. Once the ceremony is held, you will be a sergeant of the Temple and, while it is possible for a full brother or sister to leave the order, it is rare and complicated. Now is when you need to be certain.'

Arnau nodded. 'I *am* certain. I wasn't until yesterday, but I feel I was given clarity in that fracas, clarity I had lacked before. This is where I should be.'

He looked across at Titborga, who was in close conference with the preceptrix. She seemed destined to become Ermengarda's second, filling the place of fallen Catarina.

'Will I be made your squire?' he asked Brother Ramon.

'Perhaps. Now is not the time to worry over such things.'

'Rourell is going to be unpopular,' Arnau sighed. 'Della Cadeneta was right about that one thing. He was committed and sure that we would not risk ruining the high nobles' plans for creating a strong house out of two lesser ones, but we did just that. His death will not sit well with them and the king. I fear the troubles for the preceptory are only just beginning. Bernat d'Entenza will be irritated that Titborga undid his plans to create a powerful lordship out of their union. Alberto de Castellvell already hates us all, and this will push him further into opposition. The king will be angry.'

'The *old* king would have taken issue with us,' Ramon replied calmly. 'But Pedro the Second is a good man, who fears God above state. He will do nothing precipitous. Indeed, there is talk of a new Crusade against the Almohads to chastise them for the dreadful mess that was Alarcos. If he is planning something big, he will need the support of the Temple. But you are correct in that our strength has waned and we are at a low ebb. Drawing souls to the houses of the order in Iberia has ever been difficult. There is, somewhat regrettably, competition between the houses for those donats who wish to join, and Rourell is rarely the prime choice, unique as we are.'

'I may have an idea about that,' Balthesar put in, narrow-eyed.

'Yes?'

'Relics.'

The other two frowned at the simple suggestion, and the older knight smiled. 'As a church with a famous reliquary draws worshippers from afar, so might a Templar house achieve a similar draw by the acquisition of such relics. And, let's face it, the order is known far and wide for the recovery of a number of sacred objects from the site of Our Lord's crucifixion in Outremer.'

'You propose a brief jaunt to Outremer?' Ramon rolled his eyes. 'Jerusalem is in the hands of the Saracen, Balthesar, and the Crusaders disbanded. Acre is our main hold there now.'

Balthesar levelled a look at his fellow knight. 'No. Not Outremer, though you must know the time is coming for that. The Holy Roman Emperor has been calling for a fresh Crusade for years, and the new pope is already supporting it. The order will be involved, and even with the situation here, the pious King Pedro will grant whatever the Pope asks.' He sighed. 'Be certain that a campaign in the sands of Outremer looms; but no, it is not to the Holy City I look right now. There are relics here in Iberia that languish uncared for and ignored under the control of the Moor. Not an easy proposition, of course, but something to think on.'

'You're as mad as Lütolf was, you know that?'

The two men fell silent, and the graveyard became peaceful once more, sizzling in the summer sun, the sound of cicadas, bees and birds a gentle hum all around.

'Come,' the preceptrix said, of a sudden. 'It is almost time for nones, and Father Diego will be insufferable if we are late.'

As the preceptrix, with Sister Titborga at her side, turned and began to make her way back towards the ruined west gate of the preceptory, Ramon smiled. 'I have to admit that having seen the preceptrix in command yesterday, with that heavy blade hanging at her side, it seems strange now to see her without a sword belt. Against all odds and reason, it sat well upon her.'

Balthesar laughed. 'She is a daughter of the church, Ramon.'

'She is a daughter of *war*, also, Brother, every bit as much as young Sister Titborga.'

And Arnau, smiling as he fell into step and followed them, pondered on that, and on the fact that the sword had not been returned to the wall of the chapter house. Had the preceptrix not yet put aside her husband's blade, fearing that there would be further use for it?

Daughter of war, indeed.

Brother Arnau chortled as he stumped towards his new home.

Historical Note

Are we not all fascinated to some extent by the Templars? The Crusades and the Templars interested me long before the idea for this book took shape. I was captivated by the tales even at school, but by adult years my knowledge was so solidly grounded in the Roman world that I had brushed off any idea of ever attempting to write something in this era. The research alone to familiarise myself with the subject was staggering.

Then Mike at Canelo (the publishers of this tome) asked me, after writing two books for them, whether I had ever considered tackling something medieval. I had, and I said so, but also that I had decided against it. The short story of *Daughter of War*'s inception involves an afternoon of beer and discussion with Mike that ended with me agreeing to do it, and only lamenting my decision on the way home. I thought more about it then. Long. And carefully. I came to a number of conclusions and put my ideas to Canelo, where they were enthusiastically received. I would do Templar tales, but not straight Crusades as they've been done so many times and by some very good authors. I would do them, but not the weird secretive Templars with their idols and mysteries. Done too much. But entirely by chance I had found the angle I wanted. I had found a reference to a female preceptor – a preceptrix, in fact – of a Templar house in Spain. Moreover, she was not the only important sister at Rourell, for she had also granted another sister entry to the order.

Yes, the two main women in this novel are real women. Ermengarda d'Oluja entered the order at Barberà in 1196 with her husband Gombau. They had received the automatic divorce that entry as brother or sister demands. They had brought considerable land and fortune to the order in the region. He had disappeared from the historical record within two years, while Ermengarda went on to be preceptrix of the small house at Rourell. There, in

1198, she admitted to the order one Titborga, daughter of Berenguer de Santa Coloma, as a full sister. This was no nunnery either. This was a Templar house. So I had real characters who truly defied the norm in the world in which they lived. It was too exciting not to explore further. For the record, Bernat d'Entenza and Alberto de Castellvell are also real characters, as is the king, of course. Ferrer della Cadeneta is not. My apologies to the residents of the tiny hamlet of Cadeneta in the Poblet hills. I have driven through the place and it is not horrible at all.

Suddenly, the whole idea seemed so much more viable. There would need to be plenty of research into the Templars of course, but I suddenly was so much more comfortable with my tale, and the uniqueness of it made the research more focused. I am very familiar with the region, and shall come to that in a moment. For the role of women in the religious and military orders and their place in north-east Iberia in the era I am particularly indebted to two works: Paula Stiles's *Templar Convivencia: Templars and Their Associates in 12th and 13th Century Iberia* and Myra Bom's *Women in the Military Orders of the Crusades*. Both are excellent works. The latter made me feel comfortable approaching the subject and the former put the perspective of time and location into my mind's eye beautifully.

So yes. Titborga and Ermengarda existed. Of course they did. I would never have named a character Titborga by choice. Not unless I was writing comedy, anyway. Their backstories are my creation and not drawn from historical record. Everyone needs a good past, eh? And Ermengarda remains so shrouded in mystery I wanted to try and give her a real tale. Besides, this is historical fiction, not a textbook.

The castle of Barberà de la Conca is a fragmentary remnant of Templar holdings in Spain. Large pieces of it stand intact in the village, but it is far from the full castles one can see in many places, including another Templar fortress at Miravet. There is some blurring in the region and time as to the form of Templar holdings. Some are clearly focused on the monastic format. Others were once Moorish castles, captured in the Reconquista and given to the Templars, who adapted them to their use. Such was Barberà. For the homes of Titborga and Arnau, I have not used specific locations. They are peripheral to the story at best. There are a number of Santa Colomas, and I have placed on the map one that stands just north of Barcelona. There, the Torre Salvana remains an enigmatic castle ruin, the town and castle both linked to the powerful Cervelló line. The linking of the Santa Coloma tied to the Templars and the family of the Cervelló is my own decision, purely for the book, and should not be taken as historical fact. Ermengarda's former home at Vallfogona de Riucorb is another fascinating fragmentary ruin to see. As for Rourell itself… well, I'll come to that shortly.

The organisation of the Templar order and its ranks are worthy of an entire book on their own. In fact there are treatises devoted to such things. The distinctions between the various levels and groupings within the order are sometimes vague, especially when dealing with such a place as north-eastern Iberia, where strict adherence to the rule seems to have been brushed aside in favour of a blend of Templar rules and geopolitical common sense. Strictly speaking, the squires of a Templar knight are generally to be found drawn from outside the order, while the sergeants are more devoted to warfare and not prayer or everyday careers. Somewhere like Rourell, though, poor by Templar standards and short on manpower as were all orders in this region through the period, cannot have been able to draw a great number of recruits from the surroundings, and their farms and mills, as in the book, would be mostly operated by Moorish slaves or forced converts. There is a distinction between full brothers, who wear the white; sergeants, who wear the black; and various federates, such as confraters, donats and assorted hangers-on. How this all worked is a matter for further investigation. Thus I am somewhat grateful that the period and region in which I have set the book were by necessity vague and unusual, with considerable blurring of lines.

It might also seem strange to have a religious house containing both sexes, and certainly it would have horrified Saint Bernard of Clairvaux, who originally set down the rules, but there *are* precedents in history. Indeed, a decade or so before this story takes place, Saint Gilbert of Sempringham died. The order he founded – the Gilbertines – consisted primarily of monasteries specifically designed to contain both monks and nuns, kept apart but within the same complex and sharing a church. A little research will turn up countless other examples, including even Benedictine ones. Still, I have given the sisters and brothers entirely separate quarters and latrines, despite the small scale of the preceptory.

I have never visited Rourell, sadly, but I have driven past it in two directions and stopped at a connected hermitage nearby, long before I knew the story of Ermengarda. I know the landscape, right up the Francoli valley from the sea to L'Espluga de Francoli and beyond. I only have to close my eyes and I can conjure up the area. I have visited many times, generally in search of the Roman remains in the region.

Rourell preceptory still sort of exists, though not in the village known as Rourell, which lies a little to the south. The preceptory lay in what is now a hamlet called La Masó, centred around the tiny square in front of the later church and the bell tower. Little remains of Templar Rourell. The lower storeys of the belfry are assumed to be Templar in origin and consequently play a part in my tale. The church there now is much later and must partially overlie the site of the Templar chapel. The building next to the church was likely the Templars' chapter house. A telltale filled-in arcade suggests its past and also points to the likely position of the church. Other buildings in that small, enclosed area seem to contain features that date back to the era, suggesting the general shape of the preceptory. Overleaf is Fuguet's map of modern La Masó and its conjectural medieval forerunner (image courtesy of Jbarberà, Wikimedia Commons):

Estat actual

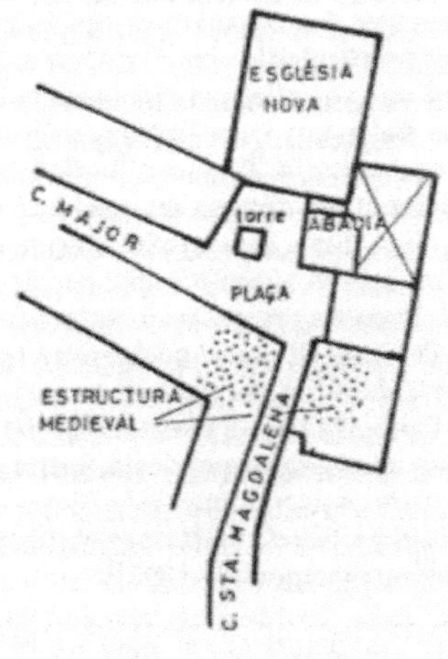

Segle XIII (hipòtesi)

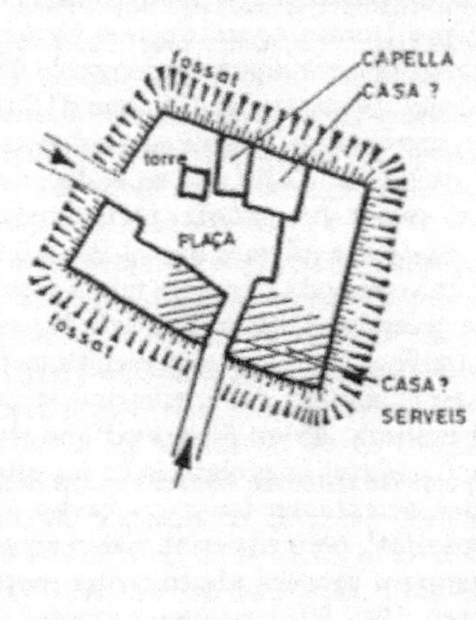

Nucli antic de la Mesó del Rourell (Dibuix: Joan Fuguet)

The problem of the sluicing of the preceptory's latrines plagued me for some time, given the surrounding ditch. Not washing away the deposits was not an option – imagine the ditch a few years down the line. And Rourell had no running water, though I gave it a fictional well. The ingenious solution of water tank, sluice gate and sloping channels is based on the remains at the abbey of Saint-Hilaire in Provence.

The mill exists. Just a quarter of a mile east of La Masó lie the ruins of the Moli de la Selva above the banks of the Francoli. Most of the extant structure is in fact a later building, but the lower areas and the vaulted cellars are considered Templar remains.

The broken bridge across the Francoli is also a true location. A brief mea culpa is due because the bridge (to be found at 41° 15' 45" N, 1° 13' 7" E) which is also an evocative ruin, was actually destroyed by a flood in the nineteenth century and not brigands in the twelfth. Still, the sight of it was enough to trigger my fight scene.

This story might seem fantastic to some extent, but it should not really. The Templars may seem an impossibly strong historical force, but just the slightest digging reveals the dissatisfaction that surrounded them and culminated in their fall at the hands of a jealous French king in the early fourteenth century. The tweaks I have made to Rourell's adherence to the standard Templar Rule of Saint Bernard of Clairvaux (who I always picture in a fur coat with a barrel of brandy around his neck) are all too realistic. The rule might have been more rigidly followed in Outremer or France, but in the lands of Iberia, which were poor in resources and men after three centuries of reconquest, there was certainly a lot of blurring of lines. Stiles's work (referenced above) goes into this at length and is something of an eye-opener. So I have bent the rules appropriately. After all, the rules say 'no women' and the historical record for Rourell shatters that immediately. Saint Bernard may have laid down the rules, but he was not a Templar and did not have to live by them, after all. A fine example of 'do as I say, and not as I do'. For the record, J. M. Upton-Ward's translation of the Templar Rule was invaluable during this writing. Without being able to quote it, my characters could not live by it, nor could they ignore and flaunt it where appropriate. It also makes a fascinating read, should you want to spend some six dollars on an ebook. Imagine that, perhaps spending more to see that source material than you spent on this book!

In my biblical references throughout I have been as careful as I can to keep the period text rather than straying into modern versions. My wording for the Psalms and other extracts comes chiefly from translations of Wycliffe's Bible (late fourteenth century). So if you're a psalm lover and you've been muttering throughout that I kept getting the words wrong, that's why.

As for Titborga's flight from an arranged marriage? It really is not as far-fetched as you might think. There were medieval women who were far from meek and passive and simply ambled through a controlled and arranged life. Some caused absolute havoc by imposing their wills on an environment not shaped to allow that. Sharon Bennett Connolly recently released her *Heroines of the Medieval World* and that book might make you think twice about the accepted subservient role of women in the era. In my research I came across astounding tales. One such is the infant daughter of Adam de Cokefield at Bury St Edmunds. As an heiress in much the same way as my Titborga, she was so sought after for her wardship that Bishop Sampson of Bury and Richard Coeur de Lion quarrelled over it. I also read that the bishop won that contest by mollifying the king, though he failed to benefit greatly anyway as the child was subsequently kidnapped by her grandfather. So you see there is plenty of evidence of tales just such as this being real.

The Templars have become one of the most studied groups in history and there is a wealth of information, though some of it is truly wrapped up in mysticism. There can be little doubt that they kept a certain level of secrecy concerning the goings-on within their order, but not to the extent of the crazed tales that led to their downfall. All in all, the Templars existed for less than two hundred years, their rule and form constantly evolving, their centre of power shifting, their very focus changing from protecting pilgrims from Turkish raiders in the Holy Land to becoming a monastic and temporal force to rival even kings and popes. Much focus is given to their activity in France, which was to some extent their heartland, and to Outremer, where they were formed, where many of their most famous events took place, and where for some time they were housed. Surprisingly little attention seems to have been paid to their activity in Iberia.

The peninsula was, at this time, split between several rival Christian nations (Aragon/Barcelona, Castile, Leon, Navarre, Portugal) and the Moorish realm of the Almohads, one of the more violent, expansionist groups of Berber-related peoples from North Africa. Where there had previously been individual Muslim taifas across Iberia, there was now one caliphate under the Almohads, and we are reaching an era of the Reconquista that becomes bloody and terrible, from the Christian losses at Alarcos in 1195 to the Christian victory at Las Navas de Tolosa in 1212. Against this backdrop of brutality and vying royals, the Templars were still on the rise, and their position in the Reconquista is fascinating, since they repeatedly took part in the push of one king or another, but never launched a campaign themselves. That was not their remit. And so they flourished, particularly in north-eastern Spain. Indeed, one of the earlier kings, Alphonso the Battler, left in his will the entire Kingdom of Aragon to the Templars and two other military orders, though the will was contested and never fully enacted.

I have gone as far as I could in trying to show the daily life of a Templar, which was HARD. These were not rich, fat or lazy men and women. They earned every ounce of their fierce reputation. Any mistakes in the text are my own. Some might, however, *not* be mistakes, but rather choices made for the advancement of the tale. I hope you've enjoyed it, and Arnau will return for another adventure, you can be sure.

Thank you for reading.

Simon Turney, December 2017

Printed in Great Britain
by Amazon

67097638R00180